Praise for Jennifer

SOMEWHERE IN FRANCE

"A tale richly steeped in the atmosphere, drama and heroism of an evolving and war-torn world. A compelling and memorable read." —Lynn Sheene, author of *The Last Time I Saw Paris*

"Utterly engaging and richly satisfying, *Somewhere in France* depicts the very best in love and war. Fans of *Downton Abbey* will devour this novel!" —Erika Robuck, bestselling author of *Fallen Beauty*

"[Robson's] deft touch as a storyteller keeps readers engaged in the story of the lovers, as well as illuminating the bigger picture of the war raging around them." —*Publishers Weekly*

"[T]he fiercely independent Lady Elizabeth Neville-Ashford (Lilly) will be sure to inspire readers." —Huffington Post

"Robson intermingles the overarching themes of love, war, and societal strictures in this appealing read that should resonate with fans of *Downton Abbey*." —*Booklist*

After the War is Over

Also by Jennifer Robson

SOMEWHERE IN FRANCE

AFTER THE WAR IS OVER

A Novel

JENNIFER ROBSON

wm

WILLIAM MORROW

An Imprint of HarperCollins*Publishers*

P.S.™ is a trademark of HarperCollins Publishers.

AFTER THE WAR IS OVER. Copyright © 2015 by Jennifer Robson. All rights reserved. Printed in the United States of America. No part of this book may be used or reproduced in any manner whatsoever without written permission except in the case of brief quotations embodied in critical articles and reviews. For information address HarperCollins Publishers, 195 Broadway, New York, NY 10007.

HarperCollins books may be purchased for educational, business, or sales promotional use. For information please e-mail the Special Markets Department at SPsales@harpercollins.com.

FIRST EDITION

Designed by Diahann Sturge

Robson, Jennifer, 1970–

After the war is over : a novel / Jennifer Robson. — First edition.
pages ; cm
ISBN 978-0-06-233463-3 (softcover) 1. World War, 1914–1918—Fiction. I. Title.
PR9199.4.R634A69 2015
813'.6—dc23

2014023121

ISBN 978-0-06-239307-4 (international edition)

15 16 17 18 19   OV/RRD   10 9 8 7 6 5 4 3 2 1

For Kate.
My sister, my friend, my inspiration.

After the War is Over

PART ONE

What is our task? To make Britain a fit country for heroes to live in.

—David Lloyd George (November 1918)

Chapter 1

By nature she wasn't a solitary person, and yet Charlotte couldn't help but relish the peace and quiet that descended on the constituency office after her colleagues had gone home. Even the ward councilor herself, Miss Rathbone, had departed after extracting a promise that Charlotte not stay on too late. With nothing but the scratch of her pen and the faint thrum of traffic outside to distract her, she'd made terrific progress, first taking care of her filing, then some overdue correspondence. Now she was making a fair copy of the notes she'd taken at the Women's Industrial Council meeting that afternoon. It was a dull task, but one that would only become less interesting the longer she let it sit.

It had only been two months since her return to Liverpool, and already she was discouraged. As tedious and unpleasant as nursing had been at times, at least she'd been able to witness the difference her actions had made: wounds bandaged, burns salved, restless spirits comforted.

She was good at her work here, for she'd been with Miss

Rathbone for three years before the start of the war, and even after a nearly five-year break she'd fit right back in, picking up the reins of her duties as if she'd never set them down. That was the problem.

Nothing had changed. Four years of limitless war, untold millions dead, millions more left wounded, bereaved, desolate. And for what? Britannia was blind and deaf to the suffering of her citizens—the men crippled by war wounds who were reduced to begging on street corners, the widows with no work because returning soldiers were given what few jobs there were, the children who went to bed hungry and were kept home from school so they might help their mothers with piecework. It was all so very, very discouraging.

"Miss Brown?"

The voice from the hall was so startling that Charlotte all but jumped out of her skin. She looked up and was relieved to see a solitary woman, her face somehow familiar, standing at the door.

"I'm ever so sorry to bother you, miss, but there weren't nobody out front . . ."

"There's no need to apologize, I assure you. I was only a bit surprised. Do come in and sit down."

Try as she might, Charlotte couldn't recall the name of her guest. The woman looked poor but respectable, her coat shiny at the seams, her shoes polished though the soles were likely worn through, her face wearied by worry and need. She might have been any age from twenty-five to forty-five.

"I feel as if we've met," Charlotte began, "but I'm afraid I can't place your name."

"Doris Miller. I met you the other week, when you was helping Miss Rathbone on her report."

"Yes, of course. I remember now. You spoke to the Pensions Committee about how hard it's been for you. I believe you lost both your husband and your eldest son?"

"Yes, miss. My husband was killed at Loos, and then Davey right at the end of it all, at Messines last year. He was . . . he was only just eighteen."

"Oh, Mrs. Miller. I am so very sorry for your loss." The words were rote, but she meant them all the same. To the bottom of her heart she did. "I recall that you haven't been able to find any steady work."

"No, ma'am. The jobs are all going to the men. Fair's fair, I suppose." Mrs. Miller looked down as she spoke, her eyes fixed on the sight of her toil-roughened, gloveless hands, clasped so tightly together the tips of her fingers had gone white.

"May I ask, Mrs. Miller, if there's any particular reason you came to see me tonight?"

"I told myself, on the way over, that you'd understand. You was ever so nice when I talked at that meeting. You didn't look down your nose like some others do."

"Thank you. I will do my utmost to help you, Mrs. Miller, if help is what you need. If that is why you've come to see me. But first you must tell me what is amiss."

"I've had a letter. From my uncle, my mother's brother. He lives in Belfast. He was widowed last year. He's asked if I might come and live with him, me and the children, and take care of him. He's had a fall or two and he don't want no stranger coming to help."

"Is he a man of means? Can he support all of you?"

"He was a welder at the shipyards, and he and my aunt never had no children of their own. So I expect they was able to save a bit over the years."

"Do you think him a decent man? Will he treat you and the children well?"

"He's nice. Quiet. I think we'll do well by him."

"Are you asking if I think you ought to go?"

"It's only that . . ." Mrs. Miller's voice trailed off and she resumed her impassioned hand twisting. And then the words came out in a torrent, so softly Charlotte had to lean forward to hear them.

"They's said there's summat wrong with my papers, that's why my pension hasn't come through, not for my husband, or for my son either. I've sent them everything I have, I even had a copy made of my marriage certificate, but they wrote me back and said it's under review, or summat like that, and how am I to feed the children?

"The steamship fare to Belfast for all of us is nigh on five pounds. I've tried but it's too much. I sold all the furniture when things got bad a few months back. We've only the one bed left, the table and a few chairs, and they won't bring enough, not hardly enough. They's only fit for the rubbish. I sold my wedding ring last year. We've the clothes on our backs and nowt else. I daren't ask my uncle for it, else he change his mind. Think twice, or worry we might make trouble for him. It'd only be a loan, until we're settled and I can take in washing or summat else. And I thought . . . I hoped . . . I thought you or Miss Rathbone might know of somewhere I might go . . ."

Charlotte knew exactly what she ought to do. By rights, she ought to send Mrs. Miller to the offices of the Personal Service Society, the charity that Miss Rathbone had recently founded for families in desperate straits. All she had to do was write down the address on a scrap of paper, pass it to the woman, and send her off.

And yet she hesitated, for assistance from the PSS would involve a daunting amount of form filling and question asking. Mrs. Miller might end up receiving the aid she needed, but not without sacrificing what few scraps of self-respect she still possessed. Charlotte had seen it before, more times than she could count, and she was heartily sick of it.

"You were right to come here," she stated in the firmest voice she could conjure. "For I do know of a fund, a rather secret fund, you see, for war widows just like yourself, and I feel quite certain that Miss Rathbone would agree if I advance you the money to cover your fares to Belfast."

Mrs. Miller went pale, and for a moment Charlotte thought the woman was going to faint, but then she rallied and sat up even straighter than before.

"God bless you, Miss Brown—"

"Let me just fetch the ledger . . . yes, there it is."

Charlotte pulled a spare notebook from the shelves behind her, and opened it to a blank page. Using a pencil, she wrote down Mrs. Miller's name, the amount of the loan, and the date; she would erase it later. Then she opened the bottommost drawer of her desk, dug into her bag, and extracted a five-pound note. It was a good thing she'd been to the bank that morning.

"Do you have a handbag, Mrs. Miller? Or would you like an envelope?"

"Can I have an envelope?"

"Of course. Here is the money, and in return I shall ask for only one thing. When you are settled, please find a way to let me know how you are getting on. Your eldest daughter is still in school, is she not?"

"Yes, miss. I'd never of took her out of school."

"Then she will certainly be able to write out a short letter and send it to me here. Just so I know that you are all safe and sound."

Charlotte tore a page from the notebook and wrote her name and the address of the constituency office upon it. "Here is my direction. I am so pleased you came to me today, Mrs. Miller. Miss Rathbone will be delighted to know we were able to help such a deserving family."

"God bless you, Miss Brown, and Miss Rathbone, too. I'll never forget how good you've been to me and my children."

"You're very kind. Now, tell me: how are you going to get home?"

"I'll walk, same as I did to get here. Shouldn't take more'n an hour to get back."

Charlotte bent again to the open drawer and fished tuppence out of her purse. "If I give this to you, will you promise to take the tram home tonight?"

"I couldn't, honestly I couldn't."

"I insist. Now off you go to your children, and I wish you a very happy journey to Belfast."

After seeing Mrs. Miller out the door, Charlotte returned to her desk and gathered her things; she'd finish her notes in the morning. As she locked up and started off down the street, she was buoyed along by a rare sense of elation, her spirits lighter and brighter than they'd been for months. She's wasn't fool enough to think that five pounds could solve the world's problems, or even make a discernible dent in them, but they would ensure a decent future for Mrs. Miller and her five surviving children.

Tomorrow she'd go to the bank and withdraw three pounds, enough to cover her room and board for the month; fortunately she had enough in reserve to tide her over until she was paid again. A few weeks without a daily newspaper or any new books wouldn't hurt her, and it would serve as a useful reminder of how well off she was in comparison to most. She had enough to eat, she had a warm bed to sleep in, and she had useful work that paid her well.

And if, alone in her narrow bed at night, so forlorn she could almost hear her soul shriveling away, she were to wonder and worry why there wasn't more to life . . . well, that was human nature, wasn't it? To want the impossible, though the sum of her experiences proved that happiness was rare, elusive, and above all, ephemeral.

Chapter 2

Charlotte walked north, her route taking her along the grand avenue that divided Princes Avenue from Princes Park. Swaths of snowdrops had emerged from the winter-dead grass of the boulevard, their blooms gleaming brightly in the gathering twilight. Once, the first flowers of spring had seemed like heaven-sent heralds of new seasons and new life. But that had been a lifetime ago, before the world had changed. Before she had changed.

She hadn't a very long commute from her lodgings to Miss Rathbone's office at the foot of Granby Street, scarcely half a mile, and on an evening like this it made for a perfectly pleasant walk. Some of the other women at work had bicycles, which they rode fearlessly through the city traffic, but Charlotte preferred to walk. Bicycles weren't cheap, besides, and were next to useless on rainy and cold days. All the same, she rather wished she'd learned how to ride one when she was still young. Not that being thirty-three made her ancient, but she was well past the age when she could frolic about like a schoolgirl.

She crossed Upper Parliament Street and continued north. Night was nearly upon her, the birds gone silent, the streetlights flickering to life. Almost home, and for a change she wasn't so late that the Misses Macleod would be worrying about her.

Miss Rathbone had sent her to the elderly sisters when she had first arrived in Liverpool, back in the summer of 1911. They were spinsters, she'd told Charlotte, and devoted to each other. No longer able to manage on their own, they'd badly needed help, but the cost of keeping a servant was beyond their modest means. So Charlotte would board with them, keep an eye on the old ladies, and her rent would cover the wages of a live-in maid-of-all-work.

When Charlotte had left for London in the autumn of 1914, Rosie Murdoch, a nurse at the Red Cross Hospital in Fazakerley, had taken over her room. Nearly five years later, Rosie was still in residence, and had been joined by two additional boarders, Norma and Meg. With the upstairs full, Charlotte had been installed in the dining room upon her return. It wasn't an ideal solution, for they all had to cram around the kitchen table for supper, and the other women's comings and goings sometimes made it difficult for her to sleep. Norma in particular was a night owl, not returning until the wee hours on the three evenings a week she went out dancing, and occasionally, rather the worse for wear, she needed to be helped up the stairs and into bed.

Altogether the house was fairly bursting at the seams, but the other boarders were a far more lighthearted group than Charlotte's earnest colleagues at the constituency office, their amusing and often boisterous dinner-table conversation just the sort of leavening she needed to elevate her spirits, or at least distract them, at the end of a long day. The lone exception was Meg, widowed during the war, whose sadness enveloped her like a cloud of too-strong perfume. Charlotte had tried, gently, to befriend the widow, but so far with little success.

Quickening her pace, she reached Huskisson Street just as the clock on St. Luke's Church rang six o'clock. She came to number 47 and let herself in, but rather than unlace her boots straightaway she lingered in the front hall and let the comforts of home seep into her bones. The house smelled of beeswax polish and Lifebuoy soap, fresh-baked bread and fried onions; standing there, she suddenly felt so tired that she wanted nothing more than to eat her supper and crawl into bed.

Instead she unlaced her boots, took off her coat and hat and gloves, tidied everything away in her room, and went down the back stairs to the kitchen, where everyone else was in the middle of supper. She didn't have to look at the table to know what was on the menu, for it was a Wednesday, and Wednesdays meant bubble and squeak, made from vegetables left over from Tuesday's supper, and served with such scraps as remained from Sunday's roast—this week it had been mutton—to round it out.

Charlotte squeezed into her place at the table and waited for Janie, the maid-of-all-work, to dole out her portion of supper.

"How was your day?" asked Miss Margaret.

"Quite good, thank you. How is everyone else? How is that poor lance corporal doing, Rosie?"

"He rallied last night. Looks like the worst of the infection is behind him. Now we only have to keep an eye on his burns, make sure none of them go septic—"

"Rosie, dear, you know how I feel about your hospital talk at the table," Miss Mary interjected mildly. "You'll give us all indigestion."

"Sorry. Will bend your ear later." Although Charlotte had left nursing behind, likely for good, she never minded listening to Rosie talk about work.

"How was your day, Meg?" Charlotte asked. "Was the shop busy?"

"I'm afraid not. Scarcely five customers all day. But Mr. Timmins says things will pick up as Easter draws near." Meg never once looked up from her supper, her answer delivered without inflection or any discernible emotion. It had been like this at every meal since Charlotte's return to Liverpool, but she could hardly fault the poor woman. Sometimes the worst wounds of all were invisible to the naked eye.

Charlotte turned to the girl sitting at her right. Not yet twenty, Norma had an abundance of youthful energy and optimism that could be grating to the nerves, especially at the end of a long day. But she was also a reliable source of entertainment at the table, especially when conversation became bogged down. "How about you, Norma? How were things at the office?"

"Well, let me tell you—it was nifty. A brick of the *dreamiest* doughboys you can imagine came in. They were sending a crate of something-or-other home to America."

"Whatever for?" asked Rosie, not sounding especially interested.

"They're only allowed to take their kit bag home on the troop ships. If they have any extra keepsakes from France—"

"Like what? A stuffed rat? A roll of barbed wire?"

"Don't be such a wet blanket, Rosie. *Honestly.*"

"Go on," Charlotte pressed. "The Americans came in and were shipping something home . . . ?"

"And they said I was so nice, and such a pretty girl—such a *doll*, they kept saying—that they had something for me. And here it is!" With a flourish, she pulled a small paper bag from beneath her chair and emptied its contents onto the cluttered table. "Can you believe it?"

It was a banana. One perfectly ripe banana, its skin scattered with just the right amount of freckles, its heady fragrance half forgotten yet instantly familiar. Neither Charlotte nor anyone else in the room had seen one since the summer of 1914.

"Where on earth did those boys find a banana?" asked Miss Margaret.

Norma had been working at a shipping office down by the docks for several years, and often came home with startling stories or unusual gifts from customers. Only last week she'd brought home an ancient bottle of Madeira, its stenciled label illegible under a hardened layer of decades-old dust. They'd polished off the bottle of dizzyingly strong fortified wine in an evening.

"I've learned it's best not to ask. They'd had an entire bunch, they said, and this was the last one. Shall we?"

They all leaned forward, crowding close as Norma peeled away the skin and set the naked fruit on a clean dinner plate that Janie placed before her. And then, as precisely as a surgeon, she cut it into seven equal portions.

Silence fell around the table as the women slowly ate the fruit, their faces a moving tableau of wonder and delight. Meg was the first to speak. "It's . . . it's just lovely. I'd forgotten . . ."

"Me, too," said Rosie. "My mum loved them. Would buy a bunch from the greengrocer whenever one of us had a birthday."

"Thank you, Norma," said Miss Margaret. "Such a treat for us all."

"You're very welcome. Now, if you don't mind, I'll excuse myself. I'm off to the pictures with one of the girls from work."

"What are you seeing?" asked Charlotte. It had been an age since she'd been to the cinema herself.

"*The Hope Chest*. It's Dorothy Gish's newest. Doris has seen it already. Says it's grand."

Soon Charlotte was the only one left at the table, and as she scraped her plate clean of bubble and squeak it occurred to her that she'd forgotten to check the table in the front hall for the day's post.

"Janie, did anything come in the post for me today?"

"Oh, yes, Miss Brown. Shall I fetch it for you?"

"No need. I'm done now. Thank you for supper. You always make everything taste delicious."

The letter was on the front hall table. As soon as she picked it up, she knew it was *the* letter, the one she'd been waiting for all week. Her heart racing, she tore open the envelope and began to read.

16 March 1919

Dear Miss Brown,

Further to your inquiry of the 12th March, I am pleased to con-firm that, as per the regulations of the Representation of the People Act of 1918, and as a graduate in good standing from Somerville College, you are indeed entitled to cast a vote in the forthcoming by-election for Oxford University. I therefore enclose a voting paper for you to return at your earliest convenience, together with instructions on its proper submission.

I remain,
Your obedient servant,
Mr. C. M. R. Hopkins
Office of the Vice Chancellor
University of Oxford

Chapter 3

She set off for work not much past dawn the next morning, her voting paper tucked securely in her handbag. How odd, that a single piece of paper could instantly make her feel more present, more engaged, as if she were somehow part of a greater whole.

Even the task she'd set herself for the morning, collating information on rents and prices from a whopping great pile of files, seemed appealing, and by the time her wristwatch read half past eight, before anyone other than Miss Rathbone had arrived, Charlotte had opened, read, and made notes from each and every file.

She took the voting paper from her bag, unfolded it, and smoothed away its creases. It was time.

She went to the door of Miss Rathbone's office and knocked lightly.

"Do come in!"

"Miss Rathbone? Do you have a moment?"

Charlotte's employer looked up from the papers that cluttered her desk and exhaled a great plume of smoke from one of her ever-present Turkish cigarettes. "Of course, my dear. Is everything all right?"

At least fifteen years Charlotte's senior, Eleanor Rathbone had been middle-aged since the day she was born. Some of the younger women who worked in the constituency office were intimidated by her, for she took no pains to hide her formidable intellect, nor did she have much patience for those who were less sure in their convictions than she. A generation ago she would have been called a bluestocking and dismissed out of hand for her ridiculous notions about equality between the sexes and the inherent value of women's work. Two decades into the twentieth century, Miss Rathbone was beginning to make her presence and politics felt on the national stage.

Like Charlotte, she had attended Somerville College at Oxford, and after finishing her studies, Miss Rathbone had returned to Liverpool and had joined her father in his work chronicling the lives of the city's working poor. She'd been elected as a city councilor for Granby Ward in 1909; two years after that Charlotte had begun work as one of her constituency assistants.

But Miss Rathbone's work as a ward councilor was only one of the many hats she wore. Elsewhere in Britain she had become known as a committed suffragist and defender of women's rights beyond the voting booth. If a cause was worthy in her eyes, she threw her considerable weight behind it. Rest could wait for the hereafter, she often told her assistants. What counted, in this life, were good deeds and hard work.

She was far from perfect, of course. She tended to bully her opponents into submission, smothering their arguments with the weighty superiority of her own convictions. She was high-minded to a fault, maddeningly humorless at times, and entirely lacking in vices apart from her addiction to tobacco.

Charlotte worshiped her.

"Yes, ma'am, quite all right. I've come about my vote."

"I don't follow you," Miss Rathbone said, stubbing out her cigarette and regarding Charlotte with an air of heightened interest.

"I can't remember if I told you I didn't vote in the general election. I wanted to, but I had to apply to the registrar at Somerville for proof of my status as a graduate, and by the time—"

"I understand. By the time you'd jumped through all their hoops, registration had closed."

"I was so disappointed. But they've since called a by-election for Oxford University, so I will be able to vote after all. I know it's one of the university constituencies, and not a proper riding—"

"A vote is a vote, my dear."

"As soon as the writ was issued, I applied for my voting paper, and it arrived yesterday." Her voice faltered; until that moment, she hadn't realized how much it had meant to her. "I was hoping, Miss Rathbone, that you would do me the honor of acting as my witness."

"The honor is entirely mine," Miss Rathbone replied, her serious face transformed by a rare smile.

Charlotte extracted her voting paper from its envelope and filled in the empty spaces where indicated.

I, *Charlotte Jocelin Brown (Somerville College, 1907),* give my vote as indicated below:

Professor Gilbert Murray, standing for the Liberal Party

I declare that I have signed no other voting

paper and have not voted in person at this election for the university constituency of Oxford.

I also declare that I have not voted at this general election for any other university constituency.

Signed
Charlotte Jocelin Brown
47 Huskisson Street
Liverpool
This day of *19 March 1919*

Her contribution complete, she handed the form across the desk to Miss Rathbone.

I declare that this voting paper (the voting paper having been previously filled in), was signed in my presence by *Miss Charlotte Jocelin Brown,* who is personally known to me, on this day of *19 March 1919.*

Signed
Eleanor Rathbone
Greenbank House
Mossley Hill, Liverpool

Miss Rathbone set down her pen, lit another cigarette, and sighed with contentment. "Normally I would not presume to discuss your choice of candidate with you, but as it is staring me in the face, I will commend you for it."

"I fear Professor Murray has no chance at all."

"None whatsoever," Miss Rathbone agreed. "The university is Conservative to its foundation. But that, my dear, is not the point. Your name has been counted. *You* have been counted. How does it feel?"

Charlotte had to think on it a moment. She'd been so intent on having her voting paper signed and witnessed that it hadn't occurred to her to dwell on the moment itself, let alone contemplate its true significance.

"Casting my vote felt familiar, oddly enough. As if it were something I'd done a hundred times before. If I think on it, I suppose I would say it felt right. As natural as breathing."

"An excellent point, for what could be more natural than an intelligent, able, and curious adult exercising her right to help determine the governance of her country? I feel this calls for a toast, in spite of the early hour."

Pushing back from her chair, Miss Rathbone went to a small drinks table at the far side of her office. She poured two modest measures of walnut-brown sherry and handed one of the tiny glasses to Charlotte.

"To you, Charlotte, on the occasion of your first opportunity to exercise your franchise in a parliamentary election, and to those who fought so valiantly for the cause of universal suffrage, but were never able to cast their own vote."

They raised their glasses and then, seated again, sipped at their sherry. It was beautiful stuff, so dry it nearly evaporated on Charlotte's tongue, and so potent that she set her glass down unfinished. It wouldn't do to fall asleep at her desk.

"I've been meaning to congratulate you on your election as president of the National Union," she said.

"Thank you. I'm afraid we have a long road ahead. With the government so obsessed with stabilizing the labor market, I worry most women in this country will soon find themselves out of work. It makes me wonder if we have all lost sight of what truly matters."

"Perhaps it's simply that people want a respite from urgency," Charlotte ventured. "They want to *be,* to live without anxiety, and if that means neglecting causes they once held dear . . ."

It was clear, from the puzzled expression on Miss Rathbone's face, that such sentiments were not only foreign to her, but also unthinkable.

"Then we are all lost. No; we will have to find a way to wake this country up—and do so before we stand at the brink of disaster again. That reminds me . . ."

"Yes, Miss Rathbone?"

"Only an idea or two for my article on family allowances. Back to work we go, my dear. I need to finish off these memos I was writing for tomorrow's meeting of the Personal Service Society. You'll be there to take notes, won't you?"

"Of course I will. Thank you again, Miss Rathbone. It means a great deal to me that you witnessed my vote."

"You are most welcome. Now shut my door tight, and leave me to think."

WHEN SHE EMERGED from Miss Rathbone's office, a little light-headed from the few sips of sherry she'd imbibed, her colleagues had all arrived and were fetching themselves cups of tea in the cloakroom.

Her closest friend in the group, Mabel Petrie, was just taking off her coat. She and Charlotte were Miss Rathbone's assistants, while the other women, six in total, worked as clerk typists. Like Charlotte, Mabel was the daughter of a vicar, and though she hadn't been to university she had received a fine education at a ladies' college in Newcastle, where she had grown up.

"May I show you something, Miss Petrie?"

It was a quirk of the office that she and Mabel were accorded the privilege of being referred to by their surnames, while the clerk typists were known by their Christian names alone. When she and Mabel went to lunch, or took a walk through Princes Park, they used each other's Christian name; but at work they were Miss Brown and Miss Petrie.

"Oh, do. That looks like something official," Mabel answered.

"It's my vote," Charlotte said, and instantly the cloakroom fell silent.

"Your vote? How is that possible?"

"I can't vote here, as I don't own any property or pay rates or anything like that. But I went to Oxford, and as a graduate of the university, I'm entitled to vote in their constituency."

"Doesn't the city of Oxford have its own member of Parliament?" asked Margaret, one of the younger clerk typists.

"It does, but for some reason the universities themselves have constituencies. Oxford and Cambridge both have one, and there's a new constituency for all the other English universities."

"Seems an odd way of doing things."

"It is, rather. But it gives me the chance to vote, so I'm not going to complain."

The other women all crowded round, all eager for a look at Charlotte's voting paper. All except Miss Margison.

Though a clerk typist, Ann Margison insisted on being called by her surname, and as she had worked for Miss Rathbone for donkey's years, no one thought to challenge her on it.

She was capable enough, and was as devoted to their employer as the day was long, but she was such a disagreeable person, all hard edges and cutting gibes. If Miss Margison had ever had something nice to say about anyone or anything, Charlotte had yet to hear it.

"Lucky you," the woman said, and it was clear she was not offering her congratulations. "Lucky to be able to buy yourself a vote so easy."

Charlotte ignored her; what could she say that wouldn't sound defensive or pandering? It was true, after a fashion, for her expensive education had set her apart, and had given her a vote when most other women were still excluded from the franchise.

"You'll all be filling out one of these before long," she said. "You know Miss Rathbone won't rest until it happens."

When the others had gone to their desks and begun their day, Charlotte returned to her little office and looked at her completed voting form until she was sure it was fixed in her memory. She folded it into the envelope she had prepared earlier, affixed a stamp, and then took it to the pillar-box around the corner. Pushing it through its slot, rather as she imagined one might insert a ballot in a voting box, was terribly satisfying, if a trifle anticlimactic.

There were no brass bands to herald her victory, no crown of laurel or medal to mark her achievement. Only the sun, shining brightly in a pale spring sky, and the joyous music of birdsong high in the trees. But for now, for today, it was more than enough.

Chapter 4

The next morning Charlotte was once again knee-deep in files when there was a knock at her office door.

"Miss Brown?" said the office's reception clerk.

"Yes, Gladys?"

"Telegram just came for you. Here you are."

"Thank you."

Charlotte accepted the flimsy, nearly transparent envelope and took a steadying breath. Something had happened to one of her parents. That was the only explanation, really. Either Mother or Father was unwell, and the sooner she opened the wretched thing, the sooner she could pack and set off for Somerset.

She tore open the envelope and extracted the single sheet, its message penciled out in neat block letters.

DEAR CHARLOTTE. LORD CUMBERLAND DIED
YESTERDAY MORNING. FUNERAL AND RECEPTION
FRIDAY AFTERNOON. HOPEFUL YOU CAN COME.
LILLY NEEDS A FRIENDLY FACE. EDWARD TOO.
REGARDS ROBERT FRASER.

Charlotte slumped a little in her chair, her heart pounding, and tried to quell the sense of relief she felt. Not bad news from home, but from London, from the fiancé of her dearest friend.

Lord Cumberland hadn't been much of a father to Lilly, nor had he been a particularly decent man. But her friend needed her, and for that reason alone she would go to London and endure what was sure to be a farce of a funeral. What could be said of a man who'd had so much and had given so little?

Once, long ago, Charlotte had been a servant in the Cumberland household. Lilly's governess, beloved by her charge but disdained by nearly everyone else in the family. Her friendship with Lilly had endured—had made every lowering moment of those years worthwhile—but the prospect of seeing Lady Cumberland and her elder daughters was singularly unappealing.

She wouldn't think of how Lilly's brother Edward was suffering, though it was a subject that had preyed on her mind ever since his near-miraculous return from the war. They had been friends, back in those years of war before his capture by the enemy. They had written to each other several times, and once, when he was home for Christmas, he had taken her and Lilly to lunch at the Savoy. As for what had occurred after lunch, she wouldn't think of that, not now. Not ever.

She had become very fond of him; perhaps too fond, given that he was engaged to another woman. Once or twice, she had even allowed herself to daydream of a future in which they were free to be more than friends.

She went to Miss Rathbone's office and knocked.

"I'm terribly sorry to bother you, Miss Rathbone. The thing is . . . I've just had a telegram from London."

"Not bad news, I hope."

"It is, rather. Do you recall my friend Lilly? She and I lived together in London."

"The WAAC? Yes, I do. Is she—"

"It's her father. He died, quite unexpectedly, and she was hoping I might attend his funeral. It's tomorrow afternoon. So I was hoping, with your permission, that I might have leave to go. I'll make up the time, I promise."

"I have no fears on that account, not least because you've worked late almost every night since your return. Do go, and please convey my condolences to your friend."

"Thank you very much, Miss Rathbone. I promise I'll leave everything in good order."

"I know you will, my dear."

"I was also wondering . . . may I use the telephone to ring London and let them know I'll be there? I'll ask the operator for the charges."

"Never mind about that. Do you wish to use my telephone?"

"No, thank you, ma'am. I'll use the one at the front desk. But thank you for offering all the same."

Charlotte hurried down the hall to the reception area at the front of the building. The main telephone for the constituency office sat at its own little desk, separate from that of the reception clerk, and for a change was not in use.

At this hour there was a chance she might find Robbie at the hospital before he embarked on rounds or disappeared into the operating theater for the day; even if he were occupied, his clerk would be able to take a message. She picked up the ear-piece and waited for the telltale burst of static that invariably preceded the operator's appearance on the line.

"Operator."

"Hello. I need you to put through a call to the London Hospital, in Whitechapel, East London."

"Yes, madam. I'll ring back once the call is connected."

Charlotte hung up the earpiece and waited, wishing she had thought to bring some work with her. At last the telephone trilled out its response.

"Operator here. I'm connecting you with the central telephone at the London Hospital. Please hold the line."

"Thank you."

A different voice came on the line, this time distinguished by an East London accent.

"London 'Ospital. 'Ow may I direct your call?"

"I need to speak to Robert Fraser in general surgery. Or his clerk, if he's not available."

"One moment, please an' thank you."

A man's voice came on the line. "General surgery."

"Good morning. Is this the clerk for the surgeons?"

"It is, ma'am."

"May I leave a message for Robert Fraser?"

"You can speak to him yourself. He's right here."

"Thank y—"

"Fraser here."

"Robbie? It's Charlotte. I got your telegram. How is Lilly?"

"Saddened, of course. And surprised, as are we all. I'd always assumed her father was indestructible."

"What happened?"

"It was yesterday morning, straight after breakfast. He got up, took a step, and collapsed. I've spoken to the physician they called and he thinks it was Lord Cumberland's heart. All but instant."

"I see. Well, I'm ringing to let you know that I shall of course come to the funeral."

"Thank you. Lilly's finding it all a bit much. As you can imagine, her mother and sisters have been quite dramatic about it all. And Edward is naturally feeling the effects of this, too."

Edward. The eldest, the heir—and now the Earl of Cumberland. "He couldn't have expected it, not so soon."

"Exactly. And on the heels of everything else he's endured. At any rate, the funeral is tomorrow afternoon, two o'clock, at St. Peter's Eaton Square, with a reception to follow at Ashford House."

"Ah," was the only response Charlotte could muster. So much for her long-ago vow never to return to that tomb of a house in Belgravia.

"I know," Robbie said. "We'll both be as welcome as ants at a picnic. But it can't be helped, and you'll have an ally in me—I promise."

Lord and Lady Cumberland had detested Robbie from the moment they had laid eyes on him, back when he and Edward had become friends as undergraduates. The idea that their son and heir should associate with the son of a Glaswegian dustman had all but induced apoplexy in them both. Their daughter's decision to then marry the dustman's son had only deepened their enmity.

But Lilly, for her part, had refused to be cowed by her family's disapproval. She had left home not long after the beginning of the war, had served with distinction in the Women's Army Auxiliary Corps, and even after her demobilization had refused to return to her parents. Instead she had moved into the same boardinghouse where Charlotte had lived during the war.

"You are a dear."

"Oh—I almost forgot. Lilly says you're to stay with her at Mrs. Collins's. It's all arranged."

"That's very kind of her. Well, then—I'll see you tomorrow."

"Shall I have a car meet you at Euston?"

"No, thank you. I can easily make my way there. And you have other things to worry about. Do give Lilly my love."

"Good-bye until then."

"Good-bye."

After they'd rung off, she sat at the desk and stared into space for long moments, unable to shake the sense of unease that had settled over her like a too-warm shawl. She had to go. She had said she would, Lilly was expecting her, and she was needed. But, oh, how she dreaded it.

She worked late, ensuring her desk was clear before she left, and arrived home just as the other women were finishing supper.

"Hello, everyone. Is there anything left from supper, Janie?"

"Yes, Miss Charlotte. I'll fill a plate for you now."

"Thank you. Before I forget, you needn't cook for me to-morrow night. I have to go to London for a funeral. For my friend Lilly's father. The service is tomorrow."

"What are you going to wear?" asked Norma.

"I hadn't thought of it. I have a black skirt and coat that more or less match. They should do."

"Those things you wear to church? I'll beg your pardon now, but they're *awful*. How long have you had them?"

"I'm not sure. I bought them just after I moved to London, so . . . early 1915?"

"Precisely. They're hopelessly out-of-date. You'll look like the help if you wear them."

If only Norma knew the truth. "But I haven't anything else that's suitable. And I don't have time to visit the shops before I leave."

"I've a suit you can wear," Rosie offered. "I had it made only last year. We're nearly the same size, I think."

"And I've a hat you can borrow," said Meg, surprising everyone when she spoke up. "Black wool felt, with a high crown and narrow brim. Perfect for the occasion."

"There you are," said Norma, who was clearly in her element. "Let's get you dressed and see how you look."

Garments were collected, Charlotte was sent into her room to change, and all awaited her return to the sitting room so they might weigh in and offer suggestions. As there was no full-length mirror in the house, Charlotte had to be content with the other women's assessment of her appearance, as well as such glimpses as she could catch with her tiny hand mirror. Rosie's suit seemed to fit well, and Meg's hat was alarmingly stylish compared to the battered wool cloche she'd worn for the past two winters.

"I suppose I'll do." The suit, which she wore with her best high-necked white blouse, was beautifully made, its lapels and pockets edged with wide grosgrain ribbon. She would never fit in, for Lilly's family could spot bourgeois impostors at a thousand yards; but at least she wouldn't embarrass her friend, and that was what mattered.

"What about your hair?" Norma asked. "You wouldn't have time to cut it, would you? Imagine how nice it would look."

If there were one concession to fashion Charlotte absolutely refused to consider, it was cutting her hair. She had a plain face, and even on her best day was never more than passably attractive—pretty *enough*, one well-meaning friend had once said—but her hair was beautiful.

"No, Norma. I'm not cutting my hair. I'll put it in a low chignon. It looks well like that, and with enough pins it will stay in place."

She raised the mirror to her face, intent on assessing Meg's hat, but her attention was caught, and held, by the woman who stared back at her. Did she always look so serious, her eyes wary, half-hidden shadows behind the metal rims of her spectacles? She attempted a smile, but it looked all wrong. It was the grimace of someone in pain, someone who carried with her the memory of joy, with none of its delight.

SHE CAUGHT THE 9:15 train to Euston the next morning. With nowhere to leave an overnight bag during the funeral service, she had only her handbag by way of luggage. Once she'd packed an extra set of combinations and stockings, and her toothbrush and comb as well, there hadn't been enough room for a book. Then again, she rarely managed to read while she was traveling, for the countryside provided too engaging a diversion. Even now, at the wan end of spring when the trees had barely come into bud and the fields beneath lay fallow, the land was beautiful, achingly so.

Alone in her compartment, Charlotte felt secure enough to nap for half an hour, her bag tucked securely under her arm, and then to eat the tinned salmon sandwich Janie had made up for her. It wouldn't do for her stomach to disrupt the funeral proceedings with a plebeian growl.

Her train arrived at Euston a little past one o'clock, which left just enough time to visit the ladies' waiting room at the station and ensure her face was free of any soot or grime. It was too far to walk, at least three miles, and she didn't dare risk taking the Underground if the trains were running behind.

She would have to splurge on a taxicab, although she was loath to spend so much for such a short journey.

The journey to Belgravia took no time at all; with motorcars and horses alike still in short supply, traffic was light. Everywhere she saw signs of rebirth, of the nascent spring: advertisements for luxuries like chocolate, bicycles, face powder, and hair pomade now adorned billboards in place of recruitment posters, while fresh paint gleamed on the façades of public houses, private homes, and shop fronts.

The cab drew to a halt on Wilton Street, just north of the church, for the street beyond was thronged with carriages and motorcars, many of them draped with swaths of black crape.

"A funeral you're going to, miss?" asked the cabbie.

"Yes. The father of a friend." She handed over her fare, together with a generous tip, and let herself out of the cab. "Thank you very much."

St. Peter's was set well back from the street and had, to Charlotte's eyes, a forbiddingly austere exterior. Inside, however, the sanctuary was warm and light, with soaring Romanesque arches, delicately carved screens, and jewel-bright chapels. The altar itself had been adorned with garlands of hothouse flowers; additional arrangements flanked the chancel entrance, their heady scent perfuming the air even yards away.

Declining the assistance of an usher, she found a seat near the back of the congregation and settled down to watch a parade of England's elite fill the church near to bursting. The prime minister and at least half his cabinet were there, together with nearly every duke, marquess, and earl in the land. Last of all the guests were the Prince of Wales and Prince Albert, and despite the solemnity of the occasion Charlotte was unable to quell a flutter of excitement as they marched past.

And then it was time for the Cumberland family to process to the front of the church. A phalanx of Lilly's relatives swept past, most of them unfamiliar to Charlotte, and then finally her friend appeared, arm in arm with Robbie. More relatives followed—several sisters and their families, as well as Lilly's younger brother, George. Finally Edward, now the Earl of Cumberland, entered the sanctuary on the arm of his mother, who looked more or less as she always did: pale, dignified, and utterly composed. He was using a cane, Charlotte noticed, but didn't seem to be putting much weight on it.

Although Charlotte's religious observance and belief had become rather frayed in recent years, she had grown up in the bosom of the Church of England, and the traditional funeral service was a balm to her spirits. Everything was exactly as it ought to have been: "Guide Me O Thou Great Redeemer," Psalm 23, and words of prayer so familiar she scarcely had to think to summon them to her lips.

The church's forecourt cleared rapidly after the service, with most of the congregants making the short journey to Ashford House by motorcar or carriage. It was no trouble to find Lilly among the thinning crowd, and before she thought better of it, Charlotte threw open her arms for her friend's embrace.

"Charlotte! You came."

"Of course I came. There was never any question of that."

"You are coming back to the house with us? I know it will be torture—"

"Never mind me. You're the one who is important today. You need me, and so I'll be there."

Now Robbie came forward, shaking her hand and offering a gentle smile. "Hello, Charlotte. How was your journey?"

"Very restful, thank you."

"I know it's easier to walk back, but I think it will be too far for Edward. Will you come with us in the carriage?" Lilly asked.

"Thank you. Although if—"

"Hello, Charlotte," came a voice from behind.

She spun around and, in her haste, nearly bumped into the man who had approached her.

"Lord Cumberland," she answered. "I am so terribly sorry—"

"Christ, Charlotte. None of that, not today. Please." He grinned halfheartedly, but there was no humor behind his smile.

"Edward, then," she replied, and shook his outstretched hand.

"Will you come in the carriage with us?" Lilly asked her brother.

"I suppose. Would rather walk."

"I know. But you'll be on your feet all afternoon, and you know what the doctors said. You mustn't overtax yourself."

"Fine. Where is the bloody thing?"

"Right behind you," Robbie answered. "So haul your miserable carcass inside and stop complaining."

The four of them were soon settled inside, the women facing forward and the men sitting opposite. Edward immediately closed his eyes, pulled off his hat, and let his head loll back against the tufted seat back, while Robbie focused his attention on his gloves. Apparently the women would have to do the heavy lifting, as far as conversation was concerned, until they arrived at Ashford House.

"How are you feeling, Lilly?" Charlotte asked.

"Well enough. I mean, I know I wasn't terribly close to Papa, but his death was a shock all the same."

"And your mother?"

"Cool. Calm. As remote as always."

"How has she been treating you?"

"More or less as she always does—which is to say that she ignores me whenever possible, and tolerates me when she cannot ignore me."

At this Edward laughed bitterly, but before Charlotte could open her mouth to reply, she felt the quelling pat of Lilly's hand upon her forearm. She turned to her friend, who shook her head minutely, and decided to swallow her retort.

Instead, she tucked Lilly's arm in hers. "When do you leave for Cumbria?"

"Late tomorrow morning. Papa's interment will be on Sunday. Needless to say I'm dreading it."

"At least we'll have this evening."

"We will. And we won't have to stay so very long, will we, Edward?"

"Not long at all," her brother confirmed. "I told Mama I will remain for one hour exactly, and not a minute more. And there's to be no reception line."

The carriage drew to a halt. As they waited for the footman to lower the step, Charlotte peered out the window, curious to see if her memories had played her false. They had not, for the icily perfect façade of the Belgravia mansion was as unwelcoming as ever. If buildings had faces, then Ashford House resembled nothing more than a humorless and rigidly austere Roman statesman.

The carriage door opened. They had arrived.

Chapter 5

It had been eight years since Charlotte had last entered Ashford House. Although Lilly was at her side, she hesitated a moment at the doorstep, her heart in her throat, her hands clammy inside her gloves.

But there were scores of people behind her, flowing out of their plush vehicles like luxe, bejeweled lemmings, and so there was nothing for it but to take a deep breath and let herself be swept along by the crowd. Across the grand entrance hall, up the cold, wide marble staircase, and into the echoing acreage of the blue drawing room.

At first she stood with Lilly and Robbie, but then Lilly went to say hello to a childhood friend, and Robbie went in search of a cup of tea for him and Charlotte both. So she stood her ground, feeling increasingly out of place, and prayed that her discomfiture did not show on her face.

She had made up her mind to approach Lilly, who certainly wouldn't have minded, when a *tap, tap, tap* of heels alerted her that someone was approaching. Charlotte turned her head and realized, to her horror, that it was Lady Cumberland and Lilly's two sisters. It was almost comical, the way they walked so preeningly, so evidently aware of people's admiration and envy. They were wearing beautiful gowns, dead black of course, as high mourning had to be, but so gorgeously fashioned and trimmed that one didn't even notice the color, or lack of it, after a moment.

Lilly's sisters had grown plump, though they kept themselves well corseted, while Lady Cumberland didn't appear to have aged at all. She had to be in her fifties at least, but looked scarcely older than her daughters, and her beauty had not diminished one whit in the eight years since Charlotte had seen her last.

It was then that she made a critical error: she looked Lady Cumberland in the eye. Without saying a word, without even glancing at her daughters, the countess wheeled about and the three of them, arranged in perfect formation, positioned themselves before Charlotte.

Once she had been expected to curtsy whenever she encountered the countess. She would not do so now. She stood even taller, lifted her chin a fraction higher, and gritted her teeth against the sudden, paralyzing fury that surged through her veins. Once she had vowed she would never expose herself to their disdain again, and to do so, now, went against her every instinct.

Lady Mary, the middle of the Cumberland sisters, fixed her with a predatory stare. The three of them, Charlotte decided, resembled nothing so much as grimly assessing ravens, glittering in their black plumage, their eyes chill and calculating.

"Have we met?" she asked, each word a precise, cutting blow.

Before Charlotte could speak, Lilly's other sister, Lady Alice, provided the answer. "Don't you remember? She was Lilly's governess—oh, it was ages ago, wasn't it? Certainly long before the war."

"She was? What on earth is she doing *here*?"

"Lady Elizabeth invited me." That was all the explanation she would give. Not one word more.

They said nothing else, which was a relief, though Lady Cumberland continued to unnerve her by looking through Charlotte as if she weren't even there. She then turned her back and walked away, back in the direction she had come, leaving her silly, spineless daughters to trail after her, whispering and giggling into their gloved hands.

It wasn't quite the cut direct of a hundred years before, for that was reserved for social equals; rather, it was an acknowledgment of Charlotte's innate invisibility and, ultimately, her complete unimportance.

It shouldn't have hurt her—she had vowed she would never let them hurt her again—but it did. Oh, God, how it did.

ROBBIE, PREDICTABLY, WAS horrified when he returned with their tea. "I ought to have known something like that would happen."

"I'll survive. It wasn't that bad, to be honest." Her hands were trembling, her mouth was as dry as dust, but she hadn't faltered. She had stood her ground. "How do you stand it? Stand *them*?"

"We hardly ever see them, to be honest. They've never quite forgiven Lilly for leaving home and joining the WAAC. Certainly they'll never forgive me for having the effrontery to imagine I'm good enough to marry her."

"You really ought to elope," she suggested. "I'm serious."

"I've considered it, believe you me. But it wouldn't be fair to my mam, nor to our friends."

"I suppose you're right. I'd forgive you, though."

"See?" he said, smiling down at her. "I knew there was a reason Lilly likes you so much."

"Who is the woman standing with Lilly? I know most of her other friends, but she isn't at all familiar."

"The woman . . . ? Ah. That's Helena, Edward's fiancée."

That girl? That young, smiling cipher—she was Edward's fiancée? It seemed impossible to credit. She was terribly pretty, of course, with fair hair and large, expressive eyes.

"What do you think of her?"

If Robbie thought her sudden interest strange, he showed no sign of it. "I scarcely know her. I'd say she's a nice enough girl. Seems devoted to him, but . . ." He hesitated, frowning at his teacup.

"Yes?"

"I'm certain she bores him to tears. I've tried to ask him about her—ask about his intentions. But he always finds a way to wriggle out of the conversation."

"They haven't set a date?"

"No, and thank God for that. Is this the first time you've set eyes on her?"

"Yes. I saw Edward once during the war, when he was home on leave, but Lady Helena wasn't with him. I hadn't expected her to be so young."

"She is that. Though she seems to be a bright girl, and can talk quite knowledgeably on a number of subjects."

"Would you say she's attached to Edward?"

"She seems affectionate enough. As far as I can tell, she's unfazed by his injuries. Though I doubt she realizes that a missing leg is the least of his problems."

"How is he?" Charlotte asked. Although she would love to know more about Lady Helena, she was far more interested in

Robbie's opinion of Edward's condition. "Today is the first I've seen of him since the day you returned from France."

"I don't know. I honestly don't know. Physically, he's improving. I strong-armed him into visiting a prosthetics clinic, so he has a leg that fits him now."

"He scarcely even limps."

"They do wonderful work there. Perhaps too good. He seems to think his recovery is complete."

"And you . . . ?"

"I think it's barely begun. A man doesn't recover from such injuries, from such horrors, in a few months. He drinks too much, for a start, and I know he doesn't sleep well."

"Before the war, he was troubled—"

Robbie shook his head. "No, this is worse. It's like . . . like a weight he can't shed. Dragging at him, pulling him—"

He looked over her shoulder, his attention caught by something on the far side of the room.

"What is it?" she asked.

"Lilly's asking for me."

Charlotte turned to follow his gaze, and saw that Lilly, now trapped in conversation with a clutch of elderly ladies, was tugging on her earlobe.

"That's my cue. Will you be fine on your own? I promise not to go far."

"I'll be perfectly fine. Lady Cumberland did her worst, and I survived."

She set down her cup and saucer on a nearby occasional table, not willing to draw attention to herself by summoning a footman, and retreated to one of the lushly padded window seats. She would look out the window, though the formal gardens below had little to recommend them at this time of year, and when she had fully recovered her composure, she would join Lilly and Robbie.

Not bothering to look at her wristwatch, she couldn't be certain of how much time was passing. Only when the sound of approaching footsteps, careful and measured, intruded on her silent meditation did she turn her attention back to the drawing room.

It was Edward.

When he'd returned from Belgium, from the enemy hospital where he'd been held for nearly the last year of the war, he'd been achingly thin, with distressingly dark shadows beneath his eyes. Less than a season later, he was better groomed, with his fair hair combed neatly off his forehead, and his fine suit expertly tailored to conceal the full extent of his frailty. But the shadows remained, lingering in his voice, his manner, and his weary gaze.

It shamed her, but in all that time she hadn't sent him a single letter. He had been suffering—she could see it now, as clearly as the lines on his face—but had she even once bothered to let him know she was glad he'd survived? To let him know she had missed him? She had asked after him in her letters to Lilly, and once or twice had asked to be remembered to him; but that wasn't enough, and she knew it.

Embarrassment had stilled her hand: a pathetic excuse, really, but it was the truth. The night of his return, she had all but fainted at his feet when he walked through the door of her and Lilly's boardinghouse. She'd known that Robbie was expected home, but the reappearance of Edward, their Lazarus risen from the dead, had been a shock she couldn't ever have foreseen.

She had recovered her composure before long, and somehow made it through the strange, rather awkward hour that followed. They had gathered in Mrs. Collins's shabby little sitting room and had, all four of them, spoken of carefully neutral items: the recent weather, the men's journey home, the peace negotiations in Paris.

So much had been left unsaid. How had he survived? Why had there been no news of him for nearly a year? Instead he had bid her good evening, thanked her solemnly for her good wishes, and had returned to Ashford House, no doubt to give his parents the shock of their lives when he walked through the door.

Consumed by the details of her coming move to Liverpool, Charlotte had left London a fortnight later without once seeking him out. She thought of him often, but she really had been so terribly busy, and of course he was occupied with his family and the many bureaucratic complications of having been declared dead and without issue.

She had meant to write to him, but the days had crept by, days that turned into weeks, and the longer she waited the heavier her pen had become.

Yet his eyes now held no trace of reproach.

"I owe you an apology," he said as he sat beside her. "Robbie has informed me that once again my mother and other sisters have behaved abominably."

"Then why are *you* apologizing?"

"I ought to have prevented their being rude to you. I assumed, wrongly, that they would be civil."

"Never mind. I've a thick skin. They weren't particularly rude, besides. Simply . . . disapproving."

"I am sorry, though. Especially since you took the trouble to come so far."

"You shouldn't worry about me, not when you have so many other concerns. How are you bearing up?"

"Well enough. Despite his faults I was fond of the old fellow. The rest of it I could do without. The solicitors, the estate managers, the hangers-on . . . most of all my mother and sisters, Lilly excepted. Moaning and complaining and clinging at me endlessly. It's almost enough to make me wish I were back in Belgium."

"Don't say that," she whispered. "Don't ever say that."

"Why not? It's true enough."

"They weren't unkind to you there, were they?" she asked, and immediately regretted her presumption. To ask him about such a thing when he was mourning his father, and when they were surrounded by a roomful of people, was the very height of insensitivity. Yet he didn't seem to mind, or even notice.

"Not at all. They cared for me very well indeed."

"Then why didn't they repatriate you sooner, or at least send word?"

"Because I refused to tell them my name. I had lost my identity disks and my uniform had been cut off and discarded. They had no way of knowing who I was."

It wasn't . . . how could it be possible that he had done such a thing? For months she had grieved for him, had agonized over his brutal end, and all the while he had been alive and perfectly able to relieve her suffering, and that of everyone else who loved him.

"How *could* you? Have you any idea what it did to Lilly? To all of us?"

He met her gaze steadily, unflinchingly. "I know. But I was certain I would die, sooner rather than later, and I didn't want anyone to know the whole of it."

"She didn't care. None of us cared about that. We only wanted you back."

"And here I am," he said, his mouth twisting into a fine imitation of a smile.

"Edward, I—"

"No more, please. Not today. I haven't slept for days, and I may just collapse in a heap if I'm forced to talk about this much more."

"Will you at least talk to Robbie?" she pressed.

"He's been grumbling to you, hasn't he?"

"I think he's right to be worried."

He sat up straight and looked down his fine, proud, aristocratic nose at her. "You think he's *right*? Whatever can you know of it?"

"I was a nurse. I took care of men like you. I saw how they suffered."

"Men like *me*? You mean the crackpots, shaking and stammering, covering their ears whenever a door slams shut? You think I'm like *them*?"

"There's no shame in it—"

"Of course there is. Everything about it is shameful, beginning with the way people like you talk about it. As if you know. As if anyone who wasn't there can possibly understand."

"I didn't say I understand."

"*Don't*. Don't even think it. Your problem, Charlotte Brown, is that you believe you can fix everything. But you can't fix me. Nothing can, save oblivion. The same oblivion I was desperate for, but was denied by well-meaning doctors and nurses like you. So save me your concern and your pity. They're wasted on me, and we both know it."

"Edward," she whispered.

He heaved himself to his feet and walked away, his limp achingly pronounced, and though his mother caught at his arm, he shrugged free of her grasp and continued on, leaving the reception behind, it seemed, for good.

If she had thought herself uncomfortable before, it was as nothing compared to now, when every last pair of eyes in the room was focused accusingly on her. She knew what they were thinking. Who was that drab little nobody in the corner? And what had she said to upset Lord Cumberland so thoroughly?

Lilly came to her then, took her arm, and, with Robbie, led her away. Soon they were in a carriage and en route to Mrs. Collins's boardinghouse in Camden Town.

Her friend tried to be reassuring. "Don't look so upset. Edward has been like this for months. I've lost track of the number of times we've been speaking about something and he takes offense and stalks off."

"I did upset him. That's the problem. I pressed at him about the war—it was so crass of me, so unfeeling. I ought not to have said anything."

"If none of us says a thing, though, how will we get to the bottom of what's troubling him?" asked Robbie. "If we care about him at all we have to press on."

"I suppose you're right. Although I won't be here to help. Perhaps if I were to write to him . . . ?"

"Let him stew," Lilly insisted. "In the meantime, we have ever so much to talk about. I want to hear all about your new friends at the Misses Macleods', and all about work, and your parents, too. And especially I want to hear what it was like when you cast your vote. I'm terribly envious, you know."

Robbie had to return to work, so it was just Lilly and Charlotte and Mrs. Collins at table that evening. Though it was heavenly to be with her friend again, and to hear of her wedding plans and her hopes for university and her happiness with Robbie, Charlotte's thoughts were never far from Edward. The brother and friend they loved, the man who had been returned to them, but whose soul, she feared, still walked among the dead, the millions of dead, who haunted the battlefields and charnel houses of Flanders and France.

Chapter 6

At first, Charlotte didn't notice the advertisement that had been pinned to the message board in the porter's lodge. The afternoon post had just arrived, and so she was preoccupied by the disappointing contents of her pigeonhole.

"Any good news?" asked her friend Celia, who was engaged to be married and daily expressed her relief at having her future settled.

"Nothing so far," Charlotte answered, tearing open the last of the four envelopes waiting for her. "'Thank you for your interest, but at present we have no suitable vacancies, although we would happily welcome you in a volunteer capacity,' et cetera, et cetera. There's also a letter from my mother, keen as ever to have me return home. So I've *that* to look forward to, I suppose."

"Sorry 'bout that. Makes me ever so glad that Rupert and I are getting married in July."

Charlotte longed to ask Celia why on earth she had spent three years at university if her highest aim was to become someone's wife, though she knew it was unfair. Her friend had done well, had learned for learning's sake, and who was she to criticize Celia's decision to marry? All the same, it wasn't the path she had chosen, or intended to choose for a number of years to come. Marriage meant the end of work, and she had plans. She was going to make a difference in the world, and she couldn't do it by sitting at home and arranging her life to suit the ambitions and desires of a man.

If ever she were to marry, her husband would have to be an exceptional man. Right-minded, interested in the sort of things that really mattered, and supportive of her views and ambitions. The sort of man who would consider her his equal.

Charlotte was fairly certain that no such man existed, not anywhere on the face of the earth.

She saw it then. A smallish piece of paper, tacked in the exact middle of the notice board, and typewritten in the blackest ink.

> **Governess Required**
> **Gentleman requires a governess**
> **for the education of his sister.**
> **Applicant must have or shortly expect**
> **to obtain a diploma in Modern Languages,**
> **English, or History as well as**
> **first- or upper-second-class results**
> **in Final Honors Schools. Liberal salary.**
> **One month paid vacation *p.a.***
> **Apply to E. Ashford, Merton College.**

It wasn't what she wanted; wasn't even remotely close to what she dreamed of doing with her life. And yet it might serve, might do as a stopgap of sorts, if only until she found something else.

Celia had wandered off, likely in search of a quiet spot where she might read the latest letter from her fiancé, who was at St. John's College only a stone's throw away. Why he wrote to her every day was a mystery Charlotte couldn't begin to fathom. Somerville students were allowed to socialize with male undergraduates, so wouldn't it have been simpler to meet at a tea shop?

She returned to her room on the top floor of Walton House and, by shifting several armfuls of books and papers to her bed, was able to clear a space on her desk. With her best pen in hand, she wrote out a reply to Mr. Ashford that outlined her qualifications and expectations, and found an envelope.

She wasn't likely to meet him, not today, but it wouldn't do to enter one of the men's colleges looking anything but polished. So she took down her hair, brushed it smooth, secured it in the same low chignon she always wore, and pinned her best hat, her Sunday hat, to her head. Then she put on her smartest coat, the one she had hoped to wear when being interviewed by dozens of prospective employers, and set out for Merton College.

Crossing Woodstock Road, she headed south along St. Giles, veering east at Broad Street and turning onto the Turl to avoid the crowds along Cornmarket, then across the High Street and down Magpie Lane to Merton, which she'd always thought the prettiest of the Oxford colleges. Not that she'd seen much of it; women weren't welcome inside its hallowed walls, charladies and cooks excepted.

She presented herself at the porter's window, just inside the college gate, and waited for him to look up from his newspaper. He'd seen her coming, so she resigned herself to waiting until he could be moved to acknowledge her presence. It was always this way at the older colleges.

"Yes, miss?" he asked after she'd silently counted to a hundred. He didn't even look up from his paper.

"Good afternoon. My name is Charlotte Brown, and I should like to leave this for Mr. Ashford."

"Lord Ashford to you."

"I beg your pardon? The notice he posted gave his name as E. Ashford. I had assumed he was a don at the—"

"Lord Edward Ashford. Undergraduate here."

"Ah," she said, thoroughly flustered. "Well, then, may I leave this letter for Lord Ashford?"

"You may. Good day to you, miss."

"Good afternoon." With that, she turned on her heel and retreated, back through the gate, into the late-afternoon sun and away from the surly porter with his red face and too-tight collar and silly bowler hat. Away from yet another man who made no effort to hide his disapproval of women at his university. Never mind that she wasn't even a true member of the university, having been barred—like all women—from matriculating, and wouldn't receive a degree for the work she had done. Never mind that she sat the same examinations as the male students and had worked every bit as hard. Never mind—

Head down, she rounded the corner onto Oriel Street and promptly collided with a young man in cricket flannels. Stumbling badly, she would have fallen but for the steadying arm he extended toward her.

"So sorry—"

"Beg your pardon—"

He straightened up, collected his cricket bat from the

ground, and disappeared around the corner. And Charlotte, her heart racing, continued on her way.

A MESSAGE WAS sitting in her pigeonhole when she returned to Somerville an hour later, having allowed herself a restorative browse through Blackwell's Bookshop. It wasn't a letter as such—simply a sheet of paper, folded in four, with a few scribbled lines within.

Dear Miss Brown,

Sorry to have missed you earlier. Are you free tomorrow morning for a cup of tea at Boffin's? Let me know and I'll collect you from the Somerville lodge at ten o'clock.

Regards,
E. Ashford

THE EVENING POST brought no offers of employment, nor did the first post of the following morning. There was nothing for it but to meet Lord Ashford and do her best to impress him. She wouldn't have to stay on in the position for terribly long, really only until she received a more suitable offer of employment, and in the meantime she would be earning her way, living independently of her parents, and possibly even establishing some useful connections.

It wasn't ideal, but things could always be worse—she could be facing a future with nothing more exciting than a fiancé to recommend it.

Arrayed in her best, just as she'd been the day before, she placed herself outside the front gate of Somerville at five minutes before the hour. At five minutes past ten o'clock she began to wonder if her reply to Lord Ashford had gone astray. At ten minutes past she was certain something was amiss.

At a quarter past ten, she admitted defeat. Likely he had found someone else for the position, or perhaps—it hadn't occurred to her before but it now seemed a likely explanation—it was a practical joke at her expense. She wouldn't be the first female student to be so duped.

She went back inside the college, stopping at the lodge for a moment to check her pigeonhole once more, and as she left, empty-handed, she came face-to-face with the same man she'd bumped into the day before, only this time he wore a wrinkled undergraduate's gown on top of his coat. He was perspiring and out of breath, though no less handsome for it.

Recognizing her, he smiled and moved out of her way. "My apologies once again. I'm very late to meet someone, I'm afraid."

Could it be? "You aren't Lord Ashford, are you? Because I'm—"

"Miss Brown," he said, his smile widening. "I ought to have known. I do beg your pardon—I overslept, and for some reason my scout didn't come to wake me early, as I'd asked. I shouldn't be at all offended if you decided to walk away and wash your hands of me."

She couldn't help but grin back at him. "I'm quite all right, Lord Ashford. Shall we walk down to Boffin's now?"

"Yes, please. I'll need at least one enormous mug of coffee before I can speak intelligibly."

It was a fine morning, as was often the case in Oxford in late May, with a sky so clear and blue it made her eyes ache. They walked side by side, Lord Ashford matching his pace to hers, and after a few hundred yards he looked at her and asked, "What course are you taking?"

"English. My finals are in a fortnight."

"Nervous?"

"A little. I did well in Honor Mods, though, so if that's any indication of what's to come, I should be fine. What about you?"

"I'm taking Greats. I sat my Honor Mods a few weeks back and scraped by, so I'm hoping they'll let me continue on."

"Do you like classics?"

"I do, oddly enough. Wasn't at all keen when I began—more a case of taking the degree because I couldn't think of what else to do—but I've warmed to it over the past two years. Though Greek still gives me nightmares," he added, and shuddered theatrically.

"Your notice said you were looking for a governess for your sister."

"Yes. Her name is Lilly. She's thirteen. Very intelligent girl, but her previous tutors have been hopeless. My other sisters are thick as mud—unkind of me, but true—and they'd have been fine with nothing more than the bare essentials. But Lilly needs more."

They were at Carfax now. Crossing the High Street, they walked east to the Oxford Restaurant, known locally as Boffin's, and found an empty table at the very back. Lord Ashford ordered them a plate of scones, a pot of tea for Charlotte, and a mug of coffee for himself, and then he continued to tell Charlotte about his sister.

"As I said, Lilly is bright. My parents, though, are as antediluvian as Noah himself. Won't allow her to go away to school, nor will they let her attend any of the good day schools for girls in London. I have managed to persuade them to take on a better class of tutor for her alone, and to let my sisters continue on with the idiot they have at present. That's what the notice was about."

"Why aren't your parents conducting the interviews, then?"

"To be bald about it, I don't think they care. I mean, they care about the final candidate, but they're profoundly uninterested in the search itself. So I volunteered, which is for the best, really. Left to themselves, they'd surely dig up someone even worse than the woman teaching the girls now."

"Your sister is fortunate to have such a caring brother," Charlotte said, deciding it was best to avoid any commentary on the relative idiocy of previous governesses.

"Nonsense. I simply can't stand the thought of her turning into a feather head like the other two."

"Would you like to see my references? I have one from my English tutor, as well as from Miss Penrose, our new principal at Somerville."

"I will look at them at one point, thank you. Right now I'd rather talk about you. Where did you grow up?"

"In Somerset. In Wells, that is."

"Do you have any brothers or sisters?"

"No, it's only me. I was, ah . . . I was adopted. So it's only the three of us."

What had just come over her? She could so easily have said she was an only child, and left it at that. Her closest friends knew the truth, of course, though she'd never discussed the precise circumstances of her adoption with anyone other than her parents. Some stories were simply not meant to be shared.

"And what does your father do?"

"He's a prebendary at Wells Cathedral."

"That sounds ecclesiastical."

"It is. He's one of the canons there."

"Why not stay in Wells? Find some charming young cleric to marry?"

"I—I . . ." she stammered, taken aback by the directness of his question.

"Forgive me. I shouldn't have asked."

"No, it's a sound enough question. I went to quite a good school in Bath, and Father tutored me as well. When my head-mistress suggested I sit the entrance exams for Somerville, we were all rather surprised. But once I had the idea in my head, I couldn't let go of it."

"Have you liked being here?"

"I've loved it."

"So why apply for this position? Surely you can aspire to something higher. Be honest—I won't fault you for it."

She folded and refolded her napkin and tried to think of how to respond. "I . . . well, I can't find anything else, to be perfectly honest. I've been looking for a position for months now."

"Would you mind working as a clerk or typist? Surely you could find a position of that sort without too much difficulty."

"I wouldn't, but it seems rather a waste. I had hoped to, well, to *do* something with my education. Silly as it may sound, I thought I could help to right wrongs. To make a better world."

"That doesn't seem especially silly to me. Do you honestly think teaching a thirteen-year-old girl is something you'll enjoy?"

"I do. Would I make the sort of governess she wants to have?"

"You would. Likely because you're the sort of woman she hopes to become."

"You don't need to flatter—"

"Not a bit of it. You're intelligent, educated, and independent. That's what she wants for herself. And that's what I'd like to show her she can become, providing of course you decide to take on the position."

"Are you offering it to me?"

He looked her straight in the eye, surprising her with the strength of will she glimpsed behind his cheerful-Charlie good looks. "Yes," he said.

"How many other women have you interviewed?"

"None. You were the first to apply, and I can't imagine for a moment that anyone could surpass you. When can you begin?"

He seemed so certain of himself—of her. "I don't . . . I mean, I hadn't thought of it," she said.

"Why don't we say the beginning of July? That will give you time to finish up here and pay a visit to your mother and father."

"What about your parents? Won't they need to meet me first?"

"Leave them to me."

He beckoned the waitress, settled their account, and steered Charlotte outside. "Do you mind if I leave you here? I'm late for my Greek tutorial."

"That's quite all right, but—"

"Let me know how you get on in finals. I'll send you your train ticket to Penrith—that's where we'll be in July, at my father's house in Cumbria—and I'll also advance the first quarter of your salary to help with your traveling costs. I thought eighty pounds a year? Ninety? Yes, ninety seems right."

"But that's at least double what I'd thought to be earning. Are you quite certain, Lord Ashford?"

"Enough with the 'Lord Ashford.' Call me Edward. May I call you Charlotte?"

"I don't think that's advisable, given that I'll be under your employ."

At that his eyes brightened. "So you'll do it? Splendid. I must go, but I'll send everything along soon. Good luck with your finals, Charlotte."

He shook her hand and set off at a run, east along the High Street and, presumably, back to Merton, his gown billowing behind him in a quite comical manner. If only the rest of their encounter had been something she could laugh away.

Somehow, without precisely agreeing to do so, she had become the governess to a sister of Lord Edward Ashford—and that, apart from his sister's name, was all she knew of him and his family. In little more than a month, she would begin work as a governess.

A servant. Despite her own upper-middle-class upbring-ing, her superior academic qualifications, the outrageous salary she would receive, and the compliments Lord Ashford had attached to his offer, she would be a servant, living with strangers, employed by aristocrats who were sure to deplore a modern woman such as herself.

It was not the grand and noble future she had once envi-sioned for herself.

Charlotte stood on the pavement outside Boffin's a minute longer, trying and failing to take everything in, and then set off for Blackwell's. She might as well begin her new future by looking up Lord Edward Ashford in *Debrett's Peerage*.

Chapter 7

Liverpool, England
April 1919

Charlotte was at her desk, trying to make sense of her notes from the Pensions Committee meeting of the evening before—why, oh why had she never thought to take a course in shorthand?—when Miss Margison stomped past. The woman didn't seem capable of simply walking; no, she telegraphed her every footstep throughout the constituency office, no matter if her mood was good or bad, no matter if she was wearing court shoes or galoshes. This morning her mood was vile, for reasons that Charlotte had yet to deduce and, frankly, had no interest in exploring.

She'd worked alongside the woman since 1911, excepting of course the interval during the war when she'd been in London, and in all that time they had never become friendly. Miss Margison didn't appear to have friends, or if she did she kept them well hidden. She never sat with the other women in the office during their break for tea, never went to the pictures after work with any of them, never in Charlotte's recollection had so much as asked after their families or beaux. At the end of the day, the woman seemed to vanish, and as no one had any notion of where she lived, or with whom, they had nothing to chat with her about the following morning.

A voice rang out from Miss Rathbone's office. "Miss Brown! Could I trouble you to come here for a minute? Miss Margison has a question for you."

Charlotte stifled a groan and got to her feet. What could it be this time? She approached Miss Rathbone's desk, studiously ignoring the third woman in the room.

"Yes, Miss Rathbone?" she said, her voice beautifully calm.

"I'm sorry to trouble you, my dear, but Miss Margison had some concerns about the invitations for the annual general meeting of the National Union. I gather the approved proofs were to have been returned to the printers last week?"

"Yes, ma'am. I put them in the outgoing post myself."

"I see. The difficulty, I'm afraid, is that Miss Margison has only now had a call from the printer, saying he didn't receive the proofs."

Not again. This was the third time an item had been pinched from the outgoing post and the finger of blame pointed at her by none other than Miss Margison.

"I assure you, ma'am, I did place them in the outgoing post." And from today onward, she vowed to herself, she would personally place every item of post that left her desk directly in the pillar-box down the road.

"I quite believe you. There you have it, Miss Margison. Now, I believe we still have a copy of the invitation at hand? Very well. Since you are at loose ends this morning, would you be so kind as to take it over to the printers? It shouldn't take you above an hour to travel there and back on the tram."

"But, Miss Rathbone—" Miss Margison protested.

"I am so glad that is settled, ladies," Miss Rathbone finished, her attention already turning to the papers on her desk. "Oh—Miss Margison?"

"Yes, ma'am?"

"Before you leave, if you could fetch me a cup of tea? Thank you."

Charlotte returned to her office, acutely aware of Miss Margison's disbelieving stare, wondering yet again what she had ever done to deserve the other woman's dislike. She knew herself to be a decent person, a friendly person, and yet for entirely mysterious reasons she had earned the enmity of another.

Before the war, she would have forced a confrontation and cleared the air with the woman, just like that, but something held her back. Everyone had their reasons for behaving as they did, and one day she would surely figure out what made her odd and unpleasant colleague behave as she did.

ALL THROUGH SUPPER that evening, Norma entertained them with stories of her day at work. Most seemed to revolve around customers who were so enthralled by her face and figure that they abandoned their brains at the door. It would have been worrying if Norma hadn't been so funny at the retelling.

"So he said to me, 'Dearie, why don't you come round that counter and show me all those darns in your stockings,' and I said, 'Not if I was on a sinking ship and you was the only lifeboat on the sea.'"

"Oh, Norma. You mustn't say such things, especially to a stranger. What if he had taken offense?" chided Miss Margaret.

"Then Joe and Daniel and the rest of the men from the warehouse out back would have had a talk with him. They don't let anyone give me guff."

"Miss Margaret's right," Rosie said. "You can't know what sort of men you're talking to, and if one of them gets it in his head that you offended him, and the men from the back aren't around—"

"Fine, fine. But you wouldn't believe the sort of things some of them say to me."

"I would. Trust me, I would. The men I deal with are lying flat on their backs in hospital beds but they still talk a load of rubbish. Best thing to do is ignore it."

"I suppose. Say—now that we've all finished our tea, does anyone feel like playing a round of cribbage in the sitting room? Rosie? Charlotte?"

"No, thank you, Norma. I'm feeling rather tired tonight. I think I'll just read in my room, if you don't mind."

All through supper Charlotte had scarcely said a word, longing only for the meal to be over so she might crawl into bed, read something comforting, and let the weight of her long and dispiriting day slide from her shoulders.

After helping Janie clear the table—it was Charlotte's task to shake out the tablecloth and fold it away in its drawer— the Misses Macleod and their boarders, all except Charlotte, moved to the sitting room. It was just across the hall from her bedroom, and even with both doors shut she could easily hear the conversation and laughter from where she sat, in her chair by the window, trying to concentrate on her new book. She had been keen as mustard to read *The Return of the Soldier,* but to-night, and the night before, too, she hadn't been able to follow the narrative for more than a page before losing steam.

She shut her book carefully, using a braided paper bookmark that Lilly had made for her years ago, and set it aside. Standing, she went to her bureau, intent on fetching a fresh nightgown.

A knock at her door, then a whispered voice she recognized as Rosie's. "Charlotte? Are you in bed?"

"No, not yet. Do come in."

Rosie shut the door behind her and sat in the chair that Charlotte had just vacated. "Are you all right?"

"Hard day, that's all. Ann Margison was at me again."

"What did she do now? Sprinkle arsenic in your tea?"

"At least that would be cut-and-dried. No, it was her trick with the outbound post again. This time it was proofs that were meant to go back to the printer. I know I've said it before, but now I mean it—from now on, no matter how busy I am, I'm to walk down the street to the pillar-box and put my post in directly."

"How did you find out?" Rosie asked.

"She said she'd had a telephone call from the printers complaining that the proof hadn't arrived. Of course the call wasn't for her; we've none of us our own telephones, apart from Miss Rathbone. But her desk is close to the one at the front, and if ever Gladys is away she pretty much leaps on the thing to answer it. For all I know they didn't even call, and she only said so because she was certain of the proofs having vanished."

"Do you have any idea at all why she's so nasty?"

"I don't know, not really. I have my suspicions, chief among them that she's jealous of me in some way. Perhaps because I left and then was welcomed back so readily by Miss Rathbone. Perhaps she thinks I'll take her place . . ."

"Isn't she one of the clerks? Who does the typing and filing and things like that?"

"Yes, and I'm one of the aides, which means I have my own office, rather than a desk in the main room. I thought of that, but it's always been that way, mainly so that I can speak to visitors, constituents and the like, with some degree of privacy. It's not as if I took her office from her."

"No, of course not. But I wonder . . . perhaps she envies how easily you were able to fit back in, as if you hadn't been away at all."

"I suppose. Though it makes no sense—no one is unkind to her, and we always make sure to invite her if we're going out as a group for lunch. I don't even go half the time, for heaven's sakes."

"Why don't you confront her? Simply ask her why she is doing such things?"

"I could, but she'd probably say it's all in my imagination and I'm simply stirring up trouble. I think, for now, I'll leave it be, and hope she eventually realizes that I've no intention of undermining her."

"A sensible approach. Now—on to more important things. Have you any plans for Friday night? Norma wants us all to go dancing at Holyoake Hall on Smithdown Road. Even Meg has said she'll come. We can have our supper here and then walk over after."

"I'm not sure, Rosie. I don't know any of the new dances."

"We can fix that easily enough."

Somehow, before Charlotte could utter a single syllable of protest, Rosie had led her across the hall into the sitting room, where the sofa and easy chairs had been pushed to the side and the rug rolled back.

"Hooray for Charlotte!" Norma cheered. "Take my hand and let's get you started. Why don't we start with the fox-trot—you do know it, don't you?"

"Yes, Norma. I haven't been living in a nunnery."

"I'll play," said Meg. "I don't feel quite like dancing tonight."

"Let's start with 'My Rainbow Girl,'" Norma suggested.

"Let me run through it first?" Meg asked. "I won't be a moment." She set her hands to the keys and joyous, heartfelt music filled the room, a tonic for their battered spirits. As she reached the chorus, she began to sing, and after a few bars they all joined in, even the Misses Macleod.

"When you are near, girl, you bring me good cheer, girl
The love light shining from your eyes
Is like a rainbow, radiant in the skies
For you're the sunlight that gleams, dear
Thro' clouds in my dreams, dear
You set my senses in a whirl
My little rainbow girl!"

It had been an age since Charlotte had listened to music, and even longer since she'd danced. When had she last stood on a dance floor and let a man hold her as they moved together? Was it as long ago as Oxford?

No . . . a memory stirred of a night at the hospital, a long, dark night in the summer of 1916, when every ward had been packed full of broken men. She and her colleagues had all been so tired, so downcast, but then someone had pushed aside the tables and chairs in the mess hall, and someone else had produced a huge old gramophone, of all things, and they'd danced for hours, all together, the nurses and doctors and orderlies. How strange that she'd forgotten it until now.

With Norma in the lead, Charlotte soon felt comfortable with the conventional fox-trot, and then with the Baltimore and the Peacock Strut, variations that her dance partner assured her were all the rage.

"Do you see the music for 'Let's Toddle at the Midnight Ball'?" Norma called to Meg. "Let's do it next. It's an older one, but they were playing it last week at the Palais. Almost exactly like a fox-trot, except you bounce on the balls of your feet, like this." She demonstrated to Charlotte, her bobbed curls bouncing against her cheekbones. "See? It's ever so easy."

"'Let's toddle, come on and toddle, toddling and waddling along. Listen to

the music of the shuffling feet, oh, what a rhythm we're going with them,' " Meg sang, her voice sweet and light, and soon they were all singing and bouncing together, even Miss Margaret, who had been coaxed out of her easy chair to dance, somewhat unsteadily, with Rosie as her partner.

As soon as Meg had played the closing chords of the tune, Norma was over to the piano, shuffling through the pile of sheet music that rested next to Meg on the bench. "Here—we have to try this one. My friend Edith played it for me on her gramophone the other night. It's 'The Tiger Rag,' straight from America."

"I've heard it, but I've never played jazz music," Meg protested. "And the music is so . . . so *different*."

"Please try—please do. You'll love the sound of it. You all will, I promise."

"Very well. But it's going to be a bit bumpy at first."

Meg ran through the piece by sight, stumbling here and there over the unusual rhythm of the piece, though normally she was an accomplished pianist who could master a tune at first viewing. As she gained in confidence, the music from the piano grew louder, the syncopation more compelling, and though Charlotte had no notion how one ought to dance to such music, her feet were simply itching to dance.

"It's a one-step," explained Norma. "Ever so easy once you get started. Dance with me, Rosie, and we'll show the others."

They danced and danced until the clock on the mantel chimed ten o'clock and the misses, who normally retired at half past eight, declared that they were for their beds. So the women rearranged the sitting room and went to their respective rooms, and Charlotte, for the first time in weeks, fell asleep as soon as her head touched the pillow.

PART TWO

How fortunate we were who still had hope I did not then realize; I could not know how soon the time would come when we should have no more hope, and yet be unable to die.

—Vera Brittain, *Testament of Youth* (1933)

Chapter 8

The Earl of Cumberland
requests the pleasure of your company
at the marriage of his sister
Lady Elizabeth Adelaide Sophia Georgiana Neville-Ashford
to
Mr. Robert Graham Fraser
The Church of Saint Mary Magdalene
Haverthwaite, Cumbria
Saturday, the seventh of June
One thousand nine hundred and nineteen
Eleven o'clock in the morning
Breakfast to follow
Cumbermere Hall

At exactly eleven o'clock, the landau glided to a halt in front of the ancient parish church of St. Mary Magdalene. Charlotte waited for the footman to help Edward and Lilly descend, then came forward to embrace the bride.

"You look beautiful," she said truthfully. "Let me straighten your gown and veil before we go in."

Charlotte handed her bouquet of sweet peas and damask roses, a smaller version of Lilly's, to the waiting footman. "There aren't any creases to speak of," she observed as she smoothed and adjusted the folds of the bride's simple handkerchief linen gown. Her own pale blue frock was similar, though it lacked the drawn-thread and white-work embroidery of the bride's, and instead had bands of organdy insertion at its middy collar and sleeves.

"How is Robbie?" Lilly asked. "Does he seem nervous?"

"If he isn't, he should be," Edward answered. "Marrying into our lot . . . God help him." For a moment Charlotte wasn't certain if he was jesting or not, but then he smiled and she was reassured.

"What are you waiting for? Take her arm and go on in," Charlotte told him. She took her bouquet back from the footman, followed them inside, and waited for the music to begin.

First the swelling chords of the organ, and then the voices of the village choir, singing a newer anthem that was a favorite of Lilly's. *"I was glad,"* they sang. *"Glad when they said unto me: we will go unto the house of the Lord."*

The congregation rose to its feet as Lilly and Edward stepped forward into the modest nave, Charlotte a few steps behind. She could just spy Robbie, standing alone at the front; once Edward had escorted his sister into the church, he would move to his friend's side as his supporter.

Robbie looked terribly handsome in his kilt and doublet, smiling broadly as his bride approached, and for perhaps the thousandth time Charlotte thanked heaven that both he and Lilly, and their love for each other, had survived the war.

The little church was full of Cumberland relations, although the bride and groom had insisted, and in this had been supported by Edward, that their friends be invited as well. Charlotte had met most of them the night before, at the prenuptial dinner at Cumbermere Hall, and found them an entertaining and friendly group, in particular Lilly's former colleagues from the WAAC.

By way of family Robbie had only his mother and several cousins present, though at least a dozen colleagues from the hospital in London had come north for the occasion, as well as friends from his days in the RAMC. Mrs. Fraser, whom Charlotte had found very warm and motherly, but also terribly shy, was doing her best to enjoy the occasion, though the poor woman likely wouldn't feel herself again until she was back home in Scotland. Cumbermere Hall and its occupants had that effect on most people.

Charlotte stood at the front as the service began, ready to assist Lilly, and though she ought to have been listening to the vicar's welcoming remarks, she couldn't help but cast her eye over the occupants of the Cumberland family pew. Lilly's mother, predictably, had not deigned to lighten her mourning for the occasion, and was dressed head to toe in deadening black, while Lilly's sisters wore complementary shades of mauve. All three bore the same expression of mild disgust, which made them appear as if they had smelled something very disagreeable but had no notion of what to do about it.

Sitting at the end of the pew, her pretty face wreathed in smiles, was Lady Helena. Charlotte had spoken with her the evening before, though only for a few minutes, and had found her pleasant, thoughtful, and surprisingly curious about Charlotte's work in Liverpool. She seemed a timid girl, constantly looking to Edward for reassurance, though Charlotte could see no evidence of the venality that so stained the character of Lilly's sisters. It would take a sturdy soul indeed to withstand life among the Cumberland women, Lilly excepted, and Charlotte rather feared that Lady Helena wouldn't be equal to it. Not, of course, that it was any of her affair.

The service flew by in what felt like seconds: the exchange of vows, with Lilly's soft voice faltering near the end; the hymn "Now Thank We All Our God"; the first lesson, read by Lilly's friend Constance Evans, one of the WAACs she'd known in France. Then the psalm, sung beautifully by the choir; the second lesson, read by Colonel Lewis, who had commanded the clearing hospital where Robbie and Lilly had worked; and a mealymouthed homily by the vicar, who was new to the parish and entirely unequal to the occasion. And, last, a moment of peace in the Lady Chapel, as she and Edward witnessed the marriage register, and Robbie, embracing his wife, bent his head so he might hear her whispered thoughts.

They assembled before the altar, ready to depart, but instead of the expected chords from the organ, a surprise: the rising, skirling notes of a single piper outside the church. They all looked to Edward.

"How could I not?" he confessed. "It will give Mama indigestion for *days*."

Outside the sun was shining, the sky was a perfect shade of blue, and a crowd of well-wishers from the village was waiting to cheer the bride and groom. Lady Cumberland and her daughters and sons-in-law, together with the ever-obedient George, retreated to their carriages, not troubling to offer a word of congratulations to the wedded couple.

Charlotte watched Edward's face as his family's carriages moved away, but he betrayed no sign of annoyance or disappointment. It wasn't as if such behavior was unexpected, after all.

He was squinting in the sunlight, his free hand shielding his eyes, and although he looked well enough in his morning suit, he was still far too thin. He had shadows under his eyes, dark smudges that gave wordless evidence of late nights and lost sleep.

"Are you—" she began, but he smiled at her and squeezed her arm fraternally.

"Shall we be off? I'm bound to take longer than everyone else. Ought to have brought my cane."

"I'll hold tight," she offered, and was immediately horrified by her boldness. What if he thought . . . ?

"That's very kind of you, but I had better offer my arm to Mrs. Fraser. My tiresome relations didn't think to offer her a ride back in the carriages, so I had best see to her. And I suppose Helena will wish to walk with me. You'll be all right, won't you?"

"Of course. I'll walk back with Lilly's other friends."

"Then I shall see you back at the hall."

She watched as he went over to Lady Helena, who really was looking very pretty, and detached her from the group of Cumberland cousins with whom she'd been speaking. He then approached Mrs. Fraser and said something that made her smile from ear to ear. She offered her arm and he set off with the two women, his pace measured and precise, along the graveled path that led back to Cumbermere Hall.

Feeling a bit like a bump on a log, Charlotte walked over to Lilly's friends from the WAAC—Constance, Bridget, and Annie—all of whom she had met for the first time the afternoon before. Most of the wedding guests, with the exception of immediate family and Mrs. Fraser, were staying at the Haverthwaite Arms, the village's modest inn. Lady Cumberland had refused to countenance hosting everyone at the hall, insisting that she was still too overwrought by the loss of her husband to bear the ordeal of having strangers under her roof.

Charlotte had been relieved to be at a distance, even if it meant she saw less of Lilly over the wedding weekend than she would have liked. As the inn was small, she was sharing a room with Constance, whom she liked enormously.

"Hello, ladies," she greeted the women. "Shall we make our way back to the hall for the wedding breakfast?"

"Would love to know why they call it breakfast when it's nigh on half past twelve," Annie grumbled. "Shouldn't it be the wedding dinner?"

"Hush, you," said Bridget. "Quit your mithering."

"I hope this breakfast is easier to make sense of than that dinner last night. Had no idea which fork to use—there were that many of them. Made a right pillock of meself."

"You did nothing of the sort," Charlotte reassured her.

"Was it me, or was Lady Cumberland looking daggers at all of us?" asked Constance worriedly.

"She looked at me like I was something nasty she'd stepped in," said Annie. "Gave me a turn, it did."

"She makes everyone feel like that," Charlotte explained. "It's nothing you did, I promise. If Mr. Lloyd George himself were to join us, she would treat him much the same. Besides, you mustn't let her ruin your fun. Edward—Lord Cumberland, that is—is delighted to have you here. He told me so himself."

"He did, did he?" said Bridget with a naughty wink. "Too bad I'm engaged to my Gordon already, otherwise I'd give him a look-in, if you know what I mean. Talks so nice, and he's ever so handsome. Shame about the tin leg, though."

"Bridget Gallagher! He might hear you," said Constance, pulling at her friend's sleeve.

"He's not the sort to mind. His mum would fall over, though. Wouldn't that be a sight? Her having to call for her smelling salts!"

"And what would that do to Lilly's wedding?" said Constance. "Behave yourselves, or I'll tell Colonel Lewis, I will."

Simply the notion of being dressed down by their former OC had a leveling effect on Annie and Bridget, who were content thereafter to talk about their lives after their discharge from the WAAC.

"We're both at Brandauer's, making pen nibs, right where we was before the war," Annie told Charlotte.

"In Birmingham, yes?"

"Hockley. Never thought I'd miss it, back when I joined the WAAC, but I was glad to come home."

"At the factory—they didn't give your jobs away to the men?"

"Nah," said Bridget. "Stamping nibs is women's work. Pay is good, too, though we don't get near as much as the men."

"I gather you're both engaged?"

"We are that," confirmed Annie.

"And when will the weddings be?"

"No time soon, I hope," said Bridget. "That'd be an end to work, at least for me. Gordon is that stubborn, he is, and once the kiddies start coming I'd have no time for it, anyways. So I'm content to wait awhile."

"Me, too," added Annie.

"And what about you, Constance? I believe you said you're from Peterborough?"

"I am. I'm living with my mum and dad again, just until I

decide what to do. I'll probably go back to being a clerk some-where. I did love the driving, but there's no hope of a job like that now. And Dad would never allow it."

"Are you still writing to that soldier who landed at the CCS last August?" asked Annie.

"No," said a blushing Constance, "but only because he's back in Peterborough as well. He was an old friend from home," she explained, turning to Charlotte, "and by some chance he ended up at our clearing hospital. He wasn't hurt all that badly, only a broken arm and some wounds from shell frag-ments, but it was enough to keep him out of harm's way until the end of the war."

"And now he's back . . . ?" Charlotte asked.

"He's back in Peterborough, working at his father's survey-ing firm, and we go out for a long walk every Sunday after church."

"That sounds wonderful."

"If you don't mind my asking, Charlotte, how did you end up working for Lord Cumberland's family? I wouldn't have expected someone with an Oxford degree to become a govern-ess," Constance said.

"Nor would I. The truth is that I needed a job and I couldn't find anything else, not then. I was very happy with Lilly, though."

"How long were you here?"

"Four years. I started in 1907, when Lilly was just fourteen, and I left when she made her debut. That's when I moved to Liverpool and began to work for Miss Rathbone."

"The suffragette?" asked Constance.

"She prefers the term 'suffragist,'" Charlotte clarified. "She's not only interested in votes for women, you know. Miss

Rathbone believes all adults are entitled to the vote, no matter how much they earn or where they live."

"So if you was working for her, how is it that you and Lilly lived together in London?" asked Annie.

"I wanted to be doing more for the war effort, so I came to London and trained as a nurse. Lilly lived with me at Mrs. Collins's when she was working as a clippie, and again after she was invalided home."

"Didn't Lilly invite Mrs. Collins to the wedding?" asked Constance. "I was sure she said she had."

"She did. But Mrs. Collins has never left London, not even for a day at the seaside. She was too anxious about taking the train up, not to mention leaving the house empty for a few days. I'm sure Lilly will take over some photographs to show her when she and Robbie return from their honeymoon." Charlotte resolved then and there to write to Mrs. Collins that evening and tell her all about the wedding.

They were through the woods now and following the other guests along the raked gravel path that led to the back of the great house. A wide, sweeping staircase led to the second floor, to a large terrace often used for afternoon tea in fine weather. Just as Charlotte reached the top of the steps, the French doors that ran the length of the terrace were opened and Mr. Maxwell, the Cumberland family's butler for many years, stepped outside.

"Lord Cumberland, Lady Elizabeth, Mr. Fraser, ladies and gentlemen," he called out. "Breakfast is served."

They filed into the galleried dining room, Lilly and Robbie leading the way, where an immensely long table had been set for the eighty-odd wedding guests. Lady Cumberland was already present, standing at the far end of the room, a brittle smile fixed on her face. A warm welcome indeed.

As the bride's only attendant, Charlotte was seated near the center of the table, with Robbie to her left and Mrs. Fraser to her right. Immediately across the table sat Lady Cumberland, flanked by her other daughters and sons-in-law; evidently she did not intend to mix with any of the other guests.

Charlotte turned to Mrs. Fraser, planning to inquire after her enjoyment of the ceremony, and was startled by the look of terror on the woman's face. Robbie's mother was staring at her plate, or rather at the menu card that had been set atop it. Charlotte looked down at her own card and immediately understood: the entire menu was written in French.

Consommé à la Comtesse
Suprêmes de Saumon à l'Écossaise
Côtelettes d'Agneau
Chapons à la Cumberland
Jambon et Langue Découpés à l'Aspic
Asperges avec une Sauce Mousseline
Crème Glacée Lady Elizabeth
Gâteau de Noces
Café

"Don't worry," she whispered. "None of it is very exotic. Soup, salmon, lamb chops, chicken, ham and tongue in aspic, asparagus, ice cream, and wedding cake. Oh, and coffee, too."

"I've never seen the like in all my life. And all these forks and knives . . ."

"Start at the outside and work your way in. Or, even better, watch to see which one Lady Cumberland uses."

"Thank you, Miss Brown. You are a dear."

"Not at all. You know, when I first came here, to work as

Lilly's governess, I couldn't sleep for a week. I was terribly nervous."

"Lady Elizabeth is very fond of you."

"She's your daughter-in-law now, and I'm sure she'd prefer that you call her Lilly."

"I know, I know. It's only . . . well, it seems so strange to me. Robbie had been friends with his lordship for years and years, but I never thought to be sitting *here*."

"You are, and may I say that you look every inch the happy mother of the groom. This is an important day for you, too. I do hope you are able to enjoy it."

"I'll do my best. Oh—here's the soup. Which of these spoons am I meant to use?"

"That one, just there."

By the end of the meal Charlotte had acquired a fine understanding of every single award, scholarship, and prize Robbie had won in the course of his academic career, as well as a detailed description of the medals he had been awarded, among them the Military Cross, for his efforts in evacuating his hospital during the Spring 1918 Amiens offensive.

Their dessert of strawberry ice cream had just been cleared away when Edward, who had been seated to Lilly's left, stood up and waited for the room to fall silent.

"Ladies and gentlemen, my honored guests, I beg your indulgence while I sing the praises of my sister Lady Elizabeth Fraser, the loveliest bride imaginable. I think you all know how dear she is to me, as indeed she is to all of us. Her courage, selflessness, and determination are a shining example of a life lived with meaning and purpose. To know that today she has married my greatest friend . . ."

Here he paused, his voice catching, and he cleared his throat before continuing, this time in a lighter vein. "Quite frankly I had no idea that they had fallen in love, not until the moment that Robbie appeared at my hospital bed, a little more than six months ago, and confessed the truth to me. I am sorry to confess it, but I very nearly flew out of my bed and throttled him. She was, after all, my youngest sister."

A chorus of nervous laughter circled the table. The new Earl of Cumberland could so easily have objected to his sister's marriage to a social nobody, but instead he had supported the match wholeheartedly. Further proof to Charlotte, if ever she had needed it, that Edward hadn't an ounce of prejudice in him.

"Fortunately for them, and for all of us who have gathered here today, I soon realized that I was wrong in my misgivings. Robert Fraser is the finest man I've ever known, and as such I believe him to be the only man in the world who is truly deserving of my sister. Nothing could give me more pleasure than to stand before you now and toast them on their wedding day. In this, I know I am departing from tradition, but I beg you to allow me: a toast to the bride *and* to the groom."

Chapter 9

As soon as Edward had finished speaking, Robbie began his own speech, which managed to be funny and moving all at once, and featured a fine recitation of "A Red, Red Rose." The guests were then directed to the music room, where coffee and slices of wedding cake were served, together with additional helpings of champagne for those in an especially festive mood.

Edward seemed to be in his element, moving from guest to guest, ensuring everyone felt welcome despite his mother's churlish behavior, delightedly sharing reminiscences of the bridal couple to anyone who would listen. He always had a glass of champagne in his hand, frequently refilled by a trailing footman, and as the reception continued he appeared, to Charlotte's eyes, increasingly frail. Having abandoned his cane, he began to rub at his temples with whichever hand wasn't holding his glass, and although he took pains to hide it, she could tell he was favoring his good leg. She longed to help, but there was nothing she could do, certainly not without embarrassing him.

Needing a quiet moment to herself, she moved to an empty corner of the room, attracted by a pair of small, dark oil paintings that she remembered from her days as Lilly's governess. They were overshadowed by enormous canvases above and to their right, both by Canaletto, but she had always preferred the Dutch burgher and his serious wife to the Venetian cityscapes. They weren't handsome people, but they looked as if they had been good-hearted, hardworking, honest, and sincere in their desire to live a decent life.

"May I join you?"

Not recognizing the voice, Charlotte turned to discover a shyly smiling Lady Helena. "Please do. I was only reacquainting myself with the Rembrandts."

"Such a shame they're hidden away here." Lady Helena peered at the portrait of the man, tilting her head as she took it in at one angle, then another. "The varnish has darkened quite badly. See here?" She pointed at the burgher's robe. "This would have been a bright blue originally, but now it's almost black."

"Yes. Yes, I can see that now."

"Do you know what I love best about Rembrandt's portraits, Miss Brown? It's the hands. Look how tightly hers are clutched together. I think she was nervous. Her husband—see how relaxed his posture is compared to hers?—had insisted on portraits of both of them, and she wanted to look her best, wanted to know she was worthy of the honor. But still she doubted . . . and Rembrandt captures that in the hands alone."

"Yes, of course," Charlotte agreed calmly, though she was quite taken aback by Lady Helena's remarks. What had happened to the young, bland cipher?

"I beg your pardon. I ought not to have spoken in such a forthright manner."

"Please don't apologize," Charlotte insisted. "You speak so knowledgeably on the subject. Are you an artist yourself?"

Lady Helena shook her head, her face flushing a little. "Not really. Not properly. I dabble, that's all."

"Isn't that how most of us begin? By discovering what we like, what we wish to do, and then learning as and when we can?"

"You're very kind. Particularly in light of your own accomplishments. I'd have loved to become a nurse, like you, but my parents were concerned that Lord and Lady Cumberland might disapprove."

"I'm sorry to hear that."

"I still tried to do my part, but it was nothing compared to what you did. Lilly, too. Just some hospital visiting. That sort of thing."

"I'm sure the men were most grateful to you."

"I like to think they were. Most of the time I did little sketches, just pen-and-ink portraits for them to put in their letters home. Sometimes I brought my camera. That sort of thing. Nothing terribly brave, I'm afraid."

Charlotte set her hand on Lady Helena's arm, hoping she wouldn't find the gesture impertinent. "I disagree. It is very brave indeed to go into a ward full of injured men, not knowing how they may react, or how they will be wounded, and offer to help them. You did a great deal of good. I'm certain of it."

"I felt I had to do something, that's all. After Edward . . . well, there were all those months of not knowing, and I had to occupy myself. But of course that's all over now. I'll be busy with a home, soon, and Edward will need me at his side, so . . ."

"I'm sure you will be very happy together."

Lady Helena smiled bravely, though she wasn't quite able to erase the sadness from her eyes. "I'm sure we will. Oh, look—Lilly is beckoning us. It must be time for the pictures."

The photographer was slow in his work, fussing endlessly over the arrangements for his portraits of the bridal couple and their families. When it came time for Charlotte and Lilly to have their picture taken together, he experienced some difficulty with his flash apparatus, and it took an age for him to sort out the problem and finish.

Returning to the music room, Charlotte walked its perimeter, intent on talking to Edward. While the photographs were being taken, his merry demeanor had flattened into a weary stillness, and she was concerned that he was feeling overwhelmed by the festivities. When she couldn't find him she approached one of the footmen and, after asking if Lord Cumberland had retired for the afternoon, learned that he had stepped outside for some fresh air.

Edward hadn't gone far, halting at the third of the formal parterres beyond the terrace. It was planted with roses, a jumble of color and scent quite at odds with the severely clipped box hedges that delineated its perimeter. He was sitting on a stone bench in one corner, his head down, a neglected cigarette smoldering between his fingers.

As she approached he looked up and winced, as if he already knew what she would say.

"Oh, Edward," she groaned. "Not again. You promised Lilly you were done with that filthy habit."

"I am sorry," he answered mildly, dropping the cigarette to the ground and crushing it beneath his heel. "I promise I'll try to give it up."

"You'll end up with a cough if you don't. And it will make your teeth quite yellow."

"I don't doubt it."

She sat next to him and let the sun warm her hair for a few minutes before speaking again. "At the risk of another set-down—"

"You mean my disgraceful behavior at my father's funeral? I had been meaning to apologize, you know, if only via the post. But then Lilly fixed the wedding date and I knew I'd be seeing you."

"You were right to be upset with me. I ought not to have presumed I understood, and I certainly shouldn't have introduced the subject. Not then, at any rate."

"All the same," he countered, "I was beastly to you, and for that I apologize most sincerely." He bent his head, his shoulders bowed, and rubbed at his eyes with one hand.

"There's no need. You were right. I don't know what happened to you, nor can I truly know how you feel. But I did care for men who were badly, badly wounded, even though their injuries weren't the kind a surgeon can repair. Some mocked them for it. Some said they were cowards."

"What do you say?" he asked, not looking up.

"They were men. Ordinary men who were trying to make sense of a world gone mad. That's all." She squeezed his forearm, still so thin beneath the camouflage of his clothing. "Tell me: why did you come out here? You seemed happy enough earlier."

"It was too loud, that's all. It was giving me a headache."

"Then why all the champagne?"

"Why not? It's a wedding, after all. Champagne makes people happy."

"A glass of it, perhaps," she said doubtfully.

He plucked a rose from one of the ramblers that overhung their bench and began to dissect it, petal by petal. "It helps with the pain. Phantom pain, they call it. In my missing leg. Helps with my headaches, too."

"Drink will only make things worse. If you're in pain you must see a physician."

"So he can stupefy me with morphine? I think not. Drink is a far safer tonic."

"Is that all? The physical pain, I mean?" she asked. "You aren't troubled by memories of the war?"

More petals fell to the ground. "Nothing to speak of. Nothing that keeps me awake at night."

"You swear?"

"I swear it, Charlotte."

"Why don't you speak with someone from your battalion? One of the other officers? Surely you're still in contact with some of them."

"I am, but we're not a talkative lot. Reliving it is the last thing any of us want to do."

"So you bury it all."

"No," he said, looking her in the eye at last. "I simply don't think of it. The war happened. It's finished. It's in the past."

"But it's all around us—it's everywhere we look," she protested. "How can you *not* think of it?"

"Practice."

The silence grew between them, heavier and heavier, until she could bear it no longer. "I ought to go. After all, you came out here for some peace and quiet, and instead I've been badgering you."

"No, don't go. I only needed to clear my head. I'm happy for the company."

Time, then, to change the subject to something less troublesome. "I had the chance to speak to Lady Helena just now. She seems very nice."

"She is."

"Have you set a date yet?" Charlotte asked, knowing full well that they hadn't.

"No." He leaned forward again, resting his elbows on his knees, and held his head in his hands. "There's so much to think about . . . if only I could empty my head of everything."

"Is this to do with Lady Helena?"

"No . . . yes . . . I don't know. It all boils down to money."

"Money?"

"Yes. You've heard of estate duty, I presume? Yes? Well, I owe His Majesty's government something like half a million pounds."

"Good Lord."

"Twenty percent of my inheritance—gone, just like that. Although it could have been worse. I gather there's talk of raising it to thirty or even forty percent."

"What does this have to do with Lady Helena?" Charlotte asked, still reeling.

"She's titled, but comes with little money. Fifty or sixty thousand pounds, I think. Mama is pressing me to break the engagement and find an American to marry instead."

Although she scarcely knew Lady Helena, Charlotte was horrified at the thought of her being set aside for such mercenary concerns. "You aren't going to give in, are you?"

"Would that be so bad? I'd only be replacing one stranger with another."

"How can she be a stranger? You've been engaged to the woman for five years!"

"I was absent for more than four of them, and I can count on one hand the number of times we've been alone together. To be perfectly honest, it was something our parents arranged."

"In this day and age?"

"It happens more often than you'd think. I had to do it, you know. I . . . well, I'd got myself into some difficulties. Had accumulated some debts. Papa and Mama agreed to sort out everything if I, in turn, agreed to find a suitable wife. So I did."

Charlotte felt quite certain that she was going to be sick. "Did Lady Helena know of this?"

"I doubt it. Certainly I never told her."

"I assumed . . . I thought that you were in love with her," Charlotte whispered.

"Of course not. I don't know her well enough to love her."

A surge of pity for the blameless Helena swept through her. The poor girl was to be picked up and set down like a playing piece on a chessboard, with no regard for her feelings or desires or anything beyond the dynastic concerns of people who didn't care a fig for her. It was positively medieval.

"So what do you plan to do?" she asked. "Marry the richest American you can find and solve all your problems?"

"I'm the one facing financial ruin. I'd have thought you would sympathize."

"Ruin? You're facing nothing of the sort. You have no idea, not the faintest idea, of what true ruin entails."

"So enlighten me. Tell me one of your depressing stories. I'm sure you have plenty to choose from," he said acidly.

"I do. There's the family I tried to help last week. Tried, but failed. The father was wounded during the war, so badly he can no longer work. The mother had just been sacked so her job might be given away to a man. They had five children at home, the eldest only eleven. All too young to go out to work—not legally, at least.

"So I went to them. I went to their flat and told them there was relief to be had, and that there was no shame in it. I promised I would not take away their children. I swore to them that I would help. They only had to come to my office and fill out some forms."

"What happened?"

"They never came to me. I waited for them—I ought to have brought the forms with me when I visited, to save them the trouble of the journey to the constituency office—but they never came. So I went back to their flat the next day, this time with everything we'd need for a relief claim, and they were gone. Had done a 'midnight flit.' They were too frightened of the debt collectors, too frightened of me, even, so they disappeared."

"I see."

"No, your lordship, you don't. Those children hadn't eaten a decent meal in days, if not weeks. Their shoes were more cardboard than leather, and there was scarcely a stick of furniture left in the flat. What will become of that family? I lie awake at night thinking of them.

"But they are only one family, one among hundreds, *thousands,* and their numbers are growing. If you could only comprehend the magnitude of the disaster I face every day . . . and yet it takes so little to help them. A pound here, a pound there. So little."

"I'd have helped. All you had to do was ask—"

"Of course I never asked. It would have been most improper. You were my friend, not my penny bank."

She got up and walked to the far side of the parterre, need-ing to put some distance between them. She couldn't breathe with him at her side.

"Go on," he goaded her. "Tell me what a failure I am. Tell me what poor use I've made of all my wealth and privilege."

"But you have—can't you see that? Can't you look beyond your own misery? The world doesn't revolve around you and your unhappiness."

He laughed, but it was a bitter sound, made ugly by its utter lack of humor. "So says Saint Charlotte, made holy by her de-votion to others. If only you could hear what comes out of your mouth. You speak as if your every word is a pearl of wisdom bestowed by the Almighty." He surged to his feet and advanced on her, one halting step after the other, but she stood her ground.

"You shame yourself with such words. You know you do." Her voice was shaking; so were her hands. She clenched them into fists and straightened her spine. She would not back down.

"So you, Miss Brown, *you* are allowed to tell *me* that I'm a pathetic, self-centered failure—no, don't shake your head, we both know that's what you meant—but you are above reproach? Or do you truly believe that your actions are beyond criticism? Are you really that perfect?"

He stood so close, looming above her, and for an instant she feared he might do something unwise. Strike her, perhaps. Or even kiss her. She wasn't certain which she feared more.

Somehow she found her voice. "At least I'm doing some-thing to help others. All you've done since you came back from the war is whine and moan and feel sorry for yourself. Isn't it time you got on with your life? Did something worthwhile? You're alive, for a start, which is more than millions can say.

And you are richer than any man has a right to be. Grow up, for heaven's sake. Simply . . . *grow up.*"

She walked away, her knees shaking, desperate to escape the anger and shame and despair that he had provoked in her. But he came after her, so she broke into an undignified run, driven by her need to escape this exasperating man she had no right to care about. A man whose troubles ought to mean nothing to her.

She stumbled on a stone that protruded from the path and fell hard on her knees. Before she could stand again he was at her side, pulling her gently to her feet.

"Stop, Charlotte. Don't run from me."

"Don't touch me. Let go of my hands," she begged, frantic in her need to be free of him.

"Look at me, won't you? Just for a minute?" he asked, sounding as wretched as she felt. Good, she thought. He deserved no less.

"I spoke in anger just now," he said, still imprisoning her hands. "You were right, as you usually are. That's why I lashed out at you. Please forgive me."

As the echo of his words floated in the air between them, it dawned on her that she had been unforgivably rude. She had never been the sort of person to give in to strong emotions; she had never, in all her life, spoken as harshly to another person as she had done, just now, to Edward.

"I beg your pardon, Lord Cumberland, for my rudeness. I spoke out of turn."

"I deserved every word of it," he insisted. "And I will find a way to sort out my silly problems. I swear I will."

She stood there, not moving, and let herself feel the warmth and strength of his hands. And she recalled the moment, only six months earlier, when he had come through the door of her and Lilly's boardinghouse in Camden Town, and she had seen with her own eyes that, by virtue of some unknowable miracle, he was not dead. That he had not vanished into the mud and muck and horror of the war.

She let herself remember the joy she had felt in that moment, at the sight of his dear, sad face, and with it she remembered all that he had suffered. If only she could take back her unkind words.

She regarded their linked hands for a moment, and then, another apology on her lips, she looked up and met his gaze. He looked almost like the old Edward, the boy she had first met at Oxford, so charming and carefree and sure of his place in the world. But that boy was dead and gone, and in his place was a man who had seen things she would never be able to know, let alone imagine. A man who was infinitely more complicated, and dangerous, than the boy he had once been.

"Do you feel up to returning to the reception?" he asked softly.

"I do. I wouldn't want Lilly to worry. I don't look too disheveled, do I?"

"You look perfect," he said, taking her arm.

As quickly as it had erupted, her anger had melted away, but wasn't that what always happened when she was around Edward? No matter what he did, no matter how he behaved, she always forgave him.

He carried such burdens, admittedly some of them of his own making, and there were so few people he could trust. Robbie, Lilly, and herself. Perhaps one or two friends, although she'd met some of his friends before and had not cared for them one whit. Even his engagement was a sham.

She felt sorry for him; that was all. He was unwell, unhappy, nearly friendless, and crippled by obligations that would have taxed the energies of even the fittest man. He needed her friendship, not her censure.

"It will all work out in the end," she said as they walked up the terrace steps. "I'm certain it will."

"If I were still the sort of man who believed in such things, I would agree with you. As it is . . ."

"Yes?"

"I'll soldier on."

Chapter 10

Cumbria, England
July 1907

There was no reason at all to be nervous. Not yet, at least. Lord Ashford had been perfectly clear in his last letter: John Pringle, one of the family's coachmen, would meet her at the train station in Penrith and bring her to Cumbermere Hall. Only once she'd had a chance to settle in would she be introduced to the family.

Charlotte had been traveling since dawn, for her journey had begun at home in Somerset, where she'd gone after the end of term. Although her parents hadn't criticized her decision to take on the post of governess to Lady Elizabeth, neither had they been especially pleased. Her mother had been particularly fretful. "After all your hard work at university . . . I don't know. It seems like a step back for you to go and work as a servant in someone else's home."

Charlotte had tried to persuade her that she wouldn't be a servant, not precisely; she would be teaching a young lady, not waiting on her hand and foot. But her mother, who herself had been taught by a governess at home, was unconvinced.

Her father had said little, and on their afternoon walks together they had both avoided the subject of her new position. Unlike some men, he wore the mantle of paterfamilias lightly, rarely imposing his wishes on his wife or daughter. If he'd had grave concerns, of course, he'd have voiced them, but in their absence he was content enough to stand back and allow Charlotte to chart her own course. In this she was fortunate, and she knew it. Every blessing in her life had come from her parents. Without them, what would have become of her? How might her life have turned out?

That morning, both Mother and Father had said good-bye and waved her off with smiles on their faces and repeated assurances that they knew, simply *knew,* she would excel at her new position. "You'll be the making of that young woman," her father had insisted. "Mark my words."

It was nearly one o'clock as the train pulled into the small station at Penrith. Charlotte alighted from the carriage and looked up and down the platform, wondering if Mr. Pringle would be there or waiting outside the station. After a moment, she spotted a man dressed in livery a few yards away, his back to her.

"Mr. Pringle?"

He turned around, a broad smile on his homely face, and came forward to take her valise and carpetbag. "There you are, Miss Brown. I was looking out for you at the wrong end of the train."

"Lord Ashford was kind enough to send me a first-class ticket, otherwise I should have been in the third-class carriages. How do you do?" She held out her hand, and after a moment's surprised hesitation, he set down her carpetbag and accepted her greeting.

"I'm very well, thank you. We're just outside on the fore-court, if you'll follow me."

Mr. Pringle helped her into a modest two-wheeled buggy, which had just enough room for the two of them, and then strapped her bags to the back of the carriage. "Your trunk arrived yesterday, so I decided to fetch you in this. Faster than the landau, and old Bill here's more reliable than any of his lordship's motorcars."

In only a few minutes they had left Penrith behind and were on the road to Ullswater. On both sides the fells towered above them dramatically, their rugged slopes dotted with boulders and the occasional cluster of bleating sheep. Raised in the south of England, where the largest hills were little more than molehills in comparison, Charlotte was used to more decorous landscapes. But this countryside had never been tamed, had never been bent and shaped to the will of man, and she couldn't help but find it a trifle intimidating.

"Thank you for coming to collect me, Mr. Pringle." It wouldn't do to seem standoffish, not with the first person she met today, and he did seem like a friendly sort.

"You can go ahead and call me John Pringle, just like everyone else does. Can't remember the last time someone called me Mr. Pringle."

"Why both names?" she asked. Was this an idiosyncrasy of all aristocratic families, or just the Cumberlands?

"Well, there were at least three or four men called John working on the estate when I started, nigh on thirty years ago. And there were more than a few Pringles, too. I suppose I could have picked another name, like some do. But I wanted to keep the names my mum and dad gave me. So that's why I'm John Pringle to everyone at Cumbermere Hall—yourself included."

"Very well, John Pringle it is. How far a drive is it to the hall?"

"Eight miles, more or less. Could have taken a shortcut, but I thought you'd like a proper view of the great house for the first time you lay eyes on it."

"I gather it's very large."

"That it is, but it's beautiful all the same. My people have lived here, and worked for the earls, for more'n a hundred years now. Feels like our home, too."

They sat in silence for another few minutes; though Charlotte was brimming over with questions, she didn't want to test John Pringle's patience or loyalty to his employers. It wouldn't do to offend him with impertinent questions—and what if such questions were reported to Lord Ashford or his parents? It was a risk she didn't care to take.

The carriage was slowing; from what she could tell they were still in the middle of nowhere, the only sign of human habitation a lattice of low fieldstone walls fencing in pastureland and the road itself. She looked to John Pringle, concerned that something was amiss.

"We're coming up to the entrance to the park, Miss Brown. Just past this bend."

The gates seemed to appear out of nowhere, but then they had been hidden from view by a stretch of especially high hedgerows. John Pringle slowed the horse to a walk and neatly guided both animal and carriage under a monumental archway that linked two halves of a gatehouse. The buildings would have looked perfectly at home in Belgravia, their neoclassical façades brightened by window boxes brimming over with petunias. The gates themselves, more baroque in style, were made of wrought iron painted a gleaming black, each half inset with a heraldic crest.

They turned onto the long approach to the great house, old Bill at a trot again, pulling at the reins in glad anticipation of home. Deer scattered at their approach, disappearing into the dappled shade cast by the park's ancient oaks. The carriage passed through deeper woodland, the drive continuing straight as a Roman road. And then they were in the sun again, and the house lay in the distance before them.

Charlotte couldn't suppress a gasp of wonderment as she saw Cumbermere Hall for the first time. Rising four stories high, it faced south, with wings stretching north at either end. Scores of windows marched in perfect symmetry the length of each wing and story, their sole interruption a majestic entrance set into the center. But rather than stop in front of the house, John Pringle steered the carriage around to the western wing, to an entrance that was many times less grand in both size and decoration, and there drew the carriage to a halt.

As he helped Charlotte down, the door opened and an older woman emerged, her status evident by the ring of keys at her waist and the lace cap that crowned her neatly arranged hair.

"Welcome to Cumbermere Hall, Miss Brown," the woman said, coming down the steps and extending her hand in greeting. "I am Mrs. Forster, the housekeeper here. Do come in."

"Thank you, Mrs. Forster."

"Your trunk arrived yesterday, and is already in your room. Menzies, take Miss Brown's things upstairs. I shall now take tea with her in my sitting room."

Charlotte followed the housekeeper inside, along a corridor that gave onto a series of kitchens and storerooms, and into a small room neatly furnished with a pair of armchairs, set on either side of an empty hearth, and a small table and chairs.

In the far corner was a rolltop desk with a set of pigeonholes above.

Mrs. Forster invited her to sit at the table, which already held a plate of sandwiches and fancies and a large earthenware teapot.

"Tell me a little about yourself, Miss Brown. Where did you grow up?"

"In Somerset, ma'am. My father is a cleric at Wells Cathedral."

"I see. Have you any siblings?"

"No, ma'am."

"Your parents must be very proud of you. How do you take your tea?"

"With milk, thank you."

"Help yourself to some sandwiches and cake. A little something to hold you until suppertime. While Lord and Lady Cumberland are at the hall you'll take your meals with the other senior staff, but after they return to London you'll be with Lady Elizabeth in the nursery."

"Yes, ma'am."

"There's no need to ma'am me, my dear. Plain Mrs. Forster will do. Now, where was I? The girls and Master George have their rooms in the nursery wing, which is overseen by Nanny Gee. Mrs. Geoffrey, but everyone calls her Nanny Gee. Lovely woman. There's the governess for Lady Mary and Lady Alice, too. Miss Shreve."

"I hope . . . that is, I worry she may take offense at my coming here."

"I shouldn't worry. Between you and me, the poor thing looks as if the next stiff wind might blow her over. A few kind words and she'll be your friend for life."

"I see," Charlotte said, drinking the last of her tea. "That is a relief."

"If you've any trouble with the other staff, let me know immediately. Not that I expect you will, though. All of us are very fond of Lady Elizabeth. Such a dear girl, and simply desperate for a little attention. I think you'll get on very well here."

"Thank you, Mrs. Forster."

"Are you ready to go on upstairs? Good. If you have any difficulty in finding your way about, simply ask one of the staff. Of course, you'll be with Lady Elizabeth most of the time, so she'll be your guide."

Mrs. Forster led them along a corridor, around a corner, along a second and even longer hallway, and then up flight after flight after flight of stairs. By the time they had arrived at the baize-lined door to the nursery wing, Charlotte was thoroughly discombobulated, and certain she would require a trail of bread crumbs to navigate henceforth.

"I'll introduce you to Nanny Gee, and then take you to your room. I expect she'll be in the children's sitting room with Master George." They stopped at a door, roughly halfway along the corridor, and Mrs. Forster knocked briskly before entering.

"Good afternoon, Nanny Gee. How are you today?"

"Very well, Mrs. Forster. Is this Miss Brown with you?"

"It is, indeed."

"Don't be shy, Miss Brown. Do come in. We've been all in a tizzy waiting for you. Miss Lilly's been that excited. I don't think she's slept for days. Come, now, Master George. Say hello to your sister's new governess."

"Hello, Miss Brown. How do you do?"

Charlotte came forward to shake George's outstretched

hand. He was a handsome boy, about seven or eight years old, and very similar in appearance to his brother. "I'm very well, thank you, and pleased to make your acquaintance. Yours as well, Mrs. Geoffrey."

"Oh, none of that, dear. Call me Nanny Gee. Your room's all ready for you. Used to be Master Edward's until he left for university. Shall I take you?"

"No need, Nanny," Mrs. Forster replied. "We'll leave you to finish your meal."

Charlotte's room was small and modestly furnished, but made pleasantly bright by a large, west-facing window. Against one wall stood a single walnut bed topped with a plain linen counterpane; her trunk sat at its foot. On the opposite wall were a wardrobe and a chest of drawers. An old armchair, its upholstery somewhat worn, sat before the window, with a desk and chair next to it.

"There's fresh water in the ewer, and the necessary is at the end of the hall," said Mrs. Forster. "If you need anything else, simply let me or Nanny Gee know."

"The room is lovely. I'm sure I won't need a thing."

"I'll send up a footman to escort you down to meet the family. They're finishing luncheon now, so I expect you'll have about half an hour. Will that do?"

"Yes, of course. Thank you for everything."

"You are most welcome, my dear. I'll see you at supper."

Charlotte wanted nothing more than to lie down and close her eyes, but time was of the essence. She might be summoned at any instant, and it was imperative that she make a good first impression on Lord Ashford's family.

She opened her trunk and drew out her best day gown, a charcoal-gray wool that she had wrapped in tissue paper for just this eventuality, and as she buttoned it up she was relieved to see the paper had protected it from creasing. After washing her face and hands, she unpinned her hair, brushed it carefully, and fixed it back into the same severe, low chignon she always wore. Her spectacles were dusty, she realized belatedly, so she washed and polished them as well.

At five minutes before the hour, a little less than the thirty minutes Mrs. Forster had promised, there came a knock on the door.

"Miss Brown? Are you there?"

She hurried to the door, certain that it couldn't be—but there he was, standing in the hall, his expression the picture of delight.

"Lord Ashford? What are you doing . . . ? That is, I mean, ah . . . I wasn't expecting you . . ."

"I bumped into Mrs. Forster and she said you'd arrived, so I told her I would fetch you myself. I'm terribly sorry I didn't greet you. We were still at table, otherwise I'd have been there myself. Are you ready? Lilly is simply beside herself with excitement."

"Yes . . . at least I think so. Do you think your parents will find me suitable? That is, am I dressed suitably?" There really wasn't any reason at all for her to be so nervous. It wasn't as if she were being taken in front of a magistrate.

"You look exactly right. And remember that *I* am your employer, not my parents. I am delighted with you, and Lilly is certain to be as well. That's really all that matters."

"You're very kind. Is your entire family here at the hall at present?"

"Only for the week. Normally my parents are in London for the summer—for the Season, that is—but they've come north to recover before the last flurry of balls and parties and so forth. We're going back on Monday, all except Lilly and George, but most of the staff will stay on here. Only Mr. Maxwell and my parents' personal servants make the journey back and forth."

"I see."

"I'll pop back in a few weeks, just to see how you're getting on. In the meantime, will you write to me? Let me know how Lilly is faring?"

"Oh, of course. I should be delighted to do so."

"We're almost there. I took the long way round so we'd have a chance to talk."

"I'm afraid I wouldn't have known the difference." She smiled up at him, grateful for his thoughtfulness. "I was expecting a large house, but nothing on this scale," she admitted.

"It is enormous, isn't it? Yet it still seems like a friendly sort of place. Perhaps because it's so old. Bits and pieces date to the Middle Ages—they're covered up by the Georgian façade, but you can still find them if you look closely."

Charlotte had grown up in the shadow of one of the greatest cathedrals in England, a building filled with history and treasure and artworks of the highest order, but she had never lived *in* it. She couldn't decide if it were a blessing to have such a heritage, or a curse.

They came to the end of a long gallery, its walls adorned with a museum's worth of Old Masters, and approached a set of double doors.

"This is the main drawing room," Lord Ashford explained. "My parents usually come here after luncheon. Are you ready?"

"I think so."

Lord Ashford ushered her in, and then led her across the vast space, which was at least as big as the entire main floor of

Charlotte's home in Somerset, until they stood several yards distant from Lady Cumberland. The countess was seated at a table in the center of the room, her skirts arranged in decorative swirls around her, and was pasting photographs in an album. Her gown, Charlotte noted with a frisson of alarm, would not have been out of place in a ballroom. It looked to be constructed of dozens of layers of paper-thin chiffon and lace and tiny silk rosebuds, and though it was beautiful, Charlotte suspected it was also very uncomfortable. Was this how the elite dressed for a typical afternoon *en famille*?

Lilly's elder sisters, Alice and Mary, sat together on a settee not far distant, and were giggling behind their hands. Likely at her, Charlotte acknowledged; she'd gone to school with similar types. Lord Cumberland was in a wing chair, a newspaper covering his face, snoring gustily.

And then there was her pupil. Lady Elizabeth was perched on one of the window seats, trying and utterly failing to hide her excitement. She was dressed in a dark blue middy dress, a rather juvenile style for a girl of her age, and her hair was pulled back and plaited tightly. She had bright eyes, either hazel or brown, a scattering of freckles across her nose and cheeks, and a shy but sincere smile. Charlotte liked her immediately.

"Mama, Papa, girls. Allow me to present Miss Charlotte Brown, lately of Somerville College, Oxford."

His mother set down the photograph she was trimming and turned her head to look at Charlotte. "How do you do?"

"Very well, your ladyship. Thank you." And then, having been briefed by her mother, Charlotte executed a well-intentioned if somewhat creaky curtsy, the first she had attempted since her childhood dancing lessons. This provoked a torrent of giggles from Lady Alice and Lady Mary, and a single raised eyebrow from the countess.

"What did you study at university?"

"English literature, your ladyship."

This was absorbed without comment. "Where are you from again?"

"Somerset, your ladyship. My father is a prebendary at Wells Cathedral."

Lady Cumberland finished trimming the photograph she was holding and pasted it into her scrapbook. "Very well. Elizabeth? Do come here. And stand still, for heaven's sake. You may take Miss Brown on a walk through the gardens, and then return with her to the nursery."

"Yes, Mama."

"I'll accompany them, Mama," Lord Ashford said. He touched Charlotte's arm, indicating that they ought to leave, though his mother hadn't said good-bye. Perhaps she didn't bother to say farewell to underlings.

"Shall we walk through the rose garden?" Lord Ashford asked once they were safely back in the gallery.

"That sounds very nice," Charlotte agreed. "But I think Lady Elizabeth and I ought to fetch our hats."

"Of course. I'll wait for you both on the terrace."

At last Charlotte was alone with her pupil. She would have to proceed carefully, for she didn't want to overwhelm the girl. At the same time, she could see how desperately the child wished to make a good first impression, and how easy it would be to crush her spirits.

"I do so hope you will be happy here, Miss Brown. When

Edward explained you would be coming to teach me, I thought I would die on the spot. In all my life, my whole, entire life, I have never been so happy!"

"What a lovely thing to say." Charlotte fixed her warmest and most encouraging smile on the girl.

"But it's true. Edward knew I was in danger of expiring from boredom, and so he found you. Miss Shreve means well, but my sisters have worn her down. We haven't done anything worthwhile in ages."

Charlotte would not be drawn into discussions of Miss Shreve's teaching abilities, but she did wish to learn more about the sort of subjects her pupil considered worthwhile.

"Tell me: what are you best at?"

"Literature and history," the girl replied instantly. "And I love composition, too, even though I'm not very good at it. I'm forever writing about things that make no sense. At least that's what Miss Shreve says."

"Is there anything you'd say you can't do? That you're hopeless at?"

"Oh, that's easy. Maths and grammar. And I've never learned biology or chemistry or geography. For all I know, I'm terrible at those subjects, too."

"I doubt that very much. In fact, I rather suspect you are good at everything. It's simply a matter of my finding the correct way to impart the information to you. I can tell you are a very intelligent girl, so that helps immeasurably."

Lilly's face flushed with pride at having been so complimented. Perhaps it was the first time anyone, apart from her brother, had told her how bright she was. Charlotte decided to press forward a little more.

"I wonder if you would mind if I set you some exams. Nothing too punishing, I promise. I only wish to see where you are. Once I have an idea of what you do know, we can turn to studying what you don't yet know. Does that seem agreeable to you?"

"Oh, yes, Miss Brown. That sounds—well, I know Edward would tease me if he were listening, but that sounds wonderful. Having the chance to sit exams, I mean, just as if I were at school."

"Well, you are at school now. But you must let me know if ever you find your lessons boring, or think them too easy or too difficult. I've never been a teacher before, so I expect I shall have a great deal to learn as well."

They reached the top floor again and were through the door to the nursery. "Do you have a sketchbook? Yes? Why don't you bring it along, together with some pencils and charcoal. I'd like to see how well you can draw."

As they went to leave the nursery and join Lord Ashford, Lilly took Charlotte's arm and gently stopped her before they returned via the main staircase. "Let me show you the other way. If you're not with Edward or me you'll want to go this way," she said, leading them to the stairs Charlotte had used when Mrs. Forster had first brought her upstairs.

"Mama has a fit if anyone uses the great stairs when they aren't with a member of the family," Lilly explained softly, and not a little anxiously. Intelligent child that she was, she likely realized that Charlotte had never been a servant before, and would have unknowingly taken the great stairs as if she had every right to do so.

Edward was waiting for them on the terrace, and together they went down its wide, sweeping steps into the formal gardens below. In the main they consisted of low, precisely trimmed boxwood parterres, their central areas filled with brightly blooming annuals. As they moved to the main beds, the flowers gave way to roses, their blooms fading, though one old rambler, its boughs almost hiding the frame of a white-painted pergola, was still heavy with blossoms.

"Shall I draw something for you, Miss Brown?"

"Yes, please. Perhaps the dovecote I spy over there?"

As soon as Lilly had hurried off to make her sketch, Lord Ashford led Charlotte to a nearby bench. It was at the very edge of an herb garden, and without thinking she snapped off a few rosemary leaves and crushed them between her fingers. If Lord Ashford noticed, or minded, he betrayed no sign of it.

"She's every bit as bright and eager to learn as you said, Lord Ashford." Charlotte lowered her voice, not wishing Lilly to overhear.

"She is, isn't she? Where do you propose to begin?"

"I need to find a starting point. Not only in terms of her general abilities, but also as far as her command of individual subjects is concerned. At a guess I would say she is a strong writer, with a good grasp of history and literature, a less good understanding of geography, and very little knowledge of mathematics, biology, and the like."

"I suspected as much." Lord Ashford rubbed at his temples, as if his sister's poor education actually pained him.

"What of languages?" Charlotte asked. "French, German, Italian?"

"I'm not sure. The girls had a French governess for several years, and I believe Lilly made good progress. But she hasn't learned any other languages, as far as I know."

"Has she been exposed to the classics at all? Does she have any Latin or Greek?"

"None whatsoever, I'm afraid."

"Then she and I have a great deal of work ahead of us."

"You must let me know how you are getting on, both of you. And you absolutely must let me know if my parents, or my other sisters, are unkind in any way, or if they interfere with your teaching. And you've only to ask if you need anything at all for the schoolroom."

"I will, Lord Ashford. Thank you."

They sat quietly in the sunshine for a while, content to watch Lilly as she worked on her drawing of the dovecote, and Charlotte wondered yet again why this man, so much a product of his class and yet so different from his peers, had taken on the task of ensuring his youngest sister received a decent education. His being fond of her wasn't explanation enough; plenty of brothers loved their sisters but didn't care a jot if they were learned or witless.

"Why are you doing this for her?"

He turned to face her, his expression unusually serious. "Alice and Mary are awful now. I mean, I love them—they're my sisters—but they're awful. They remind me of nothing more than *Punch* caricatures of brainless debutantes. But the thing is, Miss Brown, I remember when they were little, just ordinary little girls, and they weren't like that. They used to be like . . . well, like Lilly, filled with wonder and delight at the world around them, just bursting with questions. I ought to have done something, found a way to get through to them, but I was away at school, and overnight, it seemed, they changed."

"But not Lilly."

"Not yet. You represent my chance to save Lilly. With what she learns from you, she might be able to escape all this, or at least acquire enough of an education to make an interesting wife for a thoughtful man."

"I can think of many people who would be happy to live as your sisters do," Charlotte ventured.

"I know, and I don't mean to grumble. But it weighs on me, you know. This knowledge that only one possible future awaits, that only one path can be taken. I can't escape it, but perhaps Lilly can. I'm counting on you."

"I will do my very best not to disappoint."

"I can't imagine that you will. After all, you are exactly the sort of person I'd like Lilly to become. Who better than you to teach her?" He accompanied this startling compliment with a smile that managed to extract every molecule of oxygen from her lungs.

She tried to think of an intelligible reply—how on earth was one meant to answer such a remark?—but was saved by Lilly, who was approaching with her finished drawing for Charlotte's inspection.

"I hope you like it, Miss Brown."

"I do," she said, and it was the truth. "You need to work on your grasp of perspective a little, but your eye for detail is excellent."

Edward stood and then, stooping, dropped a kiss on his sister's head. "If you don't mind, ladies, I must leave you now. Lilly will need to change for dinner, but Nanny Gee will take care of that. I do hope to see you again before I leave, Miss Brown."

"Thank you for everything, Lord Ashford."

He shook her hand, and as he walked away she was struck yet again by how attractive he was. It ought not to signify; he was her employer, not a friend or potential beau, but it was difficult not to notice. His hair was impossibly fair, the sort of color one usually saw only on babies or Swedes, and at close quarters she had seen that his eyes were dark blue, so dark she had at first thought them gray. His long, straight nose and high cheekbones further underscored her realization that he was very likely the handsomest man she had ever met. So much for her assumption, only bolstered by her experiences at Oxford, that most aristocrats were inbred dolts.

"What shall we do now, Miss Brown?"

Charlotte looked to her wristwatch, a twenty-first birthday present from her parents, and saw that it was only just three o'clock. "We've hours before you need to be upstairs again. Shall we go on a walk? It seems a shame to spend a day such as this indoors."

"Yes, please. Would you like me to show you the yew walk?"

"I should love to see it. While we're walking, I thought we might discuss Linnaeus's botanical classifications. Have you studied them before? No? Then we might as well begin."

Chapter 11

Cumbria, England
June 1919

Rather to Charlotte's surprise, the remainder of the wedding reception passed in a pleasant blur, and when it came time to bid farewell to the bride and groom, she, and all the remaining guests save Lady Cumberland and her coterie, stood on the front steps and shouted their good-byes.

Edward was surrounded by other wedding guests, so she wasn't able to say good-bye properly, but she did wave at him and smile encouragingly. Perhaps she would write to him in a week or two, just to see how he was feeling. It was the sort of thing she, as his friend, ought to do.

As soon as she and the other guests arrived back at the Haverthwaite Arms, Charlotte went in search of its proprietor, Mr. Poole. She found him behind the long bar in the dining room, his usual haunt during opening hours. Not only was the Arms the village's only inn, but it was also its sole public house.

"Good afternoon, Miss Brown. How was the wedding breakfast?"

"It was lovely. I wonder if I might ask a favor of you."

"Ask away."

"I'm hoping to catch a train to Preston this afternoon. Might one of your sons be available to drive me to the station?"

"Of course, Miss Brown. No trouble at all. Give me a quarter hour to have David hitch up old Barney and you'll be set."

At this time of day the trains to Preston were infrequent, but there would be one within the hour, at the very least. She changed out of her linen gown and put on her dark brown skirt and coat, packed away her things, checked her handbag for her purse and return ticket, and went downstairs.

It was a good forty minutes, via bumpy back lanes and byways, to the station in Penrith, and when she arrived it was only to discover that the express train had left a quarter hour before. There was a local run set to arrive in a half hour, however, which would arrive in Preston at nine o'clock. According to the stationmaster, that would leave her with ample time to catch one of the evening services to Liverpool's Central station.

All that afternoon and evening, first on the train to Preston, then on the shorter run down to Liverpool, Charlotte wrote. Her conversation with Edward had been full of revelations, not least of them his admitted ignorance of the true face of poverty in Britain. If a man as educated as Edward had no notion of the extent and depth of poverty across the land, it stood to reason that many others had no idea of how badly their fellow citizens—their neighbors—were suffering.

She had two sheets of notepaper in her valise, and when she'd covered them front and back with her small, fine script, she scrabbled through her bag and found a crumpled bookshop receipt, as well as the minutes from the February meeting of the Pensions Committee. When these were exhausted she set down her pencil, folded her notes away, and committed the remainder of her thoughts to memory.

Her train rolled into Liverpool at a quarter past eleven, so late that the trams were finished for the evening and a sensible young woman would not even consider walking home alone. So she resigned herself to the expense of a motor taxi and was back at the Misses Macleods' within the half hour.

Everyone was asleep, even Janie, but Charlotte would not sleep until she was finished. There was too much to say, to explain.

"Enlighten me," Edward had said. And so she would. Not him, not directly, but as many people as she could reach. She took out her notes, copied them out afresh, and worked until dawn was breaking. Until she was satisfied with the arguments she had made and the story she had told.

She would sleep for a few hours, go to church, have Sunday lunch with her friends and the Misses Macleod, and tell them about the wedding. It looked to be a fine day, so she might even walk over to Princes Park and buy a lemon ice from one of the Italians with their pushcarts.

In such a fashion she would muddle through what was left of Sunday and then, on Monday morning, on the way to work, she would stop by the offices of the *Liverpool Herald* on Victoria Street and leave an envelope for the newspaper's editor in chief, John Ellis. He might choose not to hear her. He might simply toss her letter in the rubbish. But for now, for this morning, it was the best she could do.

ON MONDAY AFTERNOON a local letter, postmarked that morning, arrived at Charlotte's desk.

16 June 1919

Dear Miss Brown,

Thank you for your letter and submission, which I read with some interest. While the piece you enclosed is not suitable for publication in its present form, I should like to discuss it with you further, perhaps after you have finished work for the day. I keep late hours, so you are welcome to come whenever you like. No need to ring ahead.

Yours faithfully,
John Ellis

He hadn't said no. He had said he would speak to her. All things considered, it was an excellent start.

At half past six, long after everyone else had gone home, even Miss Rathbone, she judged that the hour had arrived for her visit to Mr. Ellis. Her arguments were fresh in her mind as well as his, and his office would probably be quiet at this time of day.

She knew little of John Ellis, apart from the fact that Miss Rathbone approved of his politics and thought highly of him. He'd been at his post for less than a year, having taken over from the newspaper's longtime editor in chief just before the Armistice, and in that time had made few changes to the *Herald*. It was one of two evening papers in the city, both of them poor cousins compared to the *Daily Post,* and its editorial content was not particularly engaging. Not yet, at any rate.

The *Herald* was housed in a large but ramshackle building on

Victoria Street. A row of delivery lorries was parked outside, already returned for the night, and placards with the evening's headlines were affixed to the brick-and-limestone façade.

Although the reception desk inside the front doors was empty, the ground floor was far from deserted. A young man brushed past Charlotte, a stack of reference books in his arms, and began to climb a set of stairs at the far end of the entrance hall.

"Excuse me," she called to him. "I'm here to see Mr. Ellis. Where might I find him?"

"Up the stairs, third floor, straight down the hall," he answered, not missing a beat as he bounded up the steps. "His office is dead ahead. If he's not there you'll find him out on the floor."

Mr. Ellis's office, a rather small affair given his position, was indeed empty. She turned about and retraced her steps, wishing she had asked the boy what he meant by "the floor." A few yards along was a set of wide double doors; peering through, she spied a high-ceilinged room, made bright by the setting sun, its space punctuated by large communal desks. At a round table in the center of the room a group of men was gathered, their heads bent over a newspaper that lay open for their inspection.

Charlotte approached cautiously, not wishing to disturb them. One of the men, younger than the rest, was talking, and as he spoke he wrote on the newspaper, underlining and circling, until there was more red than ink upon the pages. He had thick spectacles, pushed high into his sandy hair, and wore an expression of quiet intensity. If he was not John Ellis she would be most surprised.

She took another few steps forward, waiting for an opportune pause, until she was only a few yards away. The man she took to be Mr. Ellis looked up, frowning at the interruption, and then realization dawned.

"Miss Brown?"

"It is."

"John Ellis. I'm almost done here. Would you mind waiting for me in my office? I'll be along as quick as I can."

"Of course."

"Shall I bring you a cup of tea?" he offered, smiling broadly.

"Yes, thank you," she answered, although she'd have preferred a glass of sherry.

She had time to look around his office, which was indeed quite small, and furthermore was exceedingly untidy. She could scarcely see the top of his desk, piled as it was with editions of nearly every newspaper she'd ever read, and a good many whose titles were unfamiliar: the *Sydney Morning Herald*, the *South China Morning Post*, the *Chicago Tribune*. On the floor were stacks and stacks of magazines, academic journals, and yet more newspapers, many of them yellow and curling at the edges.

In little more than five minutes he joined her, shouldering his way through the door, a pair of mugs in his hands.

"Sorry about that. I'd have been here sooner, but I was set on finding us some biscuits. Usually there's a tin of them hanging about, but tonight our larders are bare."

"That's quite all right."

"My colleagues here are like vultures. Will strip a carcass bare in seconds." He handed her one of the mugs. "I didn't think to ask how you like it, so I added milk and sugar."

"Perfect," she fibbed, although she detested sweet tea.

"So. Your article."

"Yes. You said you didn't think it suitable at present—"

"I thought it was magnificent. Exactly the sort of thing I should like to see in this newspaper. The difficulty is space."

"I see," she said, though in truth she didn't. Was it not in his purview to decide what would appear in his paper?

"I have four pages a day, six days a week. Between advertisements, classifieds, sporting news, and all the trivia my publisher expects me to include, I have only one or two columns a day to work with. When you stop to consider everything that has been going on this year, you can imagine how difficult it is for me to find room for everything. Remember the rioting that took place last month here and in most of the other port cities? I only had room for forty inches of coverage, which barely scratched the surface. Were racial prejudices the main reason that the riots broke out? Did the rioters think of their actions as political? Or was it disaffection, plain and simple, with a dose of vandalism thrown in for good measure? With only forty inches to spare a day, I fear I was unable to do justice to the subject."

"I hadn't realized—"

"I only wish I could run your article in its entirety, but you must agree that it is long."

"It is, but—"

"May I propose, instead, that we run a series of short pieces in the *Herald*? Would once a week be too much trouble? You've enough material here to keep you going for several months."

"Are you offering me a position as a columnist in your paper, Mr. Ellis?"

"I suppose I am, after a fashion. But I can only give you twenty-five inches. Thirty at the most."

"I've no idea what that means."

"I beg your pardon. Column inches. I suppose about six hundred words or so. Seven hundred and fifty at the outside. Can you manage with that?"

"I don't know what to say. To be perfectly honest, I hadn't expected that you would be interested."

"I receive no end of rubbish in the post, Miss Brown, but what you've written is an exception. Only a fool would ignore what you have to say."

She wasn't certain how to respond to this surprisingly pleasant man. How on earth had he risen to such a position while remaining in possession of such a congenial temperament? He might be a brute away from the office, though. He might browbeat his wife and kick his dog and treat the men and women who worked for him as little more than galley slaves. Possible, though unlikely.

"I've made some notes on the pages you sent me. I'd like to see you start with the Jones family. You'll tell their story in your first article, and in your second you will propose a solution to their troubles. You have, if you'll forgive me, a tendency toward language that is a trifle too florid."

"A lamentable failing of mine," she said, smiling in spite of his criticism.

"You'll see from my notes that I have a particular aversion to adverbs. Never use five words when one will do, Miss Brown. And never let fanciful language get in the way of the story you want to tell. Plain and simple is best."

"I understand. When should I return this to you?"

"Shall we say Monday? With a view to getting it into the paper for Tuesday?"

"Monday it is, then."

"You haven't asked how much I'll pay you."

"But I don't wish to be paid. That wasn't my intent at all."

"I'll stop you there. Always insist on being paid. Know your own worth, Miss Brown. People won't respect you if you don't. Give it to charity if you like, though if I were you I'd put it aside for a darker day. We both know what happens to people who've nothing to cushion them when disaster strikes."

"You do have a point," she agreed.

"Of course I do. As you get to know me, Miss Brown, you'll discover I'm almost always right. I will pay you fifteen shillings a week, payable upon my acceptance of each article. Now shake my hand, and off home you go. Shall I ring for a taxi?"

"No need, Mr. Ellis. It's light still, and I've only a mile to go."

"Very well. Good night, Miss Brown. And thank you. With your help I may yet turn this newspaper into something worth the paper it's printed on."

Chapter 12

A Land Fit for Heroes

In my work as a constituency assistant to one of Liverpool's most respected politicians, I daily encounter families in desperate need of assistance. They are good, decent, and honest people. They have done nothing to deserve the hardships they suffer. They are our neighbors in this great city. It is my conviction that they deserve better.

Recently I was introduced to a husband and wife whom I shall call, for the purposes of this article, Mr. and Mrs. Jones. They have four children, the eldest of whom is thirteen. A fifth child is expected shortly. Mr. Jones served in the infantry, in a local regiment, for the entirety of the war. He was discharged from further service in January of this year with a spotless service record.

Mr. Jones was wounded twice by shrapnel, both times returning to action soon after, and was gassed in 1916. The effects of the phosgene have left him with a persistent cough, shortness of breath, and chronic eye infections. Before the war he worked on the grinding floor of a local brick factory, but since his discharge he has been unable to resume work because the brick dust inflames his damaged lungs.

For reasons only understandable to the officials responsible, Mr. Jones has been deemed capable of a full return to work and denied a disability pension. Mrs. Jones, who once helped to make ends meet by taking in piecework, is also unwell, and consequently is unable to work.

Having exhausted what meager savings they once had, the Jones family was recently evicted from their modest flat and are now living with Mrs. Jones's elderly parents in their very small court dwelling of four rooms. The entire family is malnourished, Mrs. Jones most of all, as she regularly goes without in order to ensure her children are fed. I fear such malnutrition may cause her to lose the child she is expecting.

The astonishing and disheartening truth is that the Jones family is among the more fortunate of those I see in the course of my work. They have received modest amounts of assistance from the Red Cross and local agencies, and this has preserved them from utter penury. They have a roof over their heads. They are clothed, if but poorly, and all but the youngest children have shoes. They are malnourished but they are not starving. They have children who are coming of age to work and may soon help to improve the family's fortunes.

If the Jones family is to be counted among the fortunate, however relative the term, allow me to pose the question: what of those with nothing? Untold hundreds, possibly even thousands, of our fellow citizens are homeless. Many more thousands go hungry every day. Many are starving.

Last year Mr. Lloyd George promised to make "Britain a fit country for heroes to live in." It was an admirable promise, but I believe it is one that he and his fellows have failed to keep. I fear it may never be kept.

This is not a call to arms, but rather a call to action. Will the people of Liverpool, of Merseyside, and of Britain respond? Will they help the Jones family and those like them? Only by putting pressure on our government can we hope to effect meaningful change and, in so doing, build a land that is truly fit for heroes.

I implore you now: write to your Member of Parliament. Write to the Prime Minister. Write to His Majesty the King. Tell them of your concern. Ask them how they mean to help those among us who suffer. Most importantly, share your concerns with your friends, your family, and your neighbors.

The Great War may be over, but another war remains, here at home, and we are far from certain of victory.

—the *Liverpool Herald,* 24 June 1919

"SO, MISS BROWN. Tell me how it has been."

"How has what been?"

"The reaction to your 'call to action.'"

Mr. Ellis had telephoned her at work yesterday, the first she had heard from him since her article had appeared in the *Herald* on Tuesday. He'd invited her to lunch on Saturday, when she was at her leisure and he was less pressed for time than usual.

He'd asked her to meet him at the *Herald* and she'd agreed, assuming he might need to finish off some task or another and didn't wish her to wait upon him if he were late. She had assumed they would go to Reece's or Lyons' or the restaurant inside Blackler's department store.

To that end she had worn her Sunday best, had borrowed a hat from Meg, and had pinned her gold and seed-pearl brooch, a gift from her parents last Christmas, to the lapel of her coat. The Misses Macleod had said she looked very smart.

But he had not taken her out to lunch. Instead here she was, sitting across the desk from Mr. Ellis, and they were eating sandwiches. Not especially good sandwiches either, for the bread was rather stale and the filling, which she took to be tinned salmon, was badly in need of some salt and pepper.

He had apologized, explaining that he was so behind in his work he couldn't afford to leave his desk for so much as an hour. Nor did he cease working after her arrival. As they ate their sandwiches, washed down by sips of weak tea, he somehow managed to edit an article while also carrying on their conversation. Not once did he fumble for words or lose his train of thought, and whenever his eyes weren't on the page before him he looked her in the eye, the solemn intensity of his gaze filtered by his spectacle lenses.

"Miss Rathbone was very pleased," she told him. "Of course I had told her about it in advance, mainly to ensure that she approved."

"She wrote to me the next morning," he said. "Receiving her seal of approval put a spring in my step all day."

"The rest of my colleagues seem to approve," she added, not troubling to factor Miss Margison into her estimation. Nothing she did would ever please that woman, who had declared for all to hear that she, unlike some, would never *dream* of calling such attention to herself. As long as Miss Rathbone was in accord with her journalistic excursions, Charlotte would continue her work with a clear conscience, no matter what anyone else had to say on the subject.

"And your friends?"

"I wasn't able to show my dearest friend, for she's away on her honeymoon. My friends here were terribly excited, though."

"Do you live with your parents?"

"No. They live in Somerset. I've a room in a ladies' boardinghouse not far from here. I lived there when I first came to Liverpool in 1911, and fortunately there was room for me when I returned after the war."

"Where did you go? During the war, that is."

"To London. I trained as a nurse, and then I went to the Special Neurological Hospital for Officers in Kensington. We treated neurasthenia patients there."

"A thankless job, I'll wager."

"Thankless at times, but not unrewarding. Were you here during the war? I mean, ah, did you . . . ?"

"I've a thick skin, Miss Brown. I wasn't in uniform. These," he said, tapping his spectacles, "prevented it. I tried to join up, but they weren't having it. So I spent the duration behind a desk in this building."

"Doing work that was every bit as worthy as—"

"You're very kind. But there's no need to jump to my defense. I wasn't the only man of fighting age left behind in Britain, after all. And the white feather brigade eventually found other ways to pass their time."

He said he had a thick skin, but it must have marked him. How could it not? Even she, so uncertain over the need to go to war, so unsure of its justice, had felt compelled to serve. She decided that if she were ever to meet anyone who confessed to having handed out white feathers, she would delightedly adorn them with a pillow's worth plus a pail of hot tar.

"What did your parents think of your having spoken out so publicly?"

"I wouldn't say they were displeased, for privately they share my convictions. But I think they were concerned I've exposed myself to public censure." That was putting it mildly, for Father and Mother were of a generation that deplored women in public life, the late queen excepted, no matter how laudable their aims.

"There's no getting around it, I'm afraid. Anyone who speaks out on such a subject is bound to face criticism."

"I did see some of the letters to the editor. The ones you ran yesterday." She ought not to have read them, but some perverse urge had propelled her to read every damning, excoriating word.

"It was exactly the response I'd hoped for."

"But they were so hateful," she protested.

"And written by idiots, to the last man."

"If you think so little of their—"

"I printed those letters for one reason only."

"To represent both points of view?"

"God, no!" He laughed. "What do you take me for? I printed those cretinous letters because it proves that people are listening. You, Miss Brown, are being *heard*."

She grinned at him, her chagrin at the memory of those awful letters to the editor beginning to melt away. Before it could vanish, however, she recalled other words, far less charitable, but no less truthful.

You speak as if your every word is a pearl of wisdom bestowed by the Almighty,

Edward had told her. "Saint Charlotte," he had called her. And it made her wonder: Had she written the article in a sincere attempt to make the world a better place? Or was it simply a self-centered attempt to draw attention to herself? She'd never before had cause to doubt herself, but now . . .

Belatedly she realized that Mr. Ellis was waiting for her to respond. "It is a fine feeling," she said at last.

"Of course it is. And with every article you write for me, more and more people will hear you."

She glanced at her wristwatch; it was past one o'clock already. "I ought to leave you to your work, Mr. Ellis."

"I'm poor company at the best of times."

"Not at all. But you need to work, and I need to finish off my article for next week." She stood, brushing sandwich crumbs off her skirt, and reached out to shake his hand. "Are you here all day?"

"On Saturdays I stay until we put the day's edition to bed. Then I go home."

"So you don't live in the attics upstairs?"

"Now there's an idea," he said, smiling ruefully. "No, I live with my mother."

"What does she think of your working all hours like this?"

"She deplores it, just as you appear to do. Insists I'm working myself into an early grave."

"It would be a terrible shame, Mr. Ellis. I doubt I'd find anyone else to publish my anarchic diatribes if you did expire."

"I doubt it, too. May I expect your next article by Monday morning?"

"You may. Good afternoon, and thank you for lunch."

CHARLOTTE SPENT THE rest of Saturday afternoon wandering

through Princes Park, not even bothering to find a bench and read the book she had brought along, as was her habit. She was too restless to settle, Edward's accusing questions a troubling refrain. *Do you truly believe that your actions are beyond criticism? Are you really that perfect?*

She arrived home at half past three and immediately went to her desk, keen to finish her next column for Mr. Ellis. No sooner had she put pen to paper than the doorbell rang. Janie was in the middle of preparing supper, and everyone else was still out and about, so Charlotte answered the door.

A young man stood at the top of the steps, an oddly shaped box in his hands. His lorry was parked, its engine rumbling, in the street beyond. "Good day, miss. I've a delivery for Miss Charlotte Brown,"

"I am Miss Brown. I'm not expecting anything—"

He handed her the box, about two feet long, unmarked apart from her name and address, and before she could ask where it was from he dashed back to his lorry and drove away.

Presumably a note or letter would be tucked inside. She carried the box downstairs to the kitchen and set it on the table.

"What's that you've got there, Miss Charlotte?" Janie asked, abandoning the carrots she was scraping.

"I've no idea. I'm not sure how to open it, even."

"Looks like the top's been tacked down. Do you want to try and lever it off? Here's the butter knife."

Inside was a layer of moss, still speckled with dew, its scent of earth and dim, deep woods instantly filling the room. Charlotte peeled it back, her heart hammering in her chest, for she'd an idea now of what she would find.

Beneath the moss lay at least four dozen roses of every imaginable variety and color: palest ivory, blush pink, apricot, cerise, a velvety scarlet. The bottom of each stem had been wrapped in damp cotton wool, which had served to preserve the blooms perfectly on their journey from garden to kitchen table.

Charlotte sat heavily on the nearest chair and tried to catch her breath. "Is there a note?" she asked, though she was certain now of the roses' origin.

"Yes, Miss Charlotte. Shall I open it?"

"If you don't mind."

"It says, 'Felicitations.' And the initial *E*. That's all."

In most English gardens, the roses were nearly done for the year, but at Cumbermere Hall, in the sheltered parterre, under the watchful eyes of a gardener who loved the flowers more than his own children, the blooms often lasted until September.

Edward had sent her the best of his roses, likely stripping bare the bushes in the process.

"What shall we do with all of them?" Janie asked.

"There are so many. I suppose we could do up a big arrangement for the sitting room. And perhaps some smaller ones for all our bedrooms. Do you have any spare jam jars?"

"I do. What if I cut some of the lady's mantle in the back garden? It'll look pretty set next to the flowers."

She and Janie worked quickly, arranging the long-stemmed hybrid tea roses in the Misses Macleods' best cut-glass vase, and trimming the stems of the damask and cabbage roses so they fit nicely in the smaller jam jars.

The other women arrived home soon after, and as soon as they discovered the flowers in their rooms, and learned from Janie that they had been delivered from a mysterious benefactor earlier that afternoon, they couldn't help but pepper Charlotte with questions.

"Who are they from?" asked Norma. "Do tell."

"My friend."

"Whatever for?" asked Rosie. "Did she hear about your story in the *Herald*?"

"Was it Lady Elizabeth who sent them?" asked Norma.

"No. A friend. And that's all I wish to say for now. A generous friend with a large garden."

"Well, all's I can say is that you've got some very interesting friends. I sure wouldn't mind meeting them someday."

"Perhaps you will, Norma. Enough of me, though. How did you spend your day? How was everyone's day?"

It was just the cue the others needed. Their chatter filled the room, banishing any more troublesome talk of admirers and mysterious friends, and Charlotte soon found herself so diverted that she was nearly able to forget about the flowers, the man who had sent them, and the gulf, as wide as the space between stars, that separated a man like him from a woman like herself.

Chapter 13

"Tell me again why we're taking this infernal vehicle instead of the train," Rosie said with a groan.

"If I'd known you'd complain so much, I'd have told you to stop at home," retorted Norma. "Two-and-six to get to Blackpool and back—if that isn't a bargain I don't know what is."

"If *I'd* known this charabanc would be so uncomfortable I'd never have agreed."

"Then next time one of the boys at work offers me cheap tickets I'll remember not to ask."

"Enough with your bickering," Charlotte intervened. "We'll be there soon enough, and thanks to Norma we'll each have a few extra shillings in our pockets. So let's not throttle one another before we get there."

They'd spent the past two and a half hours crammed into the open-topped charabanc, with at least another hour to go before they reached Blackpool. It resembled nothing so much as a gigantic coffin bolted atop the deck of a lorry, and was roughly as comfortable as one might expect of such a jury-rigged vehicle.

Earlier in the week Norma had brought home four return

tickets to Blackpool, and when Meg couldn't be persuaded to come along—she always visited her family in Manchester on Sundays—Charlotte had invited Mabel Petrie from work.

"I hope you're not finding the journey too uncomfortable," Charlotte said, noticing that her friend was looking somewhat green about the gills. "Would you like some tea from my flask?"

"I'd better not. Our driver would be sure to hit a rut just as we opened it. Thanks all the same."

Even Charlotte, whose constitution was normally as iron-clad as a dreadnought, was beginning to feel miserable, and not only because the charabanc's unyielding wooden benches had left her posterior black-and-blue. She was hot and sweaty, covered in a film of dust, and so thirsty it hurt to swallow.

"How much longer?" she called to Norma, who sat directly ahead of her.

"We're well past Preston, so not far now. Chin up!"

The view from the charabanc was pretty enough, for the Blackpool Road still bore some resemblance to its ancient antecedents, curving and winding its way through open farmland that was hedged in at intervals by tangles of hawthorn and gorse. From time to time, the horizon dipped to reveal a ribbon of startling blue, but Charlotte couldn't be sure if it were the sea or a slice of the late morning sky.

"Look, everyone!" Norma called out, pointing at a roadside sign: BLACKPOOL 5 MILES, it read. "And over there!" She pointed to a spot in the far distance.

It was Blackpool Tower, still no more than an apostrophe on the horizon, but growing larger and more impressive with every passing minute. All thoughts of charabanc-induced misery vanished; they were nearly there.

The driver led them into the heart of town, so close that the tower seemed only footsteps away, and drew to a halt on the forecourt of the train station.

"We leave at half past seven on the dot," he called out to his two dozen passengers. "Mind you aren't late or you'll be sleeping rough tonight."

"Where shall we start?" said Rosie, her good humor restored.

"Why not the beach?" suggested Norma. "We'll all have a swim, and then we can eat our lunch."

As they walked west toward the seafront, Charlotte noticed that there didn't appear to be any public change rooms, at least not along the wide promenade that ran along the shoreline and divided beach from town. "Where will we change?" she asked.

"See those bathing machines on the beach? No one uses them to bathe anymore, so they're hired out as places to change," Norma explained. "They're sixpence to use, plus another sixpence for a towel. Here we are—we'll take these steps."

She led them down to the beach, which was impossibly wide and flat, and walked directly over to the bathing machines. The proprietor was half asleep on his deck chair, but Norma soon had him laughing like an old friend.

"Come say hello to Mr. Dunbar," she called to the others. "Two-and-six for us all to use the machine at the end, plus a towel each."

"Wasn't it a shilling each?" Rosie asked.

"Yes, but I talked him down. I've got sixpence, but I need two bob from the rest of you. Hurry up now, before he changes his mind."

The machine looked to have been sitting in that exact spot on the beach since Victoria had been on her throne. Charlotte went in first, her nose wrinkling at the disagreeable odor of damp.

When she'd first had her swimming costume made, back when she was an undergraduate at Somerville, it had seemed quite daring, with its short skirt and cap sleeves that bared most of her arms. Its attached bloomers now seemed rather old-fashioned, though, and the cap that covered her hair looked like something her mother would wear.

She removed the white stockings she had worn with her frock and replaced them with black cotton ones, then pulled on an old pair of canvas plimsolls, her bathing boots having disappeared at some point over the past decade. After packing her street clothes into her bag, and satisfied that she was covered respectably, she emerged from the machine and waited for the other women to take their turn.

Much to Charlotte's relief, both Rosie and Mabel were dressed in similarly conservative suits, although Mabel's was a pretty and rather unusual shade of dark purple. The same could not be said of Norma's swimming costume.

It wasn't indecent, for there were a number of other young women on the beach wearing modern suits: scoop-necked, sleeveless, with a skirt that stopped at midthigh. But there was something about Norma's suit, or perhaps it was the way she wore it, that caused every set of male eyes on the beach to focus on her relentlessly.

The suit was, at least to Charlotte's eyes, quite astonishingly formfitting, with the knitted wool fabric revealing more than it concealed. Norma had dispensed with stockings, too, and stood on the sand in bare feet. Even her head was uncovered.

"Isn't that a bit much for Lancashire?" asked Rosie.

"I shouldn't say so." Norma was evidently delighted by the commotion she had caused. "I bought it at Blackler's. The saleslady said this is what everyone is wearing in America."

"Good for them," Rosie muttered darkly. "I'm off for a swim. Anyone care to join me?"

"We'd better not all go. I'll stay and watch over our things," Charlotte offered. "I don't mind waiting a bit."

"I'll stay with Charlotte," Mabel added.

With interest in her daring attire beginning to wane, Norma followed Rosie out to the water, which was still at low tide. That left Charlotte and Mabel to spread out the blanket they'd brought, anchor its corners with their bags, and soak up the sun.

The beach was growing more crowded by the minute, as holidaymakers finished their luncheons and came down for a stroll along the sands. There were scores of young couples walking arm in arm, some of them likely newlyweds, and no shortage of families with strings of happy, sandy boys and girls trailing after them.

There seemed to be a great many children at the southern extremity of the beach, the clamor of their voices rising and falling on the salt-kissed breeze. A herd of donkeys was corralled there, and from what Charlotte could see the animals seemed content enough. There were far worse places for a donkey to be, after all, than in the sunshine carrying children on its back.

She returned her attention to Mabel, who was looking out to sea, possibly still transfixed by the sight of Norma in her outlandish swimming costume.

"She is a good girl," Charlotte said. "A bit wild at times, but her heart is in the right place."

Mabel smiled agreeably. "I'm sure it is. If I were her age I'd probably wear a suit like that, too."

"I rather envy her," Charlotte admitted. "This awful old thing is so heavy. And it itches horribly once it gets wet."

Mabel turned to face Charlotte. "I expect it must be difficult for the younger ones. Life was so dour, and for so long. They must be desperate for some fun."

"Aren't we all? Do you know, this is the first time I've been to Blackpool. I've only ever been to the seaside at home, in the south of England."

"Where are you from again? I feel as if I ought to know."

"I grew up in Wells, in Somerset. We're only twenty miles or so from Weston-super-Mare. Mother and Father and I used to go for a week every summer. It was lovely there, and the water was so warm. I can still remember how it felt."

"It won't be warm here, that I can tell you. We've some nice beaches near South Shields, but the water is always freezing. You'd best brace yourself before we go in."

Rosie and Norma came running back a few minutes later, their goose-pimpled skin providing ample proof of the Irish Sea's hardy charms, and hurriedly wrapped themselves in the linen towels Mr. Dunbar had provided. Rather than change straightaway, however, Norma perched on one corner of the blanket and declared her intention to have a "sunbath" before getting dressed again.

Rather than grumble at Norma, as Rosie was sure to do once she emerged from the changing tent, Charlotte beckoned Mabel to come with her for a swim. It was a long walk to the water, for the tide was only just beginning to come in, and as soon as she was ankle-deep in the sea she began to doubt whether she did want to swim after all. It really was every bit as cold as Mabel had said, so much so that her legs were numb before the water had even reached her waist.

"My goodness, Mabel, you were right about the water."

"It will get better," her friend promised. "Only give yourself a moment to get accustomed to it. You're almost there—just crouch down and let it go over your shoulders. After that it's lovely. Watch out for your spectacles, though."

"Yes, of course. I ought to have taken them off, but then I wouldn't have been able to see a thing."

Charlotte forced herself to go neck-deep, and once her teeth had stopped chattering and she could breathe properly again, she decided the water was actually refreshing, if quite bracing, and exactly what she needed after those long, dusty hours in the charabanc. It had been years since she had last gone swimming, and she didn't trust herself to go out any farther, but fortunately it seemed that Mabel felt the same way. So they simply stood in the water, their feet only just touching bottom, and let the gentle waves of the incoming tide buffet them about. Before long, however, a wisp of cloud obscured the sun and they were instantly chilled to the marrow.

Once they'd waded out of the water, changed back into their street clothes, and rejoined the others, it was time for a picnic lunch. Janie had prepared sandwiches for everyone, and there were bottles of ginger beer and a basket of plums that Mabel had brought, and last of all Charlotte's flask of hot, black tea to fortify them for the rest of the day. The sandwiches were sandy, the ginger beer was warm, and the tea was tannic by the time she took a sip, but all the same it was one of the nicest picnics Charlotte could remember.

"Where next?" she asked Norma.

"Let's walk down to Pleasure Beach. It's only a mile or so from here, and we can take the tram back when we're finished."

"But we're at the beach now," Charlotte protested.

"It's not a beach, silly. It's an amusement park. With rides and games and that sort of thing. You'll like it, I promise."

While Charlotte did very much enjoy the walk south along the Promenade, she realized soon after paying her sixpence admission to Pleasure Beach that she did not care for amusement parks at all. They were too crowded, too raucous, and far, far too noisy—so noisy that she soon felt a headache coming on.

While the others queued up to go on the flying machine, Charlotte found a seat on a nearby bench and drank the last of the tea, now quite cold, from her flask. It seemed to help a little, so much so that she felt able to brave the mysteries of the river caves, which promised a journey through exotic climes and darkest jungles, but in reality was a short journey in small boats through a dimly lit and quite obviously papier-mâchéd landscape.

She drew the line at riding on the Ferris wheel, slow though it was, and was relieved beyond measure when Norma declared it was time to catch the tram back into town. It was late afternoon when they landed back in the shadow of the Tower, nearly four o'clock, so they bought lemon ices and ate them under the shade of an open-sided gazebo on the Promenade.

"What does everyone want to do next?" Norma asked. "Do we want to visit the Tower? It's sixpence entrance to the building and another sixpence for the lift to the top. There's an aquarium and a menagerie, and there's a greenhouse sort of garden, too."

Charlotte would have been content to stroll farther north along the Promenade, but Mabel and Rosie were both in favor of the Tower, and not wishing to be a spoilsport, she followed her friends into the grand entrance hall, though she declined to purchase a ticket for the lift.

"I've never been one for heights, so I'll stay here while you go up. I don't mind—really I don't."

And she didn't. It was nice to sit on a bench in the hall, in the shadow of an enormous potted palm, and think of all the lovely things she had done so far. When was the last time she'd had so much fun?

Had she ever spent an entire day having fun? She sifted through her memories, but couldn't recall a single instance—not when she was at university, not when she was Lilly's governess, not in all the years with Miss Rathbone, and certainly not during the war. There had been afternoons at the park, evenings out with friends, the occasional lazy hour or two reading a book that was entertaining rather than improving, but she'd never felt she could spend an entire day simply enjoying life.

She was thirty-three, and in the course of her adult life, she now realized, she had never, not *ever*, allowed herself an entire day of fun without being overcome by guilt or anxiety or the fear that there were worthier things to do. Having fun was for other people—people who had earned the right to be carefree.

Even as a child, she'd been set on proving her goodness to others, her parents in particular. Not because they didn't love her, for their affection was abundant and genuine, but because she had always felt she needed to earn that love. In adopting her, they had taken an almost incalculable leap of faith. And so she had decided, when she was very young, that she would never give them cause to regret their decision. She would become the daughter they deserved.

Yet such strivings hadn't made her a better person. In fact, they had done quite the opposite. Without ever meaning to do so, without really noticing, she had become—oh, the shame of it—she had become a bore. She was a high-minded, tedious, and entirely tiresome bore. "Saint Charlotte," indeed.

She was so boring she couldn't even follow her friends to

the top of Blackpool Tower. They hadn't asked her to climb the Matterhorn, only ride a lift with them to the top of a perfectly sturdy structure and enjoy the view. So what was stopping her from joining them?

Nothing.

Before she could change her mind, she paid the admission to the observation decks and joined the queue for the lifts. The ride to the top was slow and creaky and Charlotte's knees were weak with nerves by the time the doors finally opened, but she gritted her teeth and forced herself out of the lift and onto the glassed-in expanse of the main platform.

There was no sign of her friends; they must have gone to one of the upper platforms. A short flight of steps led her to the first, which a sign told her was a full 390 feet from the ground, and there she found Mabel. Here it was open to the elements, with nothing but a high wrought-iron railing to keep her safe, and in the end she decided to leave a good five feet between herself and the edge of the platform.

"Mabel?"

"Charlotte! You changed your mind."

"It seemed a shame to come all this way and not go up the Tower. Where are the others?"

"They went up to the higher decks. Do you want to join them?"

"No, thank you. I'm quite happy here."

"You don't look it, I have to say. Can you see anything from where you are?"

"Oh, yes. The view is wonderful."

"Let's walk around the perimeter, shall we? If we walk to the southeast corner we can see Liverpool, even if you're quite far from the railing."

The view really was extraordinary. It seemed as if most of Lancashire, and a good deal of the Irish Sea, was spread out around them, with Liverpool a smoky blur in the distance. If a great city like that could be reduced to a smudge on the horizon, then what was she in comparison?

By the time Rosie and Norma rejoined them, she was feeling much steadier on her feet, though no more inclined to stand at the edge of the platform, not even when they pleaded with her to come to the rail so she might look down and see the town below.

"Thank you, but I had better not risk it. Not unless you wish to carry me back to the lift after I've fainted," she joked.

It was nearly six o'clock by the time they returned to solid ground. For supper they had fish and chips, eaten straight from their newspaper wrapping, and then, with only a half hour remaining before the charabanc's departure for home, they started back for the station.

Along the way they found a souvenir shop that was still open, and Charlotte spent the last of the money she'd set aside for the day on a clutch of postcards, sticks of Blackpool Rock for Meg and her colleagues at work, a little penny bank shaped like the Tower for Janie, and a set of antimacassars, embroidered with the inscription *A Gift from Blackpool,* for the Misses Macleod.

It had been a good day, the charabanc excepted, the sort of day that everyone needed from time to time. From now on, she resolved, she would try to remember that life could be more than work and study and serious-minded contemplation of society's failings. She could know joy, and light, and relief from sadness.

She could have—she *would* have—another day in the sun.

Chapter 14

The nineteenth of July was as fine a day as anyone could have wished, dawning clear and bright, the sort of weather tailor-made for celebration. The tea party and games organized by the families of Huskisson Street to celebrate Peace Day weren't especially grand, not when compared to the parades and victory tableaux and fireworks displays taking place in every corner of the Empire, but she liked them all the more for that.

Charlotte, like most people she knew, had nearly forgotten that the Armistice last November had been just that—a setting down of arms. The war itself had not ended until the twenty-eighth of June, when the Treaty of Versailles had been signed. A few days later, the king's proclamation of peace, with its promise of a day of celebration on the nineteenth of July, had appeared in all the papers, and preparations had begun for parades and festivals and parties.

No one had questioned the rightness of such a thing, of marking the end of years of death and brutality and soul-searing loss with a *tea party*. There had been a solemn day of remembrance a fortnight before, and churches across the land had been packed to the rafters; surely that would have sufficed.

Yet today, standing in the glorious sunshine, the laughter of her neighbors' children bright in her ears, Charlotte wondered if she had been wrong to disapprove. What harm could it do, after all? The cost to everyone had been minimal—no more than a few shillings for the food and a share of the cost of the prizes. Charlotte could well afford it, as could most of the people around her. No one here was rich, and many families on the street had been driven to take in boarders to make ends meet, but all had enough to eat, had decent clothes to wear, and had sturdy shoes upon their feet. Riches, indeed, compared to many.

Every last table and chair in every house had been dragged into the street, which had first been swept and scrubbed so thoroughly that the cobbles fairly sparkled in the morning sun. Overhead, garlands of Union flag pennants crisscrossed the street, while white bunting softened the stone lintels of the houses' front doors and windows.

The tables, which stretched almost the entire block between Bedford and Sandon Streets, were covered with a draper's worth of tablecloths and bedsheets. Little could be seen of the tabletops themselves, so stacked were they with plate after plate of sandwiches, buns, biscuits, dainties, and, towering above all, the bright-hued blooms of larkspur, foxglove, and gladioli from the street's tiny back gardens. With sugar and butter still rationed, every house on the street had been saving up for a fortnight, and the results were impressive indeed.

Any stranger wandering into their midst would have thought it was May Day, for the women and girls were arrayed in their Sunday whites, the men wore their best suits, and the boys, still stinging from the Lifebuoy soap with which they'd been scrubbed, scowled and squirmed as their hair was smoothed and their collars were straightened.

The clock at St. Luke's a half mile away chimed the hour, eleven o'clock, and all fell silent. Philip Storey, a dentist who lived at number forty-nine, climbed upon a chair and began to speak. His only son had been killed at the Battle of Jutland.

"Neighbors and friends: today is Peace Day, and with it the end of the war. It's a war that has cost us dearly. So dearly . . ." At this he looked to his wife, who nodded and tried to smile.

"But they are losses we are proud to bear, for we know they are shared. Let us pray, now, for our glorious dead, for our brave men who have returned to us, for our country and Empire, and for His Majesty the King."

As soon as Mr. Storey had clambered down from his perch, he was replaced by Huw Williams, a retired actuary who lived across the street from the Misses Macleod. Welsh by name but not by birth, being a Liverpudlian down to his shoelaces, he nonetheless had a beautiful tenor voice and was the mainstay of the choir at the Methodist church on Princes Road.

Mr. Williams extracted a pitch pipe from his waistcoat pocket, sounded a note, and then, his arms beckoning everyone to join in, he began to sing the national anthem:

> "God save our gracious King,
> God save our noble King,
> God save the King.
> Send him victorious,
> Happy and glorious,
> Long to rule over us,
> God save the King!"

With formalities observed, it was time for the party proper to begin. The children were led to their seats at the long table, and soon were tucking into their sandwiches with the single-minded attention reserved for those occasions when sweets were promised at the end of a meal. Cakes and biscuits devoured, hands and faces wiped, they were shooed away so the table might be refreshed with fare for the men of the street: sandwiches again, but filled with gammon rather than egg salad, and with mugs of ale instead of the sweet, milky tea that had been given to the children.

Only when the men had eaten and the table had been cleared and set for a third time did the women sit down to eat. There was a practical reason for this, Charlotte knew, for it was the women who had cooked and prepared the food, and they had been needed during the children's and men's meals to fetch and carry. Yet it stung her, as quick and sharp as a wasp, to be last once again.

Women always put themselves last. Either it was the mothers she visited in the slums of Scottie Road who only ate after their husbands and children had had their fill, or it was the women from Huskisson Street who, after cleaning and cooking for days, were left with the rag end of the delicacies, with scarcely a slice of cake to share between them.

The men were called upon at last, given the task of clearing away the tables and chairs, and then it was time for the children's games: bobbing for apples, hopscotch, and a hard-fought tug-of-war between the north and south sides of the street. Last of all were the footraces: a hundred-yard dash for the boys and men, and a fifty-yard egg-and-spoon race for the girls. The prize for each was a commemorative mug presented by Britannia, known on common days as Mrs. Tomlinson from number forty-four, and dressed for the occasion in white robes and a coronet of aspidistra leaves.

A trill of too-loud laughter landed in a rare moment of calm, catching Charlotte's attention. She turned her head, though she already knew its author. It was Norma, once again dressed inappropriately for the occasion, once again drawing attention to herself at the most inopportune moment.

Charlotte wore her best summer frock, the same one she had worn for Lilly's wedding, and most of the other women at the party were dressed in a similar manner. The older ladies, the Misses Macleod among them, wore rather more old-fashioned frocks, with hemlines that grazed their ankles, but the younger women—Charlotte didn't feel especially young, but she still counted herself among them—sported hemlines that were a few inches higher.

Norma's dress, by contrast, stopped just south of her knees, was constructed of an alarmingly lightweight artificial silk, was an eye-watering shade of pink, and had a neckline that left absolutely nothing to the imagination. She wore no hat, only a diamanté clip in her chin-length hair, and her legs were bare.

How had she failed to notice what Norma was wearing? Her housemate had been dressed in a perfectly inoffensive outfit at the beginning of the day, at least as far as Charlotte could recall. But it had been so busy since then, with all of them fetching and serving the food, and in all those hours she hadn't spared a single thought for the girl.

If Rosie had been at the party she surely would have noticed, but she was at work, having volunteered so another nurse could spend the day with her sweetheart. Charlotte alone would have to manage this.

There was nothing for it but to approach Norma and see if she could be coaxed back inside. It wouldn't be easy, for the girl was perched on a table and was surrounded by at least a half-dozen young men, some of whom Charlotte recognized as boarders in the street's larger houses. She was sipping from a half-pint of ale, her lipstick leaving a garish crescent upon the glass, and a smoldering cigarette dangled from her other hand, though Charlotte had never before known her to smoke.

"Hello, Norma," she said in as friendly a tone as she could conjure. "I was wondering if you might help me with the clearing-up. I know the Misses Macleod would be very grateful."

"Leave 'er be, won' ya?" said one of the men. "Whas' harm in 'avin' a bit o' fun?"

The man was three sheets to the wind already. What kind of degenerate got drunk at a children's party, for heaven's sake?

"I don't mean to spoil everyone's fun, I assure you. But Miss Barnes is needed back home. It isn't fair for Janie to do all the work herself."

Norma sighed dramatically. "You're such a stick in the mud, Charlotte. Why do you always have to ruin everything?"

"You 'eard 'er," said another one of Norma's companions. "Now sod off, won' ya?"

"I beg your pardon—"

"Clear off, the lot of you." This from Mr. Williams, who now stood just behind Charlotte. "Sorry to interrupt, Miss Brown, but we can't have them spoiling the party." He jabbed a finger at the younger men, one after the other, looking each one straight in the eye. "I'll give you two minutes, then I'm calling the coppers."

"Norma," Charlotte implored. "Come inside with me. You don't know these men."

" 'Course I do. This is Bert, and this is Joe, and these are their friends from work. I'll be as right as rain with them, won't I, Bert?"

"Right as rain. Say good-bye to your nosy friend, Norma."

"Don't fuss, Charlotte. I'll knock on your door when I get in. Promise I will."

IF THE MISSES Macleod and Meg were worried for Norma's sake, they said nothing of it, and supper was occupied by pleasant recollections of the day's events. Charlotte spent an hour in the sitting room with the others before retreating to her room to work on her next column for Mr. Ellis.

It had been a lovely day, one that the children of the street wouldn't soon forget, a beacon of life and hope amid the perpetual gloom of postwar austerity. It had done no harm, as far as she could tell, and might even make the coming days easier for some.

But what of the elaborate parades of military might, the lavish luncheons for dignitaries, and the epic displays of fireworks that had taken place elsewhere across Britain, most of them paid for out of the public purse? Wouldn't that money have been better spent on the hungry and needy, among them tens of thousands of demobilized servicemen? What of the people whose only memory of this Peace Day would be the empty promises of politicians?

It might be too radical a subject for even Mr. Ellis to countenance, but she just might be able to persuade him. "The Improvidence of Peace Day," she would call it.

She had completed a fine first draft, and was ready to set down her pen for the night, when she heard an odd noise at the front door—a muffled howl, as if a stray dog or cat were in distress. She went to her window, which faced the street, and pushed aside the curtains to get a better look.

There was nothing, no trace of movement beyond. And

then . . . a rustle of fabric, an anguished moan, and she flew to the front door.

Norma. Huddled on the stoop, her head bowed, her shoulders shaking with muffled sobs.

"Ch . . . Charlotte . . ."

"My goodness, Norma. What on earth has happened to you? No—don't try to answer. Not yet. Let me get you inside and up to your room."

"No! No, please. The others can't know. They mu . . . mustn't know."

"Then come into my room. Let me help you. I used to be a nurse. I can help you."

She guided Norma to her feet and led her by the shoulders into her room, where she settled her at the edge of the bed.

"I'll have to switch on the ceiling light, my dear, so I can see what has happened."

"Don't. You'll hate me. You will."

"Of course I won't. I swear I won't. Let me turn on the light. We'll start with that."

Her desk lamp, at the far side of the room, was too dim to illuminate more than her work surface. She went to the door, to the switch that was next to it, and harsh electric light flooded the room. Returning to Norma's side, she crouched before her and, gently but firmly, pulled the girl's hands away from her face.

It was worse than she'd expected. One eye blackened and swollen almost shut. A nasty scrape on one cheekbone. A split lip already crusting over with blood.

"Are you hurt anywhere else?"

"My . . . my side. I tripped, I think. When I tried to run. He kicked me. Or it might have been his friend." She began to cry again, silently, her tears welling steadily from her eyes. She was so young, scarcely more than a child. Why would anyone do such a thing to her?

"Oh, my dear. My dear, dear girl. Did he hurt you anywhere else, Norma? In any other . . . in another way? I won't be upset with you if he did. Not in the slightest. But you must tell me."

"No . . . no. He didn't rape me."

Rape. The word sounded as evil as the act itself. "Who did this to you?"

"One of Bert's friends. The one that told you to sod off. Sorry about that."

"Never you mind. I've been called worse."

"We were out dancing, and I was having ever so much fun. And he told me, Mick told me, that I was so pretty, the prettiest girl he'd ever seen, and would I come away with him. Go to another party. It sounded fun, so I did. We went out the back way—we'd gone to the Palais, and it was full to bursting. He said it would take too long to go through the front."

"What happened then?"

"His friend followed us. And they said . . . they said I was the sort of girl who knew how to have fun. And would I have some fun with them. I didn't realize what they meant, not at first, not until he'd backed me against the wall."

For a moment Charlotte thought she might be sick. "Go on."

"So I said no. I said he was wrong. That I wasn't that kind of girl, not at all, and I wanted to go home. But he kept pulling at my frock, at my skirt, and then he ripped it. I suppose I must have screamed. He put his hand over my mouth, so I bit him, and that's when he hit me. Oh, Charlotte—it hurt so badly. I thought I was going to faint. I tried to run, but his friend tripped me, and then one of them kicked me, and . . . and . . ."

"And what?" Charlotte took Norma's hands in hers and squeezed them tight, her heart aching for the girl. She was so young, so terribly young.

"He . . . he *spat* on me. As if I were a piece of rubbish. And that's what I am. Everyone will know, Charlotte. They'll know, and they'll *see*. What am I to do?"

"Norma. You are not rubbish. You are the farthest thing from rubbish."

"You were right. I shouldn't have gone with them. I was dressed like a, like a *whore*, he said . . ."

"Norma, *listen* to me. Are you listening? Even if you had paraded up and down the street wearing nothing more than rouge on your cheeks, naked as the day you were born, you wouldn't deserve what happened tonight. They were in the wrong, not you."

"You're only saying that to make me feel better."

"I am not. It's the truth. As God is my witness, it is the truth. Now, my dear, I think we ought to get you cleaned up. It's a good thing that tomorrow is Sunday. You can rest, and the worst of the swelling will have gone down by then."

"What will I tell the others?" Norma asked, her eyes glassy with fear. Clearly the prospect of telling their landladies was terrifying to the poor girl.

"I think we'll tell them part of the story. Not a lie. Simply . . . well, simply leave out the parts that might upset the misses. We can say you went out dancing, and a man at the dance hall was rude to you, and there was a tussle, and you got caught in the middle. How does that sound?"

"Likely enough, I suppose. Though Rosie'll sniff out the truth."

"Probably, but that's a worry for another day. Now, sit here while I fetch the first-aid box from the kitchen. I'll see if I can work some magic on that eye of yours."

The kettle on the range was still warm, with enough water to fill a small basin. Armed with that, a roll of cotton wool, a pot of arnica cream, and a bottle of tincture of iodine, the only antiseptic she could find, Charlotte returned to Norma's side and set to work. She washed clean the cuts and abrasions and swabbed them with iodine as lightly as she dared, not wishing to leave a telltale brown stain. Last of all she dabbed a liberal layer of arnica cream on Norma's eye and swollen lip.

As tenderly as she had once done for her patients, she helped Norma change out of her ruined clothes and into a spare nightgown, and then she settled her friend in bed.

She would not sleep, not for hours, for she was far too angry. Not at Norma, of course, but at men who thought a young, impressionable woman was fair game simply because she was intoxicated and scantily dressed. The only thing that ought to be troubling Norma right now was a headache and the beginnings of a cold.

Charlotte had never been especially maternal in her sentiments, but she felt a mother's rage for what had been done to her friend tonight. If she had a pound for every woman she'd met in the course of her work who'd had an eye blackened by her husband, she'd have been as rich as the Queen of Sheba.

What sort of world allowed such things to happen? The same world, she supposed, that allowed millions of young men to die over a few miles of Flanders mud, and let children starve in one of the richest nations in the world.

Life was unfair; she knew it down to her bones. From time to time she forgot that essential truth, but tonight had reminded her. She wouldn't be so foolish as to forget it again.

Chapter 15

Midday already and she had barely made a dent in the reports from the pensions review. There simply wasn't enough time in the day, when it came down to it. Even if Miss Rathbone were to hire another five constituency assistants . . .

"Miss Brown?"

Charlotte looked up to find Gladys hovering at her door.

"There's a telephone call for you. From Mr. Ellis at the *Herald*." This last piece of information she imparted with a jaunty wink.

"Thank you, Gladys."

She certainly hadn't been expecting a call from him. The Monday after Peace Day, a little more than a week ago now, she had sent him the article she'd been crafting when Norma had collapsed at the front door. She had expected him to reject it, or at the very least whitewash it with a coat of anodyne paint, but once again he'd surprised her.

Her column had run yesterday, every angry, outraged word of it, and Charlotte was already dreading the arrival of that evening's edition of the *Herald* at the office. It would be brimming over with outraged letters to the editor, she was sure of it, and try as she might she wouldn't be able to stop herself from reading every last one.

Perhaps that was it. Perhaps he had called to warn her. She wouldn't be surprised if people were branding her a Bolshevik, calling for her head, demanding that she be flogged through the streets.

She went to the telephone table and picked up the earpiece. "Hello? Mr. Ellis?"

"Hello, Miss Brown. Sorry to trouble you at work."

"That's quite all right."

"The thing is, Miss Brown . . ."

He was going to sack her. The *Herald*'s publisher had finally had enough. That was it. He was calling to—

"Well, you see, it's about tomorrow evening."

"Yes?" she asked, feeling quite perplexed by his hesitant manner. Normally the man was so forthright she could barely get a word in edgewise.

"There was a dinner planned, by my publisher, and I was meant to go to it. I'd arranged things so I wouldn't have to be at the paper in the evening, and then, just now, I learned that the dinner has been canceled. So I was thinking, ah, that if you weren't otherwise engaged, that I should like to ask you to dinner instead. And the pictures, as well."

"Dinner and the pictures?" This really was most unexpected.

"Yes. At six o'clock, if you can be spared that early. We don't have to go to the pictures, you know. Not if you're tired. But I thought . . . well, it's been an age since I went to them myself."

"I see," she said, although she didn't, not really. Was he asking her as one colleague might ask another? Or was his intention rather less collegial?

"But you may well be tired at the end of the day."

"No, not at all. I should love to go." That was true enough, for she did enjoy his company. "You said six o'clock?"

"Yes. I'll come round your office and we can walk into the city center from there."

"Very well. I look forward to seeing you tomorrow, Mr. Ellis. Good afternoon."

"Good afternoon, Miss Brown."

She hung up the earpiece on the telephone but made no move to stand. Could it be . . . ?

"Don't look so surprised," said Gladys, who had returned to her desk. "You'd think no one'd ever asked you to the pictures."

She ought to have chided Gladys for eavesdropping, but she only shrugged and walked back down the hall, back to her tiny office, where she fell into her chair and stared, her eyes unfocused, at the papers littering its surface.

The truth was that she hadn't ever been asked to the pictures. She'd had male friends when she was at Oxford, and later when she'd first moved to Liverpool, but none had ever showed an interest in her beyond the platonic. And then the war had come, and the most she'd ever hoped for was a few more hours of sleep, a cup of tea that was a little stronger, a day on the ward that was a little less taxing.

But now the war was over, and with or without her, the world would continue to spin on its axis. Life went on, a man she liked and respected had asked her out to dinner and the pictures, and she would go with him and enjoy every minute.

And not once, not even for an instant, would she spare a thought for another man who had never been hers, who would never be hers, though he had never left her thoughts or fled her dreams, not in all the years she had known him, despaired for him, and longed without hope or expectation for his wounded, solitary soul.

THE NEXT EVENING she waited outside for Mr. Ellis, not wishing to endure the giggles and whispers of her younger and sillier colleagues. It was a beautiful evening, the temperature pleasantly cool after the heat of the day, and there was no sign of rain in the purpling sky.

He was nearly on time, only five minutes late, and after he had greeted her with a handshake and an apology, they began the half-hour walk north into the city center.

"Is there anywhere in particular you'd like to have dinner?" he asked.

"Not really," she said, not wanting to admit that the tea shop near her office represented the sum total of her dining experience in Liverpool.

"Then let's go to the Phil on Hope Street. They've good food, and the interior is . . . well, I'm not sure how to describe it."

"You, lost for words?"

"It doesn't happen often."

Their conversation continued on in a similarly light vein. He seemed younger, away from the office and the myriad pressures weighing down on him, and it was clear he was making an effort to be charming and funny and possibly less single-minded than usual.

How old was Mr. Ellis? It wasn't the sort of question she could ask him outright, nor was there any easy way of finding out. He looked to be in his early thirties at most. Most men like him, in his position, were married at that age. She couldn't divine any flaw in his character or person, at least not at this juncture of their friendship. Perhaps it truly was the case that he'd let the pressures of work take over his life. In that, at least, they were well matched.

They were soon at the corner of Hope and Hardman Streets, and facing what looked like a misplaced homage to an Oxford college. With an oriel window overhanging the street, elaborately carved stone façade, and exuberant use of architectural styles from several different centuries, the Philharmonic Dining Rooms certainly bore no resemblance to any public house that she'd ever seen.

The interior was magnificent, if not entirely to Charlotte's taste, with every visible surface decorated in jaw-dropping turn-of-the-century style. Everywhere she looked, her eyes were assaulted: jewel-bright stained glass, panels of exquisite mosaic work on the bar, intricately carved wooden trim, ornate plaster ceilings.

"You see what I mean?" Mr. Ellis said.

"I do. I've never seen the like."

"The Phil is an institution here in Liverpool, if that's a term one can properly use for an establishment that's only been around for twenty years or so."

"I've walked by it often enough, but I never had any reason to come inside before. All this for a public house."

"We'd best go along to the dining room. It isn't quite as eye-catching, but it'll do."

He led her upstairs to a chamber that was somewhat more restrained in its interior decoration. At his request, the waiter seated them at a table in the corner of the room, away from the noise of the other diners. "So that we may talk without shouting," Mr. Ellis explained.

The menu, as she'd expected, had been devised with the

tastes of men in mind, with an emphasis on meat and potatoes. She wasn't feeling terribly hungry, so she ordered the chicken-and-leek pie, while he asked for a mutton chop, roast potatoes, creamed spinach, and a pint of ale.

"Would madam care for anything to drink?" the waiter asked.

"Do you have any wine? Or cider, perhaps?"

"We have both, madam."

"Well, then . . . perhaps a glass of white wine? Thank you."

Rather than pick up the threads of conversation immediately, she looked around the room, which was rapidly filling with diners. Some of them were wearing evening dress—long gowns for the women, black tie for the men—which seemed rather grand for a public house, even one as finely appointed as the Phil.

"Is it me, or are we rather underdressed for the occasion?" She was wearing her second-best summer frock, a dove-gray linen with white trim, and had thought herself perfectly dressed for the occasion until a few minutes before.

"The people dressed to the nines? They're about to go to a concert at the Philharmonic across the road. You wouldn't have preferred that to the pictures, would you? I mean, I could see if there are any tickets still available—"

"I'm quite happy to go to the pictures. And besides, we don't know what is on the program at the concert hall. It may be an evening of Stravinsky and the like. All atonal squeaking and bleating."

"You aren't an aficionado of modern music?"

"Of some, yes. I rather like the new jazz music from America. But I prefer my classical music to be less experimental. A legacy of my upbringing, I suppose."

"Was your father a musician?"

"A cleric. He's attached to Wells Cathedral. I grew up in a house a stone's throw away."

"Are your parents still living?"

"Yes, fortunately. You said you live with your mother. Is your father . . . ?" She left the question unsaid, for it seemed indelicate to simply come out and ask if the man were dead.

"He died nearly a decade ago. I came home from school to live with my mother—I have two sisters, but they'd married and moved away already."

So he was in his early thirties, just like her. "Had you finished university?"

"I had my undergraduate degree. I read history at Edinburgh, and then the plan was for me to follow my father into law. He was a barrister here in Liverpool."

"But instead . . . ?"

"I decided I'd had enough of school. I went to the *Herald* and climbed on the bottom rung of the ladder. Became a subeditor and general dogsbody to the rest of the staff."

"From there to editor in chief in a decade. Very impressive."

"More like twelve years. The war helped, of course. I mean . . . that is, I hope you know what I mean. So many men were gone, and those who might have competed for positions with me had left the paper."

"Don't apologize. You served your country, too. And I'm not saying that as a sop to your feelings."

Their drinks came, then, and their food shortly thereafter, and as they ate and drank they talked of the strange summer it had been so far. Mr. Ellis was particularly troubled by the rioting that had flared up in Liverpool and other port cities at the beginning of June, only to be quelled in days. Quelled, not resolved.

"The dock workers' anger and discontent that fueled the riots, especially the ones the police have characterized as racial in nature, hasn't gone anywhere," he noted. "A day or two of fistfights and rocks through shop windows isn't enough to solve the problems this city is facing."

"I agree. I thought it deplorable, the way the papers—yours excepted, of course—characterized the riots. As if the color of a man's skin is the only thing worth describing about him."

"You're right, but you also can't deny that race was a factor in the riots."

"You don't mean to say that the rioters ran amok because they were black, or Indian, or—"

"Not at all. The dock workers rioted because they are treated like the lowest of the low, are expected to survive on wages that would have been regarded as criminally low a century ago, and then are blamed by their white neighbors for depressing the job market. There's only so much a man can take before he cracks."

"They didn't do much for their cause, I'm afraid."

"No, they didn't, but I can't blame them for it. In any case, it's only the beginning. Look what happened in Luton on Peace Day—their town hall burned to the ground, the city center laid waste."

"You think the same could happen here?"

"I'm almost certain it will. Parliament has just introduced legislation that will bar the police from unionizing, and already there's talk of their going out on strike. Can you imagine what would occur? Anarchy, pure and simple."

It was a terrible thought. The riots in June had been frightening enough, but if unrest like that were to spill beyond the confines of a single district and consume the city as a whole, or even the nation . . .

"Don't look so downcast, Miss Brown. I shouldn't have sounded so definite about it. Times are hard, yes, but we've all pulled through worse. We may well do so again."

"I suppose so. Everyone seems content enough where I live."

"In your boardinghouse?"

"Yes. On Huskisson Street."

"Not far from here."

"Not far at all."

"Do you like it there?"

"I do. My landladies are two sisters, the Misses Macleod, and there are three other women at the house besides me."

"A happy place?"

"I would say so. Certainly we're very chummy with one another. Do you live in the city center, too?"

"I'm afraid not. It would be rather easier if I did, but my parents lived in Grassendale, on Salisbury Road. It would be sensible to live nearer to work, but my mother is very attached to the house, and to her garden, so we've stayed put. It's not far on the train, at any rate."

They had finished their meal; rather to Charlotte's surprise, she had eaten every bite of her pie. It was nearly half past seven; the pictures would have started already, and if they wished to see the newsreels they would have to hurry.

"Is there any film you're especially keen to see?" he asked as they crossed Ranelagh and arrived at the foot of Lime Street.

"It's been so long since I went to the pictures that I couldn't even hazard a guess."

"I confess the same. Shall we try this cinema? It looks nice enough."

The Scala's program had already begun, although the man at the box office assured them they had only missed some old

Charlie Chaplin shorts. Their seats were good ones, on the aisle no more than six or seven rows back, and although it was only a Thursday night there were musicians in the pit at the front—not an entire orchestra's worth, but more than the single pianist who played at most cinemas.

They arrived just in time for the newsreels, which seemed to please Mr. Ellis to no end. The Peace Day celebrations took pride of place: the nation's armed forces parading past the king, bonfires the length and breadth of the land, and joyous pageants and tea parties in the smallest villages and largest towns. The destruction of Luton's town hall was not featured, nor were more recent incidents of rioting and unrest in the United States and Canada. As seen through the lens of a newsreel editor, the world was a marvelously untroubled, calm, and united place.

The pictures themselves, though terribly silly, were very entertaining. The first was a paper-thin romp entitled *The Irresistible Flapper,* in which a wild young thing came to the rescue of her sister, and whose eponymous heroine bore an unfortunate resemblance to Norma. The second was *The Artistic Temperament,* and from what Charlotte could discern, for the plot was never very clear, it told the story of a young woman who rejected a rich nobleman, took up the violin, and married a poor artist.

She was beginning to yawn, the sort of huge yawns that were almost impossible to stifle, when Mr. Ellis turned to her and, grinning, bent his head to whisper in her ear.

"Have you had enough of this?"

"Yes, please."

He took her arm as they left, likely only to guide her through the darkened cinema, although he didn't let her go as they began the walk back to Huskisson Street.

"I wonder if perhaps we ought to have risked the Philharmonic instead," he said. "Those films were absolute nonsense."

"Perhaps, but I enjoyed them. I enjoyed every minute."

It was true. The films had been ridiculous, but the newsreels had been interesting, and their meal and conversation beforehand had been lovely. He was lovely, she realized suddenly. He was a thoroughly decent, intelligent, morally upstanding, right-minded man. So why wasn't her pulse racing? Why were her palms not damp in anticipation of the moment he would say good night to her?

They walked in silence, her arm tucked in his, the streets so quiet that it seemed as if Liverpool itself, in its very stillness, were holding its breath. It was late, of course, and most people were abed by now. She couldn't recall the last time she had been out so late during the week.

He walked her to her door and waited as she fished in her handbag for her keys, all the while saying nothing. Charlotte looked up and held out her hand for him to shake. He ignored it. Instead he took a step forward and dropped a kiss on her lips, light and fleeting, his mouth a pleasantly warm contrast to the cool evening air.

"Thank you," she whispered. "I mean, that is, thank you for tonight. I very much enjoyed your company, Mr. Ellis."

"Isn't it about time you called me John?"

"John, then. Thank you."

"Thank you, Charlotte."

"Shall you take the train home? Are they still running?"

"Not at this hour. But I can find a taxi at the station. Remember what I said about the police striking. It could happen any day now, so do your best to stay alert and aware."

"I will. Good night, then."

"Good night."

She let herself in, listened for his departing footsteps, switched off the hall light, and got ready for bed. She slept poorly, waking again and again, her dreams invaded by another man, the wrong man, a man with a crooked smile and a thousand-yard stare and a beguiling voice that beckoned her so sweetly, so enticingly, but faded to hollow echoes whenever she approached.

She woke with a start at dawn, sunlight streaming in through curtains left half open the night before. It promised to be a beautiful day, but as she lay in bed, thinking of the hours to come, Charlotte couldn't shake a feeling of unease, of dread, even. The air in her room was heavy and close, and it had a scent to it—nothing tangible, nothing she could attach to a thing or place or even a memory, but it was there, lingering at the borders of her waking mind.

It smelled like a storm. Just like those summer storms that come on quickly, charge the air, and leave one feeling headachy and dull. That was it. A storm was coming, one that had nothing to do with the weather, nothing at all, and she was powerless to do anything, apart from cower and tremble and wait for it to unleash its fury on them all.

Chapter 16

All day long, mindful of what John had told her the night before, Charlotte was on her guard, alert to even the slightest noise from the street, the merest hint that all was not well. At lunchtime she ventured out, walking up to Princes Avenue and back, but could discern nothing out of the ordinary. August the first, as far as she could see, was a perfectly ordinary day.

She was at her desk when Gladys came to her door, her face pale with worry.

"I'm sorry to bother you, Miss Brown, but Constable Johnson is here. He asked for Miss Rathbone, but as she's away in London I thought . . ."

"Of course. I'll come straight out."

Constable Johnson was their local bobby, a fixture of the neighborhood for as long as anyone could recall, and his homely, earnest face was normally the picture of solid reassurance. Today he was sweating and anxious, his demeanor so out of sorts that Charlotte's heart sank into her boots.

"Good afternoon, Constable Johnson. May I help you? I'm afraid Miss Rathbone is in London for the next few days."

"Are you aware of the strike action taking place, Miss Brown?"

"Taking place? So it's happening?"

"It is. I won't be leaving my post, but I can't say the same for many of my fellow constables. The thing is, Miss Brown . . . it's spreading. At first it was only a few districts, but the strikers are going from station to station now. Soon the looting will start up, as sure as night follows day. I fear it won't be safe for you and the other ladies to stay on here."

"I see."

"It'd be best if you all went home, and stayed home until it's blown over. Will you do that for me? I'll keep an eye on the premises as best I can."

"Is there anything we should do before we go? Board up the windows, that sort of thing?"

"I don't think there's time for that, but you might want to hide anything valuable. The typewriters, and the telephone, too, if it can be unhooked from the wall. They'll be the first things to go if anyone does break in."

"Very well. We'll take care of things here and be gone within the hour."

"Thank you, Miss Brown."

"Thank you, Constable. Please have a care for your own safety."

As soon as he had let himself out, she turned to Gladys and asked her to gather everyone in the reception area. They hadn't any time to spare.

"Constable Johnson has just advised me that a large proportion of the city police has gone on strike. He's asked us to secure the office and go home. I will telephone Miss Rathbone in London, to advise her what is happening, but in the mean-

time I need you to take the typewriters to the cellar and conceal them as best you can. If you come across anything else of
value, please hide it, too."

"Is it safe to be out in the streets?" asked Bessie, the youngest of the typists.

"It is, otherwise Constable Johnson would have told us to
stay put. But not for long, I think. Hurry, everyone."

Knowing time was of the essence, Charlotte went to Miss
Rathbone's office and picked up the earpiece of the telephone
on her employer's desk.

"Operator."

"Hello. I'd like to place a call to London, to Whitehall 4—"

"I'm very sorry, madam, but all the lines to London are engaged. Shall I ring back once a line becomes free?"

She hadn't the time to wait . . . what should she do? "Are the
local exchanges available?"

"Yes, madam. What number would you like?"

"Central 331."

It took several minutes for her call to be transferred from
the *Herald's* front desk to John's office, minutes in which she
grew steadily shakier and more anxious.

"John Ellis."

"Mr. Ellis—John. It's Charlotte."

"Tell me you're not still at work."

"Only for a few more minutes. Constable Johnson came
around and told us we need to go home. Will we be safe?"

"Yes, but not for long. As soon as the sun goes down the
remaining police won't be able to keep a lid on this. You need
to get home as quick as you can."

"I will. I wonder—I tried to ring Miss Rathbone at her flat
in London, but the lines are all busy. Could I trouble you to—"

"We've a telegraph here at the paper. I'll send one to her now."

"Thank you so much."

"Lock up the office, and be on your way home."

They said good-bye, but as soon as she replaced the earpiece the telephone trilled out an incoming call.

"Hello, Miss Eleanor Rathbone's office. Charlotte Brown speaking."

"Charlotte, it's Rosie. You've heard?"

"Yes. We're locking up the office now. What about you?"

"I'll stay at the hospital. We've a set of high gates to keep out any rioters, and our watchmen will keep us safe. Don't worry about me."

"I'll tell the misses."

"Thank you. Will you ring up Norma and Meg and make sure they know to go home?"

"I will. I'm not sure if there's a telephone at Meg's shop. But it's not that far away. I'll see that she comes home with me."

"Good. Stay safe and I'll see you when all of this settles down."

Charlotte placed one last call, this time to Norma's workplace.

"Good afternoon, Peterson Brothers Shipping, Miss Barnes speaking."

"Norma, it's Charlotte. You've heard about the strike."

"Just now. The men in the warehouse are running around as if they expect the Germans to invade."

"How are you getting home? You are leaving work, aren't you?"

"Yes, yes. Mr. Peterson is giving me a lift back to the house. I'll be home for supper. Promise."

They rang off. Charlotte found the spare key to Miss Rathbone's office in the top drawer of the desk, locked the door behind her, and slipped the key back under the door. It wasn't much, but it might deter someone from investigating further.

The typewriters had been stowed away: hidden under old crates in the cellar, Mabel informed her, and the women were all ready to go. Charlotte fetched her handbag, switched off the last of the lights, and locked up after everyone else had left.

She and Mabel walked north to Upper Parliament, at which point her friend headed east, to catch the tram to her home in Wavertree, and Charlotte continued along to Lord Street, where Meg worked.

The proprietor of À La Mode Chapeaux, Mr. Timmins, was standing on the doorstep as she approached, his demeanor that of a man waiting for the tumbrel. As Charlotte had never visited the shop before, she introduced herself before asking for Meg.

"The constable who patrols the neighborhood around my office was very insistent that we all go home, so I thought I would see if you could spare Mrs. Davies."

"Yes, of course. No one will be buying any hats today. Do you know if all the police are striking?"

"Not all, but enough to leave us in danger overnight. Are you taking any precautions with the shop?"

"We've locked away all the stock in the attics, and cleared out the workrooms upstairs."

"Were you going to cover the picture window? One brick and they'd be in."

"My son is fetching some wood from home. I hope it will be enough, Miss Brown."

Meg was reluctant to leave, perhaps worrying that Mr. Timmins would think ill of her, but he was perfectly understanding, promising that he and his son could manage and that she wasn't to come back until Monday at the earliest, and only then if order had been restored.

"What if it all amounts to nothing?" Meg asked as they made their way home.

"Then we'll all feel a trifle embarrassed for overreacting. But I don't think it will blow over. I think the next few days will be very difficult indeed."

The streets were far from empty, but most of the shops they passed had shut their doors already. The people they passed all had the same look about them, a strained, horribly apprehensive expression, as if they were bracing themselves for a blow. News was spreading, from street to street and block to block, and with it a coverlet of fear and nervous anticipation was descending upon the city. Anything could happen. Anything might happen.

Soon they were all, Rosie excepted, gathered in the kitchen at home, hands clutched around cups of tea. The house was old enough to have interior shutters, the sort that recessed into the side of the window casings, and those had all been drawn and latched. The front door was locked and barred. There was nothing to do but wait.

"I ought to have asked before, Janie, but do we have enough food to last through till Monday?"

"Oh, yes, Miss Brown. I did the marketing this morning, same as always. We might run low on milk if the milkman doesn't come, but that'll be the worst of it."

"Well done. You see, Miss Mary and Miss Margaret? We are well prepared, and perfectly safe now that the house is secured."

"If you say so, Charlotte. But what if mobs start rampaging through the streets?"

"That isn't going to happen," Charlotte said firmly. "There will likely be some looting overnight, but the extent of it depends on how many constables are striking. As we live in a residential district, I can't imagine we have anything to fear. We're taking precautions, that's all."

"It's so gloomy down here," Norma complained. "Can't we go up to the sitting room? We could open the shutters a little. Just to brighten the room."

"Best to keep them latched," Charlotte insisted. "But we should go upstairs. Would you mind if we switched on the electric lights for a while, Miss Mary?"

"Not at all. A spell in the sitting room will do us all good. You, too, Janie. Come along now."

They trooped upstairs, cups of tea in hand, and settled in at their regular places: the misses in their wing chairs, now adorned with their Blackpool antimacassars, Charlotte and Norma on the sofa, Meg at the piano, and Janie, who only saw the room when she came in to clean, perching on a footstool in front of the empty hearth.

Charlotte had her book, the misses had their knitting, Meg was working her way through the sheet music for "Roses of Picardie," Janie had some mending, and Norma fidgeted. Didn't the girl have any way to pass the time apart from dancing and going to the pictures?

"Surely you can find something to do," Charlotte told her. "Why don't you read one of your magazines?"

"I couldn't read, not now. When we're all about to be murdered in our beds—"

"Rubbish. No one is going to be murdered. Some shops may

be looted, and there may be a few scuffles in the street, but that will be the sum of it. Do find something to busy yourself, won't—"

There was a knock at the door, not especially loud or forceful, but Norma seemed to think it worthy of a bloodcurdling scream.

"Good heavens, Norma! It's only a knock at the door. You'll frighten us all to death."

"Don't open the door—what if it's—"

"Do I look like a fool? You wait here."

Charlotte went into the front hall, placed herself before the door, and waited for another knock.

"Yes? Who is it?" she called out in her best imitation of Miss Rathbone.

"It's John Ellis."

Her hands fumbling with the lock and dead bolt, she opened the door to his familiar, comforting face. "Come in, come in. Whatever are you doing out?"

"I wanted to make sure you are safe, and that the house is secure."

"Will you come into the sitting room a moment, just to say hello to the others?"

She introduced him to everyone, explaining that he was the editor of the *Herald* and had stopped by to ensure they were safe. This resulted in raised eyebrows from Norma and expressions of rapt adoration from the others.

"If you'll excuse me, ladies, I must go."

Back in the hall, they pitched their voices low enough that they wouldn't easily be overheard.

"Is it bad?" she asked.

"Quite bad in some areas. Down Scottie Road and up in

Everton there's hardly a shop window that hasn't been smashed, even though the sun won't go down for hours yet. Can you believe it? Shops looted in broad daylight."

"I've shuttered the windows," she said. "But I'm worried about downstairs. The windows lock, but that's all."

"Are they big enough that a man might crawl through?"

"No, none of them."

"Then you'll be fine. Draw the curtains, if they have them, or pin up some cloth to cover them. Don't go out tomorrow, not even if all seems well."

"But surely—"

He took a step toward her, his voice little more than a whisper. "HMS *Valiant* has been called down from Scapa Flow, and will be anchored in the Mersey by tomorrow. The government is calling in men from the barracks in St. John's Gardens."

"How many of the police are striking?"

"Enough. At least half of them."

"What about the rest of England?"

"A few spots of trouble, here and there, but it's only in Merseyside that the strike has spread. No thanks to the antediluvian tactics of the Watch Committee that oversees the force. That's what happens when you pay your police officers a third of what most workingmen make, never give them any time off, and dock their pay for even the slightest infraction. Did you know that a loose thread on his uniform can cost an officer a day's pay? It's a wonder they haven't walked off the job long before now."

"What will happen to the men who've gone on strike?"

"They've all been sacked."

"Already?"

"Any man who failed to report for duty today was sacked.

The *Herald* is running advertisements on Monday for new recruits, as are the other papers."

"It seems terribly harsh. Although it's hard not to feel a little angry with them for putting us in such danger."

"Just as I imagine it's hard to put your life in danger every day, work ungodly hours, and accept wages that are barely enough to keep your children in shoes."

"I didn't mean . . . that is, I'm not unsympathetic to their cause."

"I know you aren't. It's a bloody mess, that's what this is."

"What of your mother?"

"I rang her earlier. Thank God I had a telephone installed at the house last year. She'll be fine. The servants are staying with her, and Grassendale is well removed from the trouble spots."

"I suppose you ought to get back to the paper."

"I must."

"Thank you for coming."

"Will you promise to stay inside, you and everyone else, and on no account open the door unless you're certain who is on the other side of it?"

"I will."

"Good-bye for now. I ought to have asked before—does anyone on the street have a telephone?"

"I think Mr. and Mrs. Atwater do. They're next door."

"If you need me, don't hesitate to ring. Now bolt the door, and do your best to entertain the others."

As soon as he was gone and she'd fastened the dead bolt, she closed her eyes and stood, shivering a little, in the dark, empty hall. He was such a lovely, kind man. Really he was. She could be happy with a man like John Ellis, a good man, a man whose aims in life seemed to dovetail so perfectly with her own.

But try as she might, she couldn't marshal even the scarcest wisp of romantic feeling for him. Couldn't begin to imagine him in such a context. What was *wrong* with her?

She listened and waited, holding her breath, wishing against hope for a lightning bolt of truth to descend and reveal the path she ought to take. She never prayed, hadn't for years, nor was there anyone to whom she could turn and unburden herself. Perhaps, if Rosie had been home, she might have tried . . . but they had only known each other for a matter of months. It would be an impertinence to confide in her.

She was alone in this world, as she would always be, and it was time she accepted it. Happiness didn't turn on romance or marriage or motherhood, after all. She was alone, as she was meant to be, and she would survive.

She went back into the sitting room and, taking her place on the sofa again, picked up her book, a much-loved copy of *Persuasion,* and opened it to the first page.

"Shall I read to you all? I think I have just the book for the occasion."

Chapter 17

"Has Meg said anything about the shop?" Charlotte asked. She and Rosie were returning home after a long and delightfully aimless walk through Princes Park, its gardens a riot of late-summer color. It seemed like months since they'd spent any amount of time together, for their days off didn't often coincide.

"Not to me, she hasn't. I'm worried about her. The repairs seem to be taking forever."

For five weeks, ever since the riots at the beginning of August, Meg had been living on half pay, and she was fortunate to receive even that. À La Mode Chapeaux had been thoroughly vandalized, its stock pilfered and interior fittings destroyed, but Mr. Timmins had vowed to reopen. Many other shops, especially in the poorer districts of Toxteth and Everton, had shuttered their doors for good.

"I know. And even if she were having trouble with her rent, she'd never say so. Do you want to have a quiet word with her? Just to be certain she's all right?"

"It can't hurt," Rosie said. "Though I doubt I'll get very far."

It seemed to Charlotte that Meg had warmed to her housemates over the past months, joining in their conversations more and more, staying in the sitting room with them after supper, even accompanying the other women to a musical evening where the Misses Macleod had sung with their church choir. Small steps, to be sure, and Meg's smiles were as rare as hen's teeth, but it was a start.

They were steps from home, still engrossed in their conversation, when Charlotte belatedly realized a large motorcar was stopped in the street ahead of them. No one on the street had a motorcar, not on this block at least. Certainly no one had an immense, gleaming, purring beast of a motorcar that surely ran on crumpled-up pound notes instead of petrol.

"Will you look at that? Do you suppose the king is having his tea at Huskisson Street today?" Rosie said.

"It's not the king," Charlotte answered. "It's Lilly's brother." Even from a distance, she recognized the chauffeur's livery.

It made no sense. If he had wished to contact her, he might have written, or sent a telegram, or even telephoned her at work. There was no reason for him to be here.

Rosie caught her arm and chivvied her along. "You and he are friends, aren't you? Best not to keep him waiting. Goodness only knows how long he's been here."

"I look a fright. We should go in the back way. Just so I can wash my face and brush my hair—"

"I'm sure he won't mind. Come on, now."

No sooner had they opened the front door than Janie, her face flushed and her eyes suspiciously red, rushed up to them.

"Oh, Miss Charlotte, Miss Rosie! I dunno what to do. There was a knock at the door, so I come out of the kitchen to answer it, and there was a man stood there in a funny suit. He asked if you was here and I said no, you'd gone out. And then he went back to that big motorcar outside and *she* come in."

"She?" Charlotte asked, though she already knew the answer. It wasn't Edward, after all. It was, instead, the last person in the world whom she ever, ever wished to see.

"She didn't say who she was. She went right past me into the sitting room. The misses had gone to their choir practice and everyone else was out. I didn't know what to do, Miss Charlotte."

"I quite understand."

"I did go in to ask if she needed anything, a cup of tea or summat, and I was ever so polite, but she didn't even look at me. Just told me to get out."

"Oh, Janie. I'm so very sorry. Let me speak to my, ah, guest, and then we'll all have a cup of tea together."

It was time to beard the dragon.

Without bothering to remove her hat or coat, she opened the door to the sitting room. There, seated in Miss Margaret's chair, was Lady Cumberland.

Charlotte sat on the sofa, ensured her back was ramrod straight, and looked the countess directly in the eye.

"Good afternoon, Lady Cumberland."

The woman said nothing. She didn't even blink. She simply stared at Charlotte.

"May I ask why you have installed yourself in my sitting room?"

"*Your* sitting room? Perhaps I am mistaken, but I thought you were nothing more than a boarder here."

"I may be a boarder, but this is my home all the same. So allow me to ask you again: why are you here?"

For an instant, Charlotte saw the room through Lady Cumberland's eyes. The worn upholstery on the misses' easy chairs. The spots of damp on the ceiling. The furniture that was just old enough to look outdated, but not old enough or good enough to be antique.

"You know very well," the countess answered, her gaze flickering to a point on the wall behind Charlotte's left ear.

"No, Lady Cumberland, I do not know. Please enlighten me."

"Insolent girl. Do you know how much of my time you have wasted already? First at your place of employment, if one can charitably call it such, where I was informed you were not at work."

"Saturday and Sunday are my days off."

"Two days off? I've never heard of such a thing," the countess sputtered.

"Possibly because you have never worked a day in your life."

A positively arctic silence descended upon the room. This would never do; if she were to hear the woman out, and then extract her from the house, Charlotte would have to adopt a more diplomatic tone.

"I presume that one of my colleagues was kind enough to supply you with my address?"

"Yes, and I have been sitting here for nearly an *hour*."

"If you had taken the trouble to advise me of your plans, I would have suggested a mutually convenient time. Now, believe it or not, I am a busy woman and I have things to do. May I ask you to clarify your purpose in coming here? Otherwise I shall have to ask you to leave."

Her hands were trembling, her mouth had gone dry, and there was every chance that her knees would give way if she tried to stand. But she would not be cowed.

"It's all your fault," said Lady Cumberland. Her gaze moved across the room, to a towering aspidistra next to the piano, and she began to fuss with her gloves. Could it be that the countess was nervous? Perhaps even fearful?

"He hasn't been himself, not since Elizabeth's wedding. He says it is nothing, but I know the truth. I know you are to blame."

"By 'he,' do you mean Lord Cumberland?"

"I do."

"May I ask what you believe to be wrong with him? Beyond the obvious difficulties, I mean."

"He was recovering well, I thought. At first he seemed to be improving . . ."

Lady Cumberland now sat perfectly still, as immobile as one of the china figurines on the misses' mantelpiece, but the expression on her face was a portrait of torment. It was impossible not to feel a twinge of sympathy, if fleeting and really quite minimal, for the woman.

"How is he different, in your estimation?"

"He won't go out. Not to dinner, nor to any other sort of social engagement. He sleeps the day through, every day, and at night he roams through his house and drinks himself senseless and the servants have to carry him upstairs to bed."

"His house? Is he not living at Ashford House?"

"He said he couldn't bear it, so he removed himself to Chelsea."

"Where he lived before the war?"

"Yes."

"So he is sleeping all day and drinking himself into a stupor each night?"

"Yes."

Why had Lilly told her nothing of this? Where had Robbie been all this time? "Have you spoken to him of your concerns? Reminded him of the ruinous effects of drink?"

"Of course I have, but he only laughs at me. He says that if I am very lucky he will drink himself into the grave so the earldom might pass to George."

He had not been so poorly when she'd seen him at the wedding. He could not have been, surely, or she would have known it. "I am very sorry to hear it, Lady Cumberland. Truly I am. Yet I fail to see how I can be to blame."

"He broke his engagement because of you."

"Broke his engagement? When? I had no idea." Could she have pushed him to it? Could her words, so horribly caustic in the remembrance, have set him on such a course?

"He came to me last week and told me he had spoken to Helena and broken things off. I know it was because of you. Don't deny it."

"I do deny it."

"He has some strange sort of attachment to you. He's always had an affinity for those who are beneath him. Why else would he have allowed that Glaswegian upstart to presume upon their friendship for so long?"

"You're speaking of Robbie? That upstart is the only reason your son was returned to you. He spent months searching for Edward, or have you managed to forget?"

"Edward would have come to his senses eventually."

"Given the state he's in, I doubt it very much. Now, I cannot be certain of why he ended his engagement with Lady Helena, but I presume it has something to do with it having been forced on him when he was younger. And I further presume that he has no wish to ruin her life by trapping her in a loveless marriage."

At that, Lady Cumberland actually flinched. "You would rather he married a nonentity like yourself?"

"I would rather that he be happy, just as any friend would wish for him. I promise I have no call upon his affections."

Lady Cumberland closed her eyes and bowed her head, her pose so convincingly dejected that Charlotte very nearly reached out to pat her hand. "Is that why you came here?" she asked instead. "To warn me off, à la Lady Catherine de Bourgh?"

"De Bourgh? I know no one by that name, I assure you."

"I was only making reference to—" Charlotte began, but stopped short. Lady Cumberland had never approved of novels, and particularly not ones written by women. "Never mind. I was mistaken."

"We thought him lost. For so long we thought him dead. Vanished, never to have a grave. We lost . . ."

Lady Cumberland's voice broke, and Charlotte could only watch, stricken by pity, as her adversary fought to regain her composure. "When he returned, as if risen from the dead, after we had all lost hope . . . it seemed miraculous. Yet now I fear we are going to lose him again."

"To the drink?" Charlotte asked. "Or to despair?"

"To both, I think."

It was time to put on her nurse's hat. "Do you know what I did during the war?"

"Of course not," replied Lady Cumberland, her nostrils flaring delicately. "Why should I know such a thing?"

"I was a nurse at the Special Neurological Hospital for Officers in Kensington."

"Shell shock," whispered the countess.

"Yes. I haven't seen much of Lord Cumberland since his return, but it may be possible that he is suffering from some degree of nervous shock, if you will. Not because he is lacking in courage or moral fiber, but because he has been forced to endure the unendurable."

It was a mark of Lady Cumberland's desperation that she didn't immediately reject Charlotte's suggestion. "I've brought in doctors. He refuses to talk to them. He won't even talk to Mr. Fraser."

"He might talk to me. Not because of any sort of romantic attachment, I assure you. Edward trusts me to tell him the truth. That is all."

"I see," the countess said. "If you were to agree to help him, what fee would you charge?"

"I beg your pardon?"

"You're a nurse, aren't you?"

Of course. Charlotte was the hired help. She would always be a servant in the eyes of Lady Cumberland. "Not any longer. If I did agree to speak with him, I would be acting solely as a friend."

"Will you help him?"

"I shall try."

"Very well. When will you visit him?"

"I shall have to speak to Miss Rathbone, my employer, and arrange to take a day or two off. Once I know, I'll telephone Lilly. Will that do?"

"Yes." The countess rose to her feet and went to the door of the sitting room. Curiously, she made no move to open it. Was she waiting for a footman to materialize from the ether?

"Thank you, Miss Brown."

"I promise to do my best."

Lady Cumberland extended a gloved hand, and Charlotte realized, to her astonishment, that she was meant to shake it. She did so, feeling very glad indeed that she had not removed her own gloves, and watched as the countess opened the door and swept from the room.

Charlotte returned to the sofa. It seemed best to get her thoughts in order before she did anything else.

"What on earth was that?" Rosie asked from the doorway. "I heard her leave just now. Are you all right?"

"I'm not sure. That was an exceedingly strange conversation."

"Was that Lilly's mother?"

"It was. She . . . I can barely make sense of this." Charlotte stood, feeling steadier already, and straightened the lapels of her coat. "I need to speak to Lilly. I'll tell you everything when I return, but I must get to the post office before they close."

WHEN SHE ARRIVED at the post office on Upper Parliament Street, breathless from having run most of the way, the telephone kiosks were all occupied. Nearly ten minutes passed before one became free, time that she used to compose herself, suppress her indignation at Lilly's having said nothing, absolutely *nothing* to her, and concoct her request to Miss Rathbone for yet more time off.

It was the first occasion she'd had to telephone Lilly at her and Robbie's new home in Chelsea, for they'd only moved in a fortnight earlier. She passed on their number to the operator and waited for the call to be connected. It was a clear line, for once, and the answering voice might easily have come from an adjacent kiosk.

"Hello, Fraser residence. Ruth speaking."

"Oh, hello. May I speak to Lady Elizabeth? This is Miss Brown ringing from Liverpool."

"Yes, ma'am. Right away, ma'am."

A blur of background voices, and then, "Hello? Charlotte?"

"Lilly."

"I've been meaning to call. How are you?"

"Feeling rather dazed after a visit from your mother."

Lilly gasped in dismay. "From Mama? Oh, Charlotte. I *am* sorry. Was it about Edward?"

"Yes. Why didn't you tell me?"

"I meant to, honestly I did. But we were away until July, and then there was all the bother with the painters and movers and so forth, and getting settled in the house. We scarcely saw him all summer."

"When did he break his engagement?"

"Last week, I think. It was long overdue, of course, and fortunately Helena took it well. I saw her the other day and she told me she was relieved."

"And the drink?"

"We'd been worried. But we honestly hadn't realized the extent of it until just the other evening. Robbie went to visit him and Edward emptied the better part of a bottle of brandy."

"Has this been going on all summer?"

"I think so. Perhaps even for longer."

"Has he mentioned having any headaches? Any dizziness?"

"He has, yes. He complains of his head pounding day and night. But when I ask him if he's spoken to a doctor about it, or if he'll agree to let Robbie examine him, he simply walks away. When poor Mama asks, he shouts at her. I was going to ring you, just to ask if you might suggest anything else. If perhaps you had any advice as a result of your work during the war."

"I do. At least I think I may."

"Thank heavens."

"I told your mother I would come to London and speak to

Edward. See if I can persuade him to accept help. I haven't yet spoken to Miss Rathbone, but I feel certain she'll give me a few days of leave."

"Thank goodness."

"I'll ring again as soon as I know more."

"You will stay with us, won't you? The house is a shambles, boxes everywhere, but I'm ever so keen to show it off."

"Of course I'll stay. Give Robbie my regards, and I'll see you soon."

Chapter 18

The train was slowing, shunting from track to track, the hiss and grind of its locomotive descending to a statelier register as it approached Euston station. As soon as it had lurched to a stop, Charlotte pulled her valise from the luggage rack above her seat, shouldered her handbag, and set forth along the platform, intent on arriving at the station's taxi rank before the queue stretched down the street.

On the other side of the barrier, however, Lilly and Robbie were waiting for her.

"I told you I would take a taxi," Charlotte protested.

"You did. I then said I preferred to collect you," Lilly replied, embracing her friend.

"You can't expect her to pass up a perfectly good opportunity to drive her new car," added Robbie as they walked outside.

"New car?" Of course Lilly had been an ambulance driver while she was in the WAAC, but Charlotte had assumed her friend's interest in motoring had ended at the same time as her demobilization.

"My wedding present from Robbie. There she is." Lilly pointed to a Model T Ford parked just beyond the taxi rank.

"It's a 1915 model, but she runs like new. Go on and sit in the front."

After stowing Charlotte's bags in the backseat, Robbie cranked the engine while Lilly started the car via a series of entirely mystifying actions. Having never ridden in the front seat of a motorcar, Charlotte had little notion of how one worked. Once the engine was purring away nicely, Lilly nodded to her husband and he climbed into the backseat, albeit rather awkwardly, as the motorcar's single door was shared by both banks of seats.

"I wish you could have seen my face when Robbie had Henrietta delivered. I nearly fell over," Lilly said, steering them between the massive pillars of the great Euston Arch and into the London traffic with the calm assurance of an old hand.

"Henrietta?"

"Well, actually she's Henrietta the Second. I named her after my little ambulance—the one I crashed while we were evacuating the Fifty-first. Who in turn was named for Henry Ford."

"I see," said Charlotte, although she couldn't imagine why anyone would give a motorcar a name. "You really are a very accomplished driver."

"Thank you. Practice makes perfect. I was nervous at first—I hadn't driven since I was invalided home—but it really is ever so much easier driving here. The roads are in far better shape, to begin with. Now, tell me," she said, downshifting as they swung into a huge roundabout, "if you had any difficulty getting time off work. I mean, it was such short notice."

"I called Miss Rathbone yesterday afternoon. I told her what was happening—that is, I told her that a friend of mine had fallen ill and his family had asked me to visit. It's a version of the truth, I suppose."

Skirting the truth with Miss Rathbone had made her desperately uncomfortable, but the details of Edward's condition were not hers to share with anyone outside his family.

"So Miss Rathbone didn't object?" asked Lilly.

"Not in the slightest. I was well ahead with all my work, which helped, and I'll be back for Tuesday morning."

They turned off one large road onto another, and almost immediately Lilly swung right onto a small street of Georgian cottages that ended in a cul-de-sac. The houses, charmingly, were painted in a spectrum of pastels, from palest pink to a vibrant primrose yellow. The Frasers' house was at the end of the street, its frontage rather narrower than the rest, its paint the exact hue of a robin's egg.

Once they were through the front door, Robbie carried her bags upstairs while Lilly led the way into the sitting room. It was large and beautifully proportioned, and had been sparely furnished with older pieces, their upholstery soft and faded, their wood warm with age.

"Almost everything came from the attics at Cumbermere Hall," Lilly explained. "Edward told me to help myself. You wouldn't believe how much was stuffed up there, all covered in dust and spiderwebs, simply because it had fallen out of fashion. There was enough for ten houses at least."

"Where is the shambles you spoke of on the telephone?"

"As soon as I knew you were coming we carried all the unopened boxes into the garret," Lilly admitted. "We still have to unpack our books, and there are crates of paintings and photographs and so forth to set out, but otherwise we're feeling quite settled."

Robbie set a plate of sandwiches on the occasional table next to Charlotte. "Ruth made these up before leaving for the night. And I've a pot of tea brewing in the kitchen."

As if by mutual consent, their conversation that evening entirely avoided the subject of Edward. Instead they spoke of the Frasers' honeymoon in Cornwall, Robbie's return to work at the London Hospital, and Lilly's studies with a dauntingly serious tutor.

"I've begun to have nightmares about my Latin and Greek, but Mr. Pebbles insists we press ahead."

"Mr. Pebbles? Is that honestly his name?"

"It is." Lilly giggled. "Dorian Pebbles."

"Poor man. Is he a good tutor?"

"Excellent. Very patient. He thinks I have a good chance of passing the entrance exams for university in the spring."

"Of course you will," Robbie said. "I've no doubt at all."

"Have you thought of where you'd like to study?"

"Yes." Lilly took Charlotte's hand in hers and squeezed it tight. "You must know that you've always been an inspiration to me. So I've decided to apply to the London School of Economics, and do a degree in social policy."

Lilly thought *her* an inspiration? She opened her mouth, about to respond with praise for her friend who had been so courageous, so stalwart in her every endeavor since leaving home, but the words, or perhaps they were tears, clogged her throat and left her mute. She found the handkerchief she'd tucked in her sleeve earlier, wiped her eyes, and blew her nose.

"Thank you, Lilly. I . . . I feel the same about you. Both of you."

"I think it's high time we are all off to our beds," Robbie interjected. "Charlotte's had a long day, and we'll all be on tenterhooks tomorrow. Let's get some rest while we can."

"Shall you come with me to see him?" Charlotte asked.

Lilly looked to her husband for confirmation. "Not right away. Not unless you need us. I don't want him to feel as if we're press-ganging him. Perhaps once you've spoken with him, and possibly made some headway, you could ring us here?"

"I'll work from home tomorrow morning," added Robbie. "We'll be straight over if you need us."

"That sounds very sensible. Good night, then. Until tomorrow."

NATURALLY IT WAS raining again in the morning, and although Charlotte wore her mackintosh and carried an umbrella, her skirts, and nerves, were thoroughly dampened by the time she reached Edward's house, though it was but ten minutes away by foot.

Only a few hundred yards from the Thames, it was part of a row of comfortably imposing town houses, their brick-and-stucco exteriors as plain as Puritans. She knocked, listened for footfalls inside, knocked again. At last the door was answered.

She recognized the man who greeted her, though she couldn't recall his name. He'd once been a footman at Cumbermere Hall.

"Good morning."

"Good morning, Miss Brown. Do come in."

"I beg your pardon, but I can't quite—"

"It's Andrews, ma'am. I see to Lord Cumberland when he's in residence here at Cheyne Row."

"Of course. Mr. Andrews. I've come to see his lordship, although I suspect he's still abed."

"That he is."

"Would you be so kind as to inform him that I am here and will not be leaving until he agrees to see me? I've come at the behest of Lady Cumberland and Lady Elizabeth."

A spark of hope flared in the man's eyes. "I will, ma'am. Would you care to wait in here?" He took her coat and hat and showed her into the sitting room, a dull and somber chamber that looked to have been furnished with the contents of an undertaker's parlor.

When Mr. Andrews returned, only a few minutes later, his deflated expression told her everything.

"He's awake, ma'am, but he won't come down. I don't know what to do."

"Then I shall have to go up. Don't worry," she called back as she started up the stairs, "I'll say I barged past when your back was turned."

"Good luck, Miss Brown. It's the door to your right on the first-floor landing."

At this time of day most houses, especially those of the aristocracy, were a ferment of activity, with much cleaning of hearths, beating of carpets, making of beds, and so forth. Here, by contrast, a deathly quiet prevailed, without even the gentle sounds of belowstairs activity drifting up to puncture the atmosphere of funereal decay.

She knocked once, sharply, and let herself into Edward's bedchamber. The draperies were drawn tight, and it was so dark she could barely see, so she stood at the threshold and waited for her eyes to grow accustomed to the gloom. The air felt close and suffocating, and as she took her first tentative steps forward her nose was assailed by a wretched miasma of cigarette smoke, spilled brandy, and stale coffee.

She could see better now, if imperfectly. Edward was in bed, facing away from the door, one hand flung over his eyes. His prosthetic leg lay on the floor.

"Did you send her away?" he mumbled.

"He did not."

When he said nothing further, she moved to his bed and, emboldened, sat gingerly on its bottom corner.

"Aren't you going to throw back the curtains? Shout at me to get up?"

"No, because that would only make things worse. I think you ought to stay where you are, just for now, and tell me what is wrong."

"Well, you see," he began, "back in the summer of 1914 the Archduke Franz—"

"Don't make a joke of it. Not today, at least. What are your symptoms? Tell me exactly."

"Splitting headache, nearly all the time. Not from the drink; this is different."

"Go on."

"Light-headed, though not so regularly I can predict it."

"Have you fallen because of it? Fainted?"

A pause. "Yes."

"What of light? Does it hurt your eyes? Do you have difficulty reading—not in making out the words, but in focusing on the page without it hurting you?"

"Yes to both. Any light bothers me—sunlight, lamplight. Feels like an ice pick at my temples."

"Are you exhausted by simple activities? Exclude anything that has become more difficult since you lost your leg. I mean things like having a conversation on the telephone or getting through a meal in company."

"Yes."

"Are you able to sleep?"

"Only once I'm at the point of exhaustion. Even then I wake up after a few hours."

"I see. Why are you answering my questions so readily? You've refused to speak to Robbie about this."

"Meddling Scot. Always thinking he knows what's best for me."

"You've decided it can't possibly get any worse. That's what I think," she said.

"It might. You're about to tell me I have something incurable, aren't you? Don't be shy. I'd welcome it."

"No, you wouldn't. I need to ask you a few more questions. The night you were taken prisoner, you were knocked down by a shell that exploded nearby. Is that correct?"

"Yes. We were cutting wire, well into no-man's-land. It was our own artillery that shelled us. I heard it hit, about eight or nine yards distant, and I was knocked down. That's all I recall."

"I know your leg was injured, but do you recall if you hit your head as well?"

"I might have. Can't be certain."

"How did your head feel when you woke up? It might be difficult to distinguish that pain from—"

"Sore. It felt like someone had taken a cricket bat to the base of my skull."

"And what of your neck?"

"Stiff, I suppose. Painful."

"How long did the pain persist?"

"I don't know. Weeks? When my leg became infected, and then they took it off, the pain of that drowned out everything else."

"Of course. Understandably so."

He turned, just enough to grasp her hand. His skin was cool and unpleasantly clammy.

"What's wrong with me? You must tell me. Nothing can be worse than living like this."

"Bear in mind that I'm not a physician, and as such I'm not qualified to make any sort of diagnosis. But I will say that I've seen men with symptoms similar to yours. They had suffered severe concussions, as I suspect you did when you were first injured. Amid the chaos of your capture, and then the loss of your leg, the concussion went untreated."

"That's all? A concussion?"

"You'll need to be seen by a physician. We could ask one of the doctors at my old hospital to assess you."

"No."

"Then what about Robbie? He won't tell a soul. We *must* get to the bottom of this."

"If it's a concussion, won't it go away on its own?"

"Not without help. I'm going to telephone for Robbie now, and then we shall all discuss what is to be done. While I'm gone, I should like you to get out of bed and get dressed. Pajamas and a robe are fine if that's all you can manage."

She hurried downstairs and was shown to the library and its telephone by Mr. Andrews. She relayed the heartening news to Lilly, who sounded as if she were holding back tears.

"We'll be there straightaway."

"Good. Can you ask Robbie to bring some aspirin? I doubt Edward has any proper medicine on hand."

Mr. Andrews was hovering, clearly hoping for some good news, but the battle was not yet won. She only smiled and asked him to bring her some tea, hot buttered toast, and a soft-boiled egg. "I'll wait here and take it up."

"Thank you ever so much, ma'am. It'll be the first thing he's eaten since yesterday."

Edward was sitting in a chair by the time she returned. He had put on trousers and a shirt, and was wearing his prosthetic leg, but hadn't on any shoes or socks. The contrast between his bare foot and the dull aluminum form of his prosthesis was faintly obscene.

"That smells horrid," he said as she advanced with his breakfast tray.

"Only because you've been starving yourself. You should be glad it isn't bread and milk."

"God help me."

"Is there anywhere you might eat properly?"

"There's a table in the drawing room next door," he admitted.

"Lead the way."

It was just as dark there, though the air was a trifle fresher, and as Edward picked at his food and grumbled about the absence of coffee she busied herself by opening both of the room's large windows, though she was careful to draw the draperies almost shut once she'd finished.

She pulled out the table's other chair, sat down, and stared at him, trying to assess what she observed in a strictly clinical fashion. She saw a man so thin that his clothes hung upon him. Skin that was dreadfully pale. Eyes sunken by dehydration and shadowed with pain. Hands that shook as they reached for a piece of toast or lifted the teacup.

She said nothing, only waited and watched him eat a few bites of toast, one or two spoonfuls of egg. Not enough to sustain a two-year-old child, but it was a start.

"There," he said, pushing his chair back from the table. "Are you happy now?"

"I am pleased. When was the last time you ate a decent meal?"

"I can't remember."

"When did you last venture outside? Feel sunlight on your face?"

He shrugged and began to fuss with a button at the cuff of his shirt.

She heard a motorcar pulling to a stop on the street below, and then the muffled noises of arrival and welcome in the front hall. Footsteps on the stairs, taken two at a time from the sound of it, then Robbie appeared at the door, his doctor's bag in hand.

"Hello, Charlotte. Hello, Edward. Up with the larks today, hmm?"

"Bugger off."

"Here's the aspirin you wanted," Robbie said, and pressed a bottle into her hand.

Charlotte poured Edward a fresh cup of tea and handed him two tablets. "Swallow these. You can wash them down with your tea. Doctor's orders."

"Have you finished your breakfast?" Robbie asked.

"As much as I can stomach."

"Good. Charlotte, would you mind waiting in Edward's bedchamber while I examine him?"

"Not at all."

She knew Lilly was downstairs, waiting for news, but she wanted to be nearby in case she was needed. So she busied herself with nursely duties: stripping the bed, opening the windows wide, and collecting a mountain of dirty dishes, empty brandy bottles, and overflowing ashtrays in the only available receptacle, an empty hearth bucket. Carrying this downstairs to the kitchens, she exchanged it for a set of fresh sheets from a startled and apologetic Mr. Andrews.

"I used to be a nurse," she explained. "I can make a bed in no time at all."

By the time Robbie called for her to return, perhaps a half hour later, Edward's bedchamber was in perfect order, if not as clean as it ought to be. But then the poor housemaids likely had been banished from the room for months.

"It's impossible to be certain without doing a series of X-rays," Robbie began, "but I suspect that you have, in addition to your other, more obvious injuries, a skull fracture that has healed indifferently, a degree of whiplash to the upper cervical spine, and almost certainly the remnants of a severe concussion. How severe, it's impossible to tell at this late juncture, but I think it serious enough to have kept you bedridden for months even if your leg had remained uninjured."

Robbie turned to Charlotte. "Was this what you suspected?" She nodded. He heaved a great sigh and rubbed at his temples.

"This is all my fault. In my eagerness to bring you home I never considered a physiological explanation for your troubles. The physicians in Belgium never said anything about a head injury, and fool that I am, I never thought to ask. I am more sorry than I can ever say."

"Don't apologize. I forbid it." Edward leaned forward and grasped hold of Robbie's near hand. "Do you hear me? You have nothing to be sorry for. *Nothing.*"

"May I ask what made you consider traumatic neurasthenia?" Robbie asked Charlotte.

"It was his persistent headaches and dizziness. Of course it could have been a host of other things, but we saw it often enough at the hospital. Men whose nervous shock was overlaid by concussion."

"It's been more than a year," Edward said quietly. "Will I never recover?"

Charlotte looked to Robbie, but he seemed content for her to answer. "I believe you will, but the truth is that you have been making it worse. Everything you do, and have done since you returned home, is interfering with your recovery. Shall I tell you the only cure for something like this?"

"Go on."

"It's an old-fashioned rest cure. Perfect quiet and calm until you are recovered."

"I'd rather be dead than go to a sanatorium. I swear it, Charlotte."

"Who said anything about a sanatorium? What you need is nothing more complicated than fresh air, nourishing food, exercise, and plenty of sleep. And quiet. Above all you require quiet."

"Up north, perhaps?" Robbie asked.

"Not Cumbermere Hall. Mama would install herself and badger me from dawn to dusk."

"Think of your estates. Isn't there anywhere you could go?"

"What about Cawdale Cottage?" Robbie suggested.

Edward closed his eyes and let his head fall back against one wing of his chair. "It might do."

"Cawdale Cottage?" Charlotte asked, though admittedly she was no expert on the smaller properties on the Cumberland estates.

"My bolt-hole when I was younger and needed some peace and quiet. I haven't been there in years."

"Let me telephone the estate manager," Robbie suggested. "He'll know if it's been kept up."

"Wait a moment. Who will go with you? You can't do this alone," Charlotte said.

"Mr. Andrews?"

"Thank you, Robbie, but no. I am fond of the man, but if his face were all I had to look upon I should expire after the first day."

"Perhaps we could hire a—

"You, Charlotte. I'll do it if you accompany me."

If he had slapped them across the face, one after the other, he couldn't have shocked them more.

"She couldn't possibly—"

"You can't ask such a thing of—"

"I'll get Lilly." This from Robbie, who practically ran out of the room to fetch his wife.

Once again Edward had confounded them all. Rather than mulishly refuse help, as she'd been certain, he was accepting it—with one impossible condition.

"I can't do it," she said at last.

"You can."

Lilly came in and sat next to her on the sofa. "So. Robbie has explained everything, though I'm not certain why you're insisting on Charlotte. Can't we hire a nurse to accompany you? Or perhaps an ex-RAMC medic?"

"No. It's Charlotte or nothing."

"But why, Edward? You'll be turning her life upside down."

"Not necessarily. Her Miss Rathbone has been accommodating in the past. I don't see why she'll balk at this."

"It may take weeks. Months. It isn't fair of you to ask."

"I know it. God help me, I do. But I won't go without Charlotte."

"Charlotte?" Robbie prompted. "If you were able to arrange a leave, would you do this for him? We'd ensure you were paid in the interim, of course."

"I don't care about that," she said. "It's only . . . what if word got out? That he and I were alone in that cottage? I doubt even Miss Rathbone would have me back then."

"No one would have to know," Lilly said. "We could arrange for provisions to be delivered. John Pringle would help."

"And the cottage is remote?"

"Exceedingly so," Edward answered.

Still Charlotte hesitated. Not to anyone, not even Lilly, could she voice her truest, deepest fear: that in helping Edward to restore his future, she would lose her own.

She looked him in the eye, though it hurt her to do so. "Edward, I—"

"I would kneel before you, Charlotte, if there were a prayer of my getting up again."

"Don't."

"I'm at your mercy. I need you."

"Stop. All of you *stop*, just for a moment. If I agree, and I'm not saying I will, but if I do, you must accept whatever measures I impose."

"Understood."

"That includes no drink. Of any kind."

He swallowed hard. "Agreed."

"If at any point you reject my treatment, or refuse to comply with any of the measures I impose, I will leave immediately."

"Yes. Yes, of course. Will you help me?"

It was madness, the acutest form of self-delusion, to imagine that she could spend weeks alone in his company and not be forever changed. It was impossible to remain unaffected by his charm, his kindness, his easy grace, even his maddeningly blinkered view of the world.

That day in Oxford when they'd first met, so long ago now, he had crashed into her—and she was still reeling, never to be sure of herself again.

"Yes, Edward. I will help you."

Chapter 19

A month's leave, you say?"

"If not more. His recovery is still so uncertain. His family has asked me to accompany him on a rest cure."

Miss Rathbone didn't seem so much perturbed as mystified by Charlotte's request. "And you say he will allow no one else to nurse him?"

"I'm afraid Lord Cumberland is quite intransigent. He's had a very bad time of it, you see, and he'll only accept someone he trusts as his nurse."

There had been no recourse but to tell her employer the truth, or at least most of it. Miss Rathbone already knew of her connections with the Cumberland family, so it was a straightforward enough matter to explain that Edward's health had taken a turn for the worse and required a period of convalescence.

"If you feel you must dismiss me, I understand."

"Of course not. You are far too indispensable. As such, I am prepared to make do without you for a month if I can be sure you'll return."

"You can, Miss Rathbone. Of that I am certain."

"Excellent."

"The Cumberland family has offered to cover my wages while I am gone. I ought to have said so already."

"How very kind of them. I'm sure we can put the money to good use. When were you thinking of leaving?"

"Not until the end of the week, and only then if everything here is arranged perfectly. Perhaps I might train up Gwen Vickers to take over some of my duties? Miss Petrie could easily take responsibility for anything directly involving constituents."

Miss Rathbone steepled her hands beneath her chin and thought for a moment. "No. Gwen is very good, but she's only been here a matter of months. I'd rather you ask Miss Margison. She knows the workings of the office better than almost anyone."

Charlotte acquiesced, for what else could she do? Instruct Miss Rathbone on the running of her own office? So she nodded, and agreed that it was for the best, and said she would show Miss Margison where everything was before Friday was at an end.

Of course she put it off for as long as possible, working late each night so that nothing would be left half done. Friday dawned, and her desk was nearly clear.

She went to the woman's desk, in the big room where all the clerk typists sat, and cleared her throat lightly. "Excuse me, Miss Margison. Might you have some time to go over things with me before I leave?"

"Oh, right. You're off on holiday, aren't you?"

"Not on holiday, no. A leave of absence."

"All right for some."

Never had Charlotte experienced such a punishingly penitential day. With every new file that she opened, every binder of meeting notes that needed to be transcribed, every letter that required a response, Miss Margison's expression grew more and more smug, presumably from the satisfaction of seeing so much work left undone.

Of course she had no notion of the true burden of Charlotte's duties, for she'd never had to go into people's homes and speak to them of their troubles, or go cap in hand in search of aid for those same families. Sitting at her typewriter all day, her mind preoccupied by petty jealousies and resentments, a woman like Miss Margison could not possibly understand the sort of work Charlotte did.

She stopped by the *Herald*'s offices on her way home, knowing that John would be at his desk until ten or eleven that night. He already knew she was going away, for she'd written to him at the beginning of the week. But it seemed only right to speak to him directly, and assure him that her column would not be delayed.

"You did receive my letter?"

"I did. It's a family friend who has taken ill, you say?"

"Yes. He was injured during the war, but has recently suffered a relapse. I've offered to supervise his recovery."

"That is kind of you."

"His family has been very good to me," she said, wincing a little. That was rather too close to a lie for comfort.

"Will you write to me while you're away? Not simply about your work, but to let me know how you're getting on? I ask as your friend, that's all."

"I know."

"I, ah . . . well, I might as well admit that I did hope, when we were first becoming acquainted, that we might one day become more than friends. We get on so well together, you see . . ."

"I do. I felt that way, too," she admitted. "And I did try. I promise I did."

"Don't look so mournful, Charlotte. I ought not to have said anything."

"I don't mind, not at all. As long as we remain friends."

"We will. Of that I am certain. Will you stay and have a cup of tea with me?"

"I should love to, but I leave first thing tomorrow."

"When you're back, then."

"Of course. Good-bye, John. I'll see you when I return."

"Farewell, Charlotte. Good luck."

SHE WAS MORE forthcoming with her friends at the boarding-house. They knew that Lilly's brother, wounded during the war, was experiencing a relapse, and that she was going to Cumbria to nurse him there. Unlike her colleagues at work, they also knew that Lilly's brother was a young, handsome, and exceedingly wealthy earl. Norma all but swooned at the romantic possibilities this presented.

"It's like something out of a film." She sighed. " 'Injured war hero finds a reason to live in the caring arms of his nurse.' "

Well-meaning words, so why did they feel like a stiletto jabbing between her ribs? "Please don't talk like that of him. Lord Cumberland is my friend and nothing more."

"Besides, anyone who thinks we nurses are constantly falling in love with our patients should walk a day in our shoes," said Rosie. "It's hard to look at a man with stars in your eyes after you've emptied his bedpan."

"Rosalind *Murdoch*."

"Sorry, Miss Margaret. I was just trying to prove a point."

"Have you finished packing yet?" Norma asked. "Don't forget to take something for the evening. They all dress for dinner, you know."

The notion of her and Edward, dressed to the nines as they ate their supper in a tiny country kitchen, was comical enough to make her smile. "We won't be dining formally. But thank you for the suggestion."

With her doing the cookery, their meals would be far from the gourmet fare that usually graced Edward's table. She knew the basics, for her mother had been adamant that Charlotte learn some rudimentary cooking skills before she went to university, but it had been years since she'd done anything more than butter a slice of toast.

In her small trunk there were no evening gowns, only the warmest of her frocks, the shawl she wore when reading on cold days, her sturdiest boots, and her winter coat, still smelling faintly of mothballs. There were her favorite books, too, some wool and knitting needles, and enough writing paper and envelopes for dozens of letters. If she'd forgotten anything it would be easy enough to ask John Pringle to fetch it for her.

HE WAS WAITING at Penrith station when she arrived the next morning. She'd slipped away at dawn, having said good-bye to the Misses Macleod and her friends the night before, and taken the day's first train north to Preston. From there it was only another two hours by local service to Penrith.

"Good day to you, Miss Brown."

"And to you, John Pringle. How are you?"

"Can't say as I have any complaints."

"And your parents?"

"Keeping well, and thanks for asking. You've only brought the one trunk?"

"Just this."

"Then give it here, and let's load it on the back."

It joined a number of boxes and crates already in the back of his lorry, a rather tumbledown affair that looked to have been on the roads since time immemorial, and they set off.

"I'll get you settled, then come on back with Lord Cumberland when his train gets in later today."

"I don't mind waiting," she protested, but he shook his head. "Only room for the two of us here, and you'll be wanting some time to look through the cottage."

"I really am very grateful to you, and your family, for your help. I'm not sure what we would have done otherwise."

"No need to thank me. Lord Cumberland needs us, and that's that."

Although John Pringle wasn't the most talkative of men, he was happy to tell her about his work at the garage in Penrith, his vegetable garden, and the new strain of dahlia he was planning to show at the county fair at the end of the month.

"How long have you been at the garage?" she asked.

"A little more than four years. Ever since . . . well, you remember. The bother with his lordship's parents."

What had she been thinking to ask such a question? The bother to which he referred had been his summary dismissal, which included the loss of his tied cottage, when Lady Cumberland had discovered that he had taught Lilly how to drive. Edward had found John Pringle a job at the garage, and Lilly had sold her jewelry to buy him a cottage of his own, so he and his family had escaped destitution. But still. Reminding the poor man of such a sorry period was inexcusable.

"Do forgive me for mentioning it."

"I don't mind. We're better off where we are, even if we do have to live among town folk."

"Are we far from the cottage?"

"Not far. It's right at the northern edge of his lordship's estate. We'll be at the turnoff in a minute or two."

"Was the cottage in poor condition? Lord Cumberland said he hadn't been there in years."

"It was all right. Estate manager had kept an eye on it. Needed a good scrub, top to bottom, so I got in my sister to help with that. Cut back the garden, too. Thought you might like to sit out on fair days."

They turned onto a secondary road, its gravel worn thin, and continued south for about a mile. John Pringle slowed the lorry almost to a crawl, and then directed the vehicle through a narrow gap in the hedgerow. Fruit-laden brambles arched over the lane, brushing at the sides of the lorry, their sun-warmed berries fragrant and infinitely tempting. She would have to bring a basket and collect some for after supper.

"Do you know who lived here originally?" she asked.

"Can't say as I do. Someone who liked his peace and quiet, that's for certain."

The lane curved to the right, and as it straightened out, and the brambles thinned, she caught a glimpse of the cottage. Its steep-pitched slate roof arched low over deep-set windows, and its rough stone walls had once been whitewashed. Closer still, and she saw the stream beyond, rushing headlong to the depths of the Ullswater, and the late-summer blooms that were massed against the cottage's sheltering southern wall.

"You go ahead and have a look around," John Pringle told her. "I'll bring in your trunk and these here supplies."

There was no lock on the door, only an old-fashioned latch. She went in, wiping her feet carefully, and inspected her home for the next month. To her left was the kitchen, to her right was the sitting room, and straight ahead was a steep flight of stairs. Would Edward be able to manage? If not, she supposed they could set up a bed for him in the sitting room.

She went into the kitchen and heaved a sigh of relief when she saw the relatively modern coal-fired range. There was running water, too, although it came from a pump next to the sink and not a faucet. A building of this age wouldn't have a WC, she realized, and when she looked out the back door her suspicions were confirmed by the outhouse some yards distant. She would have to make sure there was a chamber pot set up in Edward's room.

John Pringle came into the kitchen. "Everything in order? I made sure the chimneys are clean and the range is working properly. The coal bin's in the shed, and there's wood for the sitting room fire stacked against the back wall."

"Everything is perfect. Please thank your sister for all her hard work."

"She made sure you've all the food you'll be needing, and my mum made up a pot of soup for you. Just so's you wouldn't have to cook tonight."

"How very kind."

"I carried up your trunk. Put it in the smaller room, if that's all right with you."

"Of course."

"I'll be by tomorrow with fresh milk and a newspaper for Lord Cumberland. When you need anything laundered, give it to me and my sister will do it."

"Thank you so much."

"Best be on my way. Just in case his lordship decided to catch an earlier train. I'll see you again in a bit."

Charlotte went upstairs and unpacked her things, brushed her hair, and then pulled out her old nursing apron and put it on, though it was very creased and would never have passed inspection by any nursing sister worth her salt. She was going to do some baking.

As a child, she had loved making currant scones with her mother. Duckie, as Charlotte always called their housekeeper, hadn't minded their occasional forays into her domain, secure in the knowledge that her own confections were unlikely to suffer in comparison. They had always made scones, never anything else, but that was part of the fun. Knowing exactly what ingredients they would need, teasing Mother when she pretended to forget the currants, getting flour all over her pinafore as they rolled and cut the scones.

She found everything she needed quite easily, and as the range was already lighted she only had to add a small amount of coal to heat up the oven. In no time at all she'd made the scones and put them in to bake, washed up the dishes she'd dirtied, and cut enough Michaelmas daisies and astilbes from the beds outside to fill two small pitchers. One of these she set on Edward's bedside table; the other on the kitchen table, where they would take their meals.

The scones were out of the oven and cooling on a rack set over the draining board when she heard the rumble of an engine. She went to the door and saw that Edward had already alighted from the lorry. As she watched, he and John Pringle shook hands, and then the latter drove away.

"I hadn't expected you until later."

"I took the express north."

"Did you only bring the two cases?"

"Yes. I didn't think I'd need much more than a change or two of clothes."

"You won't," she said, and then she remembered to smile. "Come along in. I've made some scones, and the kettle is singing."

"Lovely."

"You must be tired," she said. "Go on into the sitting room. I'll deal with your things."

She picked up his bags, and then set them down again right away. Far too heavy for a few changes of clothing.

"Edward?"

"Yes?"

"I must ask if you brought any spirits with you."

His answering smile was brittle. "What do you think?"

"Very well. Do I have your permission to go through your bags?"

"What if I say no?"

"Then I will leave immediately."

"Very well. Do your worst."

She took his bags upstairs, one at a time, and set them upon his bed. She unpacked his clothes and put them away, and then she transferred the half-dozen bottles of brandy she had discovered, and the packets of cigarettes, into one of the now empty cases. This she brought back downstairs.

Working quickly, fearful that he would come in and object, she poured the brandy down the sink. The cigarettes went into the rubbish.

That accomplished, she poured cups of tea for them both, and piled a plate high with currant scones, which she split and buttered.

"Will you have some tea and scones?" she asked as she brought in the tray.

"I'd rather have coffee."

"We don't have any. Milk and sugar?"

"I take it black. You know, Nurse Brown, you could have taught Torquemada a thing or two."

"Perhaps," she admitted, sipping her tea.

After a moment he opened his eyes and reached for a scone. He ate it, and then another, and he even drank his tea.

Charlotte sat opposite him, in her own rather battered old armchair, and let the contentment of the moment wash over her. The cottage was really quite charming, far nicer than she had hoped. Edward had allowed her to confiscate his brandy and cigarettes without raging at her, or abandoning the entire enterprise before they had even begun.

She hadn't burned the scones.

This wasn't forever. It wasn't a life she could ever allow herself to miss, or to love. But for now, for today, it was enough.

Chapter 20

Cumbria, England
July 1911

"I can't bear the thought of your leaving," Lilly grumbled for at least the tenth time that day.

"I know. I'm very sorry to be going, but you're eighteen now. We always knew this day was coming."

"If only Mama would allow you to remain as my chaperone . . ."

As much as Charlotte would miss Lilly, she was more than ready for a change; but it wouldn't do to admit such a thing to her pupil. "I'm certain there are other ladies better suited to such duties. Besides, it's time that we both made our way in the world."

"I suppose you're right."

"I shall always be your friend. *Always*. And if we are to be friends, you must call me Charlotte. Will you do that for me?"

"Yes, please—Charlotte."

"Thank you, Lilly. See? We are peers now, both of us women grown."

They were returning from a walk to Haverthwaite, the

closest village to Cumbermere Hall, having posted some letters and bought some new stationery for Lilly. Tomorrow was
Charlotte's last day, for she was catching a train home to Somerset in the morning. Not without regrets, of course, for she
was justifiably concerned for Lilly. All attempts at persuading
Lord and Lady Cumberland to allow their daughter to attend
university had failed; even Lord Ashford had been unable to
move them. University for women, according to the countess,
was a lamentably middle-class conceit, and that was that.

"I don't think I would be quite so upset about your leaving
if I had something to look forward to. Something worthwhile
to anticipate."

"I know," Charlotte soothed. "But there's no harm in having
a bit of fun. That's what being eighteen is all about."

"Would you have wanted this for yourself when you were my
age?"

"To be perfectly honest, no. I never did. But then I was a bit
of an odd duck."

"It's so unfair."

"Perhaps. But many things in this world are unfair, and a
great deal of them are far more unpleasant than putting on
pretty clothes and going to balls and parties. And, besides, it's
only for a few weeks. By the middle of August the Season will
be over and you can return here for the winter."

"I suppose you're right."

"Of course I am. Now, I need to finish packing my things,
and you need to have a rest before dinner. Your brother—"

"Here he is now! Look, there's his motorcar coming up the
drive."

Moments later the four-seater coupe roared past them, covering both women in a layer of dust from the road, and nearly

deafening them with the roar of its engine. Lord Ashford pulled to a halt at the foot of the front entrance to the hall, not even bothering to park the motorcar properly, and jumped out.

"May I run to him? Please?" Lilly begged. "It's been ages since his last visit."

"Of course you may. I'll be right behind you."

Not for anyone, excepting perhaps the reanimated spirits of William Shakespeare or Jane Austen, would Charlotte embarrass herself by running pell-mell down a country lane. She took her time, instead, keen to retain some measure of personal dignity in front of Lord Ashford and his friends.

He was swinging his sister around in circles, lifting her high, just as one might treat a small child, but rather than interfere, Charlotte simply waited for him to set Lilly down. She was leaving in a matter of hours; what was the point of arguing with the man?

"Charles, Seymour, Billy: allow me to present my youngest sister, Lady Elizabeth Neville-Ashford."

Lilly shook their hands and greeted them prettily, which would have pleased Charlotte had the men she was meeting been of better character. They answered her charmingly enough, but there was an air of dissipation about them, a determined sort of indolence, that made her skin crawl. What was Lord Ashford thinking to bring such men to stay with his family?

"Edward, did you know that Miss Brown is leaving tomorrow?"

"I did, sweet pea, and I'm sorry to hear it. Is she—"

"Good afternoon, Lord Ashford."

"Miss Brown, I do beg your pardon. I'm afraid I didn't see you there. How are you?"

"Very well, thank you."

"All set for your journey home?"

"I believe I am."

"Gentlemen, allow me to present Miss Charlotte Brown. Miss Brown has been my sister's governess for these past four years, but is leaving us tomorrow. Miss Brown, allow me to present Lord Charles Milford, Seymour Ardley, and William Thorpe-Davison."

His friends came forward, each shaking her hand in turn, but one of them—Mr. Ardley, if she remembered correctly, looked her over from hat to hem and then, one eyebrow raised, gifted her with a revoltingly oleaginous grin. It was all she could do not to wipe her hand against her skirts.

"If you would excuse us, Lord Ashford, we ought to be on our way."

"Of course. Forgive me for delaying you. I do hope to see you again before you leave."

Charlotte could think of no correct way to respond to such a statement, for he had only spoken out of courtesy. Not for a moment did she believe he truly wished to see or speak to her, no more than he might wish to sit down and take tea with the housekeeper. So she nodded, and smiled, and led Lilly up the front steps and out of the too-bright afternoon sun.

AFTER LILLY HAD gone to bed that evening, and once Charlotte had packed away the last of her things, there was nothing much to do. She hadn't the heart to go downstairs and sit with Mrs. Forster one last time, nor could she bear to sit in her little bedroom, which would soon show no evidence of her having lived in it for much of the past four years.

She had left out the airiest of her summer shawls, and

after drawing it about her shoulders she hurried down the back stairs to the kitchens and, without stopping to chat with anyone, slipped outside into the cool, soft air of a midsummer evening. She would go to the pergola in the corner, the one nearly smothered in honeysuckle blossoms, and look at the stars for a while.

She had only been there for a quarter hour when she heard the men she'd met that afternoon, their voices blurred by too much wine and port. Lord Ashford was with them, his speech familiar and yet somehow foreign. But then, she'd never encountered him when he was intoxicated. Tonight he spoke as if someone had erased the edges from his voice, leaving it sibilant, persuasive, even sensuous.

She drew herself deeper into the shadows, praying they would not notice her as they passed by, but instead they stopped at the parterre that backed onto her pergola. She would have to go; it wouldn't do to—

"Saw that little governess making calf eyes at you earlier," said one of the men. "You know you need to watch out for ones like her. The maids're easy to buy off, but one like that—"

"Essackly," hiccuped another friend. "She's one a' those respec, restec, respectable types. Might even have some ideas about climbing a few rungsh a' the shocial ladder."

Charlotte couldn't move, couldn't breathe. She might as well have been glued to the pergola. If only she could stand, run away, even raise her hands to cover her ears—

"She's plain, but those types have hidden depths," said a third man, the same one, she realized, who had looked at her so avidly that afternoon. "You never know what's lurking beneath a set of spectacles and a shabby gown."

Why were they saying such things? And why was Lord Ashford not defending her? He had insisted, more than once over the course of their acquaintance, that he was her friend. So why would he remain silent at such a moment?

At last he spoke up, his voice so languid and carefree he might have been talking of the weather. "Miss Brown is pretty enough, but she's as cold as charity. Trust me."

His friends roared with laughter, hooting and barking like the jackals they were. "Turned you down flat, did she?"

"In a manner of speaking. At any rate, she's not worth your bother. I assure you of that."

His admission was followed by more gales of laughter at her expense, and without conscious thought Charlotte found herself on her feet, running silently back the way she had come, back to the safety and sanctuary of her room.

SHE SAID A private good-bye to Lilly the next morning, the two of them alone in the nursery sitting room; the poor girl had not wished for anyone else to see her crying, and though they had both done their best to be brave, a great deal of tears were shed before Charlotte was able to pull away.

"I shall write to you the instant I arrive in Somerset, and you must promise to send me a reply by return post. Do you promise?"

"I do. Bon voyage, Charlotte. And thank you for everything."

She was waiting at the side door downstairs, having made her farewells to the other servants, when the rumble of a motorcar caught her attention. John Pringle had said he would be taking her to Penrith in the two-seater carriage, for he knew how much she disliked riding in motorcars. Perhaps old Bill had gone lame again.

She stepped down, hauling her carpetbag and valise with her, and only belatedly realized that Lord Ashford, not John Pringle, was driving the car.

"I thought I would take you into Penrith myself."

"No, thank you. I'm quite all right."

"No choice in the matter, I'm afraid. I've already told John Pringle not to come. The horse isn't even harnessed. If you don't come with me you'll miss your train."

As much as she loathed the notion of going anywhere with him, and couldn't even bear to look at the man, there was nothing for it but to get into his damnable motorcar. She had told her parents she would be arriving on the evening train, and they would worry terribly if she were delayed.

The one good thing about motorcars was the loudness of their engines. This vehicle was particularly noisy, which meant they passed the entire journey without exchanging a word. Only once they had pulled into the station forecourt, and Lord Ashford had switched off the ignition, was any kind of conversation possible.

"Let me carry your bags to the platform," he offered.

"I'm quite all right—I don't need your help. Good-bye, Lord—"

"What is wrong, Miss Brown? You aren't crying, are you?"

"No," she lied. "I've some dust in my eyes. That's all."

"I don't believe you." He took her bags, led her to a bench by the station doors, and offered her a handkerchief.

"Are you upset about Lilly? I will keep an eye on her, you know. Or are you sad to be leaving? I did try to persuade my parents, but they were adamant that she make her debut. Although, really, you never know. She might end up meeting a decent enough fel—"

It had to come out. She couldn't bear it anymore. "I heard you. Last night in the garden, I heard what you said about me. I didn't mean to—I was sitting there, and your friends just started talking about me."

Every particle of color drained from his face. "Oh, God. What an ass you must think me."

Charlotte let silence be her answer. He cleared his throat, and then scrubbed his hands through his hair.

"I am sincerely sorry. I had absolutely no right to speak of you in such a discourteous fashion. I say that wholeheartedly, Miss Brown. Although I only said what I did because I wanted . . . I didn't want them to think . . ."

Again she said nothing, preferring to watch him flounder about like a fish at the bottom of a boat.

"The truth is that I don't think you're plain or unattractive or—"

"Cold as charity?"

He winced, screwing his eyes shut at the memory of his words. "Please forgive me. I was honestly trying to protect you. I was worried, you know, that if they were to see you as I do . . ."

"And how is that?" she asked, her anger suddenly smothered by curiosity.

"As a friend, of course. But also as an intelligent, capable, and lovely young woman. Not as a servant, no matter what they and my parents might think."

"But I am a servant. Or I was, until a few minutes ago."

"Never to me. You must know that."

"I . . . I suppose I do."

"Can you forget what I said? Allow us to part as friends?"

"Yes. If only because the ones you have aren't worthy of you." It was madness to speak so boldly to him, but what did she stand to lose?

"Perhaps not, but they make me laugh. They're fun."

"But you're all grown men. Surely it's time you stopped thinking about such childish things."

"And what?" he asked, irritation sharpening his voice. "Seek out employment somewhere? See if any of the collieries are hiring?"

"Yes, if only to teach you the value of hard work, and open your eyes to the world around you."

He shook his head unhappily. "You don't understand."

"I think I do. Your parents have indulged your every whim, your every desire, and like a glutton at a feast you've sated yourself. You're bored, and you haven't the faintest idea what to do with yourself. So you float through life, spending your time with men who are beneath you, spending your father's money as if it's water flowing from a tap, and ignoring anything and anyone that might direct you to a life of purpose and worth . . ."

As the full measure of what she had just said rang in her ears, Charlotte's mouth went dry with fear. He couldn't sack her, but he might decide to withhold his letter of reference. Why, oh why, had she said such things to him?

"I don't think anyone has ever spoken to me so passionately before," he said, his voice surprisingly gentle, a rueful smile on his face. "With the possible exception of Robbie, that is."

"Your friend from Oxford? The doctor?"

"Yes. He has never indulged me, nor do you. And as much as I should like to continue this conversation, I can hear your train approaching."

"Oh, goodness. I must go. Will you promise to take care of Lilly for me?"

"I promise. Good-bye, Miss Brown. Good-bye, and good luck."

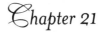

Chapter 21

18 September 1919

Dearest Lilly,

This is to let you know that your letter and parcel arrived safely and were delivered by John Pringle yesterday morning. Thank you so much for the copies of Punch. I read the entirety of "The Essence of Parliament" from an April issue to Edward last night, after supper, and he found it very amusing.

He has made great progress this past week. He is still not sleeping as well as I would like, for he was very nearly nocturnal when we arrived here and such habits are most troublesome to correct. There is also the matter of his nightmares, about which you know already, though they have been diminishing in frequency of late. As per his wishes I do not intrude when he is in the midst of one, although I do listen attentively in case he might require my assistance.

His appetite is improving in spite of my limited culinary repertoire, and he eats well and heartily at each meal. He has put on weight and each day looks more and more like his old self. Mrs. Pringle keeps us well supplied with soups and stews, and I even prepared a roast chicken the other day. My skills as a baker have improved out of all expectation, as well, and it has been several days since I last burned anything. Mother would be so proud!

It rained nonstop yesterday and the day before, and both of us are feeling horribly restless and cooped in. Today, however, the sky promises to remain clear, so we will go on a walk after lunch. His prosthesis no longer pains him, he says, although he will not allow me to inspect the stump of his leg for pressure sores. Perhaps he will allow Robbie to do so the next time we see you.

You asked how we spend our time in the evening. For the most part I read to him, for his eyes are often very sore by the end of the day, and reading taxes them further. Once I have finished with the copies of Punch, I will return to Barchester Towers, which he complains about but, I believe, secretly enjoys.

I am not sure if he is yet ready for visitors; perhaps in another fortnight? At that point I will be at the end of my agreed leave with Miss Rathbone and we shall have to make some decisions about what to do next.

You said you were worried for me, but I assure you I am well and perfectly content. Edward can be ill-humored at times, as is only to be expected given the circumstances, but for the most part he is excellent company.

I can't think of anything else we need, apart from more letters. We both enjoy your accounts of life in London and, most particularly, your studies with dear Mr. Pebbles.

Please give my fond regards to Robbie,

With love from your devoted friend,
Charlotte

It was just past ten o'clock in the morning, a fine morning, and if the weather did hold she would insist on their taking a walk. Perhaps they would go as far as the sheepfold at Malkin's farm. She'd been up for ages already; never in her life had she been comfortable with the notion of lying abed all day. Otherwise how were there enough hours to accomplish everything one wanted done?

She would wake him in five minutes exactly. He would groan and fuss and swear she was trying to murder him from lack of sleep, but she knew if she stood at the door of his room long enough he would eventually get up and begin his day. It was simply a matter of patience.

Each day was a little easier; each day he did a little better. It wasn't wishful thinking, moreover, for she had kept a detailed log of every aspect of his convalescence, and in its pages was the evidence of how far he had come. She tracked how many hours he slept, when he had nightmares, how much he ate, and the time and duration of his headaches, together with his estimate of their severity on a scale from one to ten. She recorded his complaints regarding dizziness, eyestrain, and any other ache or pain that might be related to his concussion. She made note of how often and for how long he read, walked, and napped.

In every respect he was improving. The first week had been terribly difficult, of course, for he was going without alcohol, tobacco, and caffeine, all at once, for the first time since his return from France some nine months earlier. Had his reliance on drink been of longer standing, she knew, his recovery would have been far more difficult.

As it was, he spent a good deal of that week nearly prostrate from nausea and crippling digestive pain, and his headaches abruptly worsened. At one point he had all the symptoms of a fever—he was perspiring, he couldn't stop shaking, and he complained alternately of being hot and then cold—but his temperature was perfectly normal when she checked.

And then, one day, he had felt a little better, and the next day even better. He had gone from strength to strength since then.

Charlotte consulted her wristwatch: it was now a quarter past ten. Yesterday she had woken him at half past the hour; tomorrow she would wake him at ten sharp. In such a fashion she hoped to restore his hours of sleep to a more reasonable schedule.

She tramped up the stairs, not bothering to lighten her steps, and knocked on his door.

"Edward? It's time you were out of bed."

"Bugger off."

"I thought we had agreed you would refrain from such puerile insults. Robbie may not mind, but I do."

"Please go away and leave me bloody well alone. Is that better?"

"No. I shall stand here and speak to you for another five minutes. If you are not out of bed and on your feet by that time, I shall come into your room, open your curtains, and open the window. I shall then remove the bedclothes from your bed and leave you to freeze."

"It's not that cold. I lived through worse in the trenches."

"I don't doubt it. But you didn't have warm scones and café au lait in the front lines, did you?"

"I thought coffee was forbidden."

"It was. But Lilly sent some coffee beans, together with a grinder and a strange little pot. A percolator, I think she called it. She said I was only to allow you a half cup of it and that it was best mixed with warm milk."

"I'm sure it will be revolting."

"It isn't. I had some already and it was delicious. You have three minutes left, by the way. Are you up yet?"

He groaned theatrically, and after an endless pause—had the wretched man actually fallen back asleep?—the bedstead creaked as he sat up and pulled his prosthetic leg from the chair next to his bed. She could hear him fastening it on, though the exact manner in which he did so remained a mystery to her; he refused to let her see him without the leg attached, and even more stoutly denied her requests to examine his stump.

The door opened. He was dressed in his usual attire: moleskin trousers, very worn and patched, an old linen shirt, and a woolen jumper that looked to have been knitted sometime in the last century. His hair, rather charmingly, was standing on end, and his days-old beard had a thread of lint caught up in the hairs.

"Wait," she said, catching at it with her fingertips, "you have something caught in your whiskers."

He stood stock-still, his eyes wary, as she drew the thread away. "Thank you," he said after a moment.

He seemed to enjoy his breakfast, even his woefully milky coffee, and polished off nearly half a jar of Mrs. Pringle's blackberry preserves with his scones. When she suggested they take advantage of the improved weather and go for a walk, he agreed so readily that she was taken aback. Normally she had to badger him into doing anything apart from sitting by the fire in his chair. They made it as far as the bluebell wood, still a quarter mile short of Malkin's farm, before she noticed a slight hitch in Edward's gait and, suspecting that his prosthesis was paining him, asked if they might turn back.

The rain returned in the afternoon, so he stretched out on

the sofa and read aloud from *Punch* while she fussed with her knitting and tried to recall, with limited success, the steps involved in turning the heel of a sock. He was a natural mimic, and when he recited the magazine's fictitious exchanges between notables—David Lloyd George lambasting underlings, for example—he perfectly captured the rolling Welsh cadences of the prime minister's voice.

There was no electricity in the cottage, only kerosene lanterns, and as the afternoon light faded he put aside the magazine and shut his eyes, wincing, but he didn't complain.

"Is it your eyes? Or a headache?"

"Both."

"Will you let me try something new to help?"

"Is it painful? Embarrassing?"

"Neither. Let me fetch it from the kitchen."

As well as the coffee and magazines, Lilly had sent a tiny blue bottle, unlabeled, but instantly recognizable as lavender oil when opened. In the first-aid box in the kitchen, Charlotte found some olive oil, normally to be used for earache. She poured off a teaspoon's worth into a teacup and mixed it with several drops of the lavender oil. This she carried back to the sitting room.

"Would you mind sitting up? And can you take off your jumper? I don't want to stain it."

"With what?" he asked, sounding more than a little apprehensive, but he pulled the jumper over his head and tossed it aside.

"Lavender oil. Now, turn to me and close your eyes. I'm going to rub some of it into the skin at your temples, then some more at your neck and shoulders."

"You'll leave me smelling like my grandmother," he grumbled.

"Very likely. But it should help with your headache."

She dipped her thumbs in the oil, wiped away the excess on the rim of the teacup, and began to massage his temples with the lightest possible touch. She moved her thumbs in circles, arching them low over his cheekbones and then up and over his brow.

"Bend your head toward me," she told him, and after scenting her fingers anew she began to rub behind his ears, slowly and soothingly, until his shoulders sagged and his head dropped forward in relief.

"Turn away from me, now, but keep your head bent," she said, and began to massage his shoulders, only so far as she could easily reach through the open collar of his shirt, as well as the straining tendons and muscles of his neck.

"Christ, Charlotte . . . you'll put me on my knees."

"Is it helping with the headache?"

"Yes . . . at least I think it is. May only be that you're distracting me."

"Do you think you could rest now? Only for a half hour or so, otherwise you won't be able to sleep tonight."

"Yes, I think so. Thank you."

"You're welcome. Put on your jumper so you don't catch cold. I'll wake you in time for supper."

He didn't stir again until the golden glow of dusk had crept past the deep stone windowsills and into the room, its gentle light softening everything it touched.

"You look so lovely sitting there," he whispered. "There's a sort of halo around you, from the sun. So lovely."

"Are you hungry?"

"Not yet."

"I should probably—"

"Don't. Not yet. I . . . I used to dream of you. When I was

in that hospital in Belgium, half out of my mind with fear and pain and shame, I would call for you. They told me I was calling for you. And you would come to me, in my dreams, and you looked just as you look now. An angel sweeping low to greet me. An angel with a halo of gold."

"Did it comfort you?" she asked, hoping he could not see her reddening nose, or the tears that threatened to fall.

"Yes. You comforted me."

"I was thinking of you, too. Praying that you were still alive."

"Did you mourn me? Weep for me?"

"You know I did."

"I so longed to die. I was desperate for it."

"Why? It will never make sense to me."

"I knew how disappointed you would be, all of you. It seemed easier to simply slip away."

"I was never disappointed in you," she promised.

"Really? I always assumed it was a chronic state where I was concerned."

"You mistook me. I was dismayed by your behavior. Not you. I knew you were, and are, a good man. Not without your faults, but a worthy man all the same. I know I told you differently at Lilly's wedding, but I was wrong."

"You weren't, though. Look at me, Charlotte. *Look* at me." He sat up, swung his feet to the floor, and folded up his right trouser leg, revealing the artificial limb beneath. It was made of aluminum, the metal scratched and dull, and was held in place with the help of canvas and leather strapping.

His fingers trembling, Edward loosened a buckle at the side of his knee, then one on the other side, and pulled the prosthesis away. His stump was covered by a kind of knitted sleeve or sock; this, too, he tossed aside.

"I know you've been curious. Go ahead. Tell me that it doesn't look all that bad. Offer up some well-meaning platitude."

His leg had been amputated just below the knee, which explained his ability to walk with such apparent ease. Whoever had done the surgery had been skilled, for the scarring was minimal and his stump had healed well.

"As a nurse, I'd say it looks very good. It's healed properly and you're evidently comfortable with your prosthetic."

"Doesn't it disgust you?"

"No. Not in the slightest."

"It should," he insisted. "I can barely look at it myself."

"It doesn't," she insisted, hating the expression of self-loathing on his face.

"Open your eyes, Charlotte. I'm half a man. A failure in everything I do. A stranger to his family and friends."

"Not to me. *Never* to me."

She couldn't bear another moment of this, not one more moment. The room was so charged with emotion, hers as much as his, that if she were to open a window she feared she would go soaring off into the sky, a firecracker fizzing with pent-up grief and regret.

"Don't—"

"Please—"

They both stopped short, waiting for the other to go on, and the terrible tension that made it so hard for her to breathe began to loosen its hold and melt away.

"Sorry," he said. "When I woke up I felt so peaceful, and look where I ended up. Whining about myself again. Do forgive me."

"Of course I do."

"Shall we think of something else to talk about?"

"Very well. Would you like to hear about my work with Miss Rathbone on the Pensions Committee?" She winked, hoping he recognized it as a rather feeble attempt at humor.

"Ha. It would serve you right if I agreed. But perhaps we could try for a less lofty topic? Say . . . I don't know . . . I could tell you something you don't know about me, and you could do the same. Tell me something that I couldn't possibly know about you."

"I don't follow. There are so many possibilities."

"Try. Tell me something surprising. Something you are certain I can't know. It doesn't have to be earth-shattering. Only interesting."

"How will I know if it's—"

"Try."

What could she tell him? He really did know so little about her; it would be easy to think of something. Her fear of thunderstorms, perhaps? Her childhood pet having been a tortoiseshell cat named Adelaide? Her having written a paper about *Pamela* in her second year at Somerville, though she'd read only the first hundred pages?

And then it came to her. "I'm named after a man. My middle name, that is."

"I beg your pardon?"

"My name is Charlotte Jocelin Brown. Spelled *l-i-n*, not *l-y-n*. After Jocelin of Wells, a thirteenth-century bishop. My father is an expert on him, and always thought he'd name his son after Jocelin. Instead he had me."

"Ah. Well, that is, ah, very interesting. I certainly had no idea."

"Your turn. What is something about you I don't know?"

"Let me think, let me think . . . oh, here's something. I detest chocolate."

"Chocolate? Who dislikes *chocolate*?"

"I do. Hate the stuff," he insisted.

"My goodness. I'm glad I haven't been serving you cocoa at bedtime. Is it my turn again? I'm not sure if—"

"May I go again?" he asked, and this time there was something odd about his voice. Suddenly he seemed remote, absent, his thoughts many miles away. "It isn't funny, though. Not funny at all."

"Go on," she said, a serpent of anxiety coiling tight around her rib cage.

"I am a coward."

"Do be serious."

"I am. I'm a coward through and through."

"Why would you say such a thing?" she asked fearfully.

"The night I was captured . . ."

"What happened? I only know the barest details. That you were taken prisoner in no-man's-land after being wounded, and brought to an enemy hospital."

"That's the gist of it." He was fidgeting with his trouser leg, pleating and unfolding the fabric that was hitched close around his stump.

"Why on earth were you out in no-man's-land?"

"It wasn't something I'd normally have done, but morale had been low. A few weeks before, my battalion had been transferred to a pioneer division. In essence it meant we were no longer a frontline fighting unit, but a support battalion that took over fatigue duties like trench digging and the setting up of barbed-wire defenses. The rank and file saw it as a demotion, and so naturally there was a lot of grousing. Certainly the men in my company were pretty miserable about it.

"We were in no-man's-land that night to repair some coils of barbed wire that had been cut. So, no, I wouldn't normally have accompanied my men on something routine like that, but I wanted to give a show of support. Let them see that I didn't consider such work a demotion, so they shouldn't either. That was the plan, at least."

"What happened? Did you come under fire?"

"We were shelled. One moment all was calm, and the next it felt like the world was ending. We didn't understand what was happening—all day and all evening, everything had been so quiet along that stretch of the front. Then one of my subalterns, Lieutenant Jerrold, marked the trajectory of an incoming shell, and he realized it came from the west. From our side."

"Surely it wasn't deliberate."

"Deliberate, no. Cretinous and foolhardy? Yes. I learned not so long ago that one of the brass hats at GHQ had got to boasting, earlier that evening, about some new long-range guns that were looking quite promising. So he decided to conduct a little experiment. See how far the things would go. Turns out they could lob shells exactly as far as the section of no-man's-land where we were repairing barbed wire."

"Good heavens," she whispered, wishing she were bold enough to say what men did when they were upset. A bad word, a filthy word, would better match the horror she felt.

"I know. We hit the ground and waited for someone to realize they were making a mistake. We didn't dare shout for help, or even stand up, otherwise the light from the exploding shells would have made it easy for the German snipers to pick us off. So we simply lay in the mud and waited.

"The worst part was the sound as the shells came close. It was a terrible sort of whine that got louder and louder and louder and then—*boom*. If you heard the explosion, you knew you were alive, at least for another few seconds."

"Was your group hit?"

"Yes. Several of the men were killed outright, as well as Lieutenant Jerrold. I was knocked back, into a shallow sort of crater. The force of the blast burst my eardrums, and it seemed to paralyze me, too. I couldn't hear, I couldn't speak or shout, and I couldn't move, not one muscle. So I lay in that muddy crater and let fear consume me. I lay on the ground and listened as my men died around me.

"I didn't do a thing to help them, Charlotte. I wallowed in a puddle of my own piss and tried not to choke on my fear. That's all I did. That's what cowards do, you see."

She sprang from her chair and went to him. Kneeling at his feet, bruising her knees on the cold flagstone floor, she took his hands in hers.

"I know nothing of being a soldier. I admit it. And I cannot truly understand what happened that night. But I am certain that you are *not* a coward. Fear doesn't make one a coward—if that were the case, then I, too, am a coward."

"Why didn't I act? Why did I react like a mewling child?"

"Because you had been stunned senseless by the shell that knocked you down. You were paralyzed not by fear, but by the concussive effects of the explosion. To *not* be terrified in that instant—that would have been the act of a fool."

"I wept. I wept and prayed and begged God to save me."

"I'm not surprised you did. I should have, too." Her knees

were feeling awfully sore, so she got up and sat next to him on the sofa. She didn't let go of his hands. "At some point, my dear friend, you are going to have to face up to a simple fact: you survived. Others perished, but you survived."

"Of course I face it. I face up to it every day."

"What are you going to do about it, then? There's no use feeling sorry for yourself or fretting about the past. You need to make the most of the life that has been given to you."

She smiled at him, her gentlest, most reassuring smile. If only he would believe. If only she could *will* him to believe.

"Charlotte the philosopher," he murmured, not meeting her gaze.

"Of course. It was one of my favorite subjects in school. Shall we turn to thoughts of supper, though, and leave our serious thinking for another time? There's always tomorrow."

"Yes, of course. There's always tomorrow."

Chapter 22

Christmas, 1916
The Savoy Hotel, London

They were just finishing their pudding when Charlotte thought to look at her wristwatch.

"What time do you have to be at work, Lilly? Because it's already half past two."

"Bother. I start at four o'clock. I must go—it will take me almost an hour just to get up to Willesden."

"Irvine can drive you," Lord Ashford said.

"No, thank you. I'm quite all right getting there on my own." Lilly came round the table and kissed Charlotte on the cheek. "Don't wait up for me."

"I won't. Perhaps, Lord Ashford, you might like to see Lilly out? That will give you a chance to say a more private farewell to one another."

He shot a disbelieving look at her, but took his sister's arm without protest and led her from the restaurant. Wondering if she had spoken out of turn, though she had only been looking to protect Lilly at what was sure to be an emotional moment, Charlotte picked up her fork and began to dissect the remnants of her pudding. Lord Ashford had ordered apple Charlotte for the table, no doubt thinking it was an amusing choice. If he only knew how many times she'd been winkingly presented with that particular pudding over the course of her life.

"There. Farewell effected. Happy now?" Lord Ashford said as he reclaimed his place at their table.

"I beg your pardon. I didn't mean to interfere. It was wrong of me to be so high-handed, with you and Lilly both."

He stared at her for a moment more, his expression unreadable. "No need to apologize. But it does beg the question: why are you so irritated with me? Whenever we meet, you seem to be in a state of high dudgeon, and I am your focus. What have I ever done to you to deserve it?"

"I . . . I—"

"Forgive me for speaking so bluntly, but I had hoped we could be friendly today. I mean, it's Christmas Day, Miss Brown, and in a matter of hours I'll be returning to the front. Does that signify nothing to you? Do you dislike me that much?"

"I don't dislike you at all."

"Then why not be friendly? Would it cost you so much? What is preventing us from being friends?"

Her face was red, she knew it from the way her cheeks burned, and if she could have excavated a hole in the middle of the Savoy Grill and buried herself, she would have done so forthwith. That he should say such things to her in the middle of a crowded restaurant was bad enough, but that they were true . . . that was the worst part of all.

"Forgive me," she whispered, unable to meet his gaze. When had she ever been afraid to look someone in the eye? "I've been wrong to treat you so poorly. There is no excuse for it."

"I know you think me a feckless aristocrat who's done nothing more with his life than spend his father's money and indulge himself, and until a few years ago you wouldn't have been entirely wrong. But that man is dead. Gone. Can you not see me as I am now? I'm a man, Charlotte, not a boy. If the war has done one thing to me, it's made me into a man."

"I know."

"Then treat me like one. And for God's sake don't sit there and look like you're going to cry. Just agree that we might be friends, if only for today. Agreed?"

She swallowed back her tears, and her chagrin, and nodded decisively. "Agreed."

"In that case, what shall we do now?"

"I thought you were seeing Lady Helena."

"Not until later. It's a pity the National Gallery is closed today. Otherwise we could have continued our debate over modern art."

"I really ought to go," she said.

"Not yet. What about a walk? The Embankment gardens are just across the road. And the sun is very nearly shining."

"Very well. But only if you're certain you can spare the time."

"Of course I can. Besides, we've a friendship to establish, and I'd rather do it face-to-face. Letters are a poor second in that respect. Shall we be off?"

"But we haven't paid. Shouldn't we at least wait—"

"I've an account here. But thank you for mentioning it."

A liveried attendant fetched their coats and his hat. Charlotte had worn her best dress and an almost new hat, but her coat was several winters old, and there were embarrassingly worn spots at the collar and front facing. Such a silly thing to fret over, really. Normally she never looked twice at what she was wearing, apart from her nurse's uniform, and then it was only to ensure it would pass inspection by Matron.

After Lord Ashford had asked his driver to meet them at the far end of the gardens, they set off across the road and down into the park. At first they walked side by side, but the graveled paths had grown mossy over the winter, and here and there were quite slippery, so when he offered his arm she was glad to take it.

"We were so busy talking about Lilly and her interests earlier that we never had a chance to speak of your work," he said. "I should very much like to hear about it."

"What would you like to know?"

"Tell me about the hospital. It's in Kensington, isn't it?"

"Yes. The Special Neurological Hospital for Officers. The buildings are on Palace Green, two huge old houses, side by side."

"How many patients are there?"

"Between the two buildings there are about seventy. Because we treat men with neurasthenia and other psychological disorders, each man has his own room—we don't have wards as such. And we don't do much medical nursing. By the time they come to us, the patients have been cured of any . . . well, external wounds. The only dressings I ever have to change are those of men who've hurt themselves while at the hospital. One poor fellow keeps scratching at himself with his fingernails. We keep them trimmed, but he still manages to hurt himself."

"I see. What would an ordinary day be like? Say today, for example?"

"Well, today was a bit different as I only worked a half shift. Because it was Christmas, you see. Normally I'm on for twelve hours at a stretch, from half past seven in the morning, with a three-hour break around the halfway point."

"Christ. You must be dead on your feet by the end."

"I suppose. I try not to think about it."

"What happens during those twelve hours? What do you do?"

"To be honest, at least three-quarters of it is cleaning. Washing crockery, trays, utensils. Wiping down everything with antiseptic. Dusting and tidying and making beds. There are chars for the really heavy work but we're always scrubbing away at something."

She stopped short and pulled off her gloves to reveal rough, reddened skin and fingernails cut ruthlessly short. "Look at my hands. I have to soak them in almond oil every night, otherwise they get so raw and sore I end up with chilblains."

"You said 'we,'" he noted as they began walking again. "How many other sisters are there?"

"I'm not a nursing sister."

"But I thought you'd trained—"

"I did several months' training as a VAD at the Great Northern Central Hospital on the Holloway Road. Matron there was happy with my work, so she recommended me to the War Office as a special military probationer. They then offered me a contract to work at the hospital in Kensington."

"When was that?"

"Oh, early 1915? So I'm not a nursing sister, you see. That requires three years of specialized, full-time training at a minimum. Some of the men persist in calling me 'Sister,' but they're only supposed to call me 'Nurse.'"

"I see. Very well, Nurse Brown, who else works with you?"

"There's Matron, whom I quite like. Very stern and strict but so good with the men. Endlessly patient. There are the nursing sisters, sixteen of them, and twelve probationers, of whom I'm one. The doctors come and go—they're attached to other nearby hospitals as well. And of course there are orderlies and chars and cooks and so forth."

"Are you always cleaning things, or are you able to spend time with the patients?"

"Oh, yes. I help to bathe and dress the men who are still too feeble to do so themselves, and I help them with their meals, too. If the weather is fine we take them out for walks on Palace Green. If I'm on the night shift I'll read to men who can't sleep, or even sing. Some really do enjoy being sung to."

"What sort of songs? Presumably not 'Hangin' on the Old Barbed Wire.'"

She stifled a grimace at the thought of how one or two of her patients would react to the imagery that provoked. "Hymns, mostly. Lullabies. Things that remind them of better times."

"What are they like, the patients? Is it bedlam there?"

"Not at all. We have common rooms, where we encourage the men to gather during the day, and they can be quite merry at times. But we're also careful to keep things as quiet as possible. No slamming doors or sudden noises."

"In case one of them goes off his head?"

She stopped short and glared at him. "No, Lord Ashford, in case one of them is unwillingly reminded of a horror he suffered and is forced to relive the trauma of that moment."

"I beg your pardon. That was insensitive of me."

"We do have some patients who are mildly psychotic, with conditions that may have predated their military service. They may see things that aren't there, or hear voices. That sort of thing. But for the most part our patients are suffering from what a layman would term shell shock."

"Do you like working there?" he asked.

"Do you know, no one has ever asked me? I mean, it's not as if it *matters* if I like it. We all have to do our bit, and that's that."

"But do you like it? Or do you ever wish you'd stayed with Miss Rathbone?"

"I have moments when I ask myself why I decided to become a nurse. Why I volunteered to leave a job I loved and instead spend my life washing out bedpans and the like."

"So why did you do it?"

"Why did you join up? Presumably because you wanted to do your duty and support the war effort. As did I."

"Fair enough. You still haven't answered my question. Do you like it?"

"Some days I do. Some days it seems worthwhile—when one of our patients is well enough to return to his unit, or be sent home. But then there are days when the sisters fault everything I do, Matron looks down her nose at me, the patients are all of them miserable and needing more attention than I can possibly give, and I hate it. I absolutely hate it."

"I don't blame you."

"And I know that if a man is well, and sane, there is no earthly reason why he shouldn't return to active duty—but I fear for him. It seems so unfair for a man to suffer so badly and then be thrust back into the thick of it. It . . . somehow it never seems right. But I suppose you would disagree."

"I don't, you know. Life at the front is enough to drive a man mad. Even on the good days it's a horror."

"So it's as bad as I fear it is?"

"Every bit."

"Which means that it's even worse."

"Yes."

In that one word, Charlotte discerned a lifetime's worth of horrors.

"You said there are good days. What are they like?" she pressed on.

"Do you mean a good day in the front lines, or when we're on relief?"

"At the front. What's a good day like there?"

"A day when we're just holding the line?"

"Yes."

"It's boring. Hours and hours of tedium, with the odd minute or two of terror thrown in to keep us on our toes. I spend nearly all my time in my dugout, back in the command trench, talking with my subalterns and NCOs. Matters of discipline among the men, orders from the brass hats, that sort of thing."

"So you're not in the very front lines? The front trenches?" This came as a relief, for reasons she didn't care to examine too closely.

"I spend my days a few hundred yards back from the fire trenches, though I'll come forward if needed. If I have time I try to be present while the NCOs inspect the men. I'd like to think it helps with morale, seeing me directly, although it's hard to know for certain. It's not as if I can walk up to one of them and ask."

"Why ever not? They're under your command. Surely you can speak to them directly."

"My NCOs would fall in a dead faint at my feet if I did. I speak to my company sergeant major and the CSM speaks to the ranks. I mean, if one of them were struck down by a sniper in front of me I'd offer some words of comfort. But otherwise I'm meant to be as remote as God."

"Even the men you know? Lilly told me some of them are from the estate. From the villages near Cumbermere Hall."

"Even the men I know."

"That seems very odd."

"Is it? How different is it from your hospital? Do you ever address the doctors directly?"

"Not unless they speak to me first. I talk to Sister if I have a concern, and she passes it on to Matron, who may then tell the attending physician."

"See? How different is that?"

"I suppose you have a point. Is there anyone you can speak to informally?"

"There are my subalterns, although they're all boys straight out of the schoolroom. I think the oldest is only twenty-five or so. One of them barely has a beard."

"How many men are under your command?"

"In theory there should be a hundred and forty men in the four platoons that make up my company. At present, thanks to the Somme, we're at least a score short of the mark."

"One hundred and forty men live or die at your command?"

"Only insofar as it reflects the wishes of the brigade HQ. But, yes, I suppose they do."

"Whom do you eat with?" she asked, fascinated by the picture he was drawing.

"Eat with?"

"Yes. Who sits at your table with you?"

"When we're on relief and well behind the lines, and we've an actual table in front of us, I eat with my subalterns. At the front? I sit on an upturned pail in my dugout and gobble whatever slop they've sent us before the sight and smell of it makes me sick."

"Some of the men at the hospital have talked about the rations. How horrid they are."

"If we get one hot meal a day we're lucky, though 'hot' is a subjective term. 'Not frozen solid' is better. Most days it's some kind of soup, always too thin, with bits of meat floating about. Usually horse. They serve it up in great vats that I'm sure they never wash. God-awful stuff. Sometimes there's bread, which is just as bad. Moldy, or crawling with weevils, or both. Always stale. They ran out of flour in the autumn, you know. Sent us bread that was made out of dried turnips or swede or something equally revolting. It gave every last man in my company the trots."

"Is that all you have to eat? One meal a day? No wonder you're so thin."

"They send us tins of soup and bully beef, too. That's my lunch and dinner most days. I hack open the tin and eat its contents cold. Used to have a little Primus stove, but I could never get fuel for it."

"Where do you sleep?"

"In my dugout. Sometimes it has a bed, but most of the time I sleep rough. At least I'm not out in the open."

"So that's your life?"

"That is my life. But only on the days we're in the front lines. After about eight days or so they cycle us back to the reserve lines, where things are a little better. And we do spend some long stretches in relief, well back from the front. So it's not an unending saga of misery and woe. You mustn't think that."

"Where is your company now?"

"On relief. Billeted in a village near the coast. It seemed quite pleasant, the little I saw of it before I came home."

"Is that where you'll go when you return to France?"

"Yes. We'll have another week or so there, and then we'll be given our marching orders. Did you know the men sing as they march?

" '*This war will never end, never end, never end, this war will never end, till we're all dead and gone,*' " he sang, his voice a sweetly beautiful tenor.

"Is that what you believe?"

"Yes. If I believe in anything, I believe that."

"A war that has no end?" she asked, incredulous at his certainty. "How can that be possible? We're all of us on our knees."

"Yes, but a man on his knees can get up again. That's why it won't end until we're all dead. Or as close to dead as makes no difference."

"But the papers say the Americans are sure to become our allies," she protested.

"If the Americans have any sense they'll find a way to remain well clear of this apocalypse. Ah, here we are."

She hadn't been paying attention to their surroundings, so it came as a surprise to see Lord Ashford's chauffeur and motorcar at the gardens' boundary only a few yards distant.

"May I offer you a lift home? I really am in no great hurry."

"That's very kind. Thank you."

The motorcar was warm and welcoming and about a thousand times more pleasant a conveyance than the Underground train she'd have taken otherwise. It really was very thoughtful of him to have offered—

"Aren't you meant to be seeing Lady Helena now? You'll be late if you take me all the way up to Camden Town."

"She'll be fine."

"When was the last time you saw her?"

"I can't recall. Ages ago." He looked out of the window, not seeming to focus on anything.

"Surely she'll be waiting for you. It seems most unkind—"

"Would you like to know something?" he asked, turning to her. "All this year, before every new and hopeless attack, I'd sit there in the dark, in those empty hours before dawn, and tell myself that I ought to be thinking of Helena. Before Courcelette, Morval, the Transloy Ridges, I'd sit there and try to make myself care. Her photograph was in my tunic pocket, right over my heart, just where it was meant to be. And yet when I closed my eyes I could never see her face. Never. Do you wish to know whose face I saw?"

Charlotte, who was quite certain she did not wish to know, shook her head vehemently, but he didn't seem to notice.

"The face that filled my mind's eye as I sat and waited to die, over and over again—it was your face, Miss Brown. Yours."

"You mustn't say such things."

"It's the truth. And it isn't likely we'll see one another again. So why not be honest, just this once? Because you are the woman I think of, and you are the woman whose name will be on my lips when I die."

He cradled her face in his right hand, swept away a traitorous tear from her cheek, and smiled, a smile so forlorn and bleak that her broken heart was splintered anew. She knew what he was going to do, knew with a certainty that astonished her, but rather than pull away or protest she simply waited for him.

His mouth fitted perfectly against hers, so wonderfully warm and tender, a balm for her fears, and for a moment, an instant, she was worthy of him, and he was devoted to her alone, and

248 • JENNIFER ROBSON

everything and everyone that had conspired to separate them simply fell away. She was his, his alone, and he would survive. Though millions died, he would survive, and he would come back to her.

His tongue pressed against the seam of her lips, urging them open, and the feel of him inside her mouth, the scrape of his teeth against her own tongue, was so good that her toes curled in her boots and her gloved hands scrabbled uselessly at his shoulders.

He pulled away, gasping, but rather than set her aside he drew her tight against his chest. His greatcoat was rough against her face, her back hurt from being twisted almost sideways, and her hat had vanished. She didn't care.

"We're here," he murmured against her hair. She turned her head a little, just enough so she might see out the window, and realized they were stopped in front of her boardinghouse on Georgiana Street.

"Don't rail at me," he said. "Simply say good-bye."

How was she meant to speak after such a moment? She swallowed hard, sat up, found her hat and her handbag.

How was she meant to go on?

"Good-bye, Lord Ashford."

"Please—"

"Edward, then. Good-bye."

"Good-bye, Charlotte. Adieu."

Chapter 23

Evenings were her favorite time of day. After supper, Edward would stretch out on the sofa in the sitting room, and she would curl up in the ratty old armchair, and by the light of the fire and a few kerosene lanterns they would read to each other, exchange reminiscences of Oxford, and generally keep each other amused.

Some nights, when his head was hurting and he couldn't read, and was too irritable by his own estimation to listen to any sort of narrative, he would ask her to sing. She had a fine memory for hymns, thanks to her childhood in the shadow of one of Christendom's great cathedrals, and as the cottage had no gramophone or piano or any other way to make music, her rather feeble contralto would have to do. But he never complained or ragged her about it, and in fact seemed to rather enjoy her slightly off-key renditions of such old chestnuts as "All Things Bright and Beautiful" and "Christ Is Made the Sure Foundation."

They never spoke of the war, not after his confession the

week before, and they studiously avoided the subject of what would occur at the end of her month's leave. She had less than a week to go, really only four days left if she didn't count her day of departure, and they really ought to speak of it. For what would he do once she returned to Liverpool? Would he stay on at Cawdale Cottage, either alone or with a servant to keep him company? Or would he return to London, where he had been so unhappy, and be thrust again into its glittering carousel whirl?

She very much hoped he would stay on in Cumbria, if only for another few months, for he was still fragile, still in danger of a relapse as far as his symptoms of concussion were concerned. Even worse, she feared he might turn to drink if—when—it all became too much for him.

She had done all she could; he alone would chart the path his life would take. And so she resolved to remind him that she was leaving, and that he would have to find someone else to take her place. She would tell him in the morning.

They said good night at the top of the stairs, in front of their respective doors, as they did every night. She listened, as she always did, as he undressed and got into bed. She listened until he lay quiet, and only then did she allow herself to sleep. They'd had a good day. She hoped very much that he would sleep well.

His screams woke her. Hoarse, pitiful wails that trailed away into sobs, only to be renewed with each indrawn breath. It was worse tonight, worse than it had ever been. Should she defy his wishes and go to him?

She might be able to wake him, be able to break through the terror. Allow him to sleep again. So she wrapped a shawl around her shoulders and crossed the landing to his door. "Edward? Can you hear me? Are you all right?"

But still his cries continued, rising and falling, his panic and desperation so acute that it pained her to listen. He was so alone. He ought not to be alone.

Charlotte went into his room and stood by his bed. He had left the curtains open, and a ragged patch of moonlight fell across his face, laying bare his struggle against unseen captors and remembered agony. It felt deeply wrong to stand by and watch him, but she was wary of waking him too suddenly. The men in her hospital had often had nightmares, and she had learned not to startle them out of their sleep, else risk a blackened eye.

"Edward, it's Charlotte. Can you open your eyes? I'm here now. I'm at your bedside and I'm here."

"No no nonononono . . . mustn't . . . mustn't do it. Why won't you listen . . . no, God no . . . don't do it!"

"Listen to me, Edward. I am here and you are safe. Open your eyes, now, and look at me. Listen to me."

"Oh, God . . . don't do it . . . mustn't . . . please let me go. Let me die."

He did open his eyes for a moment, but he was somewhere else, and if he saw Charlotte it was as another person entirely.

Still she hesitated, fearful to approach him when he was so agitated. It was a terrible thing, watching him like this. He would be very unhappy once he awoke and discovered that she had been a witness to his distress.

She sat on the edge of his bed and, holding her breath, touched his right forearm. When he didn't flinch or otherwise react, she took his hand in hers and squeezed it tight.

"Edward, look at me. It's Charlotte. We are at the cottage and you are safe. You need to wake up. Open your eyes and look at me. You need to wake up."

Again and again she explained where they were, that she was at his side, that he was safe. Minutes passed, perhaps a quarter hour or more, and finally, just as she was losing hope, he grew calm, and his breathing slowed. And then he squeezed her hand, opened his eyes, and looked directly at her.

"I thought I asked you never to come in while I was like this," he said accusingly.

"I know. I'm sorry. It's only that you were so upset, and you'd been calling out for so long. I couldn't *not* come in."

"I might have hurt you. I didn't hurt you, did I?"

"No, not in the slightest. As soon as I took hold of your hand you began to calm."

"All the same, Charlotte . . . don't do it again."

"You're shivering. Shall I bring you another blanket?"

"Won't help. The cold goes bone-deep. Only thing that works is time. Will you stay awhile?"

"Of course."

She sat on the bed and held his hand, but he couldn't stop shaking, not even after she'd spread another two blankets over him.

"If I were to lie next to you, on top of the blankets, would that help to warm you?" A month ago she would never have made such a suggestion, but she was desperate to go back to sleep, and for him to rest as well. "Your bedclothes would still be between us," she added.

"You're very kind to offer. Are you certain? I do promise not to pounce on you. If only because I'm as weak as a kitten."

She stretched out next to him, making sure her legs were well covered by her nightgown, and tucked another blanket over them both. "Does that seem to be helping?" she whispered.

"I think so. You're like a furnace."

"Good. Go to sleep."

"Promise not to leave."

"I won't leave. Sleep, now."

THE LIGHT WAS all wrong. Her window was to the right of her bed, but the first whispers of dawn were coming from the other side of the room. Her bed felt wrong, too, bigger and softer than she remembered. And ever so warm. It was heavenly to feel so warm.

"Good morning," came Edward's voice, still scratchy from sleep.

"Good morning," she answered happily—and then she remembered.

She opened her eyes. She was in his bed. Covered only by a nightgown—oh, heavens, half covered by a nightgown, for her legs were bare, the blanket kicked aside during the night.

She had suggested this. What on earth had possessed her? What sort of nurse simply climbed into the same bed in which her patient was sleeping?

"Don't go," he whispered. "I'm still under my blankets. Nothing happened. I didn't so much as peek."

"Peek? Peek at what?"

He simply raised his eyebrows and smiled. She had already straightened the skirts of her nightgown, so what could it be? Then she looked down and saw. Her shawl had vanished and, worse, her bodice had come undone—not entirely so, not enough to bare her breasts, but it was a near thing. A half inch more and he'd have received an eyeful.

She fumbled with the ribbons, unable to fasten them, so settled on holding the placket of her gown together. "Oh, my goodness. I do beg your pardon."

"Whatever for? I can't imagine a lovelier sight."

"You said you didn't peek."

"I'm a man, Charlotte. I'd have to be dead not to look."

"I really ought to get up. I never sleep this late."

"Stay. Let me look on you awhile."

"This isn't—"

"Your hair is so beautiful. I truly had no idea." He reached out and let a skein of it curl around his fingers. "I've never seen it unbound."

"I put it in a plait before bed, but it seems to have come undone."

"How long is it?"

"All the way down my back. I've thought of cutting it, but I've no idea how to manage short hair. It seems easier to keep it long."

"Don't ever cut it. Promise me?"

"Edward, I . . ."

"Do you remember the Christmas of 1916?"

"Yes." She remembered everything about those hours with him. *Everything.*

"I want to kiss you again."

No, she ought to say. *No,* because I am not yours to kiss and it is hopeless and what sort of decent woman acts in such a fashion? *No,* she would tell him.

"Yes," she said.

He was a little lower on the bed, so he had to arch his head back, his throat straining, to reach her lips. He fitted his hand to the back of her head, his fingers slipping through her loosened plait, and urged her mouth ever closer, until his breath was hot against her face and she could see the little flecks of silver in his dark blue eyes.

Surely he had kissed other women in the years since their

embrace in the back of a motorcar, outside her boardinghouse, on the afternoon of Christmas Day in 1916. He would not remember it as she did. He would not have honed and polished its memory until it was as bright and pure as a pearl. He would have had many other kisses to compare it with.

With aching slowness he closed the gap between their mouths. It was just as she remembered—the way their lips matched so perfectly, the drugging, velvety sweep of his tongue against hers, the almost frightening intensity with which he deepened and prolonged their embrace. It would be so easy to abandon the world that pressed in around them, to ignore how impossible any sort of shared future would be.

She had forgotten about her nightgown and its traitorous ribbons, forgotten all about it until his hand left her hair, and, tracing a hypnotic line from her earlobe to her collarbone, delved beneath the worn linen of her bodice. He cupped her breast in his hand, weighed it, let her nipple grow tight against his palm.

His lips left hers and began to follow the trail his fingers had drawn, kiss after delectable kiss. And then he was pressing his mouth to the swell of her breast, his sighs of delight hot against her shivering skin.

"Has any woman ever been so beautiful?" he murmured. "Let me kiss you. Let me make love to you."

He pulled back the covers, all but tearing them off the bed in his desperation, and pulled her even closer, shockingly close, until nearly the whole of her body was pressed to his.

Never, in all her life, had she known such pleasure. How had she lived without this? How had she survived without him? For so long she had wanted him, wanted *this,* and at last it was happening.

"Charlotte?"

She suddenly realized that Edward had stopped kissing her. "What is it? Did I do something wrong?"

"No, not at all. But we have to stop. I should never . . . I'm not a particularly decent man, but I won't dishonor you. Not if I can help it."

He was right, though it was agony to admit it. "I understand. It is better that we stop. Only . . . would you mind holding me? Just a little longer?"

Edward kissed her one last time, tenderly, regretfully, and then, rolling to his side, drew her into the shelter of his arms. Their eyes met, and in his gaze she saw every hour of hopeless longing, every barren day of aching loneliness that he had endured.

"I never thought any woman would ever want me again."

"You? The handsomest man I've ever known?"

"No man can be handsome when he's missing half a leg."

"You are. Yet you could be the ugliest man alive and I should still desire you."

He said nothing, only pressed his face against her hair and silently wept out his pain and grief for the loss of the man he'd once been.

They held each other as the last of the stars faded away and day began to bloom, and she knew this was the only time she would ever watch the sunrise with him. She knew it, as did he.

"I wish we could hope for more," he whispered. Had he read her thoughts? Or had she spoken aloud?

"I know."

"I broke with Helena because I didn't love her, certainly not as she deserves to be loved. I think she was relieved. In fact I'm certain she was."

"So what will you do now?"

He pulled away, just a little, just enough to look in her eyes. "There is a very large gap between what I want to do, and what I must force myself to do."

She nodded, and even tried to smile a little.

"What I *want* is to be with you, to stay with you for the rest of my life. I don't think I've ever known such perfect happiness before. There have been moments, over the past few weeks, when I was almost able to believe it might be possible."

"But it's not," she whispered, unable to blink away her tears.

"It isn't. And not because I think you unworthy, in any way, of becoming my wife. You must know that. If I could allow myself to marry for sentiment alone, you would be my first choice. My only choice."

"I know."

"The terrible thing is that you've always been at me to grow up, to act like a man, to shoulder my responsibilities. And now the only way I can do so is to marry a woman who is rich enough, or has a father who is rich enough, to pay off my family's debts. I wish . . . I wish I were strong enough to walk away."

"You are strong. Strong enough to face your problems head-on. I'm proud of you, Edward."

She'd read of heartache, but had never understood it before now. It wasn't her own pain that wounded her so, but his. To see him suffer, to watch him endure his anguish so bravely, was torment distilled into the purest poison. If only she might drink down his share as well as her own.

"All this year, watching my sister and Robbie together, I've been so envious of them," he admitted wretchedly. "Only now do I understand. Now I know what it's like to love someone so fully that my heart is closed to anyone else. How shall I bear it?"

One day she would be able to think of this moment, of his

profession of love, without her heart shriveling within her chest, but not today. Not yet.

"You will find happiness. I promise you will. You'll find a jolly, friendly American girl who will fall madly in love with you. And you *will* be happy with her. Swear you will, Edward. You must swear it."

"I can't."

"Does it help you to know that I love you, too? Likely since the day I answered your advertisement for a governess."

"As long as that?"

"I will be happy. I will continue in Miss Rathbone's footsteps. I will be married to my work, and I will be an aunt to Lilly's children, and yours, too, if you'll let me." Her voice broke at this admission, but she struggled on. "And we will both live worthwhile lives. No, don't look away. Our lives will be full of peace and good deeds and joy. I don't doubt it, my darling. Not for a moment do I doubt it."

It was her turn to weep, so she cried until her eyes were dry and aching, until there were no tears left to shed. He held her and kissed her tenderly and teased her, just a little, when she began to hiccup, and he was so sweetly comforting that she feared she would die from the pain of it.

"We ought to get up. John Pringle will be by anytime now."

"Will you be all right?" he asked.

"Yes. Will you?"

"I will."

She went into her room and got dressed, brushed her hair and pinned it back with shaking hands. In the kitchen, she pumped some cold water into a basin and bathed her eyes until they didn't feel quite so hot and tight, and then she set about making their breakfast.

Edward came into the kitchen not long after. He sat at the table and watched her, his expression wistful, as she set the tea to brewing and fried some eggs and sliced up the heel of yesterday's bread. They ate in silence, but companionably so, and though she came close to tears once or twice, she somehow held on to her composure.

"I told Miss Rathbone I would return by the thirtieth," she said.

"I think you must. I'll get on all right here."

"On your own? How will you feed yourself?"

"Poorly, I'm sure. Perhaps I can ask Andrews to come up from London. He can cook, after a fashion."

"Between that and Mrs. Pringle's soups you won't starve."

"See? That's all managed nicely."

"Shall I write to Lilly and let her know?"

"Not just yet. Otherwise she and Robbie will drive through the night to get here. I promise I will be fine. I won't take to drink and I won't start smoking again. I swear I won't."

She nodded, relieved that he seemed so confident, but deflated all the same. Only four more days and she would be gone.

"I had better clear up the dishes," she said, and turned away so he wouldn't see that she had succumbed to tears yet again.

She would survive, of course she would, and she would always have the consolation of knowing that he had loved her. It was less than she deserved, but more than she had ever expected.

It would have to be enough.

PART THREE

Have you forgotten yet? . . .
For the world's events have rumbled on since those gagged days,
Like traffic checked while at the crossing of city-ways:
And the haunted gap in your mind has filled with thoughts that flow
Like clouds in the lit heaven of life; and you're a man reprieved to go,
Taking your peaceful share of Time, with joy to spare.
But the past is just the same—and War's a bloody game . . .
Have you forgotten yet? . . .
Look down, and swear by the slain of the War
that you'll never forget.

—Siegfried Sassoon, "Aftermath" (1917)

Chapter 24

Liverpool, England
November 1919

As Charlotte took her place at the breakfast table, she was relieved to see the other women had chosen similarly somber clothes for Armistice Day. All of them, except for Rosie in her nurse's uniform, were dressed in unrelieved black.

"Aren't you a cheery lot," Rosie commented.

Charlotte accepted her bowl of porridge from Janie and began to eat. "I wish I had a better idea of what we're to do. The notice in the newspapers only said there would be two minutes of silence at eleven o'clock this morning. Apart from that it all seems rather vague."

"I don't think anyone knows what to do. I imagine we'll simply stop what we're doing for the two minutes. It's not as if there's any place we might gather," said Rosie.

"True enough. At least not until the war memorial is built. Have they even chosen a site?"

"Not as I know. Miss Margaret and Miss Mary, what are you going to do?"

"We thought we'd go to church. Seems the best place for such a moment."

Charlotte finished off her porridge, downed the rest of her tea, and took her dishes to the sink in the scullery. "I'd best be off. Good day, everyone."

She ought to have said something to Meg, who hadn't spoken at all during breakfast. The poor woman was likely beset by thoughts of her late husband; occasions such as this had a way of bringing the past crashing down on one's shoulders. When there was time, after work, she would make a point of seeking Meg out, just to let her know that she was concerned. Was thinking of her.

Dressed in her warmest coat, her muffler wrapped high around her face, Charlotte set off for work. It was positively arctic outside, the temperature not far north of freezing, and a misty rain was falling. Too light to warrant an umbrella, it was persistent enough to soak deeply into her coat and hat, and set her shivering after only a few minutes. Even worse, one of her galoshes had sprung a leak, and was slowly but inexorably becoming sodden with water.

Miss Rathbone, quite properly, was disinclined to waste money on the heating of her constituency office, not when such money could be better spent on her constituents. Charlotte's office was so chilly that her breath rose in ghostly plumes before her, and even after putting on her warmest cardigan, and drinking a cup of near-boiling tea, she couldn't shake the chill that had crept into her bones.

The clerk typists were gathered around the fire in the reception area, merrily neglecting their work as they warmed themselves, and as she listened to their easy banter it was hard not to feel just a little envious of them. Her little office, with its desk and bookcases and two chairs for guests, was normally something that filled her with pride. How many women had an office all to themselves? A room of their own in which to work? Today, though, its appeal was rather diminished.

The morning wore on, leavened by nothing more heartening than the occasional mug of warming tea, until the clock at All Saints chimed the quarter hour before eleven o'clock. The Great Silence, as the government had mandated the two minutes of silence be called, would be signaled by ships' guns in the Mersey, and, for those farther away, whichever church bells were closest.

Charlotte went into the hall and saw that the others, Miss Rathbone included, were putting on their coats.

"Where is everyone going?"

"Ah, Miss Brown. I was just going to call you. I thought we'd stand outside. Better to mark the silence in the open air."

"Yes. Yes, of course. I'll fetch my coat."

It did make a strange sort of sense. There was nowhere, as yet, for everyone to gather at such a moment, yet it seemed somehow wrong to be isolated from one's fellow citizens.

They stood outside and waited. Up and down the street, in front of houses and shops and even the mechanic's across the way, people set aside their work and stood, heads bowed, waiting for the chime of bells. Even the tram that ran up and down Princes Avenue had stopped, and its driver and passengers had alighted to stand at the curb. A motorcar turned the corner, continued on for a few yards, and then stopped. Its driver climbed out, looking a trifle abashed, pulled his hat from his head, and waited. They all waited.

The chime that marked the hour rang out, its bells faintly discordant, and then a single bell sounded, slow and ponderous, counting down the hours. It rang eleven times, its peals echoed by the distant boom of a warship's guns.

Where were one's thoughts meant to go at such a time? Should she silently recite a prayer? Or would it be fitting to let herself dwell on the faces of the lost, the maimed, the broken?

Charlotte thought of a young Scots captain, left mute by the horrors he had seen, his eyes so full of agony and inexpressible torment that she'd had to steel herself each time she tended to him. His wife had come to visit, only the once, for she'd been unable to recognize the changed man she found. He had once been so merry, she told Charlotte and the other nurses. Once, long ago, he had never stopped smiling.

She thought of the lieutenant colonel, an Australian, whose battalion had been annihilated at the Somme. He'd been able to converse normally enough, though his hands shook so badly he needed help to feed himself, and for a while she'd hoped he would recover. He had, but a week after his release, she later learned, he had hanged himself. There had been no note. The events of July 1916 had been explanation enough.

If she tried, she could recall almost all their faces, if not their names, the hundreds of men she had nursed and soothed and even, before she had lost the habit entirely, prayed for on her knees before bed each night.

On either side, in every direction, people began to cry, and not the polite sort of tears one shed at a funeral, but rather the great, racking sobs of acute, disbelieving grief. The end of the Great Silence must have passed, had certainly passed, but still they stood in the street, the motorcars and trams stopped in their tracks, as men and women alike wept out their sorrow for all that had been lost.

And then, although she hadn't cried since the end of September, since the morning she had wept out her despair and grief in Edward's arms, tears welled up in Charlotte's eyes. Whether they were propelled by thoughts of the war and all that had been lost, or of her own, more recent sorrows, she couldn't tell.

When she had said farewell to Edward, she had been dry-eyed, determined not to upset him any further. On the train home, she'd been surrounded by other passengers, so she had again stanched her tears. And then, alone in her bedroom at home, it had seemed wrong to cry. Self-indulgent, somehow. She had done what she knew was right. She had let him go, as she knew she must, and her life would go on. What was the point in crying about it?

It had been so very civil. They had spoken of it freely, as if they were business associates who had agreed to go their separate ways. She had asked him not to write, not at first, because it would be needlessly upsetting to both of them. If he needed to convey any information to her, she asked him to do so through Lilly.

They had also agreed to say nothing to his sister, or to Robbie, for it would only tarnish their newlywed happiness. One day, perhaps, they might share the truth, when Edward was settled and married and she, Charlotte, had gone from strength to strength in her career and had put all thoughts of marriage and motherhood behind her. Then, perhaps, they might confess the truth to their oldest and dearest friends.

She still found herself listening for him at night. A passing motorcar, or too-loud voices in the street, and she would rouse herself just enough to pray that Edward had not been awoken, too. In those moments, when she could sense him so close by, almost hear him sighing in his sleep, she was happy.

The acute pain of his loss did seem to be lessening, and after a while it didn't hurt to breathe when she thought of him, and she was able to read Lilly's letters without worrying that she might be sick. Yet a chronic sort of ache lingered on, and Charlotte couldn't decide whether she welcomed or abhorred it.

Her colleagues had begun to whisper among themselves, and Miss Rathbone had turned to go up the steps to their offices. The passengers were returning to their seats on the tram, and the motorcars on the street had driven away. The Great Silence was over, at least for another year.

In a year, where would she be? It was difficult to see how her life might change in any appreciable way. She would continue to work for Miss Rathbone, live on in her dining-room-cum-bedroom at the misses', and continue to write her column for John. There were many thousands in Liverpool who would have been grateful for such certainty in their lives.

A year from now, surely, Edward would be married. He would have repaired his family's fortunes and met his obligations to his relatives, tenants, and servants. He might even be awaiting the birth of a child. He would be happy.

She went to her desk, not bothering to remove her coat, and pulled an envelope from her handbag. It was from Lilly and had arrived the day before. Charlotte had already read it a half-dozen times.

8 November 1919

My dearest Charlotte,

I hope this letter finds you well and not suffering unduly from the early arrival of winter. Here it has been nothing but rain, rain, rain and, the other day, even a dusting of snow. I had thought myself hardened by my experiences in France, but apparently I have grown

*soft over the past year, and like being warm and dry too well to hap-
pily accept any other state.*

As I'm sure you already know, Edward returned to London a
fortnight ago, having declared that he and Andrews could no longer
keep themselves warm in the cottage. "Frozen to the marrow," was
the expression he used. Despite his grumbling about the weather, it
seems to me that he was very happy there—thanks entirely to you and
your expert care. I know you have decreed that I must stop thanking
you, but I really cannot help myself. Robbie may have brought my
brother back from France, but you restored Edward to the people
who love him, and for that I will always be grateful. More grateful
than you can ever know.

In my estimation he is very nearly the old Edward again, if not
quite so merry and jolly as he once was. Robbie and I did see him,
briefly, at the beginning of October when we went up to Cumbermere Hall for a long weekend, but it's only since his return to London
that I've been able to make a proper study of your patient. I do believe he is happier and healthier in every possible respect.

He is much given to long walks through Hyde Park, no matter the
weather, and he told Robbie the other day that he would like to get a
dog. He is rarely out in the evenings, and to my knowledge has only
accepted one invitation thus far. I have not seen him drink wine or
spirits of any kind, which is a great relief.

A few nights ago we were all at a dinner party at the Finlay-
sons'—do you remember them from my wedding?—and he spent a
good deal of time with a lovely American girl, Miss Edith Hale, who
is a friend of Violet's. I gather her father made a fortune in soap and
she is having an overdue Season in London. Edward was maddeningly closemouthed on the subject when I asked him about it afterward, and in any event I doubt he has much time for romance these
days. Much of his day is spent with lawyers and estate managers and

other bureaucratic types, for Papa left the estate in rather a shambles and it now falls to Edward to sort everything out.

I meant to tell you in my last letter, but I have taken a subscription to the Herald so I might read your columns without delay. The paper comes only a day late and I do enjoy it; you must tell your Mr. Ellis that he has an admirer in London. Your recent columns have been particularly good and I thought the one on the shortcomings of the Sex Disqualification Act was brilliant in every respect.

I must go, as dear Mr. Pebbles is coming soon and he will certainly insist on putting my nose to the proverbial grindstone. Last week he had me do a test series of examinations and I only just scraped through. I shall have to redouble my efforts if I am to gain a place at the LSE next year. Wish me luck!

With much love from
Your devoted friend
Lilly

A soap heiress. It made Charlotte wonder: flakes or bar? A choking sort of laugh rose in her throat, but she willed it away. Lilly had said the woman was friendly, and as long as Edward found her amusing that might be enough. She was sorry to hear that the Cumberland estate was in such a state, although it didn't surprise her in the least. Miss Hale's millions would certainly help to erase any lingering difficulties, at least in the short term.

Enough. She had spent enough time fretting about the past, about decisions that had been made, paths that had been chosen. Tonight, if she weren't too sad, or too tired, she would think of Edward and their month together, and she would remember how happy she had been.

Until then, however, she had work to do.

Chapter 25

There simply wasn't enough room in the budget. No matter how often she sifted through the numbers, it wouldn't be enough. She would have to let Miss Rathbone know, and perhaps they could—

"Someone here to see you."

Charlotte nearly fell out of her chair in surprise; it was so late she'd assumed she was alone in the office. "Miss Margison! Heavens—I didn't see you there. Do you know who it is?"

"Didn't think to ask. We're the only ones left, else Gladys would have asked."

"Ah . . . well, I'll be straight out. I'm sorry for any inconvenience."

"Humph."

She followed Miss Margison back down the hall. In the reception area were a man and woman; Charlotte recognized the latter, a Mrs. Dooley. Presumably she had come with her husband. She had last seen Mrs. Dooley that morning, when the woman had come in search of help. Her husband hadn't worked since his demobilization, they had a new baby due to arrive at any minute, and they had no way to pay the midwife, or even to buy nappies and gowns for the infant.

As Charlotte approached, she saw that Mrs. Dooley had been crying, and was still clutching a handkerchief. Mr. Dooley was angry, so angry the man fairly seethed with ill will. She suspected it would shortly be directed at her.

"Mr. and Mrs. Dooley. I do apologize for the wait. Perhaps we could speak in my office? I—"

"No. We'll say what we have to say and then we're gone."

"Very well. I must say I am surprised. When you departed this morning, Mrs. Dooley, you seemed quite pleased with how we had left things."

"She's not. We're not," Mr. Dooley said, his voice so loud that Miss Margison, back in the office she shared with the other clerk typists, must surely have heard.

"I come home just now, and she give me *these*," and he threw a pamphlet for the Personal Service Society, together with Charlotte's handwritten recommendation on behalf of the family, on the floor between them.

"Don't, George. Don't. You said you wouldn't make a fuss," Mrs. Dooley implored.

"I'm not making a fuss. I'm telling this woman we don't need no help from her. Not from any of her do-gooder friends either."

"Mr. Dooley, I am sincerely sorry for any upset I may have caused. I truly am. If I offended you—"

"We're in a tight spot, I'll admit it. But we don't need hand-outs. We're not that hard up."

"George, she was only trying to—"

"You hush. I know what she was trying to do. Same lot as

hands out paupers' clothes with 'charity' stamped on the back. They're all the same, these types."

"But what are we to do when the baby comes?"

"We'll manage. We always do, don't we? And you know what'd happen if anyone got wind of you coming here, cap in hand, to ask the grand ladies for their help. We'd be the laughingstock of the street, that's what."

He turned to Charlotte, fiercer than ever, and advanced on her so suddenly that she took a step back.

"You leave her alone." It was Miss Margison, of all people, come to her rescue. "Say your piece, and then go."

"Fine. We'll be off, now. Like I said, we don't want none of your charity."

"I truly only intended to help, Mr. Dooley. I am so very, very sorry for offending you."

"You do-gooders. You're all the same. Swanning about like God put you on this earth to fix everything that was wrong with it. You're not even from Liverpool, are you?" He sneered.

"Somerset, actually."

"Oh, you are, are you? 'Somerset, actually,'" he echoed, imitating her polished accent. "Well, you can go straight back there, you and your charity, and leave off meddling with my business. Come on, Mary, we're done here."

"But, George—" his wife cried, but he was already pulling her to her feet. Mrs. Dooley cast one last, desperate look at Charlotte, and then they were gone.

"Sit down," Miss Margison ordered, guiding Charlotte to the chair behind Gladys's desk.

"I . . . I can't believe that happened. I had no notion . . ."

"Let me get you a cup of tea. You stay put."

Miss Margison bustled away, and as Charlotte sat there, her face burning with chagrin, her hands shaking so badly she had to fold them in her lap, she asked herself what had surprised her most about the past five minutes: the fervor of Mr. Dooley's accusations, or Miss Margison's decision to come to her aid.

"I've put the tea to brew. Are you all right?"

"I am . . . at least I think I am. I don't understand how that could have happened. When I saw Mrs. Dooley this morning, it seemed perfectly straightforward. I had no notion . . ."

"Men are a funny lot. You never know when something will get up their nose. And it's not as if he was angry at you."

"He wasn't? He certainly put on a fine show of it."

"All bluff and bluster. He's angry at himself, poor sod, and he took it out on you."

"I only hope he doesn't take it out on his wife."

"I don't think as he will. Otherwise she'd already have a blackened eye."

"What will happen when the baby comes? She hadn't any nappies or clothes for the infant, and she was so worried about how they'd pay the midwife . . ."

"Their neighbors will see to them. You stop here a minute more. I'll fetch the tea."

Miss Margison returned with a mug for them both, and pulling the chair from the telephone across to Gladys's desk, she plunked herself down and blew at her tea to cool it.

"I've always wondered," she said, "why you up and left when you did."

"You mean during the war?" Charlotte asked, a little taken aback by the question.

"Mm. Miss Rathbone missed you so much in those early days. She was run off her feet, putting together the allowances for soldiers' and sailors' families, and managing everything else. You could have done some good here."

"I know."

"It never made any sense to me, why you did it. I'm not having a go at you," she clarified. "Only wondering why you went."

"It seems so long ago. I can hardly remember it now. I think . . . I suppose I was just swept along by all of it. I do remember that I was very upset by what was happening in Belgium. How savage the enemy seemed to be. If I'd been allowed to put on a uniform and fight, I imagine I'd have jumped at the chance," Charlotte admitted.

She'd been seized by an urge to do more, to *be* more. And there had been her terror of what could happen to those she knew and cared about, Edward most of all.

"Everyone here talked about you like you was walking the wards at Scutari with your lamp," Miss Margison said. "But it never made any sense to me. I don't mean any offense by it."

Charlotte looked her colleague in the eye. "I am sorry. I think, looking back, knowing what I do now, I ought to have stayed. The work you did here really did save lives. And I'm not so sure I can say the same for what I did."

"You, a nurse?"

"I wasn't patching up men who'd come straight from the front lines. After I'd finished the first part of my training, I went to the Special Neurological Hospital for Officers in Kensington."

"Special in what way?"

"It was a neurasthenia hospital."

"Shell shock, you mean."

"Yes. Though I've always thought the term too simple for

something so complicated. The men we cared for were broken. And I learned, very quickly, that it's harder to fix a man's spirit than his body. Sometimes the methods the doctors used there were . . . well, they didn't always sit well with me. It was a difficult time, you know, and sometimes I regret . . ."

"I'll wager you did a lot of good for those men, no matter what you say. Anyhow, it's done and dusted now, as my mum would say. No point in looking back. It doesn't help, and sometimes it makes things worse."

"You're right. Of course you're right. Thank you, Miss Margison. And if I may . . . I'm sorry if I ever treated you in a discourteous manner. If I ever failed to show you the respect you deserve."

"Shouldn't that be the other way round? I'll admit it—I made a right pill of myself, mucking about with your outgoing post when you first came back. I shouldn't have done it, and I'm that sorry for it now."

"Please, you needn't—"

"It got up my nose, that's all. The way everything always seems to turn up roses for you. I used to dream of going to school. I could've, you know. I always did well. But there wasn't any money to pay for it. So I started work when I was fourteen, at the bakery down the street. Hated it. Up at dawn six days a week. Still can't abide the smell of fresh-baked bread." Miss Margison smiled then, really smiled, and it transformed her appearance entirely.

"How did you learn how to type?"

"I saved up and started going to evening classes. Thought I'd died and gone to heaven when Miss Rathbone hired me on."

"She would be lost without you. We all would. You know this office upside down and sideways."

"Nice of you to say so. Well, I suppose I'd best be off now. Half past six and black as pitch outside."

"Will you be going north?" Charlotte asked. Perhaps they might walk awhile together, and talk of easier things. Friendlier things.

"No, I'm off down Garston way. Thanks all the same. You will be all right, won't you?"

"I will. Thank you again."

It would have been sensible to take the tram, for winter had arrived with a vengeance, the rain outside threatening to turn to sleet. But the walk home would give Charlotte the chance to be alone with her thoughts, and her doubts, and so she turned up her coat collar and continued north, though she was walking in the teeth of the wind nearly the entire way.

It had been a normal day until a half hour ago. A long day, a sad day in parts, for there was so little help she could give, and so many who were suffering. Her encounter with Mrs. Dooley had, to her mind, been a positive one. Yet . . . could she have been more understanding? Had she become so inured to requests for help that she had grown insensitive in her conduct?

A memory assailed her, as sharp as a slap across the face, of Lady Cumberland and her outings to dispense charity. Wrapped in an unbreachable aura of self-righteousness and smug entitlement, the countess had handed out baskets of food and castoffs to her family's tenants each Christmas and Easter, secure in the knowledge that none would ever dare to complain or even question the laws of God and state that had set her so high and them so low. Humiliation had been an accepted part of the equation.

Such petty humiliations were everywhere, even when charity wasn't being dispensed. Even in her own office, she realized, such class divisions were alive and well and unthinkingly accepted by everyone. The clerk typists made less than Charlotte and Mabel, for a certainty they did. They weren't even given the dignity of being addressed by their surname; only Miss Margison had been brave enough to insist on that common courtesy.

It wasn't that anyone, least of all Miss Rathbone, had consciously decided to erect a barrier between the clerk typists and the constituency assistants; it had simply been there, likely predating Miss Rathbone's election as a ward councilor.

So where should she begin? Not by suddenly addressing the clerk typists by their surnames, nor by charging into Miss Rathbone's office and demanding a rise in pay for her colleagues. But perhaps she might ask the other women if they might like to use her Christian name. Perhaps she might fetch them tea, instead of waiting for one of them to bring it to her each afternoon.

Great change comes from small steps. Her father had told her that when she was little, likely when she was bemoaning an injustice she had read about. Pit ponies, or little boys set to work as chimney sweeps, or something similarly distressing.

Change wouldn't come overnight, and possibly not in her lifetime—yet she had already cast a vote for a member of Parliament, something her undergraduate self would never have believed possible, and each year women were being accorded more freedom and greater rights. One day it might even be possible for men and women alike to be judged by their character and actions rather than the accent with which they spoke, or the God to whom they prayed, or the color of their skin. One day.

The ideas were crowding upon her; she had to get home,

had to set her thoughts down on paper. She would send the column to John in the morning, and ask him to run it instead of the piece she had submitted earlier in the week.

My last few columns have turned on instances of the government's failure to act, or its failure to act in a manner that I believe to be in the best interests of the British people as a whole. While I find no shortage of material in that regard, this week I have decided to set aside the theme of what is being done for us, or to us, and instead I wish to focus on a different matter entirely: what I can do, and what you can do, to make this country fit not only for our returning heroes, but also for every man, woman, and child who calls these islands home.

Although I do not presume to think the Christmas story is one that resonates with every reader, I do feel, in this season of Advent, that it is worth using as an example of how the very great may at once be perfectly humble as well. Who among us has not, at one instance or another, thought poorly of another human being simply because of the way he or she talks, or dresses, or because of where he or she lives, worships, or works? Who among us has not sat in judgment upon another, though we know full well that God tells us not to judge, else we be judged instead?

You may decide, if you have not already, that my words mark me as a socialist, or some other species of radical bent on the leveling of British society. I assure you I am not; my radical views, such as they are, lie in my conviction that no one of us is born superior to his others. Only by a man's actions should he be judged, I believe, and not by his origins, profession, religion, politics, or race.

I ask you to go forth this winter and spread warmth among your fellows. Offer a kind word, extend a helping hand, or offer a shilling or two to those in need. No matter how you act, treat the recipient of your kindness as your fellow. For we are all of us equal in the sight of God, and so should we be in the laws of man, and the conventions of our land.

—the *Liverpool Herald,* 9 December 1919

Chapter 26

"Where is Meg?" Miss Margaret asked as they were sitting down to supper. "Friday is her favorite. She loves fish cakes. Norma, go and tell her that we're waiting for her."

When Norma didn't return after five minutes, Charlotte got to her feet and went after her. Fish cakes might be Meg's favorite, but they didn't taste especially nice when they were stone cold.

Norma was in the hall outside Meg's room, her ear pressed against the door.

"What on earth are you doing?" Charlotte asked.

"I knocked, but she told me to go away. I think I can hear her crying."

"Let me talk to her. Meg, it's Charlotte. Is anything the matter?"

"I'm f-fine. Please leave me be."

"It doesn't sound as if you're fine at all. May I come in? Please?" She went to open the door, but it had been locked.

"Tried that already," Norma said.

"You don't have to come out. Just unlock the door and let me in. I don't think you should be alone, not if you're upset. You don't have to say a thing. Only let me sit with you."

A key turned in the door.

"Norma, you go back downstairs. Meg and I will be down in a bit. Perhaps Janie could keep our supper warm?"

Charlotte hadn't been inside Meg's room before. It reflected its occupant perfectly, or at least the cipher she knew: neat as a pin, and almost entirely bare of personal touches. The only exception was a single photograph, of a man in uniform, on the bedside table.

After unlocking the door, Meg had retreated to sit on her bed. She had evidently been crying for a long while, for her eyes were swollen and she was shivering, though the room was warm enough. Charlotte took off her cardigan and set it around her friend's shoulders, then sat next to her on the bed.

Meg seemed unable to stanch her tears, so Charlotte let her cry, rubbing her back from time to time, until the worst seemed over and only hiccuping, shuddering sighs broke the silence of the room.

"Do you wish to tell me what has upset you?" she asked in her softest, most gentle voice. "You don't have to, of course, and I won't judge you for it. But if you wish to tell me I will—"

"It's Bill."

"What about him?"

"My husband. He's dead."

"I know, my dear. He died at Passchendaele, didn't he?"

But Meg was frantically shaking her head, the tears pouring from her eyes once more, and her next words were so garbled that Charlotte couldn't make out their meaning at all.

"I don't understand . . . are you saying he's not dead? That they made a mistake?" Stranger things had happened, after all. Edward had been missing for almost a year before Robbie had tracked him down in that Belgian hospital.

"No, no . . . he *is* dead."

"I'm sorry, Meg. I don't quite follow."

Meg took a great steadying breath. "He didn't die at Passchendaele. He's . . . he's been here all this time. At the Mill Road Hospital, up Everton way. That's where I go every Sunday. I mean, where I *went*."

"He was at the hospital there?" Charlotte's nurse's mind paged through the possibilities. Paralysis, neurasthenia, multiple loss of limbs . . .

"He was burned. It was at Passchendaele—that much was true. The Germans had some sort of horrible weapon that sprayed fire. Bill and his whole platoon were burned. They all died, all except for him. I don't know how it is they kept him alive, his burns were that bad."

"Oh, my dear. I am so, *so* sorry."

"I was living in Basildon when it happened—that's where we're from—and when he was brought back to London I came up on the train as often as I could. Then they moved him up here, so I moved, too. I couldn't stand the thought of him being all alone."

"How badly burned was he?" Charlotte asked quietly.

"All over, more or less. Most of his face. His arms and hands were very bad. He lost all but two of his fingers. He couldn't move much because of the scarring. They did some operations, to make his skin less tight, they said, but it never helped. Nothing ever helped with the pain."

"Did he have any other family?"

"His parents came to visit him once, when he was still in London, but as soon as she saw him his mum started screaming, so they hustled her away. That's the last I ever heard of them. I wrote but they never wrote back."

"So all this time it was just you?"

Meg nodded. "Just me. On Sundays I'd go and spend the day at his bedside. In the beginning he could sit in a wheelchair, so I'd take him into the courtyard and we'd sit in the sun. The other patients stared at him, though. After a while he said he didn't want to go outside anymore, so we stayed on the ward. I'd read to him, tell him about my week. When the shop was closed in the summer, when Mr. Timmins was rebuilding, I went more often, of course."

"What happened?"

"I don't know for sure. When Matron called me at work, this afternoon, she only said that he'd taken a turn for the worse last night, and died in the wee hours. But I think it was the infection that got him."

"The infection? To his burns?"

"No, it was a bedsore. The past while, since the summer, I'd say, he'd been staying in bed. He barely said a word to me for months, just lay there with his eyes closed. Slept most of the time. The nurses said he was depressed."

"I'm not surprised. It must have been very hard for him."

"After staying in bed for a month or two he started to get bedsores. One of them got infected the other week. The first week of December, it was. I think . . . I think that must have been it," she said, and began to cry again.

Charlotte held her hand, and gave her a fresh handkerchief, and waited once more for the tears to subside.

"I know I should have told everyone, but I just couldn't bear to talk about it, to talk about him, so when I came here I told the misses I was a widow. It was wrong of me, I know it was, but once the lie was out of my mouth I didn't know how to take it back."

"All water under the bridge. You didn't do it to deceive anyone, only to protect yourself."

"What will I do, Charlotte? Now that's he's gone, what will I do?"

"I think that's a question best saved for another day. First things first," she said firmly. "I think we should go downstairs and tell the others—no, don't fret. I'm sure they will react exactly as I have done. Then you and I are going to eat our supper. It will be much easier to think, and plan, once we've eaten."

They sat on the bed until Meg felt a little steadier, and then they went downstairs and sat at the big kitchen table. There, surrounded by her friends, Meg told everyone about Bill and what had happened to him. Though the others were surprised, they assured Meg that they weren't at all angry and quite understood her reasons for the deception, and one by one they embraced her and offered their condolences.

"It's not as if we don't all have our secrets," Norma observed a little later as they drank their tea and nibbled at a plate of shortbread that Janie had set out.

Rosie snorted in disbelief. "You? You're an open book if ever I've seen one."

"I'm not," she insisted. "I have my secrets."

"Name one," Rosie demanded.

Charlotte braced herself for another unpleasant surprise. What was Rosie thinking? Hadn't the evening taken a dramatic enough turn already?

Norma hesitated, her face reddening, and then she spoke. "Norma isn't my real name."

"It isn't?"

"No. It's Nell."

"That's it? That's your deep, dark secret?" Rosie asked, laughing, and then they were all laughing, even Meg, even Norma.

"I always hated 'Nell,' so when I left home I changed it."

"It does suit you," Charlotte said, and reached over to pat her hand, relieved beyond measure. "It sounds very . . . well, very American."

Then she turned to Meg, who was dabbing discreetly at her eyes. "What can we do to help? Have you thought about his funeral at all?"

"Matron offered to have it on Sunday, so I don't have to take a day off work. There's a chapel at the hospital, and then they'll drive me up to the cemetery." She paused, twisting her handkerchief in her hands. "Would you come with me? It won't be a long service, I don't think."

"Of course I will." Charlotte looked around the table and took the temperature of the room. "We'll all come."

"It will be our very great honor," said Miss Mary. "We shall all of us be there."

THE MISSES MACLEOD had insisted on hiring a pair of taxis to convey the household up to the hospital, so Sunday morning saw them setting off in some style for the hospital. It had once been a workhouse, according to Rosie, and its architecture was correspondingly severe. A central building of turreted red brick was surrounded, or rather hemmed in, by huge, nearly windowless blocks that had likely once been dormitories. It was every bit as cheerless and lowering as its architects had intended it to be.

They followed Meg inside and up to the first floor, which

took a while as nearly everyone they passed had a word or two of comfort for her, orderlies and nurses and even a few patients. Although Meg seemed perfectly at ease, and the hospital was clean and tidy and none of the patients appeared to be neglected in any way, Charlotte found it unutterably depressing.

It was too quiet. Even her hospital in London, though it had been filled with men whose mental state might charitably be classified as despairing on a good day, had felt cheerier than this place. Where were the normal sounds of patients talking to their nurses and one another? Where were the visitors?

"Is it always this quiet?" she asked Meg, and though she pitched her voice to a whisper it still echoed down the corridor.

Meg nodded. "Most of the men on this ward are bedridden. And there aren't many visitors, besides. Most Sundays it was only me."

Only Meg had persevered. The families of the other patients, one could only assume, had given up. It might be the case that some lived so far away that frequent visits weren't practicable. More likely, though, they had left their loved ones here, in this cold and clean and soulless place, abandoned like so much detritus after a parade.

Matron was waiting for them, and it was a relief to see how warmly she greeted Meg, and how candidly she answered Rosie's questions about Bill's final illness. It had, after all, been an infected bedsore that had killed him. At first he had seemed to be rallying, but then, overnight, he had taken a turn for the worse and had died just before dawn on Friday.

"I thought you'd like to know that Sister Yeovil was with him," Matron told Meg. "She'll be coming with us to the service."

"I'm glad," Meg said softly. "She was one of his favorites."

"Shall we walk down to the chapel now?" Matron suggested. "Reverend Walsh will be waiting for us, and there will be a guard of honor from St. John's Barracks."

Bill's coffin was at the front of the chapel, neatly covered by a Union flag. Seeing it, Meg began to cry. The service was short, with only their party, Matron and two nurses, and Reverend Walsh in attendance. As it finished, the chapel doors opened and the guard of honor entered. They shouldered the coffin with practiced ease; likely they had performed this ritual many times before.

Accompanied only by the minister and the honor guard, for the nurses were required to remain at the hospital, they continued on to the cemetery. It seemed to go on for miles in every direction, though soldiers' burials took place in one section that had been set aside at the beginning of the war. There were many fresh graves and many white headstones as yet untouched by moss or lichen.

The soldiers unloaded Bill's casket from the horse-drawn hearse and gently placed it on the ground next to the prepared grave. Two of them removed the Union flag, folded it into a tight rectangle, and then one of the men approached Meg, knelt before her, and placed it in her hands.

The minister said his prayers of committal, Bill's coffin was lowered into the grave, and a bugler, who until then had stood quietly by the hearse, stepped forward and played the plaintive, elegiac notes of "The Last Post." All the women, even Charlotte, began to weep.

Remember this moment, she told herself. When you think you must surely die from the pain of losing the man you love, remember what it was like to stand here beneath an empty sky, next to your friend, and weep with her for a husband who took two years to die.

This was what war did to men, she thought, her heart seized anew by the agony of it all. *This* was heartbreak, *this* was loss, and she, who had arrogantly thought herself one of the wounded— she was nothing more than an insignificant bystander.

"Come, now," she said, wiping away her tears, and she took Meg's hand and led her back to the waiting cars.

Chapter 27

London, England
March 1918

"Nurse Brown?"

"Yes, Sister Barrett?"

"When were we expecting the new lot of patients?"

Charlotte had been closest to the telephone when the call had come in that morning. "Anytime now, Sister. Two ambulances direct from the station, though they didn't say how many men."

"Typical. How on earth do they expect us to be properly prepared? They might be sending two men or a dozen."

"Yes, Sister."

"Very well. Finish off Captain McGrath's dressing change, and then you can make up beds for the new men. Start in Wards H and J. Such a shame that we can't give them private rooms anymore."

"Yes, Sister."

Sister Barrett was a pleasant enough woman and not given to an overemphasis on rules and regulations. All the same, Charlotte knew better than to offer up a lazy "yes" or "no" in response. Sister had earned her title and expected underlings to use it.

The burn on Captain McGrath's forearm, inflicted by a piece of white-hot shell casing, had healed quite nicely, and only required twice-daily dressing changes. He never flinched, never complained, but then he had been rendered mute by the aftermath of his injury, when he had been buried alive in his dugout for nearly a day, along with the bodies of his commanding officer and two signalers. He was able to answer simple questions with a nod or shake of his head, but speech eluded him, even after several sessions of hypnosis.

When she had finished, she settled the captain in the patients' sitting room on the first floor. Leaving him by the window, which had a pretty view of Kensington Palace Gardens, she began to circle around the room, checking that everyone was calm and comfortable, fetching tea and adjusting blankets on laps and generally ensuring none of the patients felt neglected.

Lieutenant Stephens, alone at a table in the corner, his book forgotten, was humming to himself. It sounded like "There's a Long, Long Trail," a welcome change from "I Don't Want to Join the Army," which had been his sole musical selection for the two days preceding. She approached him quietly, and, crouching at his side, began to sing the words to the song.

> "There's a long, long trail a-winding
> Into the land of my dreams,
> Where the nightingales are singing
> And a white moon beams.
> There's a long, long night of waiting
> Until my dreams all come true,

Till the day when I'll be going
Down that long, long trail with you."

He rewarded her with a little smile, the first she'd seen since his arrival a fortnight before, so she continued to sing.

"There's a long, long—"

"What on earth is that dreadful racket?"

Of all the times for Major Pitt-Venables to embark on his fortnightly tour of the hospital. She'd heard one of the patients refer to the officer as Major Piss-and-Vinegar, and secretly she thought the name suited him perfectly. Before the war he'd been some species of physician in Brighton, but by some miracle of military efficiency had since been raised to a position that far exceeded his talents, if not his ambition. He was attached to the Queen Alexandra Hospital at Millbank, a larger facility some miles away, and undertook his inspections with the help of a junior officer.

Charlotte stood, straightening her apron, and stepped away from Lieutenant Stephens.

"I beg your pardon, sir. I was singing to one of the officers."

"Whatever for? He's not an infant. Surely you have better things to do."

"Yes, sir."

She waited until old Piss-and-Vinegar was well out of earshot before crouching next to Lieutenant Stephens and whispering in his ear. "Don't you mind the major. I'm happy to sing with you anytime."

Just then, in the distance, a mechanical trill sounded. It was the bell at the back door, and was only ever rung when new patients had arrived. Patting the lieutenant's arm in farewell, she set off down the rear stairs and waited for Sister Barrett and the orderlies to arrive.

The ambulances, made distinctive by their plain gray exteriors, had already parked. Both she and Sister breathed a sigh of relief when only four patients emerged, three from one ambulance and one from the other. The lone passenger in the second ambulance was very poorly indeed: his skin was ashen, he was perspiring profusely, and his limbs were shaking so much he had difficulty standing without assistance.

A wheelchair was brought out for the man, and the orderlies, small men who regularly astonished Charlotte with their feats of strength, nimbly carried it and its trembling passenger upstairs to J Ward. Sister Barrett, having consulted with Matron, ordered that he be bathed, changed into pajamas, fed some lunch, and put to bed for a nap.

All this Charlotte accomplished more or less on her own, and even managed to glance through the man's chart. He was Captain Soames, an infantry officer with the Welsh Guards, and had most recently been in command of a company at Cambrai. He was twenty-three years old.

There was no explanation of his condition, beyond the maddeningly cryptic NYDN designation: "not yet diagnosed; nervous." And she knew better than to ask him directly.

He ate his lunch without protest, his trembling having abated almost entirely, and when he murmured that he was done Charlotte tucked him back into bed and left him to his nap.

Sister Barrett was at her desk, likely busy with the paperwork the new patients had generated. "How is Captain Soames?"

"He's sleeping now. Was perfectly cooperative."

"Very good. Rounds are in half an hour, but you should still have time to give Major Stafford his sponge bath. Mind you don't get his sutures wet."

"Yes, Sister. I'll—"

"Nurse Brown, what is Captain Soames doing out of bed?"

Charlotte whirled around to see the captain stagger down the corridor. He had been so placid, earlier. He had even smiled at her when she had arranged the pillow beneath his head.

She and Sister Barrett rushed into the corridor and along to the sitting room at its far end. Captain Soames stood in the center of the room, swaying on his feet, and he held something in his right hand. A knife.

"Oh, God. It's the knife from his luncheon tray. I didn't . . . he must have taken it."

"It isn't sharp enough to do much damage, but we need to get it from him all the same."

Sister took a step toward the captain, then another, but before she could say anything he lunged at her, the knife a metallic blur.

Charlotte rushed forward and held out her hands in supplication. "I won't hurt you," she said. "I promise. But I need for—"

"What the devil is going on here? Why does that man have a knife?"

Major Pitt-Venables certainly had an impeccable sense of timing. Charlotte half turned to him, frantically shaking her head, but he blundered forward without even acknowledging her presence.

"Put that weapon down at once. Do you hear me?"

"Oh, I hear you all right. Major. Have you been to war?"

"Of course I have. We're all at war, you fool."

Captain Soames narrowed his eyes and extended his arm until the knife was pointed straight at the senior officer's heart.

"I'm no fool, and you know it. What I want to know is this: Have you sent men to their death? No? Of course you haven't. I have, though. I wish I could remember all their names. So many names. I tried at first . . ."

Charlotte took a tiny step forward. "Please put the knife down. You're frightening the other men. You've a perfect right to be upset, but it's not fair to let it affect the others."

"I told Colonel Watson that I needed a rest. Only a week or two behind the lines to clear my head. Do know you what he said? He said I'd let myself fall into a funk. That I lacked *grit*."

"No one here is suggesting anything of the—"

"He hadn't seen what I've seen. He hadn't done what I had to do. What does a man like *that* know of grit? Or a man like you, for that matter?"

The knife was perilously close to the major's chest. To his credit, the medical officer stood his ground, though a fine sheen of sweat had broken out on his upper lip and brow.

"He didn't know what happens when you bayonet a man, but I do. Oh, God, I do. It goes in so easily, like a hot knife through butter, but it doesn't want to come out. So you have to wrench it out, but the man you're killing, he's still alive. His hands are covered with blood, for he's grasping at the blade in his guts, and he won't let go, so you have to kick at him and scream at him . . ."

Captain Soames dropped to his knees and hugged the knife close to his chest. "I could smell his breath, his sweat, smell where he'd pissed himself . . . you've no idea. None of you have *any* idea."

Still keeping her distance, Charlotte knelt on the floor. "May I ask your Christian name, Captain Soames?"

"It's Patrick."

"Patrick, if you will put down the knife, I will listen to you. I'll sit with you and listen until you decide you have nothing more to say. But you must put down the knife."

"Do you promise?" he said, as weary as an old man at the end of his life, and Charlotte nodded eagerly.

He let the knife fall from his grasp. She opened her mouth to thank him, but before she could speak the orderlies were upon him, dragging him away, his screams echoing down the corridor.

"You promised!" he cried. "You said you would listen!"

Charlotte stood up and dusted off her skirts. Matron might allow her to speak with the captain later, and she might be able to regain his trust. But first she would have to help calm the others, some of whom were visibly unnerved by the scene they had witnessed. Lieutenant Stephens was already humming "I Don't Want to Join the Army" again.

"Nurse Brown? Are you all right?" Matron had emerged from her office; she would help calm the men. She always knew how to restore order.

"I—I think so."

Matron gave her a handkerchief. "Perhaps you might wish to wipe your face," she suggested kindly, and when Charlotte raised a hand to her cheek she realized that tears were streaming from her eyes.

"I beg your pardon, Matron."

"Not at all. It was a very distressing incident, and you handled it ably."

"I'm afraid it was all my fault. I was the one who left the knife within his reach."

"That is unfortunate, but it was a dinner knife, not a scalpel. And you ought never to have been left alone with a man whose thoughts were so disordered. So it is I who ought to apologize. Would you like a few minutes, just to gather your thoughts?"

"Only if it won't—"

"We shall be quite all right. Take half an hour for yourself before reporting back to Sister Barrett. I shall speak to her about the knife."

"Yes, Matron. Thank you."

The nurses' cloakroom was on the top floor of the hospital at the very end of a corridor, and though spacious enough, it was sparsely furnished and nearly always freezing cold. Charlotte brought up a discarded copy of *The Times* from the day before, together with a cup of tea from the kitchen, and curled up in one of the two easy chairs that some kind soul had donated.

She paged through the newspaper, her mind on her promise to Captain Soames, as well as the very real possibility that one or more of the other patients would have a setback in his treatment as a result.

She skimmed past the classified advertisements, law reports, announcements of military medals—an entire page of names, so many her eyes watered just looking at it—and several pages of unremarkable news. The Roll of Honor, blessedly short for a change; she would look at it later and see if she recognized any names.

She was about to turn the page, but some nameless impulse stopped her hand. The list was a short one; it would take her no time to read. Killed, died of wounds, wounded—she scanned the names; all strangers. And then, at the end, a single name under the banner of MISSING, FEARED KILLED:

NEVILLE-ASHFORD, Maj. E.A.G., Border Rt.

She blinked, then looked again. His name. There, in *The Times,* in the Roll of Honor. It was his name she saw; there was no doubting it.

Charlotte ran to the sink in the corner and was noisily, violently sick. She sank to the floor, on her knees for the second time that day, quite sure that she'd never be able to get up.

If there'd been any uncertainty as to his fate, he'd have been listed as "missing." She would never see him again, never, and no amount of wishing or praying, or bargains made with the Almighty, would ever erase Edward's name from that page.

"GOOD EVENING, MY dear. Did you have a nice day?"

"No, Mrs. Collins. It was . . . it was a hard day."

The afternoon had passed in a blur. Jean, one of the other nurse probationers, had found Charlotte in the cloakroom when she didn't return after the promised half hour, and rather than listen to Charlotte and wait while she washed her face and brushed her hair, the woman had gone running to Sister Barrett, who in turn had fetched Matron.

They had both been concerned, assuming that Charlotte was still upset about the incident with Captain Soames, and it was an age before she was able to escape their well-meaning clutches and return to the numbing oblivion of work. By some mercy the men were in good spirits, Matron having once again worked her brand of magic, so Charlotte had an uneventful afternoon of sponge baths and washing up and fetching of countless cups of tea.

And now she was home, standing in the front hall of Mrs.

Collins's boardinghouse, though she had no memory at all of the journey from the hospital. It had been raining, too, for her coat was spotted and her face was wet. Had it really been raining?

"I'm not feeling very well," she told the landlady. "I think I'll just go up to bed, if you don't mind."

"You poor dear. You do look done in. Oh—I almost forgot. There's a letter for you."

Charlotte didn't look at it, didn't so much as examine the envelope for clues, until she was alone in her room and sitting in her chair before the ashes of last night's fire.

The letter was from Lilly.

51st C.C.S.
France
11 March 1918

My dearest Charlotte,

Yesterday I received a letter from home (from Mr. Maxwell, not my parents) with the terrible news that Edward has gone missing. He was able to provide me with few details, apart from the information that he was last seen on March 3rd whilst conducting a raid in no-man's-land. I know nothing else but I thought I must let you know as quickly as possible. If and when I learn more I shall certainly write to you immediately.

I must go—I am very sorry to tell you so bluntly—I miss you terribly and think of you often.

With love from
Your devoted friend
Lilly

Charlotte folded the letter back into its envelope and set it on the table. It was true. His name in *The Times* and Lilly's letter, together, made it a certainty.

He was gone forever, his body lost in the wasteland, alone and cold, never to be warm again, never to see the sun again. The last time she had seen him, more than a year ago, he had promised that her name would be on his lips when he died. Yet she had pushed him away.

Why hadn't she embraced him? Why hadn't she told him the truth?

A scream rose in her throat, impossible to muffle with her hand, or even her handkerchief, so she ran to her bed and pressed her pillow to her face. She cried and raged until her eyes were dry and the pillow was sodden, and then she simply lay on the bed and let the shock and pain overtake her.

Hours later, when the street outside was quiet and still, and the room so cold her teeth were chattering, Charlotte sat up again. She changed into her nightgown and wrapped a shawl around her shoulders. She lighted her spirit kettle and made a mug of Bovril. She drank it, somehow, though her stomach roiled in protest, and then she returned to bed.

She would never see his face again. She would never hear his voice again. He was gone.

What had she been doing on the third of March? She sifted through her memories but couldn't recall anything of significance. It had been an ordinary day at work. A solitary day at home. Had she spared a single thought for him as he lay dying? She had not.

"Forgive me," she whispered, and though she had long ago

ceased to believe in any sort of hereafter, she held her breath and waited for his answer.

None came. She was alone, as she had always been, as she would always be. Alone, as Edward had been at the end, when he had taken his last breath and whispered her name and had bid her adieu forever.

Chapter 28

"All aboard for Wells. Next station, Wells. All aboard!"

Seeing no latecomers, the station guard waved his arm, and with a screech of its running gear and an enveloping burst of steam from its chimney, the locomotive rumbled forth into the night.

Charlotte was almost home. Her journey had begun before dawn, when she'd caught the train from Liverpool to Birmingham, then down to Bristol and, after one final change of trains, the branch line to Wells. It had taken her nearly eleven hours, but soon she would be home.

She hadn't spent Christmas with her parents since before the war, and though Lilly and Robbie had been keen for her to stay with them, she had known there was only one place she belonged this Yuletide. It wouldn't be a long stay, for she had missed far too much work over the preceding months, but she would be with them for a few hours of Christmas Eve, and then all of Christmas Day and Boxing Day.

It had been strange to know she wouldn't see Lilly this

Christmas, but London was far out of her way. Nor would she see Edward, of course. Lilly had asked if she might stay with them on her journey home, for the twenty-seventh was a Saturday. But Charlotte had told her friend, not altogether untruthfully, that she was terribly behind in her work and badly needed to catch up. It was true, after a fashion, though it wasn't the reason she was keeping her distance.

She couldn't risk seeing him. If she were to stay with Lilly, Edward would surely come by, wish her a happy Christmas, and ask her how she was. There was no way around it—Lilly would tell him and he would come. She knew he would, and she knew just as well that she could not bear it. Not yet, at any rate.

So she had done the right thing and gone straight home to her parents. She would leave her worries behind and let Mother and Father take care of her for a few days. They would be happy, and she would be . . . well, almost happy.

Feeling rather irritated with herself—when had fussing and worrying about something ever made it better?—Charlotte dragged her case from the overhead rack and made her way to the end of the carriage. She was almost home.

When the train finally rolled to a halt and she stepped onto the platform, she couldn't see a thing, for the locomotive had exhaled a dragon's worth of steam across the platform. At length she spied an elderly couple several yards away, but though their backs were turned Charlotte was sure they couldn't be her parents.

Then they turned, and they were her parents. It had been scarcely more than a year since she'd seen them last, but in the interim they had suddenly become old. Father was only seventy-two, and Mother only sixty-five. How could they possibly be *old*?

"Mother! Father!" she cried out, and rushed forward to embrace them. "It is so good to see you."

"You look so well," her mother said. "Doesn't she look well, Laurence?"

"She does indeed," her father agreed. "Have you only the one case?"

"Yes, Father. Only the one."

"If only you were staying longer . . ."

"I know, Mother, and I am sorry. I thought I might pop down for another visit in the spring. Perhaps at Whitsun? What do you think?"

At this, her mother's expression brightened considerably. "Oh, that would be lovely."

"We'd best get along to the car," her father urged.

"Car? Don't tell me you've learned to drive, Father."

"Goodness, no. The car and its driver belong with the dean. He was kind enough to offer."

"But we always walk from the station."

"Yes, but it's a cold night and your mother's knees are bothering her. Come, now. In you both get."

How could Mother's knees be hurting her? Her mother, who regularly walked two or three miles each afternoon? Why hadn't she said anything in her letters?

Charlotte was still fretting over the state of her mother's knees when the car pulled up at the northern entrance to Vicars' Close. Their house was at the very end, attached on one side to the chapel, and was rather larger than its fellows on the street. All dated to the fourteenth century and had, by some miracle, survived the centuries more or less in their original state, with only minor alterations made for modern convenience.

Mrs. Drake was waiting for them at the door. She had been with her parents for as long as Charlotte could remember; surely she must be considering retirement? She looked well, though, and as unchanged as the house in which they stood.

"Charlotte, my dear! Come in, come in!"

"How are you, Mrs. Drake?"

"Since when am I Mrs. Drake to you?" the housekeeper asked in mock affront.

"Duckie, then," Charlotte said, and let herself be enfolded in a comforting embrace.

"Mrs. Drake, indeed. Come in, come in, and your Duckie will take your coat and see you settled. Come on, all of you, through to the kitchen."

The kitchen, like Duckie, was mercifully unchanged. A huge pot of soup was bubbling away at the back of the range, loaves of bread had just emerged from the oven, and trays of Christmas delicacies were stacked on every available surface: mince pies, buttery shortbread, dark and fragrant loaves of gingerbread, and Duckie's fruitcake, the only kind Charlotte had ever liked.

"You won't have met the new girls, will you?" her mother asked.

"What happened to Annie and Ruth?"

"Well, Annie went off to London—do you remember why, Mrs. Drake?—and Ruth got married."

"I still miss Ruth," Father chimed in. "Lovely girl."

"Here they are now," said Duckie. "Frances, Betty, this is Miss Charlotte, come down from Liverpool to spend Christmas at home."

"Pleased to meet you, Miss Charlotte," said one of them.

"Happy Christmas to you, Miss Charlotte," said the other.

"Home you go to your families, now, and we'll see you again on Boxing Day. But first take Miss Charlotte's case up to her room."

"Yes, Mrs. Drake. Happy Christmas, Reverend Brown, Mrs. Brown."

Looking around the kitchen, Charlotte felt the last of her exhaustion melt away. She sighed happily.

"It looks as if you and Mother have been very busy," she said to Duckie.

"That we have. Couldn't have you come home to an empty larder. Mrs. Brown, what are you wanting to do for your supper? Have it now, or wait awhile?"

"Ah, yes. Supper. It depends on what Charlotte prefers. Did you want to come to midnight Eucharist with us? If so, I think we ought to eat around nine."

"I wouldn't miss it, not for the world."

"Then I'll have your supper ready for nine," said Duckie. "In the meantime, what do you say to a spot of tea and some mince pie?" Without waiting for a response, she slid the kettle onto the range and started to assemble a tray of delicacies. "Go on into the sitting room, all of you. I won't be a minute."

One of the maids, or likely both of them working together, had readied the sitting room fire; the hearth was huge, and burned logs the approximate size of a lamb, so a proper fire took some effort to build. Father soon had it blazing away, and by its light the room looked very pretty indeed. Mother had arranged sprigs of holly and boughs of evergreen on the mantel, and the wooden crèche had been set out in its usual place on top of the Pembroke table. There even was a little Christmas tree before the window, its boughs bare of ornaments.

"I'm just going to run upstairs and change," she said. "Perhaps we could decorate the tree when I come down?"

Her room was at the very top of the house, up two flights of stairs made almost comically crooked by age. Nothing had been moved or changed, though it had been fifteen years since she had left home for university, and looking around she could almost imagine herself eighteen again, excited and terrified and curious beyond belief at what life had in store for her.

Her narrow bed was still set against the wall, her old dolls and books were still on their shelves, and her dollhouse, too, had its place in the corner where ancient oak beams swept low and converged. The view was as entrancing as ever, looking south along the Close to the Chapter House and the inescapable mass of the great cathedral itself. If she opened the window she would be able to hear the music of its organ, she knew; it had been her lullaby for many childhood bedtimes.

She changed out of her travel-tired garments and put on her favorite frock, a dark blue wool, which was several years old but had the advantage of a rather longer hemline than her newer dresses. Her father was a forward-thinking man in many ways, but she didn't want to alarm him by adhering too closely to current modes.

Their evening passed quietly, just the three of them together, for Duckie had gone to visit her sister in town and wouldn't be back until the morning. They decorated the tree with paper chains and the folded birds and stars that Charlotte had made when she was little, and then they ate their supper of soup and bread in the kitchen.

As ever, the conversation revolved around Charlotte and her work. Rather to her surprise, Mother seemed to have taken a keen interest in her column for the *Herald*.

"What sort of a man is this Mr. Ellis?" Mother asked as they were doing the washing up.

"A very good one," Charlotte answered. "Resolute in his determination that—"

"Yes, yes, of course. I mean, what is *he* like? Is he married? Does he have any . . . well, personal eccentricities that might, ah . . ."

"He and I are friends, Mother. That is all. And even if I were interested in him—which I'm not, I assure you—he and I would never suit. We're far too alike. Too earnest about the things we value. We'd suck the air out of every room we inhabited."

"Leave her be, Davina," Father ordered. "Now, tell me, my dear, how is Lilly and that new husband of hers?"

"Very happy. They have a sweet little house in Chelsea, scarcely big enough for the two of them. Robbie is back at the London Hospital, where he was before the war, and Lilly is hoping to go to university next year."

"And what of Lord Cumberland? Has he recovered his health?"

There had been no question of not telling Mother and Father about her month in Cumbria, though she had only furnished them with the barest of details. As far as they knew she had been asked to assist in his recuperation from injuries suffered during the war, and that was that.

"He is quite well. I haven't seen him since the end of September, but I believe his convalescence is complete."

"Thank goodness." Her mother sighed. "When you think of all that poor man has suffered, it simply beggars belief."

"He did suffer," Charlotte said, her throat suddenly tight, and she wondered if she would be forced to excuse herself.

Fortunately the clock on the cathedral chose that moment to ring the half hour.

"Half past eleven already?" her father muttered, drawing his watch from his waistcoat pocket. "Best be on our way."

After emerging from the Close, they turned to the right and followed the crowds that were hurrying, like so many ants, toward the immense western front of the cathedral. They sat in the nave, its scissor arches and rood cross looming high above their heads. Just beyond were the choir and high altar; tomorrow she and Mother would sit there, watching Father as he assisted the bishop at Eucharist, but tonight they were ordinary parishioners, made humble by the soaring heights and ineffable beauty of the building that embraced them.

The organ sounded the opening bars of "Adeste Fidelis," the congregation stood, and nearly a thousand voices rang out in praise, Charlotte's among them. She ought to have felt like a fraud, for she hadn't counted herself as one of the faithful for years, yet somehow, in this place that felt as familiar as home, she couldn't bring herself to doubt.

CHRISTMAS DAY WAS as it had ever been: presents opened in front of the sitting room fire, a light breakfast of toast and tea, back to the cathedral for Eucharist, home again to help Duckie with Christmas lunch—Father remained for Matins—and then roast goose with all the trimmings at one o'clock.

Charlotte helped with the clearing up, for Duckie was expected back at her sister's for three o'clock, and then, feeling rather at loose ends, she went in search of her parents.

"Would anyone like to go on a walk? To the Bishop's Garden, perhaps?"

"I'll come," said Father. "Do you feel able, Davina?"

"Perhaps tomorrow. Do wear your warmest coats, my dears."

Charlotte and her father maintained a companionable silence at first, touring around the east lawn before wandering over to a bench by the reflecting pond, which boasted a perfect image of the cathedral in its still waters.

Her father looked out over the pond, then he looked at Charlotte, and then, his voice very soft, he asked her the question she had been dreading.

"What is wrong, my darling? Don't say, 'oh, Father,' and tell me I'm imagining things. You are unhappy and I should like to know why."

"I don't wish you to—"

"Is it Mr. Ellis? Had you perhaps been hoping for something more from him?"

"No," she said, shaking her head. "It's not John. I'm afraid I am the disappointment there. He's a lovely man, a true friend, but I cannot feel anything for him beyond the platonic. And I know that's not enough for marriage."

"For some it is," her father said easily, "but not, I think, for you." He took her hand in both of his and held it tight. "Who is he, then? The man you love?"

"Please, Father . . . we ought to go back. Mother will fret, you know she will."

"Charlotte Jocelin Brown," he said in his churchiest voice, though he softened it by smiling at her.

"It's . . . it's Edward."

Her father furrowed his brow, not quite understanding, or perhaps he did understand and wished very much that he didn't.

"Lilly's brother. Lord Cumberland," she admitted, and she winced at the look of horror and dismay on her father's face.

He knew, after all, that she had recently spent a month with Edward. Thank goodness he was ignorant of the precise circumstances.

"No, Father, you mustn't think that. Edward is an honorable man."

"But he is engaged to be married, is he not?"

"He was. Not anymore."

"Do you believe he loves you?" her father asked.

"I know he does."

"Then why . . . ?"

She knew what he was thinking. "It's not that. He does know you adopted me, but that's all. He certainly doesn't think me unworthy in any way. The problem is that his father left the estate in some disarray, and so Edward needs to marry someone who can fill the family coffers."

"Oh, my dear," her father whispered, and in that moment he looked every bit as miserable as she felt. "In all my life I have never wanted to be a rich man, not once, not until this moment. I am so sorry, my darling. So very sorry."

"I'll be all right," she promised him, and set her head against his shoulder. "It is something, after all, to know that one is loved. But please don't tell Mother. Better if she thinks me married to my work."

"It will be our secret," he said, and if his voice shook a little Charlotte pretended not to notice. "Shall we walk by the gatehouse and see if the swans are being fed? I remember how you used to love watching them ring their bell and wait for their dinner."

"Yes, please. And, Father?"

"Yes?"

"I hope I haven't disappointed you."

"Never, my dear. You and your mother are the lights of my life. Never forget that."

THE NEXT DAY, as was their tradition every year, her parents attended the bishop's Boxing Day luncheon, and since Charlotte was visiting an invitation had been extended to her as well. As soon as they were seated it became apparent that her mother and the bishop's wife had been talking about Charlotte's future, for eligible bachelors had been placed at both her left and right.

Of the two, Charlotte far preferred Daniel Heydon, a widowed curate from the nearby church of St. Cuthbert, to the young and ridiculously self-important deacon from Bath, seated to her right, whose name she forgot almost immediately. Mr. Heydon was intelligent and curious, and not only listened to her but also asked reasonable and informed questions about her work.

She was friendly and warm to Mr. Heydon, though she excused herself from a visit to St. Cuthbert by explaining that she was leaving early the next morning and felt, at least for this visit, that she needed to remain with her parents.

As soon as they had returned home, Mother marched into the kitchen, put on an apron, and began to make biscuits. Soon she was kneading the dough with such vigor that flour flew in clouds around the kitchen.

"Mother, don't. The biscuits will be as hard as roof tiles if you keep on like that."

"It's either this or I will shout at you, Charlotte. As I've never once shouted at you, I prefer to make biscuits."

"What have I done?" Charlotte asked, though she knew full well.

"Leaving aside your behavior at luncheon today—I know Rupert Lewis can be tiresome, but Daniel Heydon is a dear man, you know he is—I simply don't understand what you want."

"I had a perfectly agreeable conversation with Mr. Heydon."

"I'm not talking about luncheon. I'm talking about your *life*. What normal woman doesn't want a husband and children? Your father and I admire the work you do, but neither of us expects you to sacrifice yourself at some . . . some altar of charity."

"Nor do I. But work offers my best chance at happiness. Please don't cry, Mother."

She came around the kitchen table, and, taking her mother's hands in her own, led her to the chairs at its far end. Once they were both seated, she pulled a handkerchief from her pocket and wiped away her mother's floury tears.

"I did not set out on this path deliberately, you know. My life led me to it, and I cannot regret any of the decisions I made along the way. Of all people, you and Father know why I feel compelled to do this sort of work. You know why I am happy for it to be everything to me. Were it not for the kindness of strangers, what would have become of me?"

"I know. But I can't help but worry. I've been so happy in my own marriage, and I only want the same for you. I want you to have the joy of a child you may call your own. I only wish the same happiness for you."

"I know, Mother, but happiness may be achieved in many different ways. And I *am* happy," she promised. "Shall we try to bake those biscuits, or would it be best to start over?"

"I suppose if we ladle on enough jam your father will never know the difference," her mother said, sniffling a little.

"There you have it. I'll put the kettle on, too, and we'll have biscuits and jam and some of Duckie's fruitcake. Who could ask for anything more?"

She had fibbed to her mother, but only to spare her further hurt. She might not be happy at present, but Charlotte had every intention of being happy one day. She had the memory of it, which helped, and she had family and friends who loved her. It was more than enough, and more than many others had.

It would be enough.

Chapter 29

Liverpool, England
April 1920

"Hurry up, everyone—I daren't be late!"

It was half past seven already and she was meant to be going onstage at eight o'clock. They'd have left a quarter hour before if Norma hadn't gone back to change her hat twice. What was the girl thinking? It wasn't as if she'd end up dancing with one of the trade unionists.

"Calm down, calm down. We're almost there. The Davy Lou is just at the next corner," Norma reassured her. "How are you feeling? Nervous?"

"A little," Charlotte admitted.

In early March one of her columns had caused a sensation among readers. A passionate defense of trade unions, it had ended with a plea to the unions that they not marginalize women workers, and in its wake she'd been invited to address the Easter Congress of the Liverpool Trades Union Council. It had all been arranged through John and the newspaper, so she was fairly certain of a warm reception, but she couldn't help feeling a little unsettled. There were bound to be a lot of people in the theater at the David Lewis building, and not all of them would be keen to hear what she had to say.

"I was there for a show at Christmas," Norma said, "and there must have been a *thousand* people in the audience. That theater is enormous—"

"Norma, do you want Charlotte to keel over in the street? Look at her face," Rosie cautioned.

"You'll be fine," Meg said, coming closer so she might take Charlotte's arm. "You'll have all those men under your spell in no time at all."

They rounded the corner of Upper Parliament Street and turned onto the open triangle of Great George Place. Looming over the other buildings was the inescapable and faintly stolid redbrick mass of the David Lewis Hostel and Club, otherwise known as the Davy Lou.

John and Miss Rathbone were waiting for her just inside the door. She only had time for a quick embrace from each of her friends before they hurried inside the theater and she was led, feeling ever so slightly like a lamb to the slaughter, to a parlor where she and the other speakers for the evening had been asked to gather.

"We've still got some time," John explained. "They're finishing off some resolutions now, so the speeches won't start for a quarter hour at least. How are you feeling?"

"A little apprehensive," she admitted. "I've never spoken in front of such a large gathering."

"I feel certain you will be splendid, and I know Eleanor does as well."

"Quite," said Miss Rathbone. "If you feel at all anxious, simply pick a face in the audience and speak directly to him or her. That's what I always do, and I never feel the slightest hint of nerves."

Of course she didn't; nothing and no one could ever make Miss Rathbone nervous. But Charlotte smiled, and thanked her, and prayed that the tightness at the back of her throat didn't mean she was about to be sick.

"Do you want anything to drink?" John asked. "I'm sure they could fetch you a cup of tea."

"No, thank you. I think I might just read through my speech one last time."

"It's still a version of your column?"

"Yes. Since that's the point of my coming here, to try and ensure that women's concerns aren't swept aside, I thought I should cleave to that subject."

"Perfect. I'll leave you to it."

She read through it once, then a second time, and soon felt a little steadier. As soon as she had folded her speech back into her handbag, Miss Rathbone approached and asked if she might introduce Charlotte to the evening's other speakers, all of them senior members of the Trades Union Council. She shook their hands and thanked them for inviting her and promptly forgot every last one of their names.

Moments later an usher, or perhaps it was the theater manager, led all of them out of the parlor—the green room, he called it—and along a dark hall, and then quite unexpectedly onto the stage itself. They were seated on a row of chairs, right under the hideously hot and blinding lights, and within seconds Charlotte felt perspiration gathering at her temples and nape. If only she'd allowed Norma to powder her face before they'd left.

It had been agreed that John would introduce her, so he went to the lectern at the front of the stage, and then, finding it not to his liking, stood to one side and waited for the audience to fall silent. He was perfectly at ease, entirely in his element, and it struck her, then, that he ought to run for Parliament. A Britain run by men like John Ellis would be a fine place indeed.

"Good evening, ladies and gentlemen. My name is John Ellis, and I am the editor in chief of the *Liverpool Herald*." He paused for the round of applause this provoked, waiting patiently until the hall was silent again.

"Thank you very much. I have come here tonight to introduce a young woman whose name, I believe, will be recognizable to those among you who are regular readers of the *Herald*.

"Nearly a year ago, I received a letter from Miss Charlotte Brown. She spoke of the suffering she was witnessing among the people who came to her office in search of help, and she asked me to give voice to their troubles. She wished for them to be heard. I was so impressed by her letter that, on the spot, I offered her a weekly column in my newspaper. To my great relief she agreed, and in the ten months since she has never once disappointed me.

"Ladies and gentlemen, it is my very great honor, and my distinct pleasure, to introduce Miss Charlotte Brown to the members of the Liverpool Trades Union Council."

While John had been speaking, Charlotte had removed her gloves and extracted her speech from her handbag. Leaving the bag on her chair, she walked across the stage, shook John's hand, and stood behind the lectern. It was several inches too tall for her; she could barely see across it. So she did as John had done: she moved to the side and looked out across the theater. It was packed full—nearly a thousand people, Norma had said. She swallowed once, twice, and waited for her nerves to settle and the pounding heartbeat in her ears to fade.

People were looking at her expectantly, though, and the theater was perfectly silent. She would have to begin.

"Good evening, ladies and gentlemen. Thank you, Mr. Ellis, for your most gracious introduction. I will add only that it is my honor to be associated with your newspaper, and that I am deeply grateful to you for having given me a platform for my thoughts and concerns.

"As some of you may know, I work as a constituency assistant to Miss Eleanor Rathbone, and though the scope of my work is varied, I daily encounter people who, through no fault of their own, have fallen on hard times and need help of one sort or another." She drew a deep breath; it really was going well so far.

"As a result of my work, it has become clear—"

"What's a toff like you to know about our problems? Who are *you* to speak for us?" came a voice from the crowd.

An outburst of jeers and catcalls followed from other members of the audience, which blessedly seemed directed at the man who had interrupted her. He was not cowed. Instead he glared at her, his arms crossed, his expression angrily defiant.

At length the theater fell silent again, those who had been standing took their seats, and Charlotte knew she had to answer. What, indeed, gave her the right to speak out? Simply to assume she possessed such a right would be to cast in her lot with those very people who stood on the backs of the poor and ignored their existence.

Yet to admit the truth of it, to answer honestly, would be to broadcast a secret to which only her parents and a few family friends in Wells were privy. None of her own friends knew, not even Lilly, for she had decided long ago never to speak of it. It was so long ago she couldn't remember why, exactly, she had decided to shut it away. Most likely she had been worried that her parents might be embarrassed.

If they were here tonight, though, what would they tell her to do? Would they tell her to hem and haw and conjure up some mealymouthed explanation that justified her presence on the stage? Or would they tell her to do what she knew was right?

"I believe I owe the gentleman in the audience an answer. Who am I? How can I possibly claim to understand such suffering? My answer is simple: I understand because I have lived it myself. I, too, have suffered, and I do know what it is like.

"Yes, I attended the University of Oxford. And, yes, when I speak I sound as if I were born with the proverbial silver spoon in my mouth. But the truth is quite different. The truth is that I spent the first four years of my life in the dockside slums of Bristol."

The theater was now so silent that she scarcely had to raise her voice. "I was abandoned in Wells Cathedral when I was four years old. I was dirty and starving and I only knew my first name. It was Bridget, by the way.

"The people who found me, Laurence and Davina Brown, later became my adoptive parents. They had always wanted a child of their own, and to them, I suppose, the wretched four-year-old they found, asleep on a pew in the choir, must have seemed like a gift from God. It took some time for the authorities to find where I'd come from, and all that while I stayed with them, with my new parents, and in the fullness of time they adopted me.

"My mother had vanished, but the story unearthed by the authorities was a tragic one. Her neighbors told of how she had taken to drink after my father had died. She was Irish,

Catholic, friendless and alone in a foreign country, and no one would employ her. No one would give her any help. So she had taken me from Bristol, where we had been living, to Wells Cathedral, for reasons we will never know. She left me with the clothes I was wearing and a ragged blanket. There was no note, likely because she didn't know how to read or write. And then she disappeared. I will never know what became of her.

"I had a very happy childhood. My adoptive parents were loving and kind and everything that good parents ought to be. They cherished me, and my ambitions, and paid for my education.

"Today I live an easy life—I freely admit it. I am paid well for the work I do, I live in a lovely home, I am never hungry, and I rarely have to go without anything I want.

"But I still remember, nearly thirty years after the fact, what it was like to be cold and hungry and alone. I recall how my mother would disappear for hours at a time, and how there was never anything to eat. I recall how cold my feet were, always so cold, because I didn't have any shoes. I remember what it was like to be utterly helpless.

"It is my belief—and in this I am certain you agree with me—that no child should live like that, nor any woman or man. So that is why I do the work I do, and that is why I presume to speak on behalf of those who have nothing."

She had . . . she could think of nothing else to say. So she took a step back, and then another, and waited for someone to fracture the deadening silence that had fallen over the hall. She would almost welcome jeers from the crowd, if only someone would—

The man who had challenged her stood up. He began to clap, and within seconds everyone else was on their feet, their applause and shouts of "hear, hear" so deafening that she couldn't hear anything else.

She felt a hand on her arm, and turned her head to see that it was John, leading her back to her seat so she might fetch her handbag, and then off the stage, into the welcome dark and peace of the wings.

"Save your speech for another night," he told her, bending close so he might speak in her ear. "You've won them over, Charlotte. The next time they'll be putty in your hands."

She nodded, knowing he was right, and in any case quite certain that she was done with public speaking forever and ever. She looked out at the audience one last time, hoping to fix the moment in her memory. It was far easier to see, standing here, than it had been onstage with all the lights shining in her face. In the gallery, in the top row, she found her friends, standing and applauding madly for her. And then she spied a flash of fair hair at the very back of the theater.

Could it be? She shaded her eyes with her hand, squinting against the glare that made it so difficult to see through her spectacles. The man was so far away, yet she recognized the way he stood, the way he carried himself, even the way he was smiling so broadly.

"John—there's someone I know in the audience," she protested, but instead he took her arm and led her to the green room.

"Sorry about that—I couldn't hear a thing back there. Why don't you sit down for a moment? May I fetch you a glass of sherry?"

Miss Rathbone, who had been right behind them, shook her hand and then, for the first time in all their acquaintance, she embraced Charlotte. "You were magnificent. Simply magnificent."

"Wasn't she? Here you are, Charlotte. Down that and you'll feel better in no time. Would you like a sherry, Eleanor?"

"Yes, please."

"Have you ever heard such a reaction? I think it quite unprecedented."

Charlotte wanted very much to join in their conversation, but her thoughts were still in the theater, still focused on the man she had seen at the very back, all but invisible, standing in the shadows.

"As I was leaving the stage," she interrupted, "I spotted an old friend in the crowd. I should so like to see if he is still there."

"They've started up the speeches again," John answered, "so I'd say you're best to stay here. But if you wait for a while he'll probably come to you."

It did make sense, so she accepted her glass of sherry and, sipping at it, waited for an usher to come and tell her that a man was waiting at the theater door and would like to see her. An usher did come, but it was only to admit Rosie, Norma, and Meg, who were perfectly happy to accept their own glasses of sherry and wait with her in the green room until all the evening's speeches were done.

But Edward never did come in search of her, and after a while she began to wonder if she had simply imagined his being there. He had been very far away, after all. It might have been another tall, slim, very fair man with a cane.

She let her friends escort her home, after a final round of handshakes and congratulations from John and Miss Rathbone and the men from the Trades Union Council. They chattered around her as they hurried through the cold night, abuzz with the excitement of Charlotte's speech, but she could find nothing to say. Instead she thought of her mother and father, and how she would have to write them in the morning and let them know what she had done. They would support her, of course, but she wished, now, that she'd asked their permission before sharing her—*their*—story with so many strangers.

She worried as she walked, and not just about her parents. Would her admission change the way others felt about her? The women at work, for instance, or her friends from university? What would Lilly and Robbie think? What about Edward?

It was a good thing there was no chance of her marrying him, for this latest revelation would surely put his mother in her grave. Robbie's origins, though humble, were as nothing compared to Charlotte's ancestry: Irish, Catholic, and quite possibly illegitimate.

Although the others wished to stay up and celebrate her triumph some more, she pleaded a headache and put herself to bed right away. It was late, after all, and they all had to work in the morning.

She fell asleep easily enough, thanks to the sherry, but was roused by the clock at St. Luke's as it chimed three in the morning. Wide awake, her mind turned and turned, obsessively mining the events of the evening like clockworks that had been wound too tight. It was silly to worry about her speech—it was done and over and she wouldn't undo it even if she could.

It hadn't been Edward at the back; surely it had not been him. And yet . . . if it were him, if he had taken the time and trouble to come and hear her speak, should she not attempt to discover the truth of it? Learn why he had come, and why he had left?

She would stop by the post office on her way to work in the morning and telephone Lilly. That was the best solution. She would call on the pretext of wishing her a Happy Easter, and she would ask after Edward. If he were in London, that would put paid to her imaginings. And if he were elsewhere? If he had been in Liverpool?

She had no notion, not the slightest idea, of what she would do.

Chapter 30

Charlotte was at the post office when it opened at eight o'clock the next morning. For such a conversation, she couldn't possibly use the telephone at the office, nor did she expect Miss Rathbone to perpetually fund her expensive long-distance conversations on matters entirely unrelated to work.

No sooner had the clerk opened the door than she was rushing past him to the telephone alcoves, all mercifully free. She went to the nearest, picked up the receiver, gave the operator Lilly's number at home, and hung up. It shouldn't take long for the connection to be made, not at this time of day.

Only a minute or so later, the telephone rang and she picked up the receiver.

"I've made the connection, madam."

"Thank you very much." She waited, unaccountably nervous, for someone to answer at the other end.

"Fraser residence."

"Hello, Robbie. It's Charlotte. I wonder if I might speak to Lilly."

"Of course. Is everything all right?" Presumably they didn't often receive long-distance calls first thing in the morning.

"Yes . . . at least I think so. It's nothing to worry about, I promise."

"She's still upstairs but I'll fetch her."

Several minutes later Lilly came on the line. "Hello? Charlotte?" She sounded as if Robbie had woken her up.

"Hello, Lilly. I'm so sorry for getting you out of bed."

She could hear her friend stifling a yawn. "No, it was time I was up. I stayed up far too late last night. Reading at first, to pass the time until Robbie came home from the hospital, and then up another hour while he told me about his day."

"He didn't sound tired at all."

"He never does, the wretch. But tell me—what is the matter? Did something happen at your speech? I do hope everyone was pleasant to you."

"Oh, they were. Perfectly pleasant. I couldn't have hoped for a warmer reception. The thing is . . ."

"Yes?"

"I think I may have seen Edward there. I mean, I can't be sure. It was quite dark at the back of the hall, and the lights were shining in my face, but I'm fairly sure it was Edward. Do you know . . . I mean, do you think it could have been him?"

Lilly didn't answer, and after the silence had stretched on for many seconds, Charlotte began to worry the line had been dropped.

"Lilly? Are you still there?"

"Yes—I'm sorry. It's only that I wasn't sure what to say. He did know about your speech. He came to dinner on Sunday night, and while he was here he asked after you. So of course I told him that you'd been invited to speak at the congress. But I hadn't realized he would go."

"Ah," Charlotte said. She had been so certain her friend would say Edward had been in London the entire time.

"Didn't he come to say hello afterward?" Lilly asked.

"No, and that's the curious thing. I mean, why come all that way and then just leave? Do you know if he might have left London on Thursday?"

"I'm sorry, but I don't. I haven't spoken to him since Sunday. As far as I know he's been here all the while. Perhaps it might be best if you spoke to him yourself."

That was the last thing she wanted, but it wouldn't do to admit it to Lilly. "Very well. Do you have his telephone number at home?"

"It's Kensington 1227. But I wouldn't call now. At this hour he's likely to be at the clinic."

"What clinic? He isn't ill, is he?"

"No, silly. The clinic he founded in Whitechapel. The Free Clinic for Disabled Servicemen."

"But I . . . I had no idea. When did this happen?"

Another pause, and although Charlotte couldn't be certain, it sounded as if Lilly might be smiling.

"I think you must speak to him directly about it. There isn't a telephone at the clinic, not yet, so you'll have to wait until this evening to ring him at home."

"You won't tell me any more?"

"No. I think it's past time you and he spoke directly to one another. Long past time. The clinic," Lilly added, "is at the corner of Fieldgate and Parfett Streets, just off the Whitechapel Road. I'm going to ring off now. Good luck, my dear."

And then, with a tinny click, Lilly was gone. Charlotte went to the counter, emptied her purse of every last shilling to pay for the call, and continued on to work, her thoughts more awhirl than ever. It simply made no sense. No sense at all.

She spent the workday that followed in a daze, jumping out

of her skin every time the telephones rang in the reception area or Miss Rathbone's office, though the calls were never for her. She spent hours toting up figures for a study on wages and expenditures, only to discover, after copying everything out in ink, that she had made a number of idiotic errors in her basic arithmetic and would have to start again.

Although it had been her practice for some months to eat her sandwich and have a cup of tea with the other women at lunchtime, she remained in her office, at her desk, for she felt quite unable to engage in any sort of lighthearted conversation. If her colleagues noticed, they were too kind to say anything.

Late in the afternoon, Miss Margison brought her a cup of tea, but rather than leave when Charlotte thanked her, she instead lingered at the door.

"If you're feeling poorly, you ought to go home, you know. There's nothing happening here that won't keep for a day or two."

"Thank you, but I'll be all right. If I can just get through today, I'll have the weekend to rest."

"Suit yourself. Let me know if you need help with anything."

"I will. Thank you, Miss Margison."

Even after the others had gone home she lingered, finishing off any number of inconsequential tasks she'd left undone for want of a quiet moment, and only when the sky outside was nearly dark and the clock at All Saints was chiming seven o'clock did she put on her coat and hat and set out for home.

The post office was still open and wouldn't close for another hour. She could call him, if she wished, though it was Friday night and he would likely have gone out for the evening. So there was no point in trying, for she'd only waste her shillings on a conversation with Mr. Andrews or one of the other servants. She would definitely try to call him tomorrow.

She might try to call him tomorrow.

At home, the others were just finishing their supper. After apologizing to the misses and Janie for her tardiness, she took her seat at table and tried, not altogether successfully, to choke down her meal of fried cod and onions. Every bite seemed to catch in her throat, rather as if the cod had been chopped into pieces and cooked with every last bone intact. It was no use.

"I'm so sorry," she said to the room at large. "I have a terrible headache. I think I had better put myself to bed."

Once cocooned in the sanctuary of her room, however, she sat on her bed, quite unable to decide on what she ought to do next. She did have a headache, likely because she had starved herself all day, and she ought to swallow an aspirin or two. Then she ought to put on her nightgown and switch off the light and go to sleep. Ought to, ought to . . .

"Charlotte?" came a voice from the hall. "It's Rosie. May I come in?"

She ought to say no; say that she had already gone to bed.

The door opened and her friend's worried face peered around it. "Whatever is the matter with you?" Rosie asked, coming in and sitting next to her. "You're not fretting about last night, are you? Because you were—"

"No, that's not it."

"So out with it. What has you looking as if the Germans won the war?" It was such a Rosie sort of thing to say.

"I don't know . . ."

"Of course you know. Or is the problem that you don't know if you can tell me? Because you can, you know. You can tell me anything and I'll still be your friend."

Charlotte nodded, for of course she trusted Rosie. And it would be so heavenly to simply talk about it with someone. To confide in her friend, and learn what she thought of everything, and perhaps, together, find a way forward.

"Last night, just as I was leaving the stage, I saw Edward. Lilly's brother."

"Lord Cumberland?"

"Yes."

"Are you certain? If it had been him, surely he would have come round afterward to say hello." Rosie was so very practical.

"That's the thing. The not knowing, if I can call it that, has been torturing me all day."

"Why do you hope it was him?" Rosie asked softly.

"It's hopeless. We agreed it was hopeless, we were both agreed." Her eyes threatened tears again. Where on earth was her handkerchief?

"What is hopeless?"

"I love him. I've always loved him, and I discovered he feels the same way."

"When you spent the month with him?" To Charlotte's relief, Rosie didn't sound at all disapproving.

"Yes, but we admitted it to one another only at the end."

"I still don't understand why it's hopeless."

"When his father died, when Edward became the earl, he was left with huge debts, and then the inheritance taxes to pay. He has to marry someone with money. It's the only way he can do his duty to his family."

"What about his duty to *you*? People falling in love with one another—that doesn't happen every day. Despite what films and books and songs may say, most people never even have a taste of it. And you're going to toss that away because of something as unimportant as *money*?"

"But there is simply no other way he can pay—"

"Rubbish," Rosie said flatly. "Rich people always have bags of money lying about, but rather than part with any they prefer to find more of it. If you truly love one another you can find a way. I know you can."

"I suppose . . ."

Rosie began to pace around the room. "I think you gave in too easily. I think you convinced yourself that you didn't measure up. That you weren't good enough for him. You listened to the poison his mother poured in your ear and you *believed* it, and then you decided it was easier to let him go." She turned to face Charlotte, her expression both accusatory and disappointed.

Charlotte was about to answer, about to defend herself and say that it hadn't been anything of the sort, when Rosie made for the door. Was she truly going to leave after saying such things?

"I need to show you something. I'll be back in a moment."

This conversation really was not proceeding as Charlotte had expected. Where was the sympathy? Where was the understanding shoulder upon which she could weep out her pain?

When Rosie returned, she sat on the bed again and handed Charlotte a small leather folder. The words *Atelier Frères Bouchard* were stamped in gold on its front.

Inside was a photograph of a young man in military uniform. He was in his late twenties, his expression serious, and he was terribly handsome. His dark hair had been combed neatly back from his brow, and he had lovely dark eyes. Intelligent, sensitive eyes, Charlotte thought.

"Who is this?"

"His name was David Cohen," Rosie answered, her voice trembling a little. "We met in the autumn of 1917. He was a patient at the hospital, though not on my ward. He'd been injured by shrapnel, quite badly, and had been recuperating for several months already when I met him.

"I was having my lunch in the garden and he came and sat with me. We got to talking, and I kept eating my lunch in the garden every day, just so I might see him, even once it was really too cold to be eating outside. By December he was nearly well enough to return to his unit. Just before he left, he told me he loved me. And although I knew by then that I loved him, it seemed impossible. I told him it was impossible."

"Why?"

"He was a Canadian, from Montreal, and he was Jewish. I knew my parents would never approve, and his family would be just as horrified. The thing is, he didn't fight me. We agreed that it was for the best, and he left. He even wrote to me, once he was back in France, and I replied, but I never told him I loved him. I never suggested that he visit me when he had leave . . ."

"What happened to him?" Charlotte asked, her heart in her throat.

"He was killed at Soissons the following July."

"Oh, Rosie. Oh, my dear."

"I wrote to the War Graves Commission last year. They were very nice. They told me where to find his grave. I think . . . I think one day I'll go. If only to tell him how sorry I am, and that I did love him. I never stopped loving him."

Charlotte embraced her friend, and then they wept together for a while. At length Rosie straightened her back, dried her eyes, and cleared her throat.

"You must go to him. This isn't something you can sort out over the telephone. Go tonight. If you go now you might be able to get on the overnight service to London."

"But what if—"

"I turned my back on the man I loved, Charlotte, and I will regret it for the rest of my life. *Go to him.*"

The time for dithering and fretting and wondering "what if" was over. She saw that now. So she pulled her valise from under her bed and went to the wardrobe. "I must pack."

"That's the spirit. Pop in a nightgown and some underthings, and a fresh blouse for tomorrow. And your brush and toothbrush and soap and so forth. I'll fetch my black suit."

"But . . . I thought I could wear this," Charlotte protested, indicating the frock she'd worn to work.

"Do I have to drag Norma into this? No. You'll want to go to him straight off, so you need to be dressed in your best. My suit is far nicer than that frock. And you can borrow my new coat, too." It was a kind offer, for the garment was made of a fine, bluebell-colored wool, and beautifully tailored.

"Should I wear the hat that Meg gave me for Christmas?"

"The navy one with the narrow brim? Yes, do. You look lovely in it. Wait here while I bring down my things, and then I'll go next door to the Atwaters' and ask them to ring up a taxi to take you to the station."

By the time Charlotte had tidied her hair and changed into her second-best blouse, Rosie's suit, and Meg's hat, the taxi had arrived.

"Thank you so much," she told Rosie. "Will you explain everything to the misses? And the others?"

"Of course I will. Good-bye, my friend. And good luck."

Chapter 31

Charlotte's train arrived in London at just past dawn the next morning. She hadn't thought to go to the bank earlier in the day, so hadn't been able to afford the fare for a sleeper berth in first class. As a result she had passed the night dozing fitfully in a third-class compartment, her sleep interrupted by the grunts and snores of the large woman seated next to her.

From the train she went directly to the ladies' cloakroom, for she badly needed to change her blouse, wash her face, brush her teeth, and restore her hair to some kind of order. That accomplished, she inspected her appearance in a full-length mirror by the bank of sinks. She wasn't at her best, her eyes ringed by shadows that her spectacles utterly failed to hide, and the stark black of Rosie's suit had a rather deadening effect on her complexion. But she would do. At the very least, she looked neat and respectable.

Her stomach was growling alarmingly, and so she decided to first have some breakfast. What had she said to Meg on that sad evening back in December? *Once you've eaten, it will be much easier to think and plan.* Or something of that nature.

There were several refreshment stands in the station's great hall, but there was nowhere to sit apart from benches, and the first kiosk she passed only had a row of tired-looking hot cross buns for sale. Instead, she left the hall and entered the station's restaurant. She had enough money left for tea and a sandwich, and then the Underground fare to Edward's house.

She took her time with her egg-and-cress sandwich and her cup of tea, for it wouldn't do to rush through her meal and end up feeling poorly for the rest of the day. It was still early, only half past seven; surely Edward would still be at home.

But there was only so long one sandwich and one cup of tea could last, and eventually there was nothing for it but to gather up her valise and handbag and go downstairs to the Underground station. Before paying her fare she took a minute to study the route map near the ticket hall's entrance, for she wasn't sure of the best way to reach Chelsea. When she'd been at the hospital she had used the station at High Street Kensington, but surely there must be other stations closer to Edward's house.

The map wasn't really to scale, but after inspection it seemed that Sloane Square would be the closest. It couldn't be that far from Cheyne Row—perhaps a half mile or mile at the most? After all that time penned in on the train, a walk in the spring air would do her good.

In a little more than a half hour she was running up the steps at Sloane Square. The weather was far from glorious, for the skies were low and gray and the temperature was unseasonably cool. It certainly wasn't the kind of day one pictured when contemplating a reunion with the love of one's life.

Her knock on Edward's door was answered almost immediately by Mr. Andrews. If he was surprised to see her there so unexpectedly, he gave no sign of it.

"Miss Brown! Do come in. How very nice to see you."

"Thank you, Mr. Andrews. I'm very glad to see you, as well. I was hoping to see Lord Cumberland. If he's in, that is."

"I'm sorry, but he's already left for the day."

"Ah," she said. She ought not to have lingered so long over her breakfast.

"He's gone to the clinic."

"Yes, the clinic. I'm not quite sure how to get there from here, I'm afraid."

"Were you thinking of taking the Underground? Or a taxi?"

What should she say? That she only had money enough for one more ticket, and after that her change purse would be empty? Perhaps she had better walk over to Lilly's and ask for her help.

"The thing is, Miss Brown, Lord Cumberland likes to take the Underground over to Whitechapel. So that means his motorcar is still here. If you don't mind waiting a minute or two for me to bring it around, I can drive you over."

"I couldn't possibly impose," she protested. "I'm sure you are very busy."

"Not at all. And he'll be that glad to see you, and have the chance to show you around. He's so proud of the clinic. Forever talking about it, he is. You sit here, and I'll be back in two shakes."

"Thank you," she said, feeling grateful beyond words. Another journey on the Underground would have taken the starch right out of her. When was the last time she had felt so tired?

In short order Mr. Andrews brought around the motorcar, a surprisingly modest creature compared to the luxury vehicles Edward had once favored, and helped her into the backseat.

"It might seem a little odd, but I'm going to cross the Thames at the Albert Bridge and then go west to Tower Bridge," he explained. "That way we'll avoid the traffic in Westminster and the City."

"Of course," she agreed. "How far is it?"

"Well, it's about five miles as the crow flies, but there's no such thing as a straight road in this city. I reckon it's about seven miles or so. Should take us about half an hour, depending on whether Tower Bridge is open or not. If you don't mind my saying, Miss Brown, you look tired. Why don't you shut your eyes and have a rest? I'll get you there safe and sound."

"You're very kind," she answered, although she knew she would never sleep. Instead she imagined what she would say to Edward when she saw him.

There was the polite version, in which she asked him how he had been and if, just perhaps, he had come to see her speech on Thursday night. There was the direct version, in which she asked him why he had scurried away without coming to see her and, furthermore, why he had opened a clinic for disabled servicemen. And there was the angry version, in which she shouted at him until he admitted the truth. The truth of what, precisely, she wasn't sure, but he was very sorry for it. At least he was in her imagined version.

Soon they were across Tower Bridge and heading west, or at least she assumed it was west, along a largish and quite busy road. They turned right, then right again, then left, until she was thoroughly discombobulated and badly wished she had a compass. Mr. Andrews pulled up at a corner, the car half blocking the street, and switched off the engine.

"We're here."

"Are you sure?" she asked, peering out her window. "That looks like a grocer's, not a clinic."

"Next door. The brick building, all whitewashed? That's the one."

"But there isn't any sign."

He didn't answer directly, for he'd got out and was coming round to open her door. "Clinic hasn't opened yet. They're still fitting up the insides. Do you want me to come in with you?"

"Oh, no. No, thank you. I've taken up too much of your time already."

"I'll wait until you're done. If you decide to stay, or Lord Cumberland has other plans, you just let me know. But I'll not leave you here until I know something's been arranged. In you go, now." And he took her elbow and urged her out of the motorcar and across the pavement to the clinic.

She stopped at the threshold, unsure of what to do next. The room was swarming with workmen, some of them repairing the plaster cornices, some painting the window frames, some scraping the floorboards. She stood there until one of the men, a painter, noticed and approached her.

"Can I help you, miss?"

"Yes, please. I'm here to see Lord Cumberland."

"One of the nurses come for an interview?"

"Something like that, yes."

"He's in his office. Go through that door and straight on to the back."

She thanked him and walked forward, the corridor stretching by some trick of light, or wishful thinking, into infinity. Yet all too soon she was at the end of it, and an open door was at her left.

She took a small step, then another, until she was able to peek round the doorframe. Edward was at his desk, immersed in his work, surrounded by piles of ledgers and account books and a huge stack of correspondence that had been anchored, curiously enough, with a piece of broken brick.

Charlotte stared and stared, desperate to say hello, but the word would not pass her lips. So she simply admired him, at his too-long hair falling over his forehead and his beautiful hands, and she noticed how the shadows had vanished from beneath his eyes. How he had put on a little bit of weight, just enough to soften the once-gaunt angles of his jaw and cheekbones. She saw and was glad beyond measure.

He stopped writing and put down his pen, and then he looked up and smiled at her. "How long have you been standing there?"

"I don't know. Not long," she fibbed. "You look well."

"As do you."

"Was it you?" she asked.

"Yes."

"You traveled all the way to Liverpool to see me, but you left without saying hello?"

"I'm sorry. I had every intention of coming to see you afterward, but then I saw . . ."

"Yes?" She sidled a little farther into the room, still clutching her valise and handbag.

"I saw how you were with Mr. Ellis. You seemed so at ease with one another, and I feared you might have formed an attachment to him."

"*Edward.* If you'd come to say hello, I would have told you that John is my friend. No more than my friend."

"Yes, well, I know that now."

"What is all of this?" She put down her valise and gestured sweepingly around the room.

"The clinic?"

"I mean, I know what it *is*. I want to know *why*. How can you afford such an undertaking?"

"It's a long story. Won't you sit down?"

There were two chairs pulled up on the opposite side of the desk to Edward. She deposited her handbag in one and sat in the other.

"I tried to do it. I came back to London and I set about finding a wife. I did meet one girl, Edith Hale—"

"Lilly mentioned her. In a letter."

He winced a little. "I assure you it didn't go very far. Edith is terribly nice, and I'm sure that if I'd never met you I could have married her without a second thought. The same could be said for Helena, too. But there was one thing I couldn't stand about both of them."

Lilly had said Miss Hale was very pleasant, and Charlotte had seen with her own eyes how friendly and inoffensive Lady Helena was. "What do you mean?"

"They weren't you."

"Oh."

"I moped about for a while—has Lilly told you how horrid I was at Christmas?—and then it occurred to me that I could do with some decent advice. I've a terrible head for figures, so when the solicitors and estate managers and various officials I spoke to all swore I was on the path to ruin, I assumed they were right. I never questioned them."

"Who was it? The person you asked for advice?"

"Robbie. He went through everything with me, every single document, and together we got to the bottom of it all. It took us weeks to find where all the money had gone, and how much was left."

"How bad was it?"

"I wouldn't say it was good. But it was far less bad than I'd been led to believe. I owed estate duty of a little less than three hundred and fifty thousand pounds, whereas I'd thought I was on the hook for half a million. That was a relief."

"I imagine so." And yet . . . he still owed a third of a million pounds. The amount was so colossal that she felt faint just imagining it.

"It was Robbie's idea to next sort out what I had, and that was very much in excess of three hundred and fifty thousand pounds. At that point it became merely a question of selling off what I didn't need." Was this Edward before her, or some oddly rational doppelgänger?

"What did your mother say to all of this?"

"She was and is very unhappy, largely because I sold Ashford House. I've always hated the place, so it was surprisingly easy. I also bid adieu to my father's dreadful hunting lodge in Aberdeenshire, a house in Brighton none of us had ever visited, and the town house in Bath. Then there were mountains of things in the attics at Ashford House and Cumbermere Hall. Paintings, sculptures, some very valuable pieces of furniture. I let my sisters and brother choose what they liked and then I sent what was left to be auctioned off." He looked as delighted as a schoolboy who had just figured out a very complicated sum.

"This is . . ."

"I know. Overwhelming."

"I feel as if I ought to lie down."

"Be my guest. Though the floors are very dusty."

Only then did she realize he hadn't answered her initial question. "Why the clinic?"

"Even after all the bills are paid, and I've taken care of allowances for my mother and George, I still have a ridiculous amount of money coming in. It's so ridiculous I'm ashamed to even say the approximate amount out loud. I mean, I'm happy to tell you if—"

"No, don't. Not yet."

"Then I won't. I will say, though, that I certainly don't need it. So I decided—inspired by you and your work—that I ought to do something useful with it.

"*How* I might do so was unclear until one night at the end of January. I was walking through Sloane Square, and there was a man standing by the Underground entrance, dressed in little more than rags, and he was begging. I handed him all the coins in my pocket, and when he looked up to take them, I realized he was a soldier from my own company. He'd been invalided home in 1916. He told me how he'd been denied a pension, no doubt for some utterly indefensible reason, but couldn't find work as he was partially lame."

"What did you do?"

"I brought him home with me, called Robbie over to see him, and then between us we found him a bed at St. Mary's in Roehampton. He's still there, and has made good progress. It made me wonder what had happened to the other soldiers I had known. And then, when I asked Robbie about it, he said the receiving rooms at his hospital are full of veterans. Hundreds of men, and no one is making any concerted, organized effort to help them."

"So you decided to help?" she asked, her eyes hot with unshed tears.

"I did. I've plans for other clinics in Manchester, Cardiff, Tyneside, Merseyside, and Glasgow. That's only to start, mind you—there's enough money to fund half a dozen more."

Edward pushed himself to his feet, came round his desk, and, moving her handbag to the floor, sat in the other chair. "I want you to know that I didn't do this to prove my worth to you, but to myself. I had to know I was worthy of you before I approached you again."

He would certainly make her cry if he persisted in saying such things. "Is that why you came to see me?"

"Yes, and also to cheer you on. You were magnificent." He reached out to tuck a strand of hair behind her ear, and then, as if he couldn't help himself, he kissed her forehead. "Can you forgive me for all the ways I have failed you? If I'd been thinking straight I'd have figured this out months ago."

"There is nothing to forgive."

"I will try to make you happy. God knows you deserve it."

"You aren't concerned by what I said in my speech?"

"About your having been abandoned? Not in the least. It only makes me all the more proud of you."

"I love you."

"And I you."

"I so wish . . . I wish I hadn't been so critical of you. I ought to have been a better friend."

"But you were. I'd never have had the courage to take this path if not for you." He took her hands in his. "Will you marry me? Even if it makes you a countess?"

It was such a comical thing for him to say that she burst out laughing. "There's no getting around it, is there?"

"No, there isn't. So . . . ?"

"Yes, Edward. Yes, I will marry you." She leaned forward, set her hands on his shoulders, and kissed him until they were both breathless.

"Shall we call your parents?" he asked a little while later. "I don't yet have a telephone here, but the post office is just down the street. Will that do?" He stood up carefully and pulled her into his arms.

"I can hardly wait to tell them."

"After you're done, we'll walk over to the hospital so I might ask Robbie if he'll stand up for me. And then we'll ask Lilly if she will do the same for you."

"Mr. Andrews is waiting outside. He refused to leave."

"I know. I recognized the sound of my motorcar as soon as you pulled up."

"So you knew I was there all along?" she asked, so giddy with delight that she was glad of his supporting arms.

"Yes, my darling. All along I knew you were there."

An Epilogue

Oxford, England
October 1920

The man at Shepherd & Woodward, the academic outfitters, had explained it all to her. She would wear her commoner's gown to the first part of the ceremony, then return to Convocation House to change into her graduate's gown and hood. As for the rest, Somerville's newly elected dean of degrees would be her guide.

Charlotte was one of forty women receiving their degrees today, for this was the first graduation ceremony, since the university's founding in the fourteenth century, in which women would be included. She was nervous, of course, though no more so than she'd been on her wedding day back in June.

It had been the simplest and nicest of weddings. Neither of them had wanted anything grand, so the ceremony had taken place in the Lady Chapel at Wells Cathedral, her father officiating, with only their immediate family and closest friends in attendance.

Those receiving degrees, as was tradition, had been asked to wait in the Convocation House that adjoined the Sheldonian Theatre. She and the other women had gathered in one corner, and there they'd set out their graduates' gowns and hoods, which they would retrieve after the first part of the ceremony.

It felt odd to be wearing subfusc again, for more than a decade had passed since she'd written the last of her examinations. For luck, she was wearing Rosie's black suit, together with the white blouse, black tie, and soft woolen cap that the university mandated for women students. The cap looked, to Charlotte's eyes, as if it belonged in a Holbein portrait, but was no less ridiculous a piece of headgear than the mortarboards worn by the men.

And then it was time. The men marched out, arranged by precedence according to their degrees, with the women following them across the rain-drenched courtyard, through the great south doors, and into one of Sir Christopher Wren's most beautiful creations.

She and the other degree supplicants were seated around and above the officers of the university, which afforded the perfect opportunity to take in the spectacle of the ceremony as a whole. Above were the glorious colors of the Sheldonian's painted dome, while below gleamed the jewel-bright gowns and hoods of the university's masters and wardens, deans and provosts, rectors and fellows.

The theater was ringed by galleries, and that is where she found her family: Edward, her parents, Lilly and Robbie, and Miss Rathbone. She'd so have loved to invite more of her friends, but each graduate was given only so many tickets. It wouldn't have been fair to ask for more.

The vice chancellor, who not long ago had opposed the granting of degrees to women, read the traditional Latin introduction, as well as an English translation. Men receiving higher degrees, doctors of divinity, philosophy, medicine, and the like, were admitted first, college by college, followed by those receiving master's and bachelor's degrees.

And then it was the women's turn. Leaving their seats, Charlotte and the others processed to the floor of the theater, where they stood before the vice chancellor as the junior proctor read out their names. When the deans had voted, by their silence, to admit the women, the senior proctor announced—he had the perfect baritone for such an occasion—that they might receive their degrees.

The vice chancellor read them the oath, which required them to swear unending obedience and fidelity to the university, and together they replied, *"Do fidem."* I swear it. He then read his invocation, which, if Charlotte's Latin hadn't deserted her altogether, meant that she and the others had been admitted to their degrees. They curtsied and were led out the east door, back to Convocation House, where their gowns awaited.

Charlotte had hired her master's gown, for it had seemed silly to waste money on a garment she would never wear again, but the black silk hood, lined in crimson, was her own. Or, rather, it was her husband's, for it was the same one Edward had worn at his own degree ceremony more than a decade earlier.

Then it was time to return to the Sheldonian, this time as graduates of the university. The women stood before the vice chancellor a final time, curtsied again, and then, although the ceremony hadn't ended and any sort of spontaneous applause or vocal approbation was frowned upon, the entire congregation began to clap and cheer and stamp their feet.

She looked up to the gallery, to where the cheers were loudest, and found the people she loved most in the world. They had come here today for her, to cheer her on and applaud her success and show her, by their support, that she was worthy of them.

The ceremony at an end, its participants and spectators converged on the courtyard outside. Cold rain was pelting down, the sky dark as dusk, and a phalanx of identical black umbrellas stood between Charlotte and her loved ones.

Without warning, a hand grasped her waist, spinning her back into a pair of waiting and wonderfully warm arms.

"Is that Charlotte Jocelin Neville-Ashford, M.A.?"

"It is. What did you think?" she asked, although Edward's smile was all the answer she needed.

"Far more impressive than my own degree ceremony. But then, you helped to make history today. Are you ready to celebrate?"

"Yes, please. Where is everyone else?"

"I sent them ahead to Somerville. You don't mind walking up, do you? Just the two of us?"

"Not at all. It may be our only chance to talk until this evening. Oh, look—the rain is stopping." Charlotte stepped out from under the umbrella they shared, still holding her husband's hand, and tilted her face to the sky. "And there's the sun. Just in time."

"If I still believed in such things, I'd say it was a harbinger of days to come."

"Such a romantic. You'll make me swoon," she teased.

"Yet it's true. We survived the storm—I hope you recognize that I'm speaking figuratively, since you are the one with a degree in English literature, and here we are—"

"Here we are, having our day in the sun. What more could any woman want?"

"The rest of her family at her side as she celebrates her achievements?"

"There is that. Shall we?"

Arm in arm, with Charlotte measuring her steps to match Edward's pace, they moved forward together. Across the gold-tinged stone of the courtyard, down onto Broad Street, and into the long-awaited sun.

Acknowledgments

I offer my sincere thanks to the following for their assistance, with the further observation that I alone am responsible for any remaining omissions, inaccuracies, or errors.

The Imperial War Museum, the Merseyside Maritime Museum, the Museum of Liverpool, the National Archives (U.K.), and the Toronto Reference Library. Their wealth of digitized holdings formed the foundation of my research for this book.

Dr. Kathryn Ferry, for her extremely helpful advice regarding Blackpool and British seaside culture in the early twentieth century.

Ms. Sue Light, for her invaluable assistance in regard to Charlotte's service as a nurse during the war. Ms. Light, herself a trained nurse and midwife, specializes in the history of the military nursing services of the early twentieth century.

Dr. Ross McKibbin, Emeritus Research Fellow, St. John's College, Oxford, and Mr. Philip Waller, Emeritus Fellow, Merton College, Oxford. I am most grateful to both of them for graciously agreeing to read and make observations on the manuscript of this book.

Major Thomas Vincent, the Canadian Scottish Regiment, for his illuminating insights into the life of an infantry officer, and for clarification on a number of details regarding command structure and military routine.

My father, Professor Stuart Robson, for his advice in regard to everyday life in the front lines, and for his careful reading and critique of the entire manuscript.

My literary agent, Kevan Lyon, and her colleagues at the Marsal Lyon Literary Agency. I am so deeply thankful for their continuing support and guidance.

My editor, Amanda Bergeron, who is simply the best writing teacher I've ever had, and my copy editor, Martin Karlow, who regularly astonishes me with the precision and elegance of his corrections; and production editor Serena Wang who has a sharp eye for detail. Thank you to Elle Keck for all of her help. I am most grateful to Camille Collins and Lauren Jackson in publicity at HarperCollins U.S., and Miranda Snyder and Sonya Koson, their counterparts at HarperCollins Canada, for their hard work on my behalf, as well as their colleagues in marketing, among them Molly Birckhead, Emma Ingram, Shannon Parsons, Alaina Waagner, and Kaitlyn Vincent. I am also very thankful to the art department at HarperCollins, most notably Emin Mancheril and Mumtaz Mustafa, for creating such beautiful covers and capturing the spirit of my books so perfectly.

My circle of friends, among them Ana, Clara, Denise, Erin, Irene, the Janes, Jen, Katarina, the Kellys, Libbie, Liz, Mary, Michela, and Rena. Thank you for believing in me, for taking care of my children (and me) whenever I needed a helping hand, and for hand-selling so many copies of my books to your relatives and colleagues!

My family, all of you, in Canada and abroad. Thank you for

your support, encouragement, and praise. Most of all I thank my sister Kate Robson, who is my inspiration in all things, and so smart, hardworking, and courageous that she puts Charlotte to shame.

My children, Matthew and Daniela, for being so patient and supportive, and whose unconditional love is the light that brightens my days.

And my husband, who is the dearest, funniest, smartest, and kindest man I have ever met. Claudio—I could turn you into a hero in one of my books, but people would say, "this character is too good to be true." You are the best.

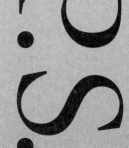

P.S.

Insights,
Interviews
& More . . .

Meet Jennifer Robson

Natalie Brown/Tangerine Photo

About the author

JENNIFER ROBSON is the *USA Today* and #1 *Globe & Mail* bestselling author of *Somewhere in France*. She first learned about the Great War from her father, acclaimed historian Stuart Robson. In her late teens, she worked as an official guide at the Canadian National War Memorial at Vimy Ridge in France and had the honor of meeting a number of First World War veterans. After graduating from King's College at the University of Western Ontario, she attended Saint Antony's College, University of Oxford, where she earned a doctorate in British economic and social history. She was a Commonwealth Scholar and an SSHRC Doctoral Fellow while at Oxford. Jennifer lives in Toronto, Canada, with her husband and young children, and shares her home office with Sam the cat and Ellie the sheepdog.

A Conversation with Jennifer Robson

Congratulations on all the success your first novel
Somewhere in France *has had! Were you surprised*
by the response from readers?

I have to admit I was! When you're a writer, you
spend years working more or less alone, and so
when you present your characters to the world it's
hard not to feel a little bit anxious, even protective.
I had become very fond of Lilly and Robbie, and
indeed of all the characters in the book (excepting
Lady Cumberland, of course), so it was terribly
gratifying when so many people fell in love with
them, too.

We first met Charlotte as Lilly's friend in
Somewhere in France. *How did you decide to*
make her the heroine of your second book?

When I was creating her character, she kept
reminding me of other women who have inspired
me, among them my grandmother, who spent her
working life as a journalist, and my late mother,
who was a lawyer and, in the last years of her life,
a judge. Both had the courage and determination to
work in fields traditionally dominated by men, and
they persevered in the face of what must often have
been quite dispiriting working conditions.

It made me wonder: although I grew up in
a family where no one ever said I couldn't do
something because I was female, what must it have
been like for women such as Charlotte and Lilly and
their contemporaries? How would it have felt to live
and work at a time when so many doors were closed
to women?

I also knew that I had to resolve the story of what
happens between Charlotte and Edward, for good or
for bad, or else risk the wrath of everyone who had
been waiting to discover what becomes of them
after the war.

During the war, many women did "men's"
work, and took on all kinds of new and exciting
challenges. Did that have an effect on their lives
after the war? ▶

A Conversation with Jennifer Robson *(continued)*

It did, but in a pretty limited fashion. Yes, some women (though not all) received the right to vote in 1918, and from 1919 onwards the Sex Disqualification (Removal) Act opened the professions to women and also made it illegal to sack a woman if she got married. In practice, however, high levels of unemployment after the war—levels that were particularly dire in the industrial north—meant that virtually all women who had been employed during the war were given the sack shortly after its end, and few were then able to find positions outside occupations that had been traditionally considered "women's work."

What the war did encourage, however, was a growing conviction among women that they were absolutely able to do the same work as men, that they ought to receive the same wages if they did the same work, and that they contributed just as much to society as did men. They saw themselves as capable, as *able*, and that perception lingered. Their daughters picked up on it, and then their grand-daughters—and so, while appreciable and measurable change did not happen until after the Second World War, it did happen. And I would say that we all owe a debt of thanks to those first women who had the courage to leave behind everything that was familiar and comfortable, and do the jobs they were asked to do.

What was your favorite part of researching After the War is Over?

Oh, definitely the portions that involved Oxford. I studied there in the early 1990s, and it was great fun to send Charlotte and Edward along streets I walked as a student, to put them in some of the same buildings I worked in and visited, and to describe the splendor of a degree ceremony. Fortunately for me, the city itself hasn't changed all that much since the turn of the last century, and the ceremonial aspects of life at the university have hardly altered at all. So it was mostly a case of re-acquainting myself with smaller details that I had forgotten over the years, and brushing up on my Latin a little bit!

Were there any historical details that were especially difficult to uncover?

So many resources are available online via digital databases that in most cases it was simply a matter of digging and asking the right questions of the right people. I did have to be very careful when I was describing the layout of certain neighborhoods in Liverpool and the East End of London, however—large swaths of both were all but wiped out during the Blitz, so I couldn't rely on modern maps as wayfinders. Instead, I turned to ordnance survey maps of the period, which showed me the streets as they existed in 1919.

I will say, though, that if I know a street or building is largely the same as it was a century ago, I find Google Street View a tremendously helpful (and entertaining) means of putting myself in the shoes of my characters—just as long as I ignore the modern signage, cars, and other evidence of the twenty-first century.

How did you research the details of Edward's injuries?

I began by reading a number of books and articles from the immediate post-war period that sought to explain and understand the phenomenon of what was then known as neurasthenia, but today we would call post-traumatic stress disorder, or

PTSD. At the beginning of the war it was understood imperfectly, to say the least. Though the number of soldiers and officers executed for cowardice—but who in fact were likely suffering from PTSD—is often exaggerated, it was nonetheless a horrible and tragic by-product of the lack of understanding that then prevailed.

By the end of the war, however, there was a growing consensus that a man might, through no fault of his own, be so traumatized by what he had suffered that he was truly not fit for duty. It was also the case that growing numbers of men were being diagnosed with traumatic neurasthenia, which recognized that a man might be badly injured by the concussive effects of shellfire, even though he bore no readily identifiable wounds. In the case of many men, their concussions were overlaid by tissue wounds or fractures, as well as PTSD, so it was difficult for their physicians to diagnose them, let alone treat them properly.

For my descriptions of Edward's concussion—its signs and symptoms, as well as his recovery—I drew upon the experiences of a close friend. After suffering a severe concussion, as well as a skull fracture, she was bedridden for many months and recovered only after a frustratingly long period of complete rest and withdrawal from work and her daily routine. I should add that most people who suffer from concussion do recover fairly quickly, but a minority—like Edward, and my friend—suffer from post-concussion syndrome. For them, recovery can take months or even years.

Do you have a daily routine for your writing?

I'd say that my routine is somewhat unusual, in that I have young children who have only just begun to attend school full time. During the week I work from the moment I drop them off at school in the morning to the moment I have to collect them, a little less than seven hours, and I try to ignore emails and phone calls whenever possible and just focus on my writing. After my children are home I'm busy with homework, after-school activities, dinner, and bedtime until at least 8:00 P.M., at which point I fire up my computer again and try to get in a few hours of research or updates to social media. Fortunately my husband often has to work in the evening, too, so we keep each other company! If I'm really pressed for time—if I have a deadline looming—I often end up working through the night, since the wee hours are wonderfully quiet. But as I get older I'm finding this approach tends to knock me flat, so I'm doing my best to put work aside and go to bed at a reasonable hour.

Do you have any advice for aspiring writers?

The best piece of advice I have ever read is to simply sit at your desk and write. Just write. You'll never be successful if you don't write—and I don't mean writing *about* writing on social media. Social media is terrific, but it can only help you if you first put in the work of actual writing.

Beyond that, I would tell them to press on in the face of rejection. I was told no any number of times before I got my first yes, and like most writers I received enough rejection letters and emails to wallpaper my bathroom.

What are you working on now? ▶

A Conversation with Jennifer Robson *(continued)*

I'm in the middle of working on a third book, also set in the same period, with a protagonist who appears briefly in both *Somewhere in France* and *After the War is Over*. This time, however, most of the narrative will take place in Paris, in the world we now associate with the "lost generation" of Fitzgerald and Hemingway. If my first two books left you dreaming of a trip to England, this one will have you packing your bags for the City of Lights. ❧

The Enduring Appeal of Blackpool

IN CHAPTER 13 OF THIS BOOK, Charlotte spends a day at the seaside with her friends. More to the point, she travels to Blackpool, that most iconic of seaside resorts, and takes in every delight it has to offer. If you happen to be British, or have spent any amount of time in Britain, Blackpool will likely be familiar, even if you've never holidayed there yourself. But I suspect there will be a number of you who will have read this chapter and wondered what all the fuss is about.

Today, many of us think nothing of hopping on a plane for a week's holiday, or jumping in the family car for a road trip to the nearest beach or national park. In 1919, however, the days of cheap overseas travel were still a half-century away, and only a wealthy few could afford to journey by ship to glamorous destinations such as Biarritz or Saint-Tropez. As well, while automobile ownership became far more widespread in the 1920s and 1930s, in the immediate post-war period only a small percentage of families had access to a car.

This didn't prevent ordinary Britons from enjoying their holidays: By 1911, historian James Walvin has observed, a little more than half the English population was visiting the seaside on day excursions and a further twenty percent was taking holidays that required overnight accommodation. Their destination was the scores of seaside resorts in England, Wales, and Scotland that grew and flourished from the mid-nineteenth century onward.

Of the many seaside resorts in Britain in the early twentieth century, Blackpool was by far the most popular. Other resorts—among them Margate and Torquay in the south, Scarborough and Skegness in the north—attracted middle-class holidaymakers, but Blackpool was happy to cater to its working-class visitors, and determinedly fostered a jolly, old-fashioned, and often somewhat low-brow atmosphere.

In the early 1920s, despite post-war unemployment and economic malaise, Blackpool attracted as many as eight million visitors a year. By the height of its popularity in the 1950s, nearly 17 million visitors flocked to the resort each year. ▶

The Enduring Appeal of Blackpool *(continued)*

These numbers were boosted considerably by the phenomenon of Wakes Week, when the mills and factories of Lancashire closed and gave their workers a week's holiday. (The closures were staggered across different municipalities, so as to avoid the disaster of hundreds of thousands of families all trying to go on holiday at once.) Although most workers received no pay for their week off, many families saved their pennies for the rest of the year in anticipation of a week by the sea—for it was often the only vacation they received, apart from Sundays and bank holidays.

While train fares from the industrial heartland to Blackpool were relatively cheap, the charabanc was an even less expensive option, though a decidedly dangerous one. Little more than an open-topped wagon bolted to the frame of a heavy-goods vehicle, the charabanc had a high center of gravity, no protection for passengers if the vehicle tipped over or was in a collision, and of course it had no seatbelts. But charabanc fares were cheap, and it was common enough for smaller workplaces, or large family groups, to hire one for the journey to Blackpool.

Once at the resort, most families stayed in a boardinghouse; the hotels in Blackpool, relatively few in number, catered to a more middle-class clientele. It was customary for guests to be locked out for nearly the entire day, ostensibly so the landlady (often of a fearsome and unyielding disposition) could clean, which meant that from mid-morning to early evening families thronged to the beach and the many amusements on offer.

At high tide, the beach at Blackpool was immensely wide and flat, and while it was pleasantly sandy the water was never especially warm. Most visitors contented themselves with a quick paddle, rolling up their trousers or holding their skirts high, and set their sights on other pastimes. It's worth noting that, in the early 1920s, people were just beginning to feel comfortable wearing bathing suits in public; the bathing machines that once sheltered people from censorious eyes had only recently fallen out of use. It helped that most suits were extremely modest in design, covering their wearers, female and male alike, from neck to knee, and (this was before the advent of stretch fabrics) were typically made of thick serge, knitted cotton, or wool.

While Norma's less modest suit would have raised eyebrows, it wouldn't have been considered scandalous as such, although she and anyone else wearing a bathing suit would have been in the minority. While Charlotte and her friends had enough disposable income to pay for such an inessential garment, many of Blackpool's holidaymakers would not have been able to afford their own suits, nor even the fee to rent one. While younger children were often clad in home-made knitted suits—which could make for a miserable paddle once the wool became sodden with seawater—contemporary photographs reveal that most people on the sands of Blackpool beach were wearing their street clothes; indeed, many seem to have been clad in their Sunday best. Today we might think it odd to be by the sea and never go for a swim, but for many it was enough to be in the sunshine, to smell the salt air, and be away from the factories, traffic, noise, and smoky air of the cities where they lived.

Of course there was more to Blackpool than its beach. There were donkey rides for the children, the rides and games of Pleasure Beach, the Winter Gardens with its Opera House, and the genteel offerings of the great piers stretching out over the sea, though the fees charged by all these attractions meant only better-off visitors could partake. Each autumn, as well, the Blackpool Illuminations drew many thousands of visitors with a dazzling display of electric lights, though the shows were halted during both world wars.

Greatest of all the attractions, however, was the Blackpool Tower. It resembles (and was inspired by) the Eiffel Tower, but where the latter stands alone on the Champ de Mars, Blackpool's tower rises from a large and rather squat brick building which houses its admissions hall, ballroom, circus, and, for many years, a menagerie and aquarium.

Today Blackpool's glories are somewhat faded, although its Tower is being expensively restored, and increasing numbers of families are traveling there rather than abroad. Vacant storefronts dot its waterfront, but its beach still welcomes thousands of visitors each summer, the donkeys are patiently waiting to offer rides to children, and sticks of Blackpool Rock may be bought and savored, just as they were a century ago. ⌒⌣

To learn more about Blackpool and its history, I recommend Beside the Seaside *by James Walvin,* The British Seaside Holiday *by Kathryn Ferry, and* The British Seaside: Holidays and Resorts in the Twentieth Century *by J.K. Walton.*

Glossary of Terms Used in *After the War is Over*

Antimacassar: A cloth placed over the headrest of a chair or sofa, ostensibly to prevent the furniture's fabric from being soiled, but also used for decorative purposes.

Armistice Day: On 11 November 1918 an armistice was declared between combatant nations and the guns fell silent. Its anniversary later became Armistice Day. In Britain and many Commonwealth nations, 11 November (or the nearest Sunday) is still observed as a day of remembrance, and in some regions is a statutory holiday.

Aspidistra: A particularly hardy form of houseplant that was all but ubiquitous in British homes in the late nineteenth and early twentieth centuries.

Bathing machines: High-sided wheeled carts that were stationed on beaches and rolled into shallow water; they offered privacy to bathers who didn't wish to be seen in their swimming costumes. By the early twentieth century they had all but disappeared from British beaches and any that remained were used as stationary changing huts.

Belgravia: A small district in central London notable for its grand squares of large Georgian houses. Edward's family lives in Belgrave Square, from which the district takes its name.

Blackpool Rock: Sticks of brightly colored, boiled sugar candy that were a popular treat at the seaside resort.

Bovril: A proprietary brand of thickened, salty meat extract, often diluted with boiling water to make a sort of broth.

Bubble and squeak: Main course dish made of fried cabbage and leftovers, typically potatoes, vegetables, and scraps of meat.

Bully beef: Popular term for the tinned corned beef that was a mainstay of the soldier's diet during the war.

Carfax: The conjunction of four major streets in the center of the city of Oxford.

Charabanc: Originally a large, open-topped wagon with bench seats for passengers; the motorized version of the early twentieth century was popular as a means of transportation from urban centers to seaside resorts.

Chilblains: Tissue injury that occurs when a person is exposed to cold and humid conditions, often resulting in swollen skin, itching, blisters, and infection.

Clippie: Popular term, first coined during the First World War, for women conductors on buses and trams.

Command trenches: Some twenty yards behind the fire trenches, the command trenches formed the rear part of the front line of British sections of the Western Front, and housed the dugouts and latrines.

Crape: A dull black fabric used almost exclusively in the production of mourning clothes and draperies for a household in mourning.

CSM: Company sergeant major; the most senior NCO in a company of men, which at full strength numbered 240 soldiers and five officers.

Debrett's Peerage: A biographical dictionary, first published in the late eighteenth century, containing information on members of the peerage and baronetage of Great Britain.

Demobilization: The lengthy process by which millions of soldiers were released from military service and returned to their homes at the end of the war.

Doughboy: Slang term for American servicemen during the Great War. The term first came into use in the mid-nineteenth century, but by World War II had largely been replaced by "G.I."

Dreadnought: The largest of the armored battleships that became the center of the arms race between Britain and Germany in the years preceding the First World War.

Estate duty: In Britain, this was the tax due on the estate of anyone worth more than £100. In 1919 the highest rate, which applied only to estates worth £1 million or more, was twenty percent.

Final Honors Schools: The final set of examinations taken by undergraduates at the University of Oxford.

Fire trenches: The first of the line of trenches that made up the British sections of the Western Front, they were zigzagged with frequent traverses to minimize the damage from enemy bombardment.

GHQ: Acronym for general headquarters; the central command of the British Armed Forces.

Greats: A popular name for the *Literae Humaniores* course of study for undergraduates at the University of Oxford. Greats students would primarily study the history of Ancient Greece and Rome, Latin, Ancient Greek, and philosophy.

The Great Silence: The two minutes of silence that were observed at eleven o'clock in the morning on 11 November 1919, the first anniversary of Armistice Day.

Guff: Slang term for unacceptable behavior or nonsensical talk.

Honor Mods: The first set of examinations taken by undergraduates at the University of Oxford.

Identity disks: Small leather or pressed cardboard tags worn by British soldiers and officers during the Great War; a precursor to the modern metal dog tag.

Landau: A four-wheeled carriage, often with a convertible top.

LSE: The London School of Economics.

Matriculation: Formal ceremony by which membership of the university is conferred on new students at Oxford. ▶

Glossary of Terms Used in *After the War is Over* (continued)

Mithering: To fuss or whine about something; popular term in central and northern England.

Moleskin: Heavy cotton material with a short nap on one side, typically in a buff or olive color.

NCO: A non-commissioned officer, for example a sergeant or warrant officer.

Neurasthenia: Medical term originally used to describe a disorder of the nervous system, but during and after the Great War was used to describe symptoms of shell shock, or what we would now refer to as post-traumatic stress disorder.

NYDN: Acronym for "not yet diagnosed, nervous"; used by medical staff when shell shock was suspected but not formally diagnosed.

OC: Officer in command, as distinct from CO, or commanding officer. Edward was the OC of his infantry company.

Peace Day: 19 July 1919, the day chosen to commemorate the signing of the Treaty of Versailles and thus the end of the Great War.

Pillock: Slang, considered quite vulgar, for an annoying person or fool.

Pioneer battalion: Soldiers in these battalions took on the "fatigue" work of trench digging, moving munitions and supplies, and the installation and maintenance of barbed wire entanglements, among other duties.

Plimsoll: Type of shoe with a canvas upper and rubber sole.

Prebendary: Senior cleric or canon in the Church of England; the title was often accorded to an administrator at a cathedral.

Punch: A weekly satirical magazine published between 1841 and 1992, with a brief revival in the early years of this century.

RAMC: Royal Army Medical Corps. Its members included medical staff such as physicians as well as support workers such as orderlies.

Representation of the People Act: Also known as the Fourth Reform Act, the 1918 Act radically expanded the franchise in Britain by extending the vote to all men over the age of twenty-one, and to women aged thirty and over who could meet certain property requirements.

Roll of Honor: The portion of *The Times* newspaper during and after the war that listed the names of soldiers and officers who were killed, wounded, captured, died of their wounds, or who went missing. In the days and weeks after major offensives it typically stretched to several pages or more.

Sex Disqualification (Removal) Act: The 1919 Act removed most restrictions to women's employment in the professions, among them medicine and the law, allowed them to serve as magistrates or jurors for the first time, and disallowed marriage as a bar to women's employment.

Shell shock: Common term for what we would now term PTSD. In 1917 it was banned as an official diagnosis and its use was censored elsewhere, with the mandate that "neurasthenic" instead be used to describe men whose nervous shock had no known physiological cause.

Special military probationer: Nurses employed in military hospitals and facilities in Britain. Many were drawn from the ranks of the VAD and had little formal training.

Subaltern: A second lieutenant in the British Army.

Subfusc: Academic dress worn by University of Oxford students for examinations and other formal occasions during their course of study.

Suffragist: A member of the suffrage movement, which sought to extend the franchise, or the right to vote, to all adults; the term is more commonly associated with those seeking the vote for women. "Suffragette" is often used in its stead, though its origins are derisive.

Toff: Slang term for someone from an aristocratic or upper-class background.

Treaty of Versailles: The treaty that formally ended hostilities between the Allied Powers and Germany. It was signed on 28 June 1919 after six months of negotiations at the Paris Peace Conference.

University constituency: A constituency in the parliament of Great Britain that represented a university or group of universities rather than a geographical area. The university constituencies were abolished in 1950.

WAAC: Women's Army Auxiliary Corps. "WAAC" was also the term used for an individual member of the corps.

War Graves Commission: Formally established in 1917, the commission is responsible for the establishment, indexing, and maintenance of the graves or places of commemoration of the soldiers and officers of Great Britain and its empire (now the Commonwealth).

WC: Water closet; informal term for toilet. Considered less polite than "lavatory" or "necessary."

Whitsun: Also known as Whit Sunday, this nominally was the observance of the Christian holiday of Pentecost in the late spring, but in practice was celebrated as a bank holiday in Britain.

A note on currency: Before British currency was decimalized in 1971—that is, before pounds and pence were measured in divisions of one hundred—it was measured in pounds, shillings, and pence. Twelve pence made up one shilling and twenty shillings made up one pound, with a total of 240 pence in a pound. Written in numeric form, a pound was symbolized by the term still in use, "£," while a shilling was "s" and a penny was "d." Other coins were circulated: the farthing (worth a quarter of one penny); the halfpenny (pronounced "ha'penny"), threepence (pronounced "thruppence"), and sixpence; the crown (worth five shillings); and the half-crown (worth two shillings and sixpence). Less commonly seen were the florin, worth two shillings, and the guinea, which actually referred to a gold coin no longer in circulation, and was equal to the amount of one pound and one shilling. ❧

Reading Group Guide

1. Although Charlotte is the Oxford-educated daughter of an upper-middle-class clergyman, she seems certain that there is a huge gulf in status between her and Edward. Do you feel that was truly the case? Or is this more a reflection of her own feelings of inadequacy?

2. Why do you think Charlotte is so devoted to her work? Do you admire her for her tenacity, or do you pity her for neglecting her personal happiness?

3. Do you agree with Charlotte's decision to keep her friendship with John Ellis purely platonic?

4. How do you think you would have coped with the difficulties of the post-war period? Would you have been able to set them aside, as does Norma? Or would you be more like Meg and Rosie, and find it impossible to forget?

5. What did you think of the inclusion of Eleanor Rathbone, a real-life historical figure, in the novel? Do you like it when writers blend history with fiction in this manner? Or do you prefer the characters in a novel to be entirely fictitious?

6. Were you surprised that it takes so long for Edward's friends and family to realize that he needs help? Do you think this is typical of veterans who suffered from psychological trauma at that time?

7. Do you feel that the gains made by women during the war were entirely lost in the post-war period? Do you think the war helped to accelerate change in any measurable way?

8. If you could choose to be poor and happy in the Britain of 1919, or wealthy and unhappy, which would you choose? And why?

9. Do you feel that Edward will be able to maintain his sobriety? Or will his experiences during the war forever haunt him?

10. Charlotte and Lilly each took action during the war in their roles as nurse and WAAC. Which of the two women is most changed by her experiences? Which role do you think you would have taken on if given the choice?

Further Reading

What follows is a selective list of books that inspired and informed me as I was writing *After the War is Over*, as well as some websites that are both interesting and reliable.

The British Seaside Holiday by Kathryn Ferris
Classes and Cultures: England 1918–1951 by Ross McKibbin
The Classic Slum: Salford Life in the First Quarter of the Century by Robert Roberts
Death's Men: Soldiers of the Great War by Denis Winter
Democracy and Sectarianism: A Political and Social History of Liverpool 1868–1939 by P.J. Waller
Eleanor Rathbone and the Politics of Conscience by Susan Pedersen
Goodbye to All That by Robert Graves
The Great Silence: Britain from the Shadow of the First World War to the Dawn of the Jazz Age by Juliet Nicolson
The Ideologies of Class: Social Relations in Britain, 1880–1950 by Ross McKibbin
Memoirs of an English Infantry Officer by Siegfried Sassoon
Music for the People: Popular Music and Dance in Interwar Britain by James Nott
Paris 1919: Six Months that Changed the World by Margaret Macmillan
Rites of Spring: The Great War and the Birth of the Modern Age by Modris Eksteins
Sites of Memory, Sites of Mourning: The Great War in European Cultural History by Jay Winter
Testament of Youth by Vera Brittain
Tuppence to Cross the Mersey by Helen Forrester
Wake by Anna Hope
A War of Nerves: Soldiers and Psychiatrists in the Twentieth Century by Ben Shephard
We Danced All Night: A Social History of Britain Between the Wars by Martin Pugh
The Women at Oxford: A Fragment of History by Vera Brittain

The Long, Long Trail
    www.1914–1918.net
The Great War Archive
    www.oucs.ox.ac.uk/ww1lit/gwa ▶

Further Reading *(continued)*

The Great War
   www.greatwar.co.uk
The Imperial War Museum
   www.iwm.org.uk
This Intrepid Band
   greatwarnurses.blogspot.com
Scarletfinders: British Military Nurses
   scarletfinders.co.uk
The Western Front Association
   www.westernfrontassociation.com ～

Discover great authors,
exclusive offers, and more
at hc.com.